Emerging from the tube station, Nigel paused to consult his A-Z before setting off down the high road.

As he walked, he found himself wondering for the umpteenth time why he bothered. He'd always dreamt of being a proper music journalist – going on tour with The Who, hanging out backstage with Bruce Springsteen, and then writing thrillingly insightful features about them that would make him the envy of his peers. But so far, the nearest he'd got to the glamorous world of rock'n'roll was the occasional freelance assignment from Deuce, a company that specialised in reissuing old records. They were the reason he was spending this particular Monday evening in Chalk Farm, interviewing the bassist from some Sixties r'n'b group he'd never even heard of. Deuce had sent him the records he was supposed to be writing the sleevenotes for, but he hadn't listened to them yet. He wasn't really into the blues.

It wouldn't be so bad if it wasn't all so predictable. A few months of working for Deuce had been enough to establish that every band's story was more or less the same; a bunch of mates start playing together, they get a lucky break, they have a hit or two, they get a bit of attention, it goes to their heads, they argue, they split up. Nigel doubted that this lot would turn out to be any different. At least there were only three of them.

Arriving at the address he'd been given, he rang the bell of the ground-floor flat. The man who answered was surprisingly young – mid-thirties, at a guess – and showed no obvious signs of rock'n'roll excess. Nigel took in the paunch, the fair hair that was starting to recede at the temples, the checked shirt and the brown corduroy trousers, and thought, he looks like a teacher. Which, he happened to know, was exactly what his interviewee was.

"Trevor Harris?" Nigel asked.

"Yes, that's right. You must be Nigel – come in, come in." He sounded eager, and slightly nervous. Nigel wondered how long it had been since anyone had wanted to talk to him about his band.

He followed Trevor through the gloomy hallway, making a mental note of the framed posters from Sixties rock festivals on the walls, and into the kitchen. Taking a seat, he waited patiently while Trevor bustled around him, making coffee (Nigel would have preferred something stronger, but he didn't like to ask – a lot of the people he interviewed turned out to be recovering alcoholics) and moving untidy piles of essays and textbooks off the table. Finally they were ready. Nigel placed his tape recorder in the middle of the table, put the microphone in front of Trevor, pressed the 'on' button and asked him to start at the beginning. He just hoped this wouldn't take long.

TIM TURNER

FIRST TIME I MET THE BLUES

A NOVEL IN 12 BARS

Snowbury Books

S^b_*

Published by Snowbury Books

ISBN 978-0-9563865-0-2

Printed in Great Britain by the MPG Books Group,
Bodmin and King's Lynn

For Lisa, with love

"Those white boys want to play the blues so bad. And they do."
(Sonny Boy Williamson II, 1963, after playing with The Yardbirds)

BAR ONE: TREVOR, 1964

In the autumn of 1964 I was fifteen, an introverted and rather intense adolescent. I blame my father for that. He was an aircraft engineer and tended to change jobs every few years. Throughout my childhood I'd been repeatedly uprooted and carted off to some unfamiliar part of the country, where I would undergo the ritual torture of joining a new school, often in the middle of the academic year. It was hard to make friends in those circumstances, so I'd learnt to occupy myself with hobbies that didn't require a companion.

We'd arrived in Croxley Green (a sleepy outpost of suburbia clinging to the western edge of Watford) in May, and I was quietly determined that it was going to be different this time. For one thing, I was starting to get bored with stamp albums and Airfix kits. Somewhere out in the wider world, the one described by the radio and the newspapers, teenagers were having fun in mysterious and exciting new ways, and I wanted to join them. I decided I was going to have to be a bit more adventurous.

Unfortunately, I spent the school holidays discovering that adventures were hard to come by in Croxley Green. I remember that summer as a series of solo cycling expeditions into the Hertfordshire countryside under slab-grey skies that held in the muggy heat, sweat gluing my shirt to my back. That, and sunnier days when I lazed on a deckchair in the back garden, working my way through Mum's collection of Agatha Christie novels or listening to the soothing drone of the cricket commentary on the radio.

By the time I went back to school, I'd lowered my sights. Never mind adventure, I just wanted to do something – anything – I'd never done before. And one morning, I was cycling to school along Rickmansworth Road and I saw the floodlights of Watford FC's ground looming over the long streets of terraced houses off to my right, and the thought popped into my head: I've never been to a football match.

My experience of football up to that point had been strictly monochrome – the pictures in the Sunday papers, the grainy highlights on the TV news – and what struck me first as I emerged from the turnstile the following Saturday was how vivid the colours were. The grass was the same cheerful shade of green as a Subbuteo pitch and the plastic seats in the ramshackle stands were bright orange, while the teams, who were warming up, were wearing yellow and black and red and white respectively. As I stood high up on the open terrace in the sunshine, waiting for the game to begin and listening to the conversations going on around me, I felt a keen sense of anticipation.

I don't remember a lot about the match itself, except that the enthusiasm of the fans in the home end was so infectious that when Watford scored what turned out to be the winning goal, I joined in the celebrations. If anyone had asked me why I was cheering and waving my arms in the air like an idiot, I wouldn't have been able to tell them – but it felt right. Maybe if the match had ended nil-nil, or if Watford had lost, I wouldn't have returned to Vicarage Road, and I wouldn't be telling this story. But they won, and I was hooked, and a fortnight later I went back to watch the next home game. And that was when I met Steve.

Inspired by the exhilaration of my first visit, I'd decided to venture closer to the centre of the terracing, directly behind the goal. In front of me, two steps down, was a broad-shouldered boy of about my age with a mop of wavy, reddish-brown hair. He was wearing a donkey jacket, the sort I'd only ever seen on workmen before, and he had a yellow and black scarf tied round his right wrist. But I probably wouldn't have noticed him at all if he hadn't been so vocal, constantly yelling at the Watford players to "get stuck in!", "wing it!", "mark up!" and so on.

Being a conscientious student, I was storing these phrases away, noting how and when they were used, with the idea of shouting them myself in due course, when I felt more confident. Meanwhile I consulted the team list in the programme at regular intervals, keen to put names to the faces of the Watford players. Actually, it wasn't a very exciting game, and I could comfortably have read the programme from cover to cover without missing any vital action. Nevertheless, I dutifully folded it in two and replaced it in my trouser pocket – the right one, where I kept my handkerchief – each time before returning my attention to the pitch.

Then, midway through the second half, Watford made a rare foray into opposition territory. The right winger dribbled past two defenders before sending a low cross zipping towards the near edge of the six-yard box, where the centre forward was charging in to meet it. The goalkeeper was rooted to his line, and for a moment a goal looked inevitable, until a defender slid in and toe-ended the ball out of play for a corner.

When the move started, I was checking the team list for the umpteenth time, until the noise from the crowd made me look up. Without thinking, I hurriedly stuffed the programme into my left trouser pocket, the one where I kept my money. A few seconds later, as Watford prepared to take the corner, I wanted to double-check the winger's name and pulled it out again – and with it, a handful of coins that went skittering down the shallow stone steps. Flustered, I quickly bent down to pick up as many of the coins as I could reach.

The corner was a good one, the ball arriving in the penalty area at the perfect height and speed for the Watford centre forward to meet it at the near post with a powerful header that sent it past the keeper's outstretched fingers and into the top corner of the net. Or so I found out later. I didn't see it. I was still groping around on the ground, and the first I knew of the goal was when the crowd roared. Before I had time to stand up, a tidal wave of spectators was surging down the steps, catapulting me forwards so that my head caught the burly teenager in front of me behind the knees. Like everyone else on that part of the terracing, he was jumping up and down, and I caught him off balance, sending him sprawling into a crush barrier.

As I was picking myself up, he turned round and snarled, "What the fuck – " Then he broke off, seeing the expression of fear on my face. Reaching out a beefy arm, he helped me to my feet and said, "Did you see that – fantastic header!"

When I mumbled that I'd missed it, he described the goal to me in painstaking detail. "It was a bit like that one he scored against Palace last season," he added. "D'you remember that?"

I explained shyly that I'd only moved into the area a few months ago, and that the game a fortnight earlier had been my first.

"What, when we beat Orient? Well, it looks like you're going to see us win again. I can't see this lot equalising." Then a thought struck him and he grinned broadly. "Hey, maybe you're a lucky mascot. You'll have to come every week."

Before I could reply, we were distracted by another Watford attack. Meanwhile, what with all the commotion on the terraces following the goal, the space I'd previously occupied was taken, so I found myself standing next to the youth in the donkey jacket for the rest of the game. I didn't really talk to him as such, but he included me unselfconsciously in the conversations he had with his friends, and I nodded and smiled at appropriate moments, and joined him in clapping the Watford team off the pitch at the end, carefully imitating his action – hands directly above and just in front of the head.

As I was turning to go, he said: "See you, then."

I knew it was just a figure of speech, the sort of thing people often said to complete strangers they never expected to bump into again. Even so, at that moment he sounded so friendly that I felt a thrill of acceptance, the sort of feeling you get as a little kid when a bigger kid says you can be in their gang.

"Yeah, see you," I replied.

I turned up at the next home game wearing the brand new Watford scarf I'd bought from a stall in the market that morning, and headed for the area behind the goal. I was unsure whether to approach my new friend, but while I was wavering, he glanced around and spotted me and said, "Hey, it's Lucky! How're you doing?"

So I went over and said hello, and actually my name was Trevor, and he said his was Steve, and then he introduced me to his companions. One of them was Frankie, his brother, four years older than him and even bigger and burlier. He had a fairly recent, two-inch-long scar on his chin, and his nose had clearly been broken at some point and then badly reset. He looked like what my parents used to call 'a bad sort', and I was instinctively scared of him. I came to learn that most people were scared of him, and with good reason – especially if they were fans of opposing teams.

With Frankie were a couple of his sidekicks who looked every bit as tough as he did. I never really talked to them, and they didn't talk to me, especially after they found out I was a grammar-school boy. I got the feeling that if it hadn't been for my yellow and black scarf, they'd probably have given me a good kicking. Not then and there, maybe, but some time, somewhere.

Fortunately, Steve's friends were more welcoming. There was a shifting crowd of them that changed from week to week, and I came to know some better than others. They all went to the same school, a secondary modern in north Watford. After all these years, most of them are just names: Mike, Alec, Robbie, Andy. But there was also Des.

The first thing you noticed about Des was his clothes. Steve and the others were on the scruffy side, but not Des. He always vehemently denied being a Mod, but even if he didn't own a baggy parka with a target on the back, he certainly thought about clothes in much the same way. You could see it in the crease in his Sta-prest trousers and the shine in his sharp-toed shoes. His haircut, too, was distinctive, a shaggy bowl cut that was favoured by the Rolling Stones at the time. Beneath it, a lively, intelligent face that seemed to reflect a constantly changing stream of thoughts and emotions.

That was the second thing I noticed about Des; after a few minutes in his company you realised that he was bubbling with nervous energy, the way a bottle of lemonade fizzes when you shake it and then slowly unscrew the cap. He couldn't stay still or silent long enough to be truly cool. During the match he was every bit as strident as Steve, screaming and yelling at the players and the referee in a voice that was surprisingly loud, given his wiry frame, and dancing from foot to foot with joy or frustration at the slightest advance or setback. But whereas Steve was serious about his football and spent the entire half-time interval discussing the game with Frankie, Des soon lost interest in the conversation and started chatting to one of the others. I was too busy trying to soak up some of Steve's football knowledge to pay much attention, but I gathered that Des was talking about music.

It was at the next match, or possibly the one after (ask Steve – he'll also be able to tell you the opponents, the result, the names of the scorers and, I dare say, how much sugar they took in their half-time tea), that I found myself gravitating towards Des rather than Steve at half-time. Frankie kept glaring at me in a way I found unsettling, so I moved down a couple of steps to where Des was standing on his own with his back to me.

When I got alongside him, I noticed that his left arm was bent at a right angle and his fingers were crooked in a variety of unnatural-looking positions, as if he'd suddenly been struck by arthritis. As I watched, he rapidly unclenched the fingers and moved them into a new configuration that looked equally uncomfortable. Then he returned to the first position.

"F sharp minor," he said without looking up.

"Er, pardon?"

"F sharp minor. It's a new chord I just learnt." He glanced at me with an expression that was unexpectedly serious, still clenching and reclenching his fingers. "I'm trying to get the progression from there to E and back again."

"Oh, you play the *guitar*," I said stupidly, belatedly realising what he was on about.

"Of course I play the bloody guitar, what did you think I was doing? Practising sign language?"

In fact, a teacher at one of my junior schools had taught us sign language, and I was about to point out that what he was doing didn't look like anything a deaf person would understand. But I thought better of it, and instead tried to cover my embarrassment and confusion in the

13

traditional English manner; I pretended nothing had happened.

"So, um, do you play in a group?"

"Yeah, we've just started a new one. Me on guitar and vocals, Steve on drums of course, Pete on bass." He nodded in the direction of a plump boy with a Beatles-type fringe who I hadn't taken much notice of before. "We're practising tonight, over at Steve's place," he went on. "You should come along."

I was about to say that I didn't think my parents would let me, but just in time I remembered that I was supposed to be trying new things. So I said yes, I'd like to come and watch them practise, and he scribbled some directions on the back page of my programme. The teams were just emerging for the second half when something occurred to me.

"What sort of music do you play, then?" I asked.

Des's eyes lit up and he smiled a joyous, knowing smile as he uttered a single word: "Blues."

Then the whistle shrilled, the crowd roared, and the game began again.

A light drizzle began to fall as I was cycling along St Albans Road, so I stopped to put up the hood of my anorak. I took the opportunity to check Des's semi-legible directions again. I'd never seen musicians rehearsing, but I had a vague notion that if I arrived late, I might disturb them at a crucial moment and make myself unpopular, and I didn't want to jeopardise my budding friendship with Des and Steve. What with that and the nagging guilt at having lied to my parents (I'd told them I was going to a schoolfriend's house to watch television), I was feeling more than a little agitated by the time I found the turning and headed slowly up a dimly-lit side street.

I needn't have worried. Des had explained that Steve's father was in the car repair business, and the garage on the corner was just as he'd described it, with its double set of steel shutters facing the street. I pulled up on the forecourt and leant the bike against a rusty petrol pump.

Now what? "We'll be in the back," Des had said. A car went past, then another, and then there was a gap in which I heard the thump of a drum somewhere nearby, followed by a descending sequence of notes played on an electric guitar. Looking around, I spotted a path leading down the side of the garage. I followed this, feeling my way along the wall in the darkness, until I found a door with a light shining under the bottom of it. A rapid series of drumbeats confirmed that I'd reached my destination, and I waited for them to stop before knocking.

"Come in!" shouted a voice, and I opened the door.

The room I entered seemed to be an extension that had been built onto the back of the garage, presumably at a time when business was booming. For now, the space where a car might have stood was occupied in part by an impressively large drum kit. Steve was sitting behind it on an upturned crate, fiddling with a cymbal, and as I shut the door he looked up and said: "All right? Take a seat, we'll be starting soon."

I found a solid-looking box to perch on and watched while the band completed their preparations. On one side of the drum kit stood Pete, with a bass guitar slung around his neck and a cigarette dangling from the corner of his mouth. He didn't seem to be doing much, though occasionally he plucked one of the strings of his bass, as if to confirm that it was still working.

On the other side of the drums, nearest to where I was sitting, Des was as restless as Pete was languid. He would play a note, then give one of the keys at the end of the guitar a minute twist and then try it again. When he was finally satisfied that all the strings were in tune, he turned round and made some adjustment I couldn't see to the small black amplifier sitting on the oil-stained floor behind him. Then he tapped the microphone a few times, strummed a couple of chords, and turned to Steve and nodded.

Pete dropped the remains of his cigarette on the floor and trod it out, muttering something that sounded like, "About bloody time." Steve held his drumsticks poised above his kit, and Des suddenly flashed me a huge grin before counting in the first song.

As it turned out, it was the *only* song for the first half-hour or so.

It was 'Dimples' by John Lee Hooker, though I didn't know that at the time. I'd never even heard of John Lee Hooker, and this music was light years away from the jangly beat-group pop I listened to on Radio Luxembourg in my bedroom in the evenings. It was more... grown-up, I suppose. The heavy, shuffling rhythm exuded a confidence that was lacking from the breathless pop rush of something like 'Please Please Me' (one of the few singles I owned). Then there was Des's voice, a pseudo-American drawl that was far deeper than you'd expect from someone so skinny.

It was obvious from the start that Des was the leader of the band. When they'd run through the song once, he gave a few instructions to Steve and Pete and then they tried it again. This time he halted them at the end of the first verse, and after that they started and stopped on Des's command, trying the song at different speeds or in different keys, or focusing on sections that he wasn't happy with. Most of it went over my head, but I did gather that Pete wasn't keeping time as precisely as he might have, and at one point I thought he and Des were going to have a row. Then Pete shrugged and said he'd try to do it the way Des wanted it done, and that was the end of it.

Eventually they moved on to a second song, Chuck Berry's 'Too Much Monkey Business'. I *had* heard of Chuck Berry, though I didn't know this particular number. It soon became apparent that the band didn't either – at least, not well enough to play all the way through. They kept attacking the song at breakneck speed, and invariably one of the three would get out of time. Or, if they all kept up with each other, Des would get the words jumbled and break off abruptly, swearing at himself. A couple of times they got as far as the guitar break, which seemed to be every bit as convoluted as the lyrics, and caused Des similar problems. He wasn't short on technique – even my untutored ears could tell that he could play a bit – but I suspected that he'd bitten off more than he could chew.

I kept this opinion to myself, of course. In fact I barely said a word, and the three of them acted for the most part as if I wasn't there. Just once, when they'd finally played 'Dimples' to Des's satisfaction, he turned to me and said: "So, what d'you think?"

"It's great – brilliant," I gushed, eager to ask him about the song and where he'd found it. But he'd already turned away to say something to Pete, and the chance was gone.

After an hour or so, Des admitted defeat. As if on cue, there was a muffled banging at the door on the opposite side of the room to the one I'd entered by.

"Get that will you, Lucky," said Steve, who was in the middle of making yet another adjustment to his drum kit. So I slid off the box I'd been sitting on and walked across the room, brushing slivers of wood from the seat of my trousers as I went.

Opening the door, I found myself face to face with the most beautiful girl I'd ever seen. True, I'd attended single-sex schools since I was eleven, and what with me being an only child as well, I didn't really get to speak to girls in the normal run of things. So yes, maybe I was easily impressed. Even so, I can honestly say that no one I've met since has taken my breath away quite so comprehensively.

It was her hair I noticed first, a vibrant shade of reddish orange, hanging straight down over her shoulders. It formed a contrast with the pale skin of her perfectly oval face, where I registered high cheekbones, a snub nose and an unusually wide mouth. I was still taking all this in when she spoke.

"If you're not going to let me in, you could at least take this off me."

Blushing at my awkwardness, I hurriedly took the heavily-laden tray she was holding and put it down on the crate Steve had placed in the middle of the floor. She'd followed me into the room, and when I dared to look at her again I was relieved to see that she was smiling.

"You must be Trevor," she said. "Stevie told me you were coming, so I made you a cup. I hope you like your tea good and strong. I'm Susie, by the way."

I had no idea how I liked my tea, since I didn't drink it at home. My parents had always implied, without actually saying as much, that tea and coffee were two of the many mysteries of adulthood which I

17

wasn't yet ready for. So I imitated the others, pouring a generous splash of milk into my mug and adding three sugar cubes. Unfortunately, I failed to notice that the others didn't actually start drinking at once. The result: an incautious slurp that burned my tongue and brought tears to my eyes. I turned away swiftly so that nobody would see.

Luckily Susie was talking to Steve, while Des was showing Pete some fingering on the guitar, so I had time to compose myself before addressing something that was puzzling me. Turning to Susie, I asked: "So, is there a kitchen out the back or something?"

She frowned. "In the house, you mean? Yes, of course."

"Oh, you live here, do you?"

"Didn't they tell you? We live right next door – or did you think I'd been lugging this tray round the streets with me?"

The others were listening to us now, and they all laughed. I blushed again, but simultaneously the penny dropped, and before I could stop myself I said: "Oh, right, so you and Steve must be related..."

This time the laughter was louder and longer, and Steve clapped me on the back and said that for an educated feller I wasn't as bright as I ought to be. But by the way he grinned as he spoke, I knew he didn't mean anything by it. And as I stood there smiling sheepishly, between the hulking brother and the slender sister, I felt the same sensation I'd experienced a few weeks earlier on the terraces at Vicarage Road – a gratifying feeling of being welcome here.

When everyone had finished their tea, Susie gathered together the mugs and took away the tray. I made sure I was nearest the door so that I could hold it open for her, and was rewarded with a smile before she disappeared into the darkness.

Meanwhile the band was gathering around Des, receiving instructions for the next section of the rehearsal. Steve fetched a small portable record player from the back of the room, and while he was looking for a suitable spot to set it up, Des explained that they were learning a new song off a record. They hadn't actually tried playing it yet, and Pete and Steve wanted to have another listen to the record first.

I leaned over to look at the seven-inch single Des was holding. It was in a plain paper sleeve, but I had time to read the label before he handed it to Steve. 'Good Morning Little Schoolgirl' was the title, and it was by a band I'd never heard of called The Yardbirds.

I know, I know. But you have to remember, when I first entered that room at the back of O'Brien's Garage, my knowledge of r'n'b, blues, call it what you like, was non-existent. It's shocking to think that I was ever so ignorant. In my defence, I should point out that I was in the majority at the time. In 1964, r'n'b enthusiasts were like members of an underground religious sect, waiting for the glorious day when the whole world would see the light.

The Yardbirds had already seen it – that much was clear from my first listen. The song opened with a catchy harmonica riff that was counterpointed by a series of staccato 'oh's from the singer, who then let out an unexpected, jubilant shriek before launching into the verse. Driving bass and guitar kept up the momentum behind the crudely harmonised vocals, and then another shriek introduced a guitar break unlike any I'd heard before, not flashy but somehow piercing, sharp, so that you felt you ought to be able to cut things with it. Then it was back to the verse, and the song quickly faded out before you had time to get tired of it. The lyrics weren't up to much, as far as I could make out, just the standard American teen pap – one couplet rhymed 'hop' with 'soda shop' – but the feel of the song, and especially that guitar solo, chimed with something inside me that I hadn't known was there. I can see now that it fulfilled the longing for novelty and adventure I'd been trying to satisfy. It hadn't occurred to me to look for it in music.

Mind you, I probably wouldn't have felt quite the same if I'd first heard 'Good Morning Little Schoolgirl' as performed by Des and co. They managed the basic riff all right with a bit of practice, and Des came up with an ear-splitting shriek which actually surpassed the one on the record. But other elements of the song proved harder to replicate. For a start, the harmonised vocals meant that Pete had to share Des's microphone, and it soon became obvious that Pete wouldn't have been able to carry a tune if you'd put handles on it. ("Look, I never said I could sing," he protested after Des had aborted the sixth or seventh

19

attempt at the first verse.) As for the guitar solo, Des seemed to be playing the right notes, more or less, but the feel wasn't there, and he knew it, judging from the look of furious concentration on his face as he played it through again and again.

There was something else missing too, something so obvious that I couldn't believe I hadn't noticed until Des pointed it out. "It's a shame we haven't got a harmonica player," he said as they were setting up for a full run-through. "Trouble is, you need someone who can play while I'm singing. It's all right for The Yardbirds, there are five of them."

"I can play the harmonica." It just came out, but I knew as soon as the words emerged that I couldn't unsay them.

"Yeah?" Des looked interested. "Can you play the blues?"

"Umm, I haven't tried. I could have a go," I added hurriedly.

"Well, when you can play that" – he nodded at the single sitting on the turntable – "let me know."

I couldn't tell whether it was an invitation, a challenge or a put-down, or all three at once. But as Des turned away to talk to Pete, I knew what I had to do. Besides, I needed an excuse to see Susie again.

I was telling the truth when I said I could play the harmonica. Well, sort of. Mum had given me one for Christmas when I was ten, and in the first flush of enthusiasm I'd learnt to play 'Three Blind Mice', 'Row Row Row Your Boat' and a couple of other simple tunes. Then I'd got bored and moved on to another hobby.

Remarkably, given the number of houses we'd occupied since then, the harmonica had survived. The morning after the rehearsal I went up into the attic and started rummaging around in the crates that no one had bothered to unpack. I eventually found one marked with a big 'T' and somewhere near the bottom, underneath the threadbare teddy bears and the lead soldiers with their dangerously sharp bayonets, down there with the spinning top and the chess set and all the other detritus of my childhood, was the harmonica.

The case was made of plastic, and there was a clown's face painted on the top. I suspected that it wasn't the sort of instrument any self-respecting blues musician would play. Nevertheless, I put it to my lips and blew. A little cloud of dust emerged from the holes at the back, together with a strangulated sound that bore little relation to any known musical note. A second, stronger puff elicited more dust and a slightly louder cacophony. Then I tried sucking. By the time I'd stopped coughing, I knew I was going to have to buy a new harmonica.

So after school the next afternoon, I cycled into town and went to Hammond's Music Shop. I'd never been there before, but my classmates had assured me that this was where you came if you wanted any kind of musical instrument, from a jew's harp to a grand piano. Sure enough, there was a glossy black baby grand in the window, flanked by a couple of uprights. A small boy in grey shorts was plinking tentatively at one of these, watched by an elderly salesman and a smart-looking woman in a twinset and pearls, both of them smiling benevolently.

The walls of the shop were lined with impressively expensive-looking orchestral instruments, and I began to feel uncomfortably self-conscious. Then I reminded myself that I was being adventurous and sauntered (or so I imagined) over to a glass-fronted case in the centre of the shop which contained the smaller instruments.

The salesman standing behind it was middle-aged, balding and rather severe-looking, though the stripy short-sleeved pullover he was wearing worked against this.

"Can I help you, sir?" he inquired gravely.

For a moment I wondered if he was taking the mickey, until I realised that my grammar school blazer doubtless marked me out in his eyes as a bona fide customer rather than just another time-wasting teenager.

"I want to buy a harmonica, please," I said.

"Certainly, sir. Do you prefer a particular make?"

It hadn't occurred to me that there'd be a choice. "Um, no, I'm sort of a beginner," I mumbled.

The salesman bent down, slid open a door at the back of the case and picked out a small rectangular box. "This is our most popular model," he said, straightening up and handing me the instrument

21

inside.

Handling the harmonica with care, I studied the shiny metal plate on the top. The words 'Marine Band' were engraved on it in big capital letters, and underneath, in a more flowery hand resembling a signature, 'M. Hohner'. On the left-hand side there was an old-fashioned picture of a man (Mr Hohner, presumably), done in profile, in an oval 'frame' surrounded by flowers. It was all very dignified for such a tiny instrument – especially compared to my old plastic harmonica with the clown's face – and I warmed to it immediately.

I was about to put it to my lips when I realised that it probably wasn't the done thing to try out instruments you had to blow into. So instead I gave it back to the salesman and said I'd take it.

"Very good, sir. Which key would you like?"

Key? Now I was completely out of my depth. I'd sat through music theory lessons at school and listened to the teacher going on about bars and staves and keys and the rest of it, but I'd vaguely assumed that these were only important if you were going to play classical music. Did blues musicians have to know this stuff too?

In my panic, I was about to pick a letter at random when the salesman took pity on me. "How about a C?" he suggested. "That's probably the most common key, whichever kind of music you want to play."

Gratefully, I agreed that this sounded like a good idea, handed over my twelve shillings and left with my new prize possession in the pocket of my school blazer. Then I headed off to WH Smith's to buy a copy of 'Good Morning Little Schoolgirl'.

Back home, I was keen to begin practising at once, but it wasn't as simple as that. Certainly, I could have started tooting away in my bedroom after dinner, but Mum and Dad would have heard me and asked what I was up to. Then I would have had to either (a) make up a story to explain this unexpected revival of my interest in the harmonica, or (b) tell the truth, with all the potential for arguments that would have entailed. My parents weren't strict or repressive by any means, and they'd always encouraged me to have hobbies, but I couldn't see them approving of me playing in an r'n'b group. So I wasn't about to give them a chance to stop me. This was mine, the football on Saturday afternoons and Des and Steve, and now the harmonica, and I wasn't about to share any of it with them.

There was another, related problem; I didn't own a record player. The only one in the house was part of the box-shaped, walnut-veneered radiogram that stood in the corner of the sitting-room. But in order to learn to play the harmonica part from 'Good Morning Little School-girl', I needed to listen to the record a few times – and I didn't think The Yardbirds would be to my parents' taste.

Still, in my new go-getting mood, no problem was insurmountable. For the next few days I invented excuses to ride off on my bike straight after dinner, and headed for the countryside. After a bit of searching on the first day, I found a small copse, well away from the nearest village, where it seemed unlikely that I'd be disturbed, and there I settled on a log and practised playing the harmonica until it was dark. Then I went home to do my schoolwork.

The weather was kind, and my progress was encouragingly quick. The harmonica came with instructions that had been folded over and over so that they fitted neatly in the bottom of the box – when I took them out, they sprang into an unruly paper concertina. By the third day I'd mastered the basics and was ready to move on to the first tune: 'Oh, When The Saints Go Marchin' In'. It was written out properly, with crotchets and quavers and everything, but fortunately it was also given in a special notation for harmonicas, with the number of the hole you needed and an arrow pointing up (meaning 'blow') or down ('draw'). The length of the arrow showed the relative amount of time you were supposed to hold the note for. It was easy to follow, and soon I was walking round the copse, leaves and twigs crunching beneath my feet as I played the tune again and again with gusto, experiment-ing with the rhythm and tempo and already imagining myself up on a stage, blasting through a solo while Des and co. looked on admiringly in the background.

I made one other important breakthrough in those first few days.

A boy I knew at school bought 'Melody Maker' every week. The paper got passed round the class, and when my turn came I discovered a photo of The Yardbirds in action. The singer, Keith Relf, was playing a harmonica in the picture, and studying it closely, I realised I'd been holding the instrument all wrong. Up until then I'd been gripping it with both hands, thumb and forefinger primly clasping the ends. But Relf was holding the harmonica in his left hand, with the thumb underneath and the other fingers on top. The right hand was just cupped over and behind the left, with only the thumb actually touching the instrument.

As soon as I reached the copse that evening I tried out this new way of holding the harmonica. It had looked right in the picture, and it felt right, like you were holding something intimate and precious. I soon found that with this grip you could make the harmonica sound different, too; by vibrating your right hand back and forth you could create a kind of tremolo that I recognised with a start as the harmonica sound I'd heard in TV series like 'Rawhide' and 'The Lone Ranger'. Opening and closing the right hand more slowly produced a different noise, a sort of wah-wah, and if you did that while blowing a nice fat chord of three or four notes, it sounded a bit like an old-fashioned train whistle. I was starting to feel like a proper harmonica player.

The next day was Saturday. My parents always went shopping on Saturday mornings, and I usually tagged along. But this time I said I had too much homework. It was the one excuse I knew they wouldn't question.

Through the net curtains I watched the car pull out of the drive. Then I switched on the radiogram and dashed up to my room, taking the stairs two at a time, to fetch 'Good Morning Little Schoolgirl'. By the time I returned, the radiogram was emitting the low hum that meant it had warmed up. I put the record on, sat back in the armchair opposite and listened. When the record had finished, I got up and put it on again, and I repeated this process four, five, six times.

To be honest, the main problem was that I kept drifting off into daydreams where I was playing concerts, making records, becoming a pop star... Then the clunk as the record deck switched itself off brought me back to my parents' living room, and the realisation that I hadn't taken anything in. Finally I forced myself to concentrate on shutting out the sound of the singer and the other instruments, so that I could focus on the harmonica. There was far more of it on the record than I'd realised on that first hearing. Although it wasn't always as loud as it was during the introduction, it was there all the way through, playing along with the guitar or echoing a line or phrase. That was encouraging. It would give me more to do, and the extra bits didn't sound very complicated.

The introduction did worry me, though. There were bits of it that didn't sound like any noise I'd produced from my harmonica over the past week, intentionally or otherwise. And when I finally stopped prevaricating, took the instrument out of my pocket and tried to find the notes, my fears turned out to be justified. It wasn't hard to work out which holes I was supposed to be playing on, but even when I seemed to have got the sequence right, it still didn't sound the way it should. I couldn't understand why.

I was slumped in the armchair, brooding on this problem, when I heard the sound of the car pulling up in the driveway. Thirty seconds later I was sitting at the desk in my room with a maths textbook open in front of me, ready for the inevitable moment when Dad shouted up the stairs: "Trevor! Come and help me bring the shopping in."

Later I decided that a blast of r'n'b might inspire me, so I walked up to the station, where there was a row of phone boxes. I dialled the number scrawled on my scrap of paper, and it was answered at the second ring. A woman's voice.

"Hello," I said, adopting my best telephone manner. "Is Steve there, please?"

"No, he's out." A pause. "This is Susie. Can I take a message?"

She too sounded as if she was straining for a level of politeness that didn't quite come naturally. As soon as I knew it was her, I wanted to reassure her, let her know she was talking to a friend. But all I could do was stammer: "Oh, hello. It's Trevor – Trevor Harris – we met last week at Steve's – I mean the band's rehearsal – you know, in the garage…"

I trailed off, reddening at my inability to utter a simple sentence to a beautiful girl over the phone. At least Susie sounded more relaxed when she replied.

"Hello Trevor," she said. "Yes, Steve's gone up to Rotherham with Frankie and some of his mates to watch the match."

"Oh, right." It hadn't occurred to me that people might want to go to Watford's away games as well as the home ones. "Well, I was just wondering, are the band rehearsing tonight?"

"No, I don't think so. I heard Stevie telling Des he didn't think they'd be back in time."

"Oh, right," I repeated, stupidly.

There was an awkward silence. "So, shall I give him a message, then?" asked Susie.

"Just, umm, just say I'll see him at the match next Saturday."

After we'd exchanged goodbyes, I put the phone down and wiped my sweaty palms on the seat of my trousers. Susie had a lovely voice, I decided, rich and unexpectedly deep; that was why I hadn't recognised it. It was another item to add to the list of reasons why I desired her, though I still had only hazy notions of how you went about fulfilling that kind of desire. All I knew was that I wanted to spend more time in her company, and to impress her, and the best way – no, let's be honest, the *only* way – I could think of doing that was to join her brother's band.

For the next week I practised whenever I could. I still couldn't crack the introduction to 'Good Morning Little Schoolgirl', but I had come up with an alternative. By cupping my right hand over the back of the harmonica and then opening and closing it rapidly, I could produce something that sounded more… well, professional. I hoped so, anyway. It wasn't exactly the same as the record, but it might be good enough.

When I joined Des and Steve and the rest of the gang on the terraces at Vicarage Road the following Saturday, I didn't say anything about what I'd been up to. I'd been so engrossed in the process of learning to play the harmonica, I'd almost convinced myself that I was practising for an official audition. But on the way to the ground, I'd had the unnerving thought that Des might simply have been joking. Maybe he wouldn't want me in the band at all – or worse still, he wouldn't want someone like me.

The thing is, I was keenly aware that I didn't really fit in with my new friends. My classmates at the grammar school had fathers who were accountants and lawyers and businessmen, not car mechanics like Steve's dad or print workers like Des's. No one had shown any outward resentment of my background – well, apart from Frankie – but that didn't mean they didn't feel it. All the more reason not to give them the chance to reject me, then; at least, not until they'd heard me play. So I just asked if they were rehearsing that evening, and if it would be all right if I came along, and Steve shrugged and said sure, why not? From that point onwards, I was so keyed up with nerves that I barely noticed what was happening on the pitch.

In the garage that evening they played the songs in the same order as last time. 'Dimples' was starting to sound quite polished after they'd run through it a couple of times, so Des swiftly moved them on to 'Too Much Monkey Business'. Before they started, he announced that he wanted to try it a bit slower than before, and once they'd all found the correct tempo, this seemed to help. By the time Des decided to take a break, everyone was in a positive mood. I hoped it was a good omen.

This time I was waiting for the knock on the door, and without prompting I hurried over and opened it. But instead of the vision of loveliness I was expecting, I found myself face to face with a stout middle-aged woman in a faded apron.

"Take this from me would you, there's a love," she said with a weary smile, handing me the tray and turning to go.

"Thanks Ma," said Steve – but the door was already closing behind her. He must have misinterpreted the disappointment that I wasn't a good enough actor to hide, because as I was putting down the tray he said: "Don't worry, I'll introduce you another time. She's worried about missing her favourite radio programme. Some daft drama serial."

Susie's absence did at least mean that I was free to concentrate on my primary objective. I waited until everyone had finished their tea, and Pete was chatting with Steve, before reminding Des of what he'd said at the last rehearsal. "Anyway, I've been practising," I concluded, as casually as I could manage. "Do you want to hear it?"

"Sure," he said, equally casually. There was no trace of mockery in his voice or his expression, and the fact that he was prepared to take me seriously was encouraging. At the same time, it made me even more nervous.

Steve and Pete were still on the other side of the room, so I quickly took the harmonica box out of my coat pocket and fumbled the lid open. As I removed the Marine Band, the piece of paper with the instructions on fell out and fluttered to the greasy garage floor like a sycamore seed, landing at Des's feet. He picked it up, glanced at it and handed it back to me without a word. I was so flustered by now that I was about to explain that they always included the instructions with harmonicas, they were just for kids, I didn't need them – but then I felt a sudden surge of impatience with myself and my lack of gumption, and that was enough. I moistened my lips with my tongue, put the harmonica to my mouth and played the introduction to 'Good Morning Little Schoolgirl'.

I'd closed my eyes so that nothing would disturb my concentration; I knew that Des's unflinching gaze would put me off. When I'd finished I opened my eyes again, and sure enough, he was studying me with an expression I found impossible to read. Pete and Steve were standing by his side, and it was Steve who spoke first.

"Good on you, Lucky!" he said. "That wasn't half bad."

Pete grunted something that could equally well have been agreement or derision, but I was more interested in what Des thought. Finally, as if he'd just completed a complex mathematical equation in his head, he said: "Let's try that again, with the band."

When everyone had moved over to their instruments I took up a position next to Des, who suddenly turned to me and asked: "What key are you playing in?"

I hadn't thought about keys since that day in Hammond's. It was C, wasn't it? A surreptitious glance at the top plate of the harmonica, where the letter was engraved in the metal, confirmed it, and I told Des.

"Right, 'Good Morning Little Schoolgirl' in C," he called out. "On four."

And so, on the count of four, I started playing, and though I was concentrating hard, I was aware of the others playing along with me, and Des singing the 'oh-oh-oh-oh' part, and it felt like nothing I'd ever felt before – like being part of something vital and dynamic, a world away from my usual solitary pursuits. Of course it was ragged, and Des stopped us at the end of the intro anyway because he wanted to try playing the guitar part in a slightly different way. But it was a good feeling, and I wanted more of it.

The next time we carried on going and played all the way up to the guitar solo, and we continued to practise the song for another half-hour. From having watched him, I knew exactly how Des liked to work, so I was able to slot right in there with the rest of them, taking instructions and responding to his cues. I wasn't given any special treatment, and it was as if I'd been accepted as one of the band, even though no one actually said as much. The only clue came at the end of the evening, when the others were packing up their instruments. I'd already returned my harmonica to its box and slipped it into my coat pocket (a process which was impossible to stretch out beyond ten seconds), so I turned to leave.

"See you next week, Trevor," said Des, just as I was opening the door.

"Yeah, see you," I said, and left quickly before they could see me blushing with pleasure.

Even then, I wasn't confident enough to feel that I'd been completely accepted by the band. But by the time I arrived at the garage the following Saturday, I had an ace up my sleeve, and as soon as they stopped for the tea break I played it.

"Listen, I think I've got us our first concert," I announced. (Notice how I slipped that 'us' into the middle of the sentence.) Gratified to have their full attention, I explained that the grammar school was having a Christmas dance at the end of term. The main attraction was a trad jazz band, but they were looking for a couple of other groups to play in the intervals between sets. I'd told the organisers I knew the perfect band.

The others clamoured round me, their questions overlapping each other. How long would we get? When was it? How many people would be there? Would we get paid? In the midst of all this, Susie came in with the tea – looking back, I can see that I'd subconsciously planned it this way, so that she'd see me being the centre of attention. When she found out what was going on she was as excited as the other three and insisted that we all clink our tea mugs as if they were champagne glasses, to toast the good news. Then she frowned.

"If you're going to play in front of an audience you're going to need a name, aren't you? Have you thought about that?"

We hadn't, and we immediately agreed that we ought to. That was just about the only thing we did agree on over the next half-hour. For a while we were on the verge of being the Des Armstrong Blues Band. It was Des himself who suggested that – modesty was never his strongest suit. Fortunately the rest of us managed to persuade him, as tactfully as possible, that it wasn't the snappiest name in the world.

"All right then, let's think of something else," he said, grudgingly. "But we've got to have the word 'blue' or 'blues' in there – all the top bands do."

"What about The Beatles?" asked Pete.

"I meant r'n'b bands, you prat," said Des, giving Pete a look that would have wilted flowers. "You know," and he started counting them off on his fingers, "Blues Incorporated, The Blue Flames, The Bluesbreakers..."

I hadn't heard of any of these bands, and I'm pretty sure Steve and

Pete hadn't either. Nevertheless, we were impressed enough to take his point – and I was too meek, given what had happened to Pete, to point out that Des's favourite group, The Yardbirds, was an obvious exception to his rule. So we started suggesting names that followed the formula 'the Blue somethings'. After all these years, I can't remember any of them. It's probably just as well.

We were going round in circles, and it was Susie who came to our rescue. She'd been sitting there in silence while we batted stupid names to and fro, but finally she decided to inject some feminine logic into the proceedings.

"Maybe we should be thinking about this another way," she said. "For instance, what have you got in common?"

"We go to the same school," said Steve at once. "But you're not suggesting we should name ourselves after *that*, are you?"

"I'm not, and anyway Trevor goes to a different school, so that's no good," she retorted. "Look, where did you all meet?"

"That's it!" I was cottoning on now. "It was at Vicarage Road."

"There you are then," said Susie.

"The Watford Blues Band?" Des snorted. "It sounds like something organised by the council."

"Wait a minute," and I was getting excited now, "how about The Hornets?"

Nowadays every football fan is aware that Watford are known as the Hornets, but in 1964 the nickname was still fresh – the result of a contest run by the local paper a few years earlier to find a new one after the team switched to wearing yellow and black. Besides, I liked the name, and it seemed ideal for our purposes, with its connotations of liveliness (buzzing around) and aggression (the sting in the tail).

To my barely-concealed delight, the others agreed. Pausing only to tack the obligatory word on the front, the newly christened Blue Hornets went back to work, practising 'Good Morning Little School-girl' with a new urgency now they knew that someone other than the drummer's younger sister was going to hear them play.

The next few weeks tend to blur in my memory into a series of intensive band rehearsals. I'd established that our slot at the dance would only last ten minutes, so our set would be as practised in the back of O'Brien's Garage: start off at a cracking pace with 'Too Much Monkey Business' to get the audience's attention, follow up with the slower 'Dimples' and finish with the other uptempo number, 'Good Morning Little Schoolgirl'. Foolproof.

In my own mind I was now firmly established in the band. After all, I'd named us *and* got us our first booking. But it was Steve who pointed out something that hadn't occurred to me: what was I supposed to do during the first two songs, which had no call for a harmonica part? Pete suggested that I could just stand in the audience and come up on stage for the last song, but I fought hard against that. What was the point in being in the band if you weren't on stage the whole time?

Eventually someone found a tambourine that I could bash against my leg in time with the music, as I'd seen Mick Jagger doing on 'Ready, Steady, Go!'. I also got to sing along with Des on the chorus of 'Too Much Monkey Business'. That worked well enough, but even I had to admit that on 'Dimples', the tambourine was superfluous. Conscious of this, I practised looking cool in front of the mirror in my bedroom. In my fantasy, the audience would be intrigued by the enigmatic figure I cut as the tambourine player, and then blown away by my virtuosity on the harmonica at the climax of the set.

Actually, I wasn't too bothered about the rest of the audience as long as Susie was impressed. She was the focus of most of my fantasies, and I spent a lot of time locked in the bathroom with them. I'd now decided that I was in love with her. How else to explain the tightening I felt in my chest at band practice as the tea break approached and I waited for her to appear? Sometimes it wasn't Susie at all but her mother, who must have thought I'd taken a dislike to her from the way my face fell every time she brought us our tea. And sometimes it *was* Susie, but she simply handed over the tray and left. Even when she did stick around, I rarely got a chance to talk to her alone, and I didn't know what to say to her anyway. There was a yawning chasm between the current state of our 'relationship' and the way it was in my dreams, and I hadn't a clue how to go about bridging it. She was always friendly towards me, but shy, quite unlike the way she would take the mickey out of Steve, and Pete too sometimes.

Not Des, though. But then, it wasn't so easy to mock him. That was partly because of the intensity with which he focused on the music, driving us so hard in rehearsals that you'd have thought we were practising for a headlining spot on 'Sunday Night At The London Palladium'. But that was just it: in Des's mind, this was his big break. I don't think any of us appreciated at the time just how badly Des wanted to be a star, but we did recognise him as our natural leader and treat him with the appropriate respect.

The other inspirational thing about him was his enthusiasm. I remember in particular one rehearsal about a week before the dance. Des was the last to arrive, which was unusual in itself, and he explained breathlessly that he'd been listening to "the best LP in the world" and lost track of time. As he slid the record out of the brown paper bag he was carrying it in, he added: "Oh, and I'm on it."

I was ready to believe anything he said, and while Steve fetched the record player, I grabbed the LP out of Des's hand. On the front cover, five young men in suits and ties crowded together behind a padlocked iron gate, all of them looking straight at the camera. I recognised the one in the middle in a pale grey suit, with just the faintest hint of a smile on his lips: Eric 'Slowhand' Clapton, the guitar-playing prodigy whose picture often appeared in 'Melody Maker'. The title was at the bottom, in lively, beatnik-style lettering: 'Five Live Yardbirds'.

The first track was one of 'ours', 'Too Much Monkey Business', taken at breakneck speed, and I realised at once that this was why Des had been trying to make Steve and Pete play the song so fast to begin with. He'd been trying to emulate his heroes, right down to Keith Relf's strange intonation, midway between a drawl and a sneer. As the song played, Des's fingers flickered automatically from one chord shape to another. His eyes were closed, and it was as if he was in some kind of trance. The rest of us could only watch and wonder what was going on in his head.

When the song finished he opened his eyes. "Bloody brilliant, isn't it?" he said, grinning beatifically.

Meanwhile Pete had grabbed the LP sleeve from me. "I don't see your name on here," he sneered.

Des didn't reply; he just got up and went over to the record player, lifted the needle and replaced it right at the end of a track. As the final chord died and the crowd cheered, he said: "Now, listen." There was a general hubbub and the sound of one of the musicians tuning his guitar, and then a voice called out: "Eric, you're a god!" You could hear someone on stage laughing briefly, and then they launched into the next song.

"That was me," said Des proudly, in case we hadn't worked it out for ourselves. "I was there – April the thirteenth at The Marquee. God, what a night that was." I thought he was going to tell us all about it, but then he abruptly switched back into bandleader mode. "Anyway, we'll listen to the rest of it later," he said brusquely. "We need to practise."

In later years I occasionally heard Des claim that he was the first person to call Eric Clapton 'God', the nickname – if you can call it that – that got scrawled on a lot of walls for a year or two in the mid-Sixties. I don't think it's true – he was usually drunk at the time, for one thing. Then again, no one's ever come up with a better explanation.

I know. I'm putting off describing the big moment – the climax of The Blue Hornets' brief career, the Christmas dance. There's a reason for that.

As I mentioned before, the main attraction was a trad jazz band. If that sounds like an anachronism, bear in mind that the Swinging Sixties hadn't really got going in south-west Hertfordshire yet, and certainly not at the grammar school. As I watched the throng jiving cheerfully to a succession of hoary old standards, I realised how musically conservative the majority of my fellow pupils were. For the first time I began to wonder how they were going to react to our fashionable brand of r'n'b.

At least the school wasn't so old-fashioned as to make the dance a single-sex affair. Tickets had been on sale at the nearby girls' grammar school, so there were plenty of well-bred young ladies for the boys to dance with. And that was *all* the boys were going to do with them if the authorities had their way. Teachers from both schools were present to act as chaperones, and from time to time one of them would dash onto the dancefloor to separate a couple who were deemed to be enjoying an unacceptable level of physical contact. There were more teachers outdoors, guarding the playgrounds, their sentry posts betrayed by the tiny clouds produced as their breath condensed in the frosty air.

There was no danger of me being a target for the patrols, sadly. Oh, Susie was there all right. I'd managed to wangle her a complimentary ticket on the grounds that she was our 'sound engineer', though even then the teacher on the door only let her in after she'd lied about her age. I couldn't blame him for being taken in; with her tight black sweater and slacks and carefully-applied make-up she passed for sixteen with no trouble. She looked stunning, and if I hadn't already been in love with her, I would have fallen there and then.

While the jazz band played their first set, the five of us stood to one side of the hall, drinking fizzy lemonade and generally acting superior. If Des, Pete and Steve felt intimidated in these surroundings, they certainly weren't about to show it. Des occasionally wandered up to the front to watch the guitarist at close quarters, while the rest of us tried to cover our nervousness by taking the mickey out of the dancers. There was one boy in particular who couldn't move in time to the music to save his life, and after we'd ripped him to shreds for a few minutes, Susie (who hadn't joined in the abuse) said: "Ah, leave the poor bloke alone. I bet none of you lot could do any better."

We all laughed, but she wasn't to be put off that easily. "Come on then, let's see what you can do. Who's going to dance with me?" She held her hand out. "Stevie?"

"Give over, Susie, you know I've got two left feet."

She turned to Pete, who just snorted "No bloody way" before she even had time to ask. Des was up by the stage at the time, so that just left me. Susie looked at me, smiling. "It looks like you and me are going to have to show these eejits how it's done, Trevor."

Believe me, I wanted to, wanted to so badly – wanted to take her hand and lead her out onto the floor and hold her and dance with her. I could already imagine the admiring looks from my classmates, the feel of my arm around her waist, the perfect fit of her hand in mine. But. But but but but but but but. I couldn't dance. Or rather, I'd never tried. I'd never been to dancing lessons, let alone an actual dance. There was always a chance that I'd be good at it, discover a natural rhythm, but it wasn't a chance I was prepared to take. The fear of failure gripped me like a hand around my throat and the original fantasy was swiftly replaced by a nightmare vision of me making a complete fool of myself in front of everyone I knew and cared about. At that moment, all my grand resolutions about trying new things and embracing the spirit of adventure crumbled into dust.

So I lied. I was getting quite good at lying by now, after practising on my parents for a couple of months. I still hadn't told them about the band; I was planning to wait until after the dance, hoping the fact that we'd played a 'professional engagement' would convince them it was a serious enterprise. I'd explained my increasingly frequent absences in the evenings as joint homework sessions with a classmate, counting on Mum and Dad being so happy that I was making friends at school that they wouldn't question me too closely. It had worked well – too well, in fact; they'd started pestering me to ask my new friend round to tea.

So I looked at Susie and said: "Umm, I'd like to, but I can't. I've got a bad ankle, you see." I lifted my left leg and waggled my foot from side to side, as if that corroborated my story. Susie looked sceptical, but I ploughed on: "I fell off my bike a few years ago. It's all right most of the time, but it swells up if I, umm, jump up and down or anything like that. Sorry," I added as an afterthought.

I was so embarrassed and disgusted with myself that I didn't register Susie's reaction to this. I muttered something about having to go to the toilet, and once there I locked myself in a cubicle, sat down and stared sightlessly at the graffiti on the back of the door, cursing myself silently in the foulest terms I knew.

I don't know how long I was in there, but I was roused by Steve's voice calling: "Lucky, are you in there? The jazz band have just gone off. We've got to get ready."

And ninety seconds later I was up on the stage preparing for my first live appearance. In my case, preparing was simply a matter of fetching the tambourine from the wings and checking that my harmonica was in my back pocket. Meanwhile the other three were making hurried adjustments to their gear. It had been agreed that we could use the jazz band's drum kit, microphones and amplifiers, but there was still a delay while Des and Pete fiddled with the controls on their amps and Steve readjusted the drums. The waiting didn't do much for my nerves and I instinctively tightened my grip on the tambourine, terrified of shaking it at the wrong time and drawing attention to myself. As if standing on stage in the school hall with an r'n'b band wasn't attention-grabbing enough... Finally everyone was happy. Des nodded to each of us in turn and then stepped up to the microphone.

"Hello, we're The Blue Hornets," he gabbled. It hadn't occurred to me that Des might be nervous too. "This is a song by the great Chuck Berry."

Then Steve counted us in and we were off, racing through 'Too Much Monkey Business' as if trying to set a new speed record. I whacked the tambourine against my leg for all I was worth and yelled the words of the chorus into the mic, and suddenly the song was over.

Now, for the first time, I focused on the audience – what was left of it. Because what I saw was this: Susie standing in front of the stage; behind her, a couple of dozen boys and girls who looked mildly bored; at the far left-hand corner of the hall, a long queue outside the ladies' toilet; at the far right-hand corner, a constant stream of boys entering and leaving the gents'; and along the right-hand wall, another queue by the trestle tables where soft drinks were on sale. At the same time I became aware of the noise, a general hubbub that clearly hadn't just started when we stopped playing. True, there was applause, but most of it was coming from Susie, with a few of the spectators following her lead. The main response we got from the audience, though, was complete indifference.

We shouldn't really have been surprised. When the dance band took a break, it was obvious that the dancers would take the opportunity to do likewise – they hadn't come to watch us play. But we *were* surprised. Fired up by Des's enthusiasm, we'd come to spread the gospel of r'n'b, and it hadn't occurred to us that our words might fall on stony ground.

There was an uncomfortable pause while we all looked at Des, waiting to see what he was going to do. Although he was clearly put out, he wasn't ready to give up yet. Glancing around to check that we were all ready, he launched into the guitar riff that opens 'Dimples'. Pete and Des came in on cue and off we went again. This time, having nothing more arduous to do than rattle and bang my tambourine, I watched the audience more closely. 'Dimples' was the most rhythmical of our tunes, the only one people could really dance to. A few couples did start moving around the floor in a vague, loose-limbed fashion copied from TV shows. Some of the teenagers standing around the edges of the hall were showing signs of animation, too – toes tapping, heads nodding – and I desperately noted each new convert to the beat as a sign that we were winning the battle. But then we finished and received the same lukewarm response as before.

I've often wondered since what was going through Des's mind at that moment. Anger, mostly, I think. Anger at the audience for failing to fall under his spell. Anger at himself for expecting too much from his first shot at playing live. And anger at me, perhaps, for helping to raise his hopes by arranging this ridiculous three-song appearance at a dance where no one wanted to listen us. I'm guessing, of course – we never talked about it – but it seems the most likely explanation for what he did next. More likely, anyway, than sheer absent-mindedness, which was the only reason I could think of at the time.

What Des did next was simple yet devastating. Turning his back to the audience he snarled: "Let's go out with a bang. 'Good Morning

Little Schoolgirl' in E."

As I turned to the mic and put the harmonica to my lips, I registered a brief look of panic on Pete's face and a swift rearrangement of his fingers on the strings of his bass. But I was already midway through the first phrase of the intro before I realised that Des meant the *key* of E, and by then it was too late. Seconds later the other three came in – in E, obviously – and even to my unmusical ears it was obvious that my harmonica – in C, the only key I had at my disposal – was producing a sound that was just plain wrong. I saw a look of pained puzzlement on Susie's face, while people all round the hall turned to each other, presumably to ask what that dreadful noise was.

Blushing deep with shame and embarrassment, I fought the urge to stop playing and managed to complete the intro I'd been rehearsing all those weeks. Even in my moment of humiliation I was unwilling to give up my precious few minutes in the spotlight, but at the same time I didn't want to ruin the whole song. The solution hit me in a flash; I simply took three big steps back from the microphone and carried on playing. Stupid, of course, but in my mind it preserved at least a shred of my dignity. For the rest of the song I gazed resolutely at the floor of the stage, determined not to catch Des's eye, or Pete's or Steve's, and definitely not Susie's.

After what seemed like aeons, Des hit the final chord. Still without so much as a glance at anyone, I turned and walked briskly off the stage. When I was outside the building I started running, and once on my bike I sped home as if I was being pursued by a pack of baying hounds. I only stopped once, on the bridge over the Grand Union Canal, to throw my harmonica as far as I could into the muddy waters. It could have been a deeply meaningful gesture, apart from the fact that I hadn't actually heard of Muddy Waters at the time.

Fortunately term was almost over, so I only had to endure a couple of days of scorn and sympathy (but mainly scorn) from my classmates. Then, a few days later, my father came home from work and announced that he'd been promoted, but it would mean moving again. While my mother smiled a thin, resigned smile and said that was wonderful news, I was thinking, yes, it really was. Although Dad didn't know it, it was the best Christmas present he could have given me.

BAR TWO: TREVOR, 1966

WH Smith's was still where I'd left it, on the High Street near the market, and I headed straight upstairs to the record department. Usually I enjoyed browsing, but today I knew exactly what I was looking for, and I quickly found it among the other new releases.

I'd been looking forward to this for weeks: the first album by John Mayall's Bluesbreakers since Eric Clapton had joined the band. With barely a glance at the front cover, I turned the sleeve over and examined the song titles – I wanted to see which blues greats Mayall had decided to cover. I nodded my head in silent approval as I noted the familiar names: Willie Dixon, Robert Johnson, Otis Rush. I was already savouring the sound of the album, as if it could somehow seep through the packaging and into my central nervous system, and I was about to head for the counter with it when I became aware of someone standing behind me.

"Isn't that the bloke who used to be in The Yardbirds?" said a familiar voice, and I turned to find myself face to face with Steve O'Brien. Well, actually I had to look up, because he'd grown even taller since the last time I'd seen him – on stage at the grammar school, I remembered with a shudder. But if Steve recalled that evening, or resented the fact that he hadn't heard from me in the 18 months since, he didn't show it. Soon we were enthusiastically swapping opinions about the World Cup – inevitably, since the Final was taking place that afternoon. We discussed England's chances, and I told him about the house I'd passed on my way into town where there was a huge Union Jack fluttering from a makeshift flagpole in the front garden.

But eventually the conversation sputtered out, as it does sometimes when you meet an old acquaintance and you only have so much in common, and I mumbled something about having to get home for lunch. We said our goodbyes, and Steve was just turning to go when he had an idea.

"Tell you what: d'you want to watch the match at our house?" he

41

said. "We've got a few people coming."

"Yeah, that sounds good." It sounded fantastic, given that the alternative was watching the Final at home with Dad, who knew little about football except that modern players were paid far too much for running around a field kicking a ball. "I'll be there."

Thanks to Dad's latest promotion, we'd moved up in the world. No three-bedroom semi in Croxley Green for the Harris family this time. We now resided in a detached house in Chorleywood, one of the smarter outposts of suburban Hertfordshire – film stars had even been known to live there.

Unfortunately for me (since I was still using a bicycle to get around), Chorleywood was a few miles further from Watford than Croxley Green. That Saturday was baking hot, and by the time I arrived at the O'Briens' house I was red in the face and my Aertex shirt was soaked in sweat. I also had indigestion, the result of having wolfed down my lunch in order to have time to play the first side of 'Blues Breakers' before setting off.

So it was probably inevitable that it was Susie who opened the door. She smiled when she saw me and said: "Hi Trevor, Stevie said you were coming. It's good to see you. Come on in."

And that was that. My heart started thumping against my ribcage and I realised that I'd never really fallen out of love with Susie. It came as a shock, because I'd assumed that I was over her. I'd thought about her a lot in the first few weeks after leaving the area, of course, but gradually she'd receded into the background, part of a brief interlude of adventure and excitement that came to seem increasingly unreal as time went by.

Besides, the school I went to in Portsmouth was mixed, and I found to my surprise that the girls there were quite keen to go out with me. I don't know whether it was my looks, or just the lure of the exotic. No, really. Some of them had never even met anyone from outside Hampshire, and I noticed a definite increase in interest after I mentioned that I'd been to London a few times. Soon I had a steady girlfriend, a skinny brunette called Alice. Our dates involved soft drinks in seafront cafés and evenings out at the movies, generally followed by sessions of enthusiastic but clumsy snogging. Occasionally she would let me feel her breasts through her sweater as we sat on her parents' sofa on a Saturday night. (I should add that they were out at the time.) It was exciting and enjoyable, but I knew it was never going to turn into anything serious. For one thing, Alice didn't like football – she had a brother who supported Portsmouth, but that just made it worse – and for another, her idea of hard-hitting, soulful music was Dave Dee, Dozy, Beaky, Mick and Titch.

Now, standing on the O'Briens' doorstep, I realised that the image of Susie had never really faded from my mind. It had just been filed away as the standard of perfection other girls would be judged against. And that standard had risen while I'd been away. Like her brother, she'd grown, but outwards as well as upwards. These days she curved in all the right places.

As I was taking this in, Susie was turning to go into the house. "They're all in the sitting room – first door on the left," she said. "I'll bring you a cup of tea, shall I?"

The sitting room was noisy and packed, and I hovered in the doorway until Steve spotted me and called me over. As I squeezed between heavy pieces of furniture and stepped gingerly over small children, he introduced me to everyone there. I recognised Frankie and one of his neanderthal mates, and Des was leaning against the wall in the corner, and it wasn't difficult to work out that Mr O'Brien was the tall, thick-set man holding court in the armchair directly in front of the television. (He stopped talking for a moment to nod to me, then resumed a vehement argument about whether or not Alf Ramsey had been right to leave out Jimmy Greaves.) The rest of them, I gathered, were relatives and neighbours and neighbours' kids. I squashed myself into a small space on the floor to the right of the TV, leaned back against the side of the sofa, took the mug of tea that was passed across the room to me and waited for the match to start.

After all these years, I don't remember many details of the game itself. It's the atmosphere that sticks in the memory. From the moment when we all joined in the national anthem before the kick-off, that little front room in Watford was a cauldron of emotion: depression when West Germany went into the lead, elation when England equalised and again when Martin Peters' goal made it 2-1, despair when the Germans scored in the ninetieth minute. As for extra time, the tension was unbearable until Geoff Hurst's second goal, and then it got worse. Could we hold on? I never even heard Kenneth Wolstenholme's famous 'some people are on the pitch...' line, because everyone in the room was yelling at Hurst as he bore down on the German goal, and as the ball crashed into the back of the net we all rose to our feet in one movement and roared in almighty joy, and then it really was all over and everyone embraced each other, friends and strangers alike. Even in the abandonment of the moment, I found myself wishing that Susie was near enough for me to hug her. But she'd watched the match from the doorway and was jumping up and down with her mother, and now they were joining in as everyone started singing 'Rule Britannia'...

Eventually we moved outside, where Mrs O'Brien had set up a table and loaded it with sandwiches, pork pies and sausage rolls. There were also bottles of Guinness and cans of Long Life lager and those huge tins that held vast amounts of Watney's bitter, and lemonade for the children, and as afternoon cooled to evening, the scrubby back garden came alive with chatter and laughter and singing.

I naturally gravitated towards Steve, who was talking about the match with a couple he introduced as his cousins, and then Des came over and joined in, and at some point the cousins wandered off and it was just the three of us. We carried on chatting about football for a while, but I think we all knew we were going to have to talk about The Blue Hornets sooner or later. The subject was hovering in the air between us, waiting for someone to grasp it, and finally I asked if the band was still going.

"Nah, we gave that up ages ago," said Steve dismissively, and for a moment I thought that was all I was going to get. But Des wasn't about to let it rest there and told me the full story. It turned out that Pete had decided he was bored with the blues not long after our abortive debut. They'd tried to recruit another bass player, but without success, and after a couple of months they'd stopped looking and the band had fizzled out. "But I've never stopped practising," Des concluded. "I'm just waiting to find the right musicians, then I'll show them."

I wasn't sure who 'they' were, but I was beginning to suspect that Des was drunk. "The trouble is, everyone's lost the faith," he went on, jabbing his beer bottle in my direction to emphasise the point. "The Yardbirds, Manfred Mann, the Stones – none of them are playing the blues any more. 'Paint It Black', that's not the blues. I mean, I really thought they were all proper bluesmen, y'know? Like John Lee Hooker and Muddy Waters. You wouldn't catch *them* singing pop songs. That's what I want to be – a bluesman all the way, for ever and ever, amen. But no one cares. No one fucking cares."

"That's bullshit!" Even I was surprised at my vehemence, but then, I was a little tipsy myself after drinking a can and a half of lager. "There are plenty of people playing the blues, right here in England." I told him about the Bluesbreakers album I'd bought that morning, and how Eric Clapton's guitar playing was soulful enough to make you cry.

"Yeah, but I hear Clapton's leaving the Bluesbreakers," said Des morosely, unwilling to be deterred from his pessimism.

"All right, but they say the bloke who's replacing him is just as good. Peter something or other. Anyway, from what I've read, Clapton's starting a new band and they're still going to play the blues. There are other groups I've read about, too. I tell you, there's something happening, and we could be part of it."

"What d'you mean?"

I turned to Steve, who'd been listening to our rantings with increasing bemusement. "Do you still play the drums?"

"Sort of. I mean, every now and then…"

"That's good enough. Look, I've been practising too, practising really hard. So let's get the band back together."

Silence. Des took a swig from his bottle and stared at me. Steve was looking at his feet. But I wasn't going to give in just like that. This crazy idea had come to me unprompted, but at that moment I was convinced it was a good one, and this was the one chance I had to make it work.

"Come on, what have you got to lose? Steve, can we still use the back room in the garage?"

"Um, I s'pose so."

"Right. I'll meet you there tomorrow afternoon at three o'clock and show you what I mean."

And with that I stalked off into the house, to forestall any further argument and to look for the toilet.

When I turned up at the garage that Sunday I was considerably less cocky than I had been the previous evening. But I'd said too much to back out now, and besides, I wanted to show off what I'd learnt. God knows I'd spent enough time practising.

Des and Steve were already there when I arrived, so I didn't waste any time. Taking the microphone out of my satchel, I asked Des if I could plug it into his guitar amp. He looked surprised, as I'd hoped he would, but he didn't object. I squatted down to fiddle with the controls, then straightened up, produced a harmonica from my shirt pocket, wetted my lips, played a couple of exploratory runs up and down the scale – and then let rip.

The tune I played them was an old one by Sonny Terry that I'd found on a country blues compilation. It was an instrumental, a raucous number with a catchy riff, and I gave it everything I had, stomping my foot on the concrete floor to keep the beat and breaking off periodically to holler "Whoo-hoo!", just like on the record. To tell the truth, it wasn't technically all that difficult. But it sounded good.

When I'd finished I looked up to see Steve grinning broadly, while Des's face registered a mixture of astonishment and thoughtfulness, as if he was already calculating the possibilities. Then he too smiled and said: "Where'd you learn to play like that?"

"Oh, you know. Just practice," I shrugged.

Which was true, as far as it went. In fact, it had taken an awful lot of practice to get from my earlier, barely competent level of playing to my current mastery of the instrument. The funny thing was that after my disastrous live debut, I had no interest in playing the harmonica ever again. Mentally, I was ready to consign my dream of becoming a musician to the dustbin and find something else to do with my spare time. Then, one Saturday morning a few weeks after moving to Portsmouth, I was browsing through a box of second-hand books on a market stall when I came upon a much-thumbed pamphlet called 'How To Play Blues Harmonica'. God knows how it got there. I like to imagine some black guy in the US Navy, sent overseas for the first time, spending the Atlantic crossing learning to play Little Walter riffs that reminded him of the clubs he used to go to in Chicago...

Anyhow, I was leafing through the pamphlet when I came across a section headed 'Cross Harp'. As I read on, I felt a surge of excitement as I realised that this was the missing piece of the jigsaw – the reason I hadn't been able to make my rendition of 'Good Morning Little Schoolgirl' sound exactly like the record. (Basically, cross harp is a way of transposing the key of a tune so that you get more draw notes, which you can bend to make the distinctive wailing sound which is the essence of blues harmonica playing. Simple, huh?) I had to try it out for myself, so I bought the pamphlet – the best sixpence I ever spent, that was. Then I found a music shop and got another Marine Band harmonica to replace the one I'd chucked in the canal. Mum and Dad were out when I got home, so I sat on my bed, opened the book at the chapter I'd been reading, and followed the instructions.

And what do you know – it worked. Not immediately of course, but once I'd got the hang of bending notes by dropping my tongue down to the floor of my mouth in the middle of drawing in air, the rest was just a question of practice. So I went back to the beginning of the pamphlet and followed it through, lesson by lesson. That took a few weeks. Then I went looking for records recommended by the author and tried playing along with them. Gradually I learnt to distinguish between and imitate different styles. I came to love the way Jimmy Reed played high and slow to accompany his slurred vocals – it sounded utterly sexual, or at least, the way I imagined sex might sound – and the way Little Walter's powerful, rounded tones made his harp sound like a saxophone. Oh yes, and I learnt to call my instrument a 'blues harp' or just 'harp', rather than a 'harmonica'. That was what children played. I was a bluesman.

So when Des asked if I knew anything else, I could answer with complete confidence. I thought for a few moments and suggested a Jimmy Reed song, 'Baby What You Want Me To Do'. He set up a slow, loping rhythm on the guitar, Steve listened for a few bars and then joined in on the drums, I played the keening harp intro, and we were away, with Des crooning the lyrics like he'd written them himself.

That afternoon we played for hours, sometimes moving quickly from one song to the next, sometimes homing in on a particular number until we'd done all we could with it. Des and I swapped suggestions of songs we could play, and we were amazed how many we both knew. In any case, if one of us wasn't sure how a song went, we soon managed to pick it up. As for Steve, he was incredible. I don't think he was familiar with more than a handful of the tunes we played, but he had the ability to work out what kind of drumming a song needed and produce it at a moment's notice.

Right at the end, for some reason, I suggested 'Good Morning Little Schoolgirl'. Maybe I thought it might exorcise any lingering demons that might threaten our new-found togetherness. Des flashed me a strange look, but then he counted me in and we were playing that song again. And you know what? It sounded pretty good. That is, my harp part sounded like Keith Relf, and Des's rendition of the guitar solo was a lot closer to Eric Clapton's than the last time I'd heard him attempt it. As he raised his right arm high and brought it crashing down on the final chord, we all grinned at each other like idiots. No one needed to say anything. We were back in business.

If I'd had my way we'd have played every day after that. I was still on my summer holidays and I had plenty of free time. So did Des, who was about to start his second year at sixth-form college, where he was studying graphic design. (I always suspected this was a deliberate career move. He'd read that Keith Richards was an art student when he joined The Rolling Stones, and decided he could do worse than follow the same path.) But Steve had to work in the garage, helping his dad to mend cars, so we could only practise properly in the evenings after he'd finished. Not every evening, but three or four times a week, we got together and ran through song after song, trying to decide which ones we all liked and which we could do the most justice to. Des was a fan of the heavier Chicago bluesmen like Muddy Waters and Howlin' Wolf, who relied on sheer power for their impact: I was more interested in people like Jimmy Reed and John Lee Hooker, who specialised in finding a hypnotic groove that sucked you in and carried you along. I couldn't believe it when Des told me he'd seen Hooker play just a few months earlier, right there in Watford, at a social club in Garston. I thought he was winding me up until he showed me the handbill that he'd carefully preserved and stuck up on the wall of his bedroom.

I spent a lot of time at Des's house that August, listening to records and talking about the blues. We didn't talk about much else, in fact, for the simple reason that we didn't have much else in common. Still, the blues was plenty to be going on with, and swapping choice cuts from our record collections took up a fair amount of time.

Our record-buying had followed an almost identical pattern. We'd both started off collecting singles and albums by the British groups who'd got their first break playing a version of r'n'b: people like The Yardbirds, Manfred Mann, The Animals, and of course the Stones. Not that they'd necessarily carried on in that vein. Des and I agreed that the bands who'd moved into mainstream pop or other styles were contemptible. They might claim that they were 'finding their own voice': we called it betraying the blues. There were a few honourable exceptions, like John Mayall, but now that Clapton had left the Bluesbreakers we were worried that even they might go the same way.

That didn't stop us listening to British r'n'b records altogether, though mainly it was to pick up tips. That's how we'd both discovered genuine Chicago blues. After you'd bought a few records you started to notice the same writing credits turning up again and again, and sooner or later a sleevenote would give you a valuable clue – letting slip, say, that the mysterious Ellas McDaniel recorded under the name Bo Diddley. Then you could start trawling the shops for *real* blues albums.

Mind you, that was easier said than done. In those days, blues and r'n'b were classified as 'jazz', but you were fortunate if you found anything decent in the jazz sections of the big record shops. If, like Des, you were within reach of London, you could try your luck in a few specialist outlets; if, like me, you were stuck in the provinces, you had to rely on second-hand shops and stalls. As it happens, Portsmouth's backstreets yielded some precious treasures. Maybe they were the legacy of the same American sailor who'd provided my blues harp tutorial.

One of the first records I took round to Des's was a live album I'd found at the bottom of a cardboard box on one of those second-hand stalls. It was called 'Folk Festival Of The Blues', and the front cover showed pictures of the featured artists which some literal-minded sleeve designer had coloured – you guessed it – blue. Still, what artists they were: Muddy Waters, Sonny Boy Williamson II, Howlin' Wolf and Buddy Guy. The first three were the aristocrats of the legendary Chess label, and Guy was on his way to achieving a similar status when the show was recorded at a club in Chicago in 1963. I knew Des would love it and sure enough, the first time we listened to it together, he wouldn't let me say a word until the final note of the final track on side two had died away.

The second time round, though, he picked up the sleeve and started scanning it as he listened. Pointing at the picture of a bespectacled Howlin' Wolf, he said: "You know what his real name is, don't you?" He went on without giving me a chance to answer. "Chester Burdett. Doesn't sound half as good, does it?"

"Actually it's Burnett, not Burdett," I said smugly. "Anyway, none of them use their real names." I took the album sleeve from him and pointed to each picture in turn. "Muddy Waters is McKinley Morganfield, Sonny Boy Williamson is Alex Miller, and Buddy Guy is, umm..."

"George – George Guy." Des grinned. "See, you don't know it all, do you?"

I was annoyed at myself for having forgotten such an easy one. "I bet I know more blues musicians' real names than you do, anyway," I said peevishly.

"I bet you don't," Des retorted, and there was an awkward pause while we glared at each other.

Then I had an idea. "All right, let's find out," I said. "I'll say a name – the name someone records under – and you have to say their real one. Then you do the same to me, and we carry on taking it in turns until one of us can't answer."

"Fair enough. And I'll tell you what," he added, with a mischievous glint in his eye, "the loser has to drink half a pint of vodka."

I'd never drunk vodka in my life, so the amount didn't register. In any case, I was confident of victory. I studied this stuff with the same dedication I applied to my school work.

Des won the toss and got to set the first question. "Little Walter?"

"Marion Jacobs," I fired back without hesitation. "Jimmy Rogers?"

"James Lane." He sounded equally confident. "Memphis Slim?"

"Peter Chatman. Bo Diddley?"

And on we went, for longer than I'd have thought possible, as we rummaged through our memories and plucked out artists we'd heard of, but never heard. Finally I caught him out with a trick question. He didn't know, or had forgotten, that Elmore James really was christened that, and after taking a couple of minutes to think about it, he admitted defeat.

He took it well – better than I would've done, anyway – and insisted on performing his forfeit straight away. I hadn't intended to make him do it, but I followed him downstairs to the kitchen, where he took a

51

bottle of clear liquid from a cupboard above the sink, filled a half-pint glass that was sitting on the draining board, and downed it in one go. Then we went back up to his room to listen to more music. It was several years before it occurred to me to wonder whether he'd lost the bet on purpose.

Meanwhile, the three of us were gradually transforming ourselves into something resembling a real blues band, though I'm not sure we realised it at the time. A major turning point came about ten days after our 'reunion'. The jam sessions were exhilarating, but it was becoming obvious that there was something missing. It was Steve who articulated it, late one evening as we were packing the gear away.

"Look, you two," he began, with an uncharacteristically serious note in his voice, and we both turned to look at him – it wasn't often that he expressed an opinion. "I know this all sounds really good – this stuff we've been playing – but you can't have a proper band with just three people, can you?"

"Yes you can," I said. "Eric Clapton's new band is a trio. He plays guitar, Jack Bruce plays bass and Ginger Baker plays drums."

Steve wasn't about to be put off. "But that's the thing – they've got a bassist. We've only got guitar, drums and harmonica, and when you're not playing it's just me and Des. There's not enough – I don't know – enough meat in it, somehow. You know?"

I did know, and so did Des. But where were we going to find a bass player? Our old bassist, Pete Gallimore, was out of the question; apparently he'd become a hard-core Mod while I'd been away, and wouldn't listen to anything but soul music. In any case, none of us had ever really liked him. But we didn't know anyone else who might fit the bill. I suggested advertising for a bass player – sticking up a notice in Hammond's, that sort of thing – but Des wasn't comfortable with the idea of a stranger joining the band, so that was the end of that.

It was Steve (again) who eventually came up with the obvious solution that we'd overlooked: since all I was doing was playing intros, fills and the occasional solo, why didn't I learn to play the bass as well? If

I got one of those holders for my harmonica ("harp," I corrected him, automatically), like Bob Dylan used, then I could play both at once.

I found it hard to imagine playing two instruments at the same time. Then again, a couple of years ago I'd never have guessed that I'd become so proficient at the mouth harp, so anything was possible. I agreed to give it a go.

The following afternoon I found myself perched on the edge of Des's bed, nervously cradling the old acoustic guitar that Des had learnt on. The wood veneer finish was scratched and chipped, but the working parts had all been carefully maintained, and it only took a few moments to get it in tune. Only took Des a few moments, that is; I had no ear for it, and it took me years to develop one... I drew my fingers across the strings a few times and agreed that it made a fine sound. I was already beginning to have fantasies of attaining Clapton-like guitar hero status, temporarily forgetting that the ultimate aim of the exercise was for me to learn the bass. (We couldn't afford a proper bass guitar yet, so Des planned to teach me to play rhythm guitar first, just to get me started.) Then I tried playing my first chord, and my fantasies flew out of the open window. Des told me not to worry, it would get easier when my fingers hardened up. I was sceptical, but sure enough, after a couple of hours I was able to play something that sounded not completely dissimilar to 'Amazing Grace'. It was a start.

I think everyone holds in their memory one perfect summer (it's always a summer) when they were young and life, for a while at least, delivered on its promises. Mine was the summer of '66, from the World Cup Final right through to the damp day in September when I walked through the gates of the Guild School for the first time. In between, six weeks of sunshine that warmed my back as I cycled into Watford from Chorleywood; sunshine that fell through the single high window in the back room of O'Brien's Garage and lit the patches of oil puddling on the concrete floor, turning them into slick, rainbow-coloured swirls that we would soon learn to call 'psychedelic'; sunshine that bounced off the fingerplate of Des's acoustic guitar as I sat by the window in his bedroom, twisting my fingers into unnatural shapes to make chords which, when played in particular sequences, combined to create that miraculous thing called 'the blues'.

There's one day in particular that I always think of when I remember that summer. It was the Saturday of the August Bank Holiday weekend, when Mum and Dad had gone away to visit friends and left me to look after myself – a rare acknowledgement on their part that I was growing up. I spent the afternoon basking on the Vicarage Road terraces with Des and Steve, watching Watford beat QPR 1-0. Afterwards, instead of going home for my tea as usual, I put my bike in the back of the O'Briens' van and squeezed into the front seat between Frankie and Steve for the trip back to their house. We ate in the back garden; big slabs of bread spread thickly with home-made blackcurrant jam, followed by fruit cake and macaroons, all of it washed down with strong tea. I was sitting in a wonky deckchair that made every tentative sip of scalding liquid an adventure, but I didn't care. The contrast with teatime at my parents' house – a prim affair that took place at the dining table, with only occasional bursts of conversation to break the silence – was acute. All that was missing to make things perfect was Susie. Unfortunately, she was up in Liverpool, visiting relatives. But you can't have everything, can you?

Steve and I stayed in the garden, soaking up the last rays of the sun before it dipped behind the surrounding houses, while we waited for Des. He arrived clutching an LP, and I was thrilled when I saw which one it was. 'Classic Jazz Masters' it said in the top left-hand corner. Below that was a blue-tinted picture of some wooden shacks, and to the right of that, a red panel with the words 'Robert Johnson 1936 1937'. There was a list of song titles underneath, a couple of which I recognised. 'Rambling On My Mind' was the song Eric Clapton had sung on the 'Blues Breakers' LP, and I had an early Muddy Waters album where he covered 'Walking Blues' and 'Kindhearted Woman Blues'. This was a record Des and I had heard a lot about, and dreamed of owning. The bastard hadn't told me he'd actually found it.

We went into the garage to listen to it, the three of us sitting on a row of crates in front of the record player like pupils in class. Up until now, we'd assumed that the sound of electrified Chicago blues was as primitive as it got. But this was something else altogether. The twelve-bar blues structure was still there, but the instrumentation was stripped back to the bare minimum: no bass, no drums, not even a mouth harp, just a bottleneck guitar and a voice. And what a voice – edgy, pleading, raw. Sometimes, like on 'Come On In My Kitchen', Johnson sounded eager and sensual, but mainly he sounded tortured, a man at the end of his tether. It was hard to make out the words at times, but one verse stuck in my mind:

'Got to keep moving, I got to keep moving
Blues falling down like hail
And the day keeps on worrying me
Got a hellhound on my trail'

This was serious stuff, too serious for a seventeen-year-old to take in at the first listen. That evening I began to get an inkling of what the blues really meant, a state of mind that casual phrases like 'I'm feeling a bit blue today' could only hint at. But it was just an inkling at that stage. The thing is, you can't understand the blues just by listening to the music. I'm sure the others will tell you the same.

From time to time while the record was playing, I glanced at my bandmates to see how they were reacting to this revelation. Des was animated, tapping his fingers against the side of a crate in time to the music. Sometimes you could see in his face that he was trying to work out how a particular tune worked, what chords Johnson was playing. But I was surprised to find Steve listening equally intently. A frown of concentration never left his face from the moment the first song started. I wondered if he was afraid that Des was about to head off in a new direction, one that wouldn't have any call for a drummer.

There was no danger of that, but we were all keen to incorporate something of what we'd just heard into our repertoire. At Des's suggestion we decided to try the first song on side one, 'Crossroads Blues', and we spent half an hour working out a basic, mid-tempo version. We rehearsed a couple of other songs after that, but there was something lacking. At the time we put it down to the effects of a long, hot day that had turned our rehearsal room into a sweatbox, but I wonder if we weren't also suffering from the aftershock of our first exposure to Robert Johnson. The stakes had been raised, and even the ever-confident Des may have been wondering whether we were up to it.

So when he broke a string on his guitar and suggested we give it a rest for a while, no one was about to argue. Steve immediately disappeared in the direction of the house. Mrs O'Brien had stopped making our tea for us by now, on the (entirely reasonable) grounds that we seemed to be rehearsing all the time these days and she had housework to be getting on with. So we had to make our own. That wasn't such a bad thing, because when it was my turn, I sometimes got a chance to talk to Susie if she happened to come into the kitchen while the tea was brewing. I spent days beforehand anticipating these precious opportunities, and days afterwards analysing every word she spoke to me. The one thing I never quite got around to doing was asking her out. Like an actor, I had my lines prepared, but she never gave me the right cue.

When Steve came back, he wasn't carrying a tray laden with tea things, but three cans of lager, two of which he tossed nonchalantly to me and Des. (He hadn't brought any glasses, though – my mother would have had a fit if she'd seen us.) While I was juggling with mine, Des caught his in one hand, popped the ring pull and took a swig – all in a single movement, it seemed to me.

Steve grinned at my quizzical look. "Pa won't miss them," he said. "And it's a special occasion, isn't it – you staying over, I mean."

To escape the clammy air of the garage, we headed back to the O'Briens' garden and sank into the deckchairs. Dusk was falling, and for a while we sat there drinking in silence, lost in our own thoughts, watching the sky turn an ever deeper shade of blue.

It was Des who finally spoke. "D'you know the story behind that 'Crossroads' song?" he asked, knowing full well that we didn't. That is, Steve had never shown much interest in such things, and if I knew the story behind a song, I always made sure the others knew that I knew it.

"Well," he began, "back in the early Thirties, yeah, Robert Johnson used to play at dances and stuff around his local area, down in the Mississippi Delta – you know, where the blues started." I nodded impatiently. He didn't have to tell *me* where the blues started. "He was all right, but nothing special. And then one day he disappeared. People thought he'd just decided to try his luck somewhere else. Musicians travelled around a lot in those days, you see.

"But here's the thing." He paused for dramatic effect. "When he came back to town, he could play the guitar brilliantly, better than all the other guys who used to teach *him* how to play. And it didn't seem possible that he could've got that good just by practising, 'cause he was playing things that no one else could. So the story started going round that he'd sold his soul to the devil."

He paused again, and Steve took the opportunity to ask: "But what's that got to do with a crossroads?"

"I was just coming to that," said Des irritably. "Apparently there was this superstition that if you went to a crossroads at midnight, the devil would be waiting there, and he'd give you anything you wanted in return for your soul after you died. So Johnson must've gone down there, said he wanted to be the best guitar player around, and – well, he got his wish, didn't he?"

I didn't know what to say to that. The rationalist in me refused to believe in this kind of mumbo-jumbo. Still, it was a great story, wasn't it? Up until now we'd been content to worship God – in the all-too-human form of Eric Clapton, at least – but the idea that the music we loved, the music we played, was somehow the gift of the devil was an attractive one for a teenage boy at a time when it was practically compulsory to break taboos. Not that I was about to suggest that we paint pentagrams on the O'Briens' scrap of lawn, you understand, or slit the throat of their neighbours' Jack Russell and drink its blood. It just seemed like an additional validation for what we were doing, in a funny sort of way.

My reverie was broken by Steve, who'd been into the kitchen to fetch more beer. Sitting down heavily in his deckchair, he said: "So, Lucky, which crossroads did you go down to, then?"

I looked at him blankly. "What are you talking about?"

"Well I mean, it's a bit suspicious, isn't it? Last time we saw you, you could play the harmonica – harp, I mean," he corrected himself before I could do it for him, "but you weren't really much cop, were you, to be honest? Then you disappear, no one hears a thing from you, and suddenly you turn up out of the blue and you can play like – like – "

"Little Walter?" I prompted. I'd decided I was going to model my style on Little Walter. If it was good enough for Muddy Waters' band, it was good enough for The Blue Hornets.

"Whatever. The point is, did you sell your soul to the devil in exchange for being good at playing the harp?" He leant forward in his deckchair, and by the light from the kitchen window I could see that he was gazing at me intently, no hint of a smile on his face.

I hesitated. Of course I knew he was just taking the mickey, but it seemed important to stress how much practice I'd put into learning to play blues harp – and how much I wanted to be in this band.

"I – er, I mean – " I began, but then Steve started laughing uproariously, and Des joined in, and I did too a few moments later, though I wasn't sure quite what we were laughing at. It was several minutes before we all got our breath back.

"Still, it's a thought, though," said Des, scrunching up an empty can and tossing it in the general direction of the dustbin by the back door. "I mean, no offence Trev, but your guitar playing is coming on a bit slowly, isn't it?"

I didn't deny it. I was all too aware that my hard-won ability to play nursery rhymes on Des's battered acoustic wasn't going to give Bill Wyman any sleepless nights.

"So maybe we could speed things up a bit," he went on. "Take you down the crossroads, see if we can get you a bit of extra ability. It's got to be worth a try, yeah?"

And that's how I found myself squashed into the front seat of the O'Briens' van once more, heading west out of Watford. We'd stopped at Des's on the way, to pick up the acoustic. "Otherwise, how're we going to know if it's worked or not?" he said just before he vanished into the house. When he emerged, he had the guitar in one hand and a bottle in the other.

We'd taken the route I'd normally be using to cycle home at about this time, and even passed the end of my road before turning off into the countryside. Now were speeding through a maze of country lanes, guided by the light of the full moon and the van's one functioning headlamp. As high hedges rushed by, so close that you could hear them scratching the side of the van, we temporarily forgot our devotion to the blues and sang pop songs at the tops of our voices. I remember in particular a stirring version of 'I Got You Babe', with Des taking Sonny's part and me impersonating Cher. All things considered, it's a wonder we didn't crash, or collide with another vehicle. Fortunately, this was in the days before the country lanes began to teem with Volvos and Land Rovers.

A mile or two after we'd passed through Sarratt, Des, who'd been leaning out of the passenger-side window, suddenly yelled "Stop!" Steve stomped on the brake and the van came to a screeching halt which sent us all shooting forwards in our seats. I had to put both arms out to brace myself against the dashboard.

"What is it?" asked Steve.

"Look!" said Des.

We looked. The road stretched away in front of us, up a slight incline. There was another road to our right, and another to our left, and a quick glance in the rear-view mirror confirmed that we hadn't spun round in the course of making our emergency stop. We were sitting plumb in the middle of a four-way junction.

Or, to put it another way, a crossroads.

Steve manoeuvred the van onto a patch of rutted earth in front of a gate and switched the engine off, and we all got out. The warmth of the day had dissipated, and the chilly air brought up goosepimples on my bare forearms.

"So what do we do now?" I asked, suppressing a shiver.

"I know what I'm going to do," said Steve, who was already climbing over the gate. A few moments later there was a splashing sound from the other side of the hedge, and I thought I heard a low sigh of pleasure. When Steve returned, Des and I followed his example, tactfully standing a few yards apart.

When I clambered back over the gate, Steve was squinting at his watch, turning its face this way and that as he tried to read it by the light of the moon.

"It's nowhere near midnight yet," he said finally. "How're we going to pass the time until the devil shows up? And another thing," he added, "I'm freezing my balls off here."

Once again, Des was ahead of him. He'd been rummaging around in the front of the van, and now stood before us with the acoustic guitar in one hand and the bottle he'd brought from his dad's house in the other. He took a swig and passed the bottle to me. It turned out to contain brandy. "This should warm us up," he said. After I'd finished choking, and once I'd realised that the burning sensation at the back of my throat wasn't actually going to kill me, I had to admit that I did feel a pleasing glow.

Meanwhile Des was strumming chords on the guitar, and soon he launched into a familiar riff. Catching on quickly, I whipped the harp from my shirt pocket and joined in, and we chorused the first few lines together: "Good morning little schoolgirl, good morning little schoolgirl, may I come home with, may I come home with you..."

Steve, who was holding the bottle, watched us with a broad grin on his face. After we'd finished he said: "Go on, give Lucky the guitar. We need something to compare with when the devil gives him his talent, so we know what he was like before." So I took the acoustic and struggled through a ragged version of 'Amazing Grace'. Not the most appropriate song for someone who was planning to sell his soul to the devil, but in any case I was concentrating so hard on finding the right chords that it was left to Des and Steve to belt out the words.

After that, Des took his instrument back and we reverted to the blues, running through our repertoire as best we could manage with just guitar, harmonica and vocals. I'd like to be able to say that we captured something of the spirit of Robert Johnson that night, down there at a crossroads in the middle of nowhere. But the truth is that all we captured was the sound of a barely competent three-piece band making it up as they went along. And Robert Johnson, as far as I'm aware, was never accompanied by a drunken drummer keeping time with the palms of his hands on the bonnet of a Ford Transit.

We were midway through 'Bright Lights Big City', and I'd just made the wondrous discovery that it was much easier to imitate Jimmy Reed's trademark drawl if you were drunk, when I saw something over Des's shoulder. A beam of light was approaching from one of the side roads, and as it came closer I could make out the silhouette of a figure behind it. Some instinct told me this wasn't a good thing, and I stopped singing. Des stopped too once he heard the dog barking. It was an angry sound, like you'd expect from a guard dog that had spotted an intruder. For a few seconds, Steve (who had his back to us) carried on beating out a rhythm on the bonnet, almost but not quite in time with the approaching footsteps, until he too stopped and turned round.

He found himself face to face with a middle-aged man wearing a long, heavy overcoat over stripy pyjamas, with the bottoms tucked into a pair of Wellington boots. This incongruous outfit would've been hilarious (indeed, I thought I heard Des stifle a snigger) if it hadn't been for what the man held in his hands: namely a short lead, on the end of which was an Alsatian, in the left, and a shotgun in the right. What's more, the man didn't look happy. Come to think of it, nor did the Alsatian.

"What the bloody hell do you think you're playing at?"

"The blues," said Des, very quietly.

If the man with the shotgun heard him, he didn't show it. "My wife has just got the kids to sleep after three hours of trying, and then this bloody racket starts up, so I have to get out of bed and come down and find out what's going on, and I find you three herberts playing – playing – playing I don't know what."

"It's the blues," repeated Des, more loudly this time. But the man wasn't about to get drawn into a debate about musical styles.

"I don't care if it's all the ruddy colours of the rainbow. I want you out of here now or else." Just in case we hadn't got the point, he let the lead in his left hand slip through his fingers a few inches, so that the Alsatian came that little bit closer to us. Right on cue, it bared its teeth and snarled.

Then the man turned on his heel and stalked back down the road. When he'd gone we all looked at each other. Steve took a slug from the brandy bottle and then got into the driver's seat of the van. Without a word, Des and I got in the other side, and we headed back to Watford – more slowly this time, since Steve had finally realised how much he'd had to drink.

So I never did get to sell my soul to the devil at the crossroads – and I certainly never acquired a miraculous facility for playing the guitar. On the other hand, when I woke up on the sofa in the O'Briens' sitting room the next morning, I discovered that I had acquired my first hangover.

BAR THREE: TREVOR, 1966

"The first surprise was the length of the queue that greeted your reporter on his arrival at St Paul's Youth Club, testimony to the rapid rise of an r'n'b group whose Friday-night residency here began only a few weeks ago. Both in the queue and inside the hall, the audience was comprised mainly of teenagers, many of them clad all in black as if for a funeral. This sartorial oddity was explained when The Hornets took to the stage, all four of them dressed in black from top to toe. With no preamble they launched straight into their first number, a spirited rendition of the Muddy Waters song 'Hoochy coochy man'.

"Here was the second surprise: for such new arrivals on the scene, this local foursome – they've even cheekily borrowed the nickname of Watford's football team – are really rather good. The star of the show was undoubtedly guitarist Des Armstrong, who never stood still the entire time he was on stage. Whether 'duck-walking' à la Chuck Berry or playing a speedy solo in the middle of the dancefloor, his antics helped to whip the packed crowd into a state of frenzied excitement. Armstrong also sang the majority of the set, a collection of songs by some of the great blues artists from Chicago. The notable exception was 'Hertfordshire Blues', a witty original number written and performed by Lucky Harris, who also contributed some spirited solos on the harmonica.

"It all added up to a lively evening's entertainment, much appreciated by the youth of King's Langley. If we are about to witness another 'blues boom', The Hornets may well be one of its leaders. Local r'n'b fans would be well advised to catch them now, before it's too late."

I've still got the cutting, yellowing now, framed on my living-room wall. Our very first write-up. It appeared in the 'Watford Observer' on November 25th, 1966, under the byline of 'Mr Vinyl', the paper's regular record reviewer. The headline is 'Hornets sting King's Langley' – the first of many awfully predictable, and predictably awful, puns.

But we didn't care about that. We were just thrilled to get a proper review in a proper newspaper, and such a positive one too. Des was naturally the most excited, mainly because he'd been compared to Chuck Berry – well, that was how he read it, anyway. I was pleased to get a mention too, but annoyed that they hadn't used my proper christian name. Steve was the only one who ever called me 'Lucky'. Unfortunately, Steve was the one the reporter buttonholed after the gig when he wanted to get some details about the band and the songs we'd played. Steve himself was a bit miffed not to be referred to by name, while Keith didn't seem to be bothered.

Ah yes, Keith. I suppose there are a few things in the review that need explaining, aren't there? Like the name of the band. Actually, that's an easy one. Once we decided we were ready to perform in public, Steve and I assumed we were going to be The Blue Hornets again. It was Des who pointed out – much to my annoyance, as I should have thought of it first – that apart from John Mayall's Bluesbreakers, no one who mattered had the words 'blue' or 'blues' in their band name any more. So we dropped it and became The Hornets, pure and simple.

It's a shame we didn't have the foresight to drop the 'The' while we were at it, as most up-and-coming bands did over the next few months. Within a year we would find ourselves in competition with groups with article-free names like Fleetwood Mac and Savoy Brown. But we'd built a following as The Hornets by that time, and we didn't have the courage to change our name in case we lost it again.

Anyway, I'm getting ahead of myself. I was going to tell you about Keith, wasn't I? Keith Fisher was the first (and best) friend I made when I started at the Guild School in September 1966. Another new term, another new school. But this time, thanks mainly to The Hornets, I faced the prospect with greater self-confidence than ever before. So what if the Guild School sent a steady stream of boys to Oxford and Cambridge? I was in a *band*.

The school's music department consisted of a large central classroom at the end of the top floor of the arts block, with smaller practice rooms leading off it. I took to hanging around there at lunchtimes, idly riffing on my harp in the hope that someone would ask me what I was playing and give me a chance to boast about the band. Unfortunately, no one took the slightest notice of me. Most of the boys I saw there had orchestral instruments like violins or clarinets and were too busy practising for concerts or exams to bother about some new kid with a harmonica.

So when a tall, blond youth strolled in one day with a solid-looking black guitar case, he immediately had my full attention. I watched, intrigued, as he took out a gleaming black Fender bass and leaned it against a table at the opposite end of the room. Then he went over to a cupboard in the corner, unlocked it and brought out a large amplifier. What seemed like moments later (compared to the endless knob-twiddling that went on whenever Des plugged in) he was perched on the edge of the table playing delicate, jazzy runs, with a dreamy look on his face.

Despite his aristocratic appearance – I was particularly impressed by his Roman nose and wavy, shoulder-length fair hair – he looked friendly enough. After watching him for a couple of minutes, I moved closer and caught his eye.

"Excuse me, do you think I could have a go on that?" I asked. "It's just that I'm learning the bass, and I've never actually played an electric one."

"Sure, go ahead," he said, and he slipped the strap over his head and handed me the Fender. His voice was deep and sounded cultured. "Have you been learning on an upright, then? That must be tricky."

"A what?" Distracted by the unexpected weight of the sleek black guitar, I was momentarily baffled. "Oh, you mean one of those things they have in jazz bands. No, I've, um, just been learning on an ordinary acoustic guitar." I suddenly realised that I'd never tried playing the guitar standing up, and went to fetch a chair, chattering nervously all the while. "Des – that's the bloke who's teaching me, he's really good – well, he says it's the same instrument really, just with two extra strings."

Keith nodded earnestly at this platitude, as if I'd just explained some profound point of musical theory, and I suddenly wondered whether he was just humouring me. Maybe he was willing to let me make a fool of myself if it got me off his back. All this made me even more nervous as I plucked randomly at the strings of the bass.

"Go on," said Keith with an encouraging smile. "It always feels strange the first time you play a new instrument."

So, after a final bit of fumbling, I tried to play a basic twelve-bar blues in E, the way Des had shown me. It was ragged, but it must at least have been recognisable, because when I'd finished and dared to meet his eye, Keith said: "I wouldn't have thought blues progressions were the easiest thing for a beginner to learn. You might be better off playing something folkier. Bob Dylan, Donovan, that sort of thing."

"No, but I'm in a blues band, you see," I said, anxious to correct him. And then the floodgates opened and I told him all about The Hornets, and how I played the mouth harp and sang backing vocals, but I wanted to learn the bass because there wasn't anyone else to play it.

"Well look," said Keith when I'd finally paused for breath, "do you mind if I give you a few tips? You wouldn't be offended, would you?"

I assured him wholeheartedly that I wouldn't, and so he spent the next quarter of an hour showing me fingerings and transitions, handing me the bass each time so that I could try things out for myself. It was absolutely engrossing, but I soon realised that it was going to take a lot more than one lunchtime to get me up to a good enough standard to play with the band.

And that's when I had my bright idea. Keith was hesitant at first, but he was too polite to turn me down on the spot. So he agreed to come along to the garage the following evening and meet "the rest of the band", as I grandly referred to them. For their part, Des and Steve were visibly taken aback by the appearance of this genteel stranger at their rehearsal, especially as I hadn't warned them I was bringing him. I had an idea that they'd have told me not to bother, but I also knew that if they gave him a chance, he'd win them over. After all, they'd given *me* the benefit of the doubt, even though I had a great deal more enthusiasm than talent.

Keith had both in spades, though he kept the enthusiasm well hidden most of the time. That first evening, he even had the grace to look nervous as he tuned his bass. But four bars into his "audition piece", as he always insisted on calling it afterwards, it was obvious that we had our new bassist. Des had chosen 'Dimples', the John Lee Hooker song we'd first played as The Blue Hornets. But where Pete's basslines had plodded, Keith's bounced and bounded, somehow managing to sound both loose and precise at the same time. I looked at Des and knew he was thinking the same as me: we'd found the missing piece of our jigsaw.

Later, Des asked him where he'd learned to play that well. Keith muttered something about it being a knack and left it at that, and we never did get a straight answer to the question. Just occasionally, in an unguarded moment, he let slip a stray detail – his father's large collection of jazz records, long summer holidays in the country, a birthday present from a musical uncle. Eventually I realised, with a twinge of disappointment, that Keith must have practised every bit as hard as the rest of us. It was just that he'd been brought up in an environment where it was considered important not to be seen to work. Achievement was supposed to appear effortless, and he certainly made it seem that way.

Much the same ethos applied at the Guild School, which was unfortunate for me. I wasn't thick, but I did have to apply myself, as I'd switched schools halfway through the A-level course and had some catching up to do. A couple of unguarded remarks about how long I'd spent on my homework soon had me branded as a swot, and the label stuck. There was one particularly traumatic week when some wag took to writing 'Harris is a swot' on blackboards, and I had to go round the classrooms every lunchtime, erasing the offending words wherever I found them.

Unable to think of a way to respond that wouldn't make me even more of a laughing stock, I transferred my rage at the unfairness of it all into my music. I didn't realise that this was visible to the others until one rehearsal when I must have been playing my harp particularly violently, because by the time we took a break I was flushed and panting.

Des looked at me curiously. "You all right, Trev?" he said.

I didn't reply, but Keith did for me. "He's just having, like, a hard time at school, you know? It's not easy being the new boy."

"Right, right," said Des. Then, decisively: "Well, sod 'em, that's what I say. They won't be laughing when we're making hit records."

That's one thing you can say about Des; however self-centred he seemed, he could be really supportive sometimes, just when you needed it. And on this occasion he was right; my being in a band did eventually help to take the heat off me, and some other poor sod became the butt of the jokes in the sixth-form common room.

Meanwhile Des had found us a gig, and on a wet Friday night in October we appeared at the bottom of the bill in a pub in Edgware. Remembering our previous debut, we'd agreed that we wouldn't expect too much – though I don't know how seriously Des took this – and we deliberately hadn't invited any friends or family. Even so, we were all a bit jittery beforehand. Well, all except Keith, who seemed to regard this situation as the most natural in the world. It was his advice that got me through it. "Just imagine you're playing in the garage, like an ordinary rehearsal, you know?" he said as we were unloading our gear from the van. "Don't worry about the crowd. They're not here to see us anyway, so they're not going to be disappointed, are they?"

So throughout our fifteen-minute set I focused on the wall behind the audience and tried to visualise what I'd be looking at if I was in the garage: the row of spanners neatly arranged in ascending order of size, the teetering stack of hubcaps, the shiny girlie calendar on the back wall.

Afterwards we sat around a table at the back and drank pints of lager while a four-piece band a few years older than us ploughed through a set that was at least eighteen months past its sell-by date, full of Merseybeat songs. At the end of a particularly turgid version of

'Please Please Me', I turned to the others and said: "We're better than this lot, aren't we?"

No one said anything for a while. Then Keith spoke up, and it was obvious that he was choosing his words carefully. "I think we can be – I mean, they're tight enough, but they haven't got a, I don't know, a spark, you know? And we have."

"Damn right we have," said Des fiercely, and he knocked back the rest of his beer. "Now, who wants another?"

The landlord must have shared our opinion of our potential, because he booked us again the following Friday, and this time we were second on the bill and got to play for twenty-five minutes. The night after that we appeared at a youth club in Borehamwood, and soon we were regularly playing two or three gigs a week. This was mainly down to Des. He was supposed to be at sixth-form college, but he seemed to spend most days looking for venues where we could play. Pubs, clubs, scout huts, church halls – wherever there was a space that could accommodate a four-piece band and an audience, Des found out who was responsible for it and tried to persuade them to book The Hornets. Most people turned him down flat, but there were enough who didn't to allow us to get a foot in the door of the live circuit. It helped that the r'n'b scene was building momentum, and a few places were beginning to put on blues nights. Knowing Des, he probably planted the idea in more than one promoter's mind, just to make sure we got a gig.

It was around this time that I began to worry that I wasn't pulling my weight. Des was finding us gigs, Steve provided the van we carried all our gear around in, and drove it himself, while Keith – well, somehow no one expected Keith to do anything more than turn up and play his bass. Which he did, faultlessly. Meanwhile, I was left with my old role as harp player and occasional backing singer. There were periods in our set when I found myself surplus to requirements and had to resort to the tactic I'd adopted when we played at the grammar school – banging a tambourine and trying to look cool or enthusiastic, depending on how the mood took me. Sometimes I looked enviously at the other three and felt like an impostor who might be found out at any moment.

I was tentatively voicing these fears to Keith one lunchtime when he came up with a solution. After reassuring me in his usual calm, rational way that I had nothing to worry about, he added: "Mind you, if you really want to stake out a place for yourself, you could always try writing songs. All we play is covers, and that's only going to take us so far, you know?"

He had a point. All the contemporary musicians we looked up to had moved on from playing other people's songs to writing their own. They'd found their individual voices, and it was immediately obvious that we should do the same. Or rather, that *I* should. This was a chance for me to show Des that he wasn't the only one driving the band forwards.

All this flashed through my mind in the euphoric split second before reality reasserted itself. Me, write a song? I was barely past the 'every good boy deserves favour' stage of music theory. You might as well ask me to split the atom or translate 'Finnegans Wake' into Hebrew, and I said as much to Keith.

"Oh, don't worry about that," he replied, languidly biting into an apple. (Keith could do anything languidly. He really should have been a character in a Noël Coward play.) "I'll help you with the music. You just come up with some words."

I spent the next week attempting to do just that. The first decision was easy enough; since I spent a large proportion of my waking hours thinking about Susie, it was natural that if I was going to write a song, it should be about her. However, after trying out rhymes for her name, and rejecting 'choosy', 'floozy', 'boozy' and 'woozy', I was ready to reconsider. The belated realisation that Steve might not take kindly to a song about my (still unannounced) feelings for his little sister swiftly put an end to that line of enquiry.

Now I was stuck. I'd never tried to compose a poem or a song before, unless you count the 'word paintings' one particularly soppy junior school teacher used to make us write, eulogising the colour of daffodils or the magic of frogspawn. I didn't know where to begin. Of course, I only had to turn on the radio to hear a stream of classic pop songs, but those kinds of lyrics didn't seem to fit the twelve-bar blues template I was trying to work with. Whenever I found a line that did fit, I realised it was because I'd already heard it in an existing song. The nearest I came to a complete lyric was a Frankenstein's monster made up of badly stitched-together fragments of Muddy Waters, John Lee Hooker and Chuck Berry. I tried singing it to myself a couple of times, but I knew it simply wasn't good enough. If I tell you that the title was 'Louisiana Boogie', you'll get some idea of what I mean.

Once again I confided in Keith, who was becoming my personal oracle. It was a role he was born to play, seeing as how he never showed the slightest sign of self-interest.

"The thing is," he said thoughtfully, "you've got to write about what you know. You've never been to Louisiana, so why write about it? It's all very well singing other people's songs about mojos and crawling kingsnakes and all that stuff – well, actually it's a bit strange, but we'll let that pass – but if it's your song, it's got to come from something inside you, you know?"

Armed with this advice, I resolved to try again. Finally, a few days later, inspiration struck, thanks to Rupert Brooke (an inspiration I acknowledged later, to the bemusement of music journalists) and Mr Smythe, the English teacher who told us to read 'The Old Vicarage, Grantchester' as part of our homework. You probably know the poem – it's the one that includes 'and is there honey still for tea?' – but it's quite long, and most people only remember the final section.

The bit that caught my eye was where Brooke, reminiscing from abroad about his home in Grantchester, compares it favourably with other places in the area, which he's wonderfully rude about: girls from Ditton are 'mean and dirty', the people of Shelford have 'twisted lips and twisted hearts', and so on. Reading this, I suddenly remembered what Keith had said, and everything fell into place. If a famous poet like Rupert Brooke could write a humorous poem about places in Cambridgeshire, I could make up a twelve-bar blues about the area where I lived. I didn't have to write a serious song, did I? Why not have some fun?

The first words I got down on paper were: "The women down in Bushey/Are all extremely pushy", followed by: "Don't go to Chorley-wood/It won't do you any good", and it carried on from there, the rhymes and the meter getting progressively dodgier. By the time I showed it to Keith the next day, I had nine couplets and a chorus:

"I've got the Hertfordshire blues

Yes I've got the Hertfordshire blues

I've got the Hertfordshire blues

And these blues I just can't lose"

All right, so it wasn't going to win any awards. But I was rather proud of myself, and delighted to see a smile appear unprompted on Keith's face as he read the sheet of paper I'd thrust into his hands. When we met the following lunchtime in the music block, he was ready with a chugging twelve-bar tune which I tried to sing along to.

We immediately discovered a flaw that I was embarrassed not to have spotted before; even when I repeated each couplet, the format demanded another two lines at the end of every verse. After a few experiments, we came up with an all-purpose verse ending that went: "And that's why I won't be going to [place name] any more". In my mind, I could already hear the guitar line that would lead neatly into the chorus, and I felt a rush of joy at the thought that I'd actually written a song. Nothing I ever wrote afterwards gave me such a sense of achievement.

Des was dubious when I brought the song to a band rehearsal, but he soon saw the value in having a gimmick that was so precisely targeted at our audiences. At his suggestion I came up with extra verses whenever we played somewhere that wasn't already mentioned in the song, and changed things around so that the current venue was always in the last verse, and got a thumbs-up after all the slaggings administered to other places. 'Hertfordshire Blues' became our regular set-closer, incorporating band introductions and solos from each of us, and on a good night it could stretch out to ten minutes or more.

Then, if the audience called for an encore, we'd come back and whip through something fast and disappear again, leaving them wanting more. Never let it be said that The Hornets didn't know the basic rules of showbusiness.

That gig in King's Langley was only the second time we'd performed 'Hertfordshire Blues' live, and my singing was still rather tentative. Apart from that, though, the 'Watford Observer' picked the perfect moment to review us. As Mr Vinyl noted, Des had developed a range of showman's tricks – or rather, filched them from other performers – that kept audiences entertained; I was now confident enough to improvise mouth harp solos rather than learning them note for note; and the combination of Steve's powerful drumming and Keith's effortless precision on the bass made for a solid, almost funky rhythm section.

What's more, we'd played enough gigs to start developing a fan base. You'd notice someone down the front in Harrow one week, and the following Saturday they'd be watching you again in St Albans. People we didn't know would shout our names (usually Des's, actually), and sometimes they'd call out for specific songs.

Securing the residency at the youth club in King's Langley had helped, too. The first time we played there, we tried to persuade as many people as possible to come along. Keith and I asked everyone in the sixth form who had the slightest interest in music, while Des and Steve rounded up all their mates from the terraces at Vicarage Road and instructed them to shout and cheer loudly at every opportunity, as if they were at a football match. (They took this literally, even chanting "Come on you Hornets!" at one point, just like we did on Saturday afternoons, and for a glorious moment I had an insight into how the players must feel.) As we came off stage at the end of a riotous evening, the organiser approached us and asked if we'd like a regular slot.

The following week, a fair number of the people we'd cajoled into watching us came back of their own accord, and some brought friends with them, and some of them brought *their* friends the week after that… The result was that the youth club was soon packed out every

Friday with people who were there specifically to see us. Most weeks we were headlining and got to play a long set which sent the crowd home happy, but occasionally we were relegated to support act for a bigger band that was passing through. The members of more than one 'name' group were surprised to find themselves getting a lukewarm reception from a half-empty room, when they could have sworn that it was thronging with enthusiastic blues fans earlier in the evening. On nights like that, it began to dawn on me that we really might have a chance of making the big time.

I have to confess that my fond memories of that November night – the one when Mr Vinyl came to see us – aren't solely to do with music. It was also the night that I first asked Susie to go out with me.

Yes, I'd been back for over four months. And yes, it's true that I realised how I felt about Susie the first time I saw her again. It's also true that I'd seen her at least a couple of times a week since then, so it wasn't as if I hadn't had ample opportunity.

Well, look… For a start, I was shy. And I don't think it would have been so bad if I hadn't wanted Susie so desperately. With any other girl I could have manufactured an opening in the conversation and then casually asked for a date. But whenever I got close to that point with Susie I felt this dreadful compression in my chest, as if a giant hand was squeezing my internal organs, and suddenly I could barely breathe, let alone say what was on my mind.

Then there was Steve. The thing is, he was always around. Of course, I generally saw Susie at Hornets rehearsals or gigs, so it's not surprising in itself that Steve should be there. But he did seem to appear from nowhere at times, usually when I was just steeling myself to pop the question. Once, at a band rehearsal, I offered to help Susie carry the tea things back to the kitchen; Steve arrived seconds later, having apparently developed a sudden craving for a jam sandwich. Another time, while he was busy assembling his drum kit before a gig, I managed to persuade Susie to come out to the van with me to fetch some leads; Steve was there, looking for a wrench, before I'd got

74

past the opening pleasantries. I was beginning to suspect that he was checking up on me.

That was worrying in itself, as I was still a little scared of Steve. Not that he'd ever threatened me or anything. He was friendly enough most of the time, though it was true that since Keith had joined the band, a slight split had developed between the 'educated' and 'uneducated' camps. But I was uneasily aware that you wouldn't want to get on the wrong side of Steve. Occasionally, on a Saturday evening after a Watford away game, he would arrive with cuts and bruises on his hands and face. Once we arrived at the garage for a rehearsal to find him nursing a bandaged hand and apologising for the fact that he couldn't play that evening; Des lost his temper and gave him a lecture about his responsibility to the band. But even then, no one ever referred to the cause of Steve's injury. It was obvious enough not to need spelling out, I suppose. And when he asked me if I wanted to come to a game at Leyton Orient with him and Frankie, I politely declined, claiming that I had too much homework.

I kept telling myself that I didn't really have anything to fear from Steve. Yes, he was protective of his sister and wouldn't take kindly to anyone messing her about. But I didn't intend to mess her about, I – well, I was fairly sure I was in love with her. Steve couldn't possibly object to that, could he?

Even so, I preferred to wait for an opportunity to talk to Susie without having to worry about Steve interrupting us. After weeks of frustration, I finally saw my chance that evening at St Paul's. At the end of one of those packed, sweat-drenched gigs, we usually headed straight for the open air, pausing only to grab whatever we needed most at that moment – cigarettes for Keith and Steve, beer for Des and a towel for me. (All right, I usually had a drink too, but it wasn't quite such a priority as it seemed to be for Des.) But that particular night, Steve couldn't find his fags, and while the rest of us were gratefully breathing in the cool night air, he was still rummaging through his coat pockets, swearing under his breath. That was when the tall man in the suit and tie entered the tiny dressing room from the door behind the stage and politely inquired if he could ask Steve a few questions about the band.

This was the opportunity I'd been waiting for. Leaving Keith to suffer Des's dissection of our performance, I nipped round the side of the hall and squirmed through the heaving mass of bodies leaving through the front door. Sure enough, Susie was sitting on the edge of the stage, absent-mindedly playing with the tambourine. There'd been an unfortunate incident a few weeks earlier when she'd poked her head round the door of the makeshift changing room in a pub at the very moment when Keith had just taken off his trousers. She blushed and hastily shut the door, and he laughed heartily, but Steve seemed to think he'd somehow engineered the moment and took some persuading that it was an accident. So Susie was now under strict instructions to wait for us *outside* the dressing room at the end of a gig.

She stood up when she saw me coming. "That was great, wasn't it?" she said. "They loved – "

I interrupted her. I didn't know how much depth the reporter intended to go into, but I wasn't taking any chances.

"Listen, Susie," I began, then faltered for a second. "I – look, are you doing anything tomorrow evening?" Before she had a chance to answer, I ploughed on. "Because if not, I was wondering if you'd, um, like to come to the pictures with me."

And just as I'd imagined – no, prayed – she would, she smiled and said: "Yes, that'd be nice."

As first dates go, it was uneventful. There were no long, lingering kisses in the moonlight, no declarations of undying love – not even the furtive feel of a breast in the back row of the movies, the sort of thing my classmates liked to boast about on a Monday morning. We just ate at the Wimpey Bar, saw a 'Carry On' film at the Empire, and then went our separate ways.

Well, all right, there was more to it than that. For a start, that evening was the first time I began to see Susie as a person, and not just as a beautiful object I longed to possess. In the past we'd always talked

76

about the band, or about me, and even now that we were alone, away from the garage and with no risk of being interrupted by Steve (he and Frankie had gone to an away game up north and wouldn't be back until late), she still kept asking me about The Hornets. Did I think we were going to be famous? What was it like being up on stage with people clapping and cheering me? Was I going to write more songs?

This was all immensely flattering, and I answered her questions as best I could. But it only exacerbated the nagging feeling I'd had before that I hardly knew anything about *her*. So when the waitress had brought our hamburgers, I changed the subject and asked Susie about her job at Trewin's department store, where she worked in beds and bedding. What were her prospects? (I realised immediately that this was the sort of thing an elderly relative might say, but she didn't seem to notice.)

"Oh, they said when I joined that if I worked hard, I could be an Assistant Department Manager in a few years." She said it in such a way as to imply that this was never going to happen.

"But...?" I prompted.

"But – well, it's so *boring*. All I do is stack shelves all day, and remake the beds after people have messed them up trying them out. I might as well be a hotel chambermaid." She smiled, but it was a sad sort of smile, and I sensed a deep-seated dissatisfaction.

"What did you want to do when you left school, then?" I asked.

There was a pause while she took a slurp of her milkshake. Finally she said: "The thing is, I didn't really *want* to leave school. I mean, I quite enjoyed it, especially English. I would've liked to stay on and do A levels, like you, but the teachers weren't very encouraging. They said I wouldn't have much chance of getting to university, so there wasn't any point."

I searched around for something positive to say. "Well, if you really want to do A levels, there's always night school. You could study in the evenings, and if you decided you wanted to go to university, you could do it as – what do they call it? A mature student. You could be one of those."

I'd obviously said the right thing. Susie looked at me and smiled a smile of such radiance that a warm glow spread through my body. I felt as though I'd passed some kind of test, and from that point on she was much less hesitant in telling me about herself. I found out that she played the piano, practising on an old upright in her parents' front room; that she hated having red hair (though I assured her that it was one of her best features); that her favourite Beatle was George, "because he looks so sensitive"; that she got angry with her brothers for being over-protective, even though she knew they only acted that way because they loved her; and, most bewitchingly of all, that she'd felt intimidated by me at first, "because I'd never met anyone that clever before". What she really meant was that she'd never met anyone who went to a grammar school, but it sounded better the way she said it.

The conversation was rapidly approaching a level of emotional honesty I wasn't equipped to deal with, so it was fortunate that I happened to glance up at the clock on the wall and realise that we were in danger of missing the film.

The first part of the date had gone well, better than I'd dared hope, but there were still two crucial moments to negotiate. I'd already decided that I wouldn't even suggest sitting in the back row of the cinema, because of the risk that she might say no and then tell her brothers – in which case I might just as well go the whole hog, accuse her of being 'easy' and book a bed in Watford General. So we sat halfway back. I didn't take in much of the movie, because I was concentrating on finding the perfect moment to put my arm around her. Unfortunately, there aren't many romantic scenes in 'Carry On Doctor', and in the end I chickened out and took her hand instead. It was lying on her thigh at the time; I clasped it from above and was thrilled to feel her fingers part so that I could lace mine through the gaps. We stayed like that for a while, until I was reluctantly forced to let go so that I could wipe my nose with my handkerchief. Even so, I felt that I'd made my point.

Afterwards I offered to walk her all the way home, but she insisted on leaving me at the turning off St Albans Road. On the way we talked about the film a little, and established that I'd be at the garage the following afternoon for band practice, but she wouldn't be around because she was going to tea at a friend's house – and then we were there.

There was an uncomfortable silence, neither of us quite sure what to say.

"I've had a really nice time," she ventured finally.

"Oh, me too," I said hurriedly. "So would you, um, would you like to go out with me again?"

"Yes," was all she said, but it was enough. I took a step forward then and kissed her on the lips, my best kiss, soft and long, and she sort of kissed me back, but in a way that suggested she wasn't an experienced kisser. I said, "Goodnight then, Susie," and she said, "Goodnight Trevor," and turned and walked up the road, her arms swinging jauntily by her side. I watched until she was out of sight and then strolled back to where I'd left my bike, kicking up piles of leaves the way I'd seen Fred Astaire do in an old musical, and softly singing pop songs to myself.

The trouble with happiness is that we don't always recognise it when it comes along. When we're happy, we're generally too busy doing whatever it is that makes us happy to appreciate that we're happy, if you see what I mean. What I'm getting at is this: if, at any point over the nine-month period from November '66 to July '67, I'd actually stopped to think about it, I'd have realised that I was blissfully happy. But at the time, I was far too busy to notice.

For a start, I spent a steadily increasing amount of time on the road, crammed into the back of Steve's van with two bandmates (three, if Susie had come along for the ride – we always let her sit up front) and a heap of instruments and other equipment. It was freezing in winter and sweltering in summer, and I suffered from more colds and viruses at that time than I ever have since. But I didn't really care because it was all so exciting. By the summer of 1967 we'd expanded out of our original heartland in all directions, so that we found ourselves playing gigs in places like Northampton and Colchester, Maidenhead and Guildford. Better still, we'd started appearing at venues in London that we'd actually heard of; the Station Hotel in Richmond, where the Stones had had their first residency, The Flamingo in the middle of Soho, and right across the street, and best of all, The Marquee, where 'Five Live Yardbirds' had been recorded. Des was so happy the first time we played there, I thought he was going to burst. Even though we were bottom of the bill, he still made us sign the famous wall in the dressing room where countless musicians had scrawled their names. As far as Des was concerned, appearing at The Marquee meant that we'd made it.

The rest of us were level-headed enough to realise that we hadn't. Not yet. But at least we'd started to make a little money, and we didn't have a manager creaming off a percentage of our earnings. (Des was still handling all our bookings, and there wasn't much else to manage.) It wasn't a fortune, but it was enough to buy us better equipment. Des got a bigger and louder amp, partly in imitation of Eric Clapton, who by this time was bursting eardrums as one third of Cream; Steve replaced the more worn-out parts of his ancient drum kit; and I bought a Fender Telecaster so that I could practise playing guitar in earnest. Since we now had a bassist, the plan was that I'd take on the role of rhythm guitarist so as to flesh out our sound.

As for Keith, his equipment was already top-of-the-range, so I don't know what he spent his share of our earnings on. Presents for his girlfriend, perhaps, a horsey-looking blonde he introduced us to before a gig at the Ricky Tick Club in Windsor. I don't remember her name. The fact that we didn't even know he had a girlfriend was typical of Keith, though. From the way she stood at the back of the room, never once setting foot on the dancefloor, I guessed that she didn't like rhythm'n'blues.

What with playing so many gigs, and the extra travelling that was required to get to them, the band began to take up most of my free time. True, we didn't rehearse so often, unless we wanted to try out new songs. Even so, I rarely had an evening to myself. Eventually

I had to sacrifice regular attendance at Vicarage Road on Saturday afternoons, a habit I didn't get back into for a long time. Steve gave me a lot of stick about that, but it was all right for him – his dad let him do a half day in the garage on Saturdays. And he didn't have parents who expected him to go to university.

I shouldn't be too hard on Mum and Dad. The truth is, I still assumed I would go to university, too. I was doing well enough at school to be reasonably confident of getting the grades I needed to read English at Manchester. (Why Manchester, I wonder? I really can't remember any more.) The trouble was, 'doing well enough' got harder as the demands on my time and energy became greater. The only way I survived was by becoming ruthlessly organised. Every weekday evening when I wasn't with the band, I was doing homework, often until well after midnight. What spare time I had at weekends was also devoted largely to schoolwork, and I even found myself reading set texts in the back of the van on the way to gigs, illuminating the pages with a torch and trying to concentrate while the others passed the time telling jokes or talking about what they'd watched on TV the night before.

But of course, I always made time for Susie.

The day after that first date, I was feeling apprehensive when I arrived at the garage. I was fairly sure Susie had enjoyed herself, and I'd been careful not to overstep the mark. Even so, Steve might have decided that he didn't like the idea of me seeing his sister. When I opened the door, he looked up from his drum kit and fixed me with a long, cool stare, as if he wanted to make sure of something. Then he nodded very slightly and carried on adjusting his cymbals. I decided to take this as a sign that we had his blessing.

I found out later that I was the first of Susie's prospective boyfriends to make it past the initial date, and while I was thrilled to learn this, a part of me was also hurt. Was I really such a safe choice? In the list of qualities that young men aspire to, 'unthreatening' is generally near the bottom. For a wild moment, I wanted to take Steve to one side and say: "You know, I *could* treat her badly if I wanted to. I could…"

My dates with Susie soon fell into a pattern. We'd see each other on Friday or Saturday night if The Hornets weren't playing a gig, and on Sunday afternoon otherwise. On Fridays and Saturdays we usually went to a movie and then headed for a café by the pond at the top of the High Street, where we talked about everything and nothing until it was time for Susie to go home. Our Sunday afternoon routine was the same during the winter, but once the weather warmed up we started to venture out into the country on our bikes. Using my local knowledge, I led Susie along the narrow lanes, away from the villages to secluded glades and corners of fields where we could – well, 'cuddle' was the word we used. More than just kissing and stopping short of intercourse, 'cuddling' was the best a randy teenager could hope for in those days – a passionate groping session, basically. Looking back, I really don't know how I restrained myself, all those times when I was lying half on top of Susie with my tongue down her throat, my hand inside her blouse but outside her bra (she was always very firm about that), and my erection pressing against her thigh. I'd like to believe it was because I respected her, but it's probably closer to the truth to say that I was afraid of the consequences if I did let myself go. I think she felt something similar. Occasionally I'd sense a change in the way she held herself, a loosening, relaxing, as if she was about to capitulate – and then, abruptly, she'd pull herself back from the brink, push me away and start straightening her clothes, the signal that she was ready to go home. While she was making herself presentable again, I'd head off into the woods, supposedly to take a leak, but actually to beat myself off in the bushes. It never took long.

By this time we were well established as a couple. Eager to show Susie off, I'd even asked her round for tea at my parents' house. Mum and Dad weren't happy about their educated son going out with a "mere shopgirl" (as I overheard my mother referring to Susie), and I think they were expecting some trollop with too much make-up and dirt under her fingernails. Instead they met a slender, pale-skinned beauty with "lovely manners" (Mum's words again), and were quickly won over.

If I was nervous that afternoon, it was nothing compared to the trepidation I'd felt in the run-up to a similar occasion a few months earlier. At that stage, the growing success of the band meant that rehearsals and gigs were taking up more and more of my time. I was running out of imaginary friends who I could plausibly claim to be visiting, and anyway, I was getting tired of lying, so I steeled myself and told my parents the truth. There followed a long and earnest discussion during which I repeatedly and sincerely promised that I wouldn't let music interfere with my schoolwork, and Mum and Dad finally decided to believe me. But just to make sure that I wasn't "moving in bad circles" (Dad, this time), they insisted on meeting Des, Steve and Keith.

So, one dismal Sunday afternoon in January, the three of them appeared at our front door at four-thirty on the dot, dressed in their smartest clothes, as per my instructions. Well, Keith probably had smarter outfits, but he had an extensive wardrobe and didn't need to try so hard. As for the other two, I'd never seen either of them in a jacket or tie before, and had to suppress the urge to giggle when I saw them.

Once everyone was seated in the living room, Des and Steve kept their eyes firmly fixed on the carpet as if trying to memorise the pattern, and responded monosyllabically to Dad's questions about their occupations. (I was intrigued to see which of them he would be more impressed by. Judging from the look on his face, Des won points for being a student, but lost them again for studying something as arty-farty as graphic design, so Steve came out narrowly on top by virtue of being a skilled manual labourer.) Only Keith kept the atmosphere from becoming unbearably tense, with a string of blandly enthusiastic observations on the house and its contents. ("What a lovely sideboard, Mrs Harris. Did you buy it locally?" That sort of thing.) But by the time he was reduced to praising the milk jug, things were getting desperate.

Eventually we got into a conversation of sorts, on the topic of music, after Dad observed that it was all very well as a hobby, but it wasn't suitable for a long-term career, was it? Just to spite him I started arguing the opposite, citing various pop stars as evidence, and eventually he was forced to admit that, yes, well, maybe a few people made a living out of it, but they were the exceptions to the rule.

"Anyway," he added, "it's not a very healthy pastime, is it? Stuck indoors all day, deafening yourselves. It can't be good for you."

"So what do you suggest, Mr Harris?" said Keith in a tone that stayed just on the right side of mockery. "What was your hobby when you were our age?"

"Fishing," replied Dad, a faraway look coming into his eyes. "In the school holidays I'd spend days on end down by the canal, me and a couple of pals, dangling a hook in the water and coming back with nothing, more often than not. But I got plenty of fresh air, that's the point. Got some colour in my cheeks." He leaned forward conspiratorially towards Keith, who was sitting nearest to him. "I tried taking Trevor a couple of times when he was younger, but he wasn't interested. Said it was boring. Do you believe that?"

I was about to object, unhappy at the prospect of Dad ganging up with my friends against me, when Des piped up.

"I like fishing, Mr Harris."

Dad looked surprised. "Do you, Desmond? What sort of fishing?"

"Fly fishing, mainly. I used to stay with an uncle and aunt who lived near a river, and my uncle taught me to cast."

This was news to me, and the thought even crossed my mind that Des was making all this up. But by the time he'd finished a lengthy (and, it has to be said, dull) conversation with my father on the ideal kind of fly to use to catch rainbow trout, I'd come to the conclusion that Des hadn't after all spent *every* spare moment for the last ten years practising the guitar. To tell the truth, I was a little disappointed. I was also worried that the pair of them were going to take this impromptu friendship a step further and arrange to go fishing together, but fortunately it didn't come to that.

The tea party limped on for a while, a little less awkwardly than before. But the main objective had been achieved; my parents had met my friends and seen for themselves that they weren't long-haired, dope-smoking dropouts or motorcycle-riding teddy boys, or any of the other wildly inaccurate stereotypes they'd been afraid of encountering. They were just three teenage boys, a bit like me.

If there's one thing teenage boys like it's a party, and in July Keith announced that he was having one to celebrate the end of our A Levels. He was keen to stress that his parents would be away that weekend, and we all knew what that meant. Every teenager does: no parents equals no restrictions, no limits. Indeed, in the summer of 1967, some sections of the media seemed convinced that young people did in fact spend most of their free time at wild, unsupervised parties, consuming vast amounts of alcohol and experimenting with hallucinogenic drugs and group sex.

If only. It may have been the Summer of Love in California, but not in suburban Hertfordshire. I had more chance of being invited to a garden party at Buckingham Palace than to an orgy, and LSD was just the Latin abbreviation for pounds, shillings and pence as far as most people were concerned. Even so, Keith's party offered the prospect of something racier than I was used to, and I let my imagination run wild, inventing all kinds of scenarios inspired by lurid tabloid headlines.

The Fishers lived in Moor Park, an exclusive area made up of private roads lined with large detached houses. The residents apparently hankered after the life of the rural squire, which explained the gardens filled with statues and gazebos, not to mention the architectural pretensions of many of the houses themselves. Mock Tudor, neo-Georgian – think of a style and you could be sure that someone in Moor Park was living in a pastiche of it.

Keith once told me that his parents' house was built in the Palladian style – something to do with symmetry, balance, that sort of thing. It was certainly imposing, with mouldings spread at regular intervals across the frontage to look like pillars. As he brought the car to a crunching halt on the semi-circle of gravel drive, Dad let out a low whistle – the closest he would ever come to admitting that he was impressed. We got out and he fetched my holdall from the boot, then paused for a moment before getting back in the car. He was looking at me oddly, as if he'd just realised the implications of my presence at a party in a house like this, and I thought for a moment that he was going to give me a lecture about drugs or (God forbid) sex. But in the end he just said: "Well, phone me in the morning when you want me to pick you up. Don't leave it too late."

I was the first one there, and Keith showed me to the room where I was to sleep before returning to his preparations. Once he'd gone I set about transforming my appearance. As far as my parents were concerned I'd come to the party in a neat navy blue shirt, smart black trousers with a crease down the front, and the black lace-up shoes I wore to school. But along with a tightly rolled sleeping bag and my spongebag, the holdall also contained an alternative outfit consisting of two crucial elements. One was a shirt I'd bought just that morning from a shop called Ages of Adonis. It was made of thin cotton printed with a paisley pattern based on dark green, but with reds and browns and yellows swirling around in it. I've never been hugely bothered about clothes and fashion, but every now and then I see some item of clothing and know instantly that I have to have it. This was one of those times. To go with the shirt I'd brought an old pair of blue jeans that I'd been painstakingly 'distressing' for weeks now, so that the bottoms were nicely frayed. I hadn't been so sure what to wear on my feet, but I'd eventually settled on a reasonably tatty pair of Green Flash plimsolls. As a finishing touch, I tried to make my hair look a bit wilder – a waste of time, as it's naturally curly, and eventually I admitted defeat and went downstairs.

People had started to arrive, and I recognised a number of my classmates. Some were easier to identify than others, mind you. Once, in a rare outbreak of malice, Keith had described a group of our contemporaries as 'weekend hippies', and now I understood what he meant. As a general rule, plain colours in clothing had been replaced by patterns, cotton by cheesecloth, tight-fitting trousers by swaying

86

bell-bottoms, and shoes by sandals or even bare feet. In a couple of cases, habitual wearers of sensible spectacles had swapped them for wire-rimmed granny glasses, the sort John Lennon used to wear. True, I did spot a few school ties, but they were being used as makeshift belts or headbands. All in all, I decided that I'd judged my look quite well.

There were girls there too of course, many of them similarly attired in swirling, multicoloured dresses and skirts, their outfits adorned with scraps of silk and muslin. I didn't know who any of them were, apart from Keith's girlfriend (Christ, what *was* her name?), who roared up in an open-topped MG not long after I joined the party. She was accompanied by a tall, glamorous-looking brunette, and the two of them entered shrieking with laughter at some private joke. I decided not to bother trying to talk to them, and instead fetched a glass of punch and joined in one of the inevitable A-level post-mortems being conducted among my classmates.

After a while I started getting impatient waiting for Susie to arrive. She was coming in the van with Steve and Des, and I thought they should be here by now. I was looking forward to showing her off, but at the same time I was a little nervous. When we were with the other Hornets, Susie and I tended to avoid touching each other, let alone kissing. They knew we were a couple, of course, but even so... My lingering fear of Steve had something to do with it, I'm sure, and neither of us was particularly demonstrative. As a result, I wasn't quite sure how to behave with her at the party. Would it be all right to give her a proper kiss when she arrived? Could we walk around hand in hand? It sounds ridiculous now – but I was young and inexperienced, and still at that stage in a relationship when you're terrified that one false move will bring it to an abrupt end.

In the event, I didn't get to greet her properly at all. I was standing on the patio, watching the reflection of the sunset eddying on the surface of the swimming pool, when Keith came to find me.

"Des is in the kitchen with the others," he said. "Apparently he's got something important to tell us."

I followed Keith back through the house, arriving in the kitchen just in time to see Des empty the last drops of a half-bottle of vodka into the punch. Keith shot him a disapproving glance, but said nothing. I smiled at Susie, who was wearing a sleeveless white dress that showed more of her slender legs than she usually revealed. Before I had time to compliment her, Des cleared his throat. He looked extraordinarily pleased with himself.

"Okay guys," he began. "I hope you're not doing anything on the twelfth of next month."

"Why, have you got us a gig?" I asked, surprised that he'd gathered us all together just for that.

"I certainly have," he grinned.

"So, where is it?"

"Windsor."

"What, the Ricky Tick again?" asked Keith.

"No, somewhere different."

I still hadn't cottoned on. None of us had, so Des added: "It's a good gig, but there's just one thing: we'll be the support act."

That wasn't so unusual either, and I was about to tell him to stop messing around and give us the details. But Keith was still willing to play along. "Anyone we might have heard of?" he asked.

"Well, I don't know." Des paused for effect. "Have you heard of The Jeff Beck Group? Chicken Shack? John Mayall's Bluesbreakers?"

I looked at him open-mouthed. Finally I managed to gasp: "The Windsor Festival? We're playing the Windsor Festival?"

"You bet we are," said Des, his grin now practically splitting his face in two. "And there's one other act I haven't mentioned. Eric Clapton and his band, Cream. Eric fucking Clapton!"

So that was it. Now that we'd all grasped the significance of the announcement – a place on the bill of the biggest blues festival in the country – there was enthusiastic handshaking all round, and I hugged Susie, and then we all drank a toast to Des with the punch he'd just spiked, and another one to 'fame and fortune', and then Des started singing 'Mannish Boy' and we all joined in, with Steve drumming on the surface of the kitchen table, while bemused teenagers stood around the edge of the room wondering what was going on.

Eventually we left the kitchen to explore the rest of the party. Susie and I ended up in the front room, where people were dancing to The Monkees and The Beatles, and we joined in, bopping around enthusiastically. We stayed there for ages, until Des came in and insisted on putting on a BB King album. The floor cleared rapidly until it was just me and Susie and Des (who was wearing his black stage outfit, and thus looked less like a hippie than anyone else at the party), and soon after that we left him to it.

A little later I left Susie on her own while I went to join the lengthy queue for the upstairs loo. (There was someone being loudly sick in the downstairs one.) By the time I returned, Susie was nowhere to be found. I thought she might be dancing again, but the front room was now full of weekend hippies sitting cross-legged on the floor, passing round a suspicious-smelling hand-rolled cigarette and listening intently to 'Sergeant Pepper's Lonely Hearts Club Band'.

While I was waiting for Susie in the kitchen, I got into a conversation with a girl called Melanie. The older sister of one of the gawkier boys in our class, she was surprisingly pretty, and when she turned out to be fascinated by the fact that I played in a band, I almost forgot about Susie for a while. Then I caught sight of her out of the corner of my eye, watching me from the doorway. I wondered guiltily how long she'd been standing there, and quickly excused myself.

I was half expecting a telling-off, but all Susie said was: "Did you remember to bring your swimming kit, like Keith said? I've just been upstairs to put on my costume. I thought we could go in now, before the pool gets too full."

"Oh, right. Right." I was momentarily confused. Had anyone said anything about swimming? I hadn't brought my trunks, but I was sure I could borrow some from Keith. After a lengthy search I found him in the driveway, kissing his girlfriend enthusiastically on the bonnet of her MG. I had to stand there for a minute or so, clearing my throat diplomatically, before he became aware of my presence.

"Swimming trunks? Yeah, sure," he said, his voice betraying a rare hint of irritation at the interruption. "In my bedroom, chest of drawers by the door, you know?"

I thanked him and ran upstairs to his room, where I ignored the semi-dressed couple writhing on the bed and started rummaging through drawers full of underwear, socks and sports kit. Minutes later I walked out onto the patio wearing nothing but a pair of maroon swimming trunks which were tied tightly at the waist to make up for the fact that they were too big for me. I was rather shy of displaying my pasty, hairless and not especially athletic torso, but no one seemed to notice. They were all wrapped up in the pursuit of a particular boy or girl, or of a particular level of drunkenness or stoned oblivion.

Susie was in the corner talking to a tall, handsome youth with a mane of curly brown hair. He practically had her pinned against the wall, and now it was my turn to try to catch her eye. But before I could, Steve caught mine. He'd just appeared in the frame of the French windows, and with the merest nod to me he strode over to his sister, tapped her on the shoulder and pointed in my direction. She came over at once, smiling. I couldn't tell whether she was glad to see me or just amused by the sight of my baggy trunks.

"Thank God you're here," she said. "That bloke kept spouting poetry at me. I told him I didn't understand a word of it, but he wouldn't stop." As she was talking, she kicked off her shoes and pulled her dress over her head to reveal a black one-piece bathing suit.

"Go on, then." She gestured towards the pool, where half a dozen people were already splashing about. "You first."

I obediently placed myself on the lip on the pool, waited for clear water in front of me and dived in. It was a warm night, but the water was icy cold and I shuddered as it enveloped my body. As soon as I surfaced, I swam a couple of lengths of front crawl as fast as I could, to warm myself up. When I stopped, I found Susie looking down at me.

"How is it?" she asked.

"A bit cold, actually," I gasped.

She squatted down and dipped a toe in the water, balancing gracefully on one leg. "I see what you mean. Not too bad, though." And

90

with that she slid seal-like into the pool and breaststroked up to the shallow end, keeping her head above the water the way women usually do.

We swam up and down for a while until we'd warmed up, then paddled to one side of the pool. It was filling up now. A couple of people had been thrown in fully-clothed, and there were splashing fights going on around us, but I barely noticed. The sun had long since gone down and the garden was illuminated by dozens of candles. We were standing at a depth where only our heads were out of the water, and Susie's long red hair was spread out on the surface around her, glowing and rippling in the flickering light. I thought (but didn't say) that she looked like the doomed heroine of a Pre-Raphaelite painting.

"You're beautiful," I said, and stepping forward through the water, as if in slow motion, kissed her as tenderly as I knew how.

When we stopped I saw that she was looking at me mischievously.

"What is it?" I asked.

"I was just thinking… Have you ever kissed underwater?"

I was taken aback. "No, I haven't. Have you?"

"No. Shall we try?"

And so we locked lips, held each other tight and ducked under the surface. Unfortunately, it was difficult trying to kiss without taking in water, and after no more than ten seconds we surfaced again, spluttering and laughing at the same time.

"Maybe we should stick to the normal kind of kissing," I suggested, and she smiled and moved into my arms again.

I'd forgotten all about the temperature of the water by now, and evidently my body had too, for I soon had an erection that I could feel pressing against Susie's thigh. The next thing I felt was more unexpected. While we were still kissing, Susie reached under the water, untied the neat bow on my swimming trunks, and then reached inside and pulled out my penis. She started squeezing the top of it, and if I hadn't had so much punch I'd probably have come there and then.

I was so surprised that I pulled away from the kiss.

"What's the matter?" said Susie, a look of concern on her face.

91

"Did I hurt you?"

"No – no, not at all," I said hurriedly. "It's just that, well, maybe we should do this somewhere else."

"You're right. Let's go inside – upstairs, I mean."

So we clambered out of the pool and slipped past all the people who were still talking and kissing and drinking and smoking, through the living room and the hall and up the stairs to the room where I'd left my stuff, and all the while I was thinking, does she really mean what I think she means?, and wondering if she was drunk, and if I was *too* drunk, and a thousand other things. Then she closed the door behind us, switched on the bedside light and peeled off her swimming costume so that she was standing naked in front of me, the light glistening on her breasts, and I was left in no doubt at all about what she meant.

I was about to take off my trunks when I thought of something. "Hang on a sec, I'll be right back," I said, and dashed down the hallway to Keith's room. The couple on the bed were asleep now, but I wasn't bothered about waking them. I yanked open the top right-hand drawer and found the packet I'd seen earlier, then hurried back to Susie.

She was still standing by the bed when I got back and looked relieved to see me, even though I'd only been gone thirty seconds. Before she could say anything, I showed her the packet of Durex.

"I thought these might come in useful," I said, trying to hide the quiver in my voice. Then I stripped off my trunks and went to her and held her tighter than I'd ever held her before.

BAR FOUR: TREVOR, 1967

We're standing in the wings, silent now as the announcer appears from the other side of the stage and ambles out into the middle. His face is unfamiliar, but when he opens his mouth I recognise the voice as one I've heard many times on pirate radio – and for a few moments, despite the nerves, I'm in my bedroom at home, listening to a transistor radio under the bedclothes, hoping to catch the latest single by The Beatles or the Stones.

My attention snaps back into the present just in time to hear the announcer say: "… and the one and only John Mayall's Bluesbreakers. But that's all later on. To start off we've got a young group who are making their first appearance at the National Jazz and Blues Festival. So please welcome onto the stage – The Hornets!"

There's a modest round of applause as we bound out from the wings, as instructed by Des. Though I can't help noticing, as I hurriedly arrange my collection of harps on top of the nearest amp, that Des is not so much bounding as strolling. The effect is to produce a small but significant pause between the time when the rest of us are ready and the moment when Des, having slung his guitar over his shoulder, nods at Steve, who beats a count of four with his drumsticks, which in turn is my signal to blast out the five-note signature riff of 'I'm Your Hoochie Coochie Man'. Then the other three join in and we're up and running. And now, as I lean into the mic to blow my harp, there's just one thought running through my mind: we've made it, we've bloody well made it.

There may only have been four of us on stage that day at Windsor, but by that time there were actually five Hornets. I mean that in the sense that every great Sixties band had its 'extra member', someone who became far more than just a paid employee. The Beatles had their manager, Brian Epstein, and with the Stones it was pianist Ian Stewart. The Hornets may not have been quite in the same league, but we had one too: Jacko Jones.

We didn't advertise for him or anything like that. He was just there one evening when we turned up at the garage; a thickset bloke in his mid-twenties with a mop of curly hair, the beginnings of a beer gut and an accent I'd only ever heard on TV. Steve explained that he was a relative who was staying with the O'Briens for a while – some sort of cousin, as far as I could make out. His presence in Watford was never properly accounted for, but I gathered that he'd left Liverpool in something of a hurry.

Jacko's claim to fame was that he'd been the rhythm guitarist in a rock'n'roll group. They were called Ray And The Romantics, and they were fairly popular in Liverpool for a while – they even had a couple of tracks included on a Merseybeat compilation album. Then, just as the big time was beckoning (according to Jacko, at least), Ray defected to another group. The Romantics folded soon afterwards.

Des was initially suspicious, but he relaxed once he learned that Jacko was a fellow musician. Jacko watched us practise and somehow, by the end of the evening, we'd hired him as our driver and roadie. From the look on Des's face as they shook hands on the deal, I guessed that he was thinking the same as me; we must be getting somewhere if we could afford to employ someone to carry our gear for us. (Never mind that Jacko's wages amounted to little more than beer money to begin with.)

So it was Jacko who took us on a tour of the Berkshire countryside that Friday night in August, with Keith leaning over from the back of the van to give him directions as we lurched from one small town to the next. We'd arranged to stay with Keith's girlfriend in Maidenhead for the weekend, but even though her parents were away, there was no question of any drunken revelry. Des saw to that. In the weeks leading up to the festival he kept telling us earnestly that this was our "shot at the big time", and he approached the entire weekend with great seriousness. Much to my annoyance, he'd even barred Susie from coming with us, though she was at least allowed to watch us play.

Funnily enough, I remember that Friday evening more clearly

than any other part of the weekend. Keith's girlfriend – I wish I could remember her name – cooked us spaghetti bolognese, which we ate sitting round a highly polished table in a dining room full of oil paintings and antiques. To go with dinner she opened a bottle of Bordeaux, which we sipped suspiciously, and afterwards she made us coffee and left us on our own in the equally opulent sitting room. The conversation was fitful, and after Des had proudly passed round a poster advertising the festival, with the Bluesbreakers and Cream and the rest of the star turns in big letters at the top and our name squeezed onto the bottom line, we were even more nervous than we had been before. Even Keith looked pensive.

It was Jacko who rescued us from our torpor. "Look at yoose lot," he said abruptly, breaking a particularly long silence. "Anyone'd think you were soldiers in the trenches, waiting to go over the top. No one's going to get killed here, like. You're just a bunch of blokes who're going to play some music to some people in a big field. Enjoy it while you can, that's what I say. It won't last for ever, like."

And with that he was off into reminiscences from his glory days playing at The Cavern, where the sweat dripped off the walls and it was so hot that the girls took off their blouses and danced in their bras, and one of his mates snogged Cilla Black when she was still working as the coat-check girl... When he'd finished we were ready to jump in with anecdotes from our own brief career, and even Keith joined in with a story about being taken to a jazz club when he was thirteen, and being offered a joint by a friend of his parents. By the time we went up to bed we'd completely forgotten our nerves.

They came back the next day, of course, but once we got out on the stage, everything was all right. Susie was up at the front, dancing and singing along and smiling at me whenever she could catch my eye. She wasn't the only one dancing, either. We'd built up more of a fan base than we'd realised, judging from the enthusiastic response of the first few rows. Behind that, it's true, there were plenty of denim-clad youths standing stock still, watching us with expressions that suggested they were only tolerating our presence because someone more famous was coming on afterwards. And behind them there were wide empty spaces that would only fill up later in the day.

We didn't care about that, though. Remembering what Jacko had said, we played our hearts out, relaxing into the music and discovering that we were actually enjoying ourselves. Des adapted to a stage that was much larger than we were used to by running through his full repertoire of tricks, including a prolonged duckwalk that raised a big cheer. And in the middle of one song where I had nothing to do but rattle a tambourine, I was surprised to find that I was dancing – not just tapping my foot in time to the music, but grooving around the stage. I must have looked like a right idiot – Susie said later that it was "rather sweet" – but at that moment I didn't care.

We finished with a song we'd rehearsed specially for the occasion, a slow, heavy version of Otis Rush's 'I Can't Quit You Baby' that included a gut-wrenching solo from Des, complete with facial contortions the great god Clapton himself would've been proud of. Then, suddenly, it was all over and we were in the wings again, being told that we couldn't go back for an encore because we'd already overrun. The applause wasn't particularly loud or concerted anyway, so we didn't argue. Instead we wandered off into the area behind the stage, hoping to bump into someone famous. Unfortunately, most of the big names weren't due on till much later, and one of the roadies told us in awed tones that Cream planned to arrive by helicopter just ten minutes before they went on stage. Still, Des did spot Jeff Beck coming out of the portable toilets, which seemed to make him happy.

After a while I went back out into the audience to find Susie, who hugged me tightly and told me how wonderful we'd been. We divided the rest of the afternoon between watching other bands perform and strolling around the site, where there were stalls selling everything the fashionable festival-goer could need, from patchouli oil to sheepskin waistcoats, paisley-patterned cravats to op-art posters. Later we linked up with the rest of the band and at one point, while the six of us were sitting together munching greasy hamburgers, a group of girls who couldn't have been more than a year or two younger than us came over and shyly asked for our autographs. We were more than happy to oblige, and I couldn't help noticing that Susie looked very thoughtful after that.

Much later, when the sun had gone down and Cream had finally appeared from the skies, I sat huddled under a blanket with Susie near the back of the audience, among the drinkers and the dope-smokers and those who, like us, were just young and in love. Since Keith's party we'd entered that stage of a relationship best described as 'rampant'. The trouble was, what with Susie working full-time and me being busy with the band, the extent of our lust significantly outweighed the opportunities we had to indulge it. So we were both looking forward to the night ahead, when Susie was coming back to stay at the house in Maidenhead. She was supposed to be sharing a room with Keith's girlfriend, as I was with Keith, but it hadn't been too difficult to negotiate a switch. (This would of course happen after everyone else was safely tucked up.) With the delicious prospect of a whole night of passion ahead of us, we warmed up by playing with each other under the blanket while Ginger Baker distracted the audience with a ten-minute drum solo.

I didn't know it at the time, but that performance on the Saturday of the Windsor Festival marked the end of a chapter in the history of The Hornets. A fresh one began the next day, with a plot devised by Des. Although the band was supposedly run on democratic lines, I'd often suspected that Des assumed he was the leader; by the end of the week I was sure of it.

For the rest of us, the events of that Sunday were mildly baffling. The first sign that there was something going on came while we were enjoying a leisurely breakfast, reliving the events of the previous day. The phone rang in the hall; the call was for Des and he was out there for ages. I shot him an enquiring glance when he reappeared, but he didn't volunteer any information. He was wearing an irritatingly smug expression, though, and I wasn't about to give him the satisfaction of asking who he'd been talking to.

Later, when we'd parked backstage at the festival site, Des told us he was just nipping off to see someone, and said we shouldn't stray too far. He returned a few minutes later, out of breath.

"Good news," he panted. "We can play today – in the artists' tent, I mean." This was a small marquee at the far end of the site where entry was by invitation only. I'd been past it a couple of times the previous afternoon, but nothing much seemed to be happening. I wondered why the organisers wanted us to play there, but once again, Des wasn't inclined to explain. Still, he implied that this was a very good thing for us to be doing, and after all it was no skin off our noses. None of us thought to ask whether we'd be paid any extra. For better or worse, we always left the financial side of things to Des.

We went on early in the evening, in front of an audience that looked significantly older than the one we'd played to the previous day. Des had given us to understand that there were lots of "movers and shakers" from the music business present, and I did notice that while we were playing, he kept looking anxiously at one particular area of the crowd. Following his gaze, I eventually worked out who he was watching: a man of around thirty, with shoulder-length brown hair and a moustache, who seemed to be watching us especially intently, nodding his head in time to the music. I mentioned this to Keith later, and he said that after we'd come off stage he'd seen Des and Jacko disappearing round a corner with the same man. We were pushing through the crowd in front of the main stage at the time, trying to find a good spot to watch John Mayall's Bluesbreakers play. Whatever Des was up to, we soon forgot about him, other than to wonder aloud what he'd think of Mayall's latest guitarist.

As it happened, Des told us exactly what he thought of him the next time the band met, in the garage on Wednesday. ("Not a patch on Eric or Greenie – he won't last long.") But that was later in the evening, after he'd dropped his bombshell. Well, I say 'dropped', but in fact we practically had to prise it from his hands, given his penchant for dramatic build-ups.

"Trev," he began, while we were setting up our gear, "you doing anything on Friday morning?"

"No, nothing I can think of," I said.

He turned to Keith. "How 'bout you?"

Keith shook his head.

"Steve, can you get your old man to give you the morning off?"

Steve thought for a moment. "Yeah, I s'pose so. We're not too busy right now."

"Great." Des paused, waiting for the inevitable question. When it didn't come, he looked annoyed. "Well, isn't anyone going to ask me why?"

Keith sighed. "I suppose you're going to tell us you've wangled us onto the bill at another festival. Though I don't know why you can't just come out and tell us, you know?"

"It's better than that," Des smirked. There was another pause, and it only ended when he realised that we were starting to get seriously irritated. "All right, all right, I'll tell you. The fact is, this Friday we're going up to the West End to sign a deal with a record company. We're going to make an album!"

In the commotion that followed, I managed to glean the information that we were signing with a company called Natchez, and specifically with the label's boss, Charlie Maynard. Des told us he'd been "conducting negotiations" (he really could be quite pompous at times) at Windsor, so this Maynard character must have been the bloke with the moustache who'd been watching us in the artists' tent.

It was only in the days and weeks that followed that it occurred to me to be angry with Des for doing all this behind our backs. Surely all four of us should have been involved in these "negotiations"? We might even have been able to strike a better deal. After all, how much financial acumen did Des actually possess? True, he'd always booked our gigs and dealt with promoters, but that couldn't be too difficult, could it? And anyway, who did he think he was to make decisions for us?

But at the time, all I could think about was how incredible it was. Naturally, like all musicians, we'd talked about our chances of "making it". Well, Des had talked about it, but I'd always taken his assessment of our prospects with a pinch of salt. To find out now that he'd been right all along – I have to say, it took a major mental adjustment. I never did quite get into the habit of thinking of myself as a rock star. Des, of course, had never thought of himself as anything else.

While Steve and I were quizzing Des about the details of this amazing deal we were going to sign, Keith remained slightly off to one side, saying nothing. Eventually he cleared his throat.

"Listen guys," he said, sounding uncharacteristically apologetic, "I'm afraid you're going to have to do this without me. The thing is, I'm going back to school next month to study for my Oxford entrance exams. I can't do this full-time, you know? I'm sorry."

I instinctively looked at Des, expecting him to throw a fit.

"Keith, you can't do this to us now," he said through clenched teeth. "Not now we're going big-time. Who's going to play bass if you leave?"

"Well, it's not up to me, you know, but I think you should let Trevor have a go."

"Me?" I hadn't intended to say it out loud, but I couldn't help it.

"Yeah, why not? You've been getting a lot better on the guitar, and I'll give you some help if you want. You'll be fine. Anyway," he added when none of us showed any sign of welcoming this idea, "three-piece bands are the in thing now, aren't they? You know, Cream and all that?"

I'm sure this was just a throwaway remark intended to make the rest of us feel better. But as soon as Keith said it I saw Des's expression change, and I knew we weren't going to have a row after all.

"Yeah, you're right," said Des thoughtfully. "They were pretty awesome at Windsor, weren't they? And Jimi Hendrix plays in a trio, too. You know, I've been thinking for a while now that we should go in that sort of direction, play something a bit heavier. This could be just what we need..." He went on in this vein for a while, and by the time he'd finished I think he'd convinced himself it was his idea that Keith should leave. That was fine by the rest of us, keen as we were to avoid falling out just when things were going so well.

There was one awkward question left to answer, which surfaced when we finally decided to start the rehearsal: should Keith stick around, given that he'd effectively resigned from the band? He was all for leaving there and then if it made things easier, but I practically begged him to stay and play once more, "for old times' sake". To my relief, the others backed me up – for I had a feeling that if we practised as a three-piece there and then, Des's confidence in the concept of The Hornets as a power trio might be irretrievably damaged.

So for the next couple of hours we enjoyed a relaxed run-through of all our favourite songs, and Des didn't even pull us up when we played the occasional bum note. Afterwards, Steve filched a bottle of Bell's from his dad's drinks cupboard, and we toasted Keith and drank to the future, and anything else we could think of. We were all quite emotional by the end of it. It's silly really – Keith had been with the band less than a year. But we were all still in our teens, and a year at that age seems like a huge slice of your life. The instinct for nostalgia sets in early.

Two days later, freshly reconstituted as a trio and wearing our smartest outfits, we rode into London on the Metropolitan Line to meet our destiny, jouncing through suburban Northwood and Pinner on our way to the heart of the action. Well, Baker Street at any rate. From there we took another tube train to Oxford Circus and then threaded our way through Soho to a narrow mews just around the corner from what we liked to think of as our spiritual home, The Marquee.

The Natchez label was housed at the top of a tall, dilapidated block whose other occupants, to judge from the signs by the street door, included at least two prostitutes. (Even I knew what 'French lessons' meant when it was written next to a doorbell.) By the time we'd trudged up three flights of stairs we were all a little out of breath, and we were taken aback when Charlie Maynard himself met us at the door to the Natchez offices. Actually, these barely merited the plural; there was just an outer room where a pretty brunette sat typing and chewing gum, and then the office itself. Charlie ushered us in and invited us to sit down on a row of hard chairs that had been arranged in front of the desk.

It wasn't anything like what I'd imagined – something plush and bright and altogether more modern – but I was encouraged by the framed posters on the walls. One advertised the 1963 Folk-Blues Festival at The Marquee, featuring Muddy Waters, Sonny Boy Williamson II, Memphis Slim and Lonnie Johnson; the other was a plug for the LP that Sonny Boy had made with The Yardbirds while he was in England that same year.

Charlie must have noticed me studying them, because he pointed to the latter and said: "I was the junior engineer on that, you know." He sounded rather proud of the fact. "Sonny Boy was awfully difficult to deal with, of course, but the music was really something else."

And with that we were off into an enthusiastic discussion of Chicago bluesmen that put us entirely at our ease. Charlie was very good at doing that – making you feel that he was one of you. It wasn't an act, either. As we got to know him, we realised he was every bit as much a blues fanatic as Des and I were, but with the advantage of ten years' head start. It was only much later that I understood that he used his passion for the blues as a way of avoiding talking about himself, to the extent that I never did find out anything about his personal life. I once tried questioning his secretary, an Eastender called Tina, but she didn't know much and wasn't interested in finding out more. "Nah, 'e's not married," she said through a wad of gum. "I think 'e lives in a big 'ouse up in St John's Wood, but I ain't never been there. Anyway, what 'e gets up to in 'is own time is 'is own business, innit?" I couldn't argue with that.

Soon Charlie was telling us about the label, which was part-owned by one of the big record companies. "I chose the name myself," he added. "Of course, you know where it's from, don't you?" He leaned forward across the desk and looked as us expectantly.

Des was first out of the blocks. "Natchez… It's a town in Mississippi, right?" he ventured.

I jumped in straight away. "Yes, but it's also in the title of a song by Howlin' Wolf – 'The Natchez Burning'."

Des shot me a filthy look as Charlie nodded enthusiastically.

"That's right," he said. "One of my favourites, as it happens. Anyway, as you can see – " he gestured vaguely at the room around us – "I haven't got millions to spend, I won't pretend I have. But what I have got, I intend to spend on producing bloody good blues records by British bands, records that capture the spirit of what's going on at the moment. And that's where you come in."

There was plenty more in this vein, designed to stoke our egos and generally make us feel good about signing for Natchez. As for the deal itself, there was a studio booked in a couple of weeks' time for us to record an LP, and when it was ready for release we'd go out on a nationwide tour. We'd even be paid a weekly wage.

"Anyway, look, I know this is a lot to take in," he concluded, "and I don't expect you to sign the contract on the spot." He reached into a desk drawer and pulled out a sheaf of papers. "There are two copies here for each of you. Take them home, have a read through, and when you're happy, sign the top copy and send it back to me. Okay?"

We took the papers he handed us and got up to leave.

"Oh, and one more thing," said Charlie, as if the idea had just occurred to him. "Those stage outfits, the black shirts and jeans – very sharp, but a bit 1964, don't you think? Here's some money to buy yourselves some new gear, since you're up in town anyway." He opened another drawer and emerged with a bundle of banknotes. "You don't all have to wear the same thing, just whatever you feel comfortable in. That's what the blues is all about – self-expression, right?"

A minute or two later we were back out in the street, clutching the cash and our copies of the contract, the three of us in a collective daze. It was Steve who spoke first. "Well, it looks like we're going to be making a record, then." He sounded as if he couldn't quite believe it.

"Yeah, it looks that way," I agreed, failing to suppress a grin.

As for Des, he could hardly contain himself. "Shall we go and celebrate, then?"

So we headed for the nearest pub and stayed there till closing time. Des bent the barmaid's ear for ages, telling her we were going to be the next number one band and all that. It didn't earn us any free drinks, but it kept us amused. We never did get round to buying any clothes that day.

As for the contract, I did read my copy all the way through when I got home, though there were sections I didn't really understand. I suppose I should have got an expert to study it, but Charlie seemed trustworthy enough. Besides, I didn't really *want* there to be anything wrong with it, not when we were about to start making an album. So at the next rehearsal, along with the others, I signed my copy, and Des posted them off to Charlie. I don't think he and Steve ever did any more than glance at theirs.

There was one more thing I had to do before embarking on my recording career; tell my parents. Mum and Dad had been fairly tolerant of what they called my 'hobby' over the past few months, reassured by the fact that I'd still managed to put in many long hours studying and revising for my exams. But the unspoken assumption was that, like Keith, I'd be leaving the band when I went to university. Now I had to tell them it was going to be the other way round.

My chance came during Sunday lunch, two days after the trip to London. Dad started talking about my A Level results, which were due to arrive in the next few days, and I knew I had to step in.

"The thing is," I began tentatively, "well, the thing is that I don't think I'm going to be going to university. Not this year, at least."

"Now Trevor, I know you don't think you've done particularly well," said Dad patiently, "but let's wait until the results arrive. We can talk about your options then. There are plenty of other universities if you don't get into Manchester."

"No, that's not what I mean, Dad. I'm going to be a musician – full-time." And then I told them about Charlie Maynard and Natchez, and the album and the tour and the weekly salary, taking care to make it all sound as professional as possible. They weren't convinced, though. Dad kept saying that it wasn't like a proper career, the sort you needed a university degree to get into, while Mum just shook her head and said what a shame it was.

"Look," I said finally, still trying to find ways to soften the blow, "if it doesn't work out with the band, I can always go to university next year. Lots of people take a year off between school and college. Just think of this as my year off, if it makes you any happier."

I could tell that it didn't, but they didn't persist in trying to change my mind. As for my A Levels, it turned out that I'd missed my target by a couple of grades, so I wouldn't have got into Manchester anyway. Somehow, I don't think this was much comfort to Mum and Dad.

For the next two weeks I had daily bass guitar lessons with Keith and spent much of the rest of the time practising in my room. I had a lot to learn, but Keith managed to convince me that I could make the grade. Having spent a year or so trying to master a six-string guitar, the four-string bass did seem easier. So I plonked away every evening, while Mum and Dad watched television downstairs and wondered sorrowfully what was to become of me – or so I imagined, at least.

Des wasn't idle during that time either, as I discovered when I arrived for the final practice session before recording was due to begin. Leaving aside the teasing build-up for once, he handed me and Steve a plastic bag each and said: "I've got presents for you. Have a look." He was uncharacteristically shy about it.

Inside my bag was a brand new denim jacket, and I was just thinking how nice it was of him to buy it for me when I turned it over and saw what was on the back. It was a picture – no, an embroidering – of a cartoon hornet playing an oversized harmonica. I looked up in delight. Steve was holding up his jacket, on which a similar hornet was sitting behind a stylised drum kit brandishing a pair of sticks.

"And mine's playing the guitar, see?" said Des, displaying a third jacket. "They should fit all right. I took the measurements from your coats."

They did too, and while Steve went and fetched a mirror so that we could admire ourselves, Des told me how he'd worked up the designs himself, and then found a woman who'd do the embroidery cheaply in return for a credit. "I thought we could use these on the album cover, you see," he explained. "It's something distinctive, to make us stand out from other bands."

I agreed – it was a really good idea. But I couldn't entirely suppress the nagging resentment that here was yet another decision Des had made without consulting the rest of us.

There was someone else who'd been putting their time to good use. Later in the afternoon I went into the house to take a leak. I was just about to head upstairs when I heard the sound of the piano coming from the front room. And not just any old tune; it was 'Mannish Boy', and it sounded pretty damn good. I gently pushed open the door and stood at the back of the room until it finished, then crept forward and flung my arms around Susie's neck. She jumped, but relaxed when she saw who it was, and turned to kiss me.

When we'd finished smooching, I stepped back and studied her. "Why didn't you tell me?" I asked. "I know you said you'd been prac-tising a lot, but I didn't realise you were, well, that good. Can you play anything else – blues songs, I mean?"

"Oh yes, lots." She was blushing, but there was a confident edge to her voice that I hadn't heard before. "The thing is, what with the band being signed up and everything, I realised that I might not see much of you any more. And I don't want that to happen. So I thought that if I got good enough at the piano, you might take me on tour with you. Then we could be together all the time."

I thought for a moment. "Does Steve know about this?"

"Yes, but I made him promise not to say anything."

That figured. Steve was definitely the man to go to if you wanted a secret kept; he never told tales. Susie went on to confess that she'd been waiting for one of us to come into the house so that we'd 'overhear' her playing, because she hadn't been able to pluck up the courage to ask to join the band.

"But it's all up to Des in the end, isn't it?" she added with a sigh.

"No it is *not* up to bloody Des," I said, exasperated. "It's not just his band. Listen, this is what we're going to do…"

The next morning we all piled into the van and drove to a studio in a side street just off Kilburn High Road. This was to be our second home for the next few days. Our visit to Natchez HQ had comprehensively lowered our expectations, so we weren't surprised to find that Avenue Recordings was tiny. The front door opened directly onto an untidy lounge with a sofa, a couple of chairs, and a table in the corner with a kettle, a jar of instant coffee and a few chipped mugs. From there a door led into a corridor with two small rooms off it; the first was the control room, the second the studio itself. At the end of the corridor was a narrow staircase that led up to a deeply unpleasant toilet and an office no one ever seemed to use. And that was it. It was hardly Abbey Road, but we didn't care. This was our gateway to the big time.

Charlie had appointed himself as our producer. This was flattering at the time – the label boss taking personal charge of his protégés – but looking back, it's obvious that he simply couldn't afford to pay anyone else to do the job. He was assisted by an engineer called Adrian, a tall, long-haired bloke barely older than us, with a droopy moustache and a cigarette permanently dangling from the corner of his mouth. He rarely spoke, at least in our presence, and I couldn't help thinking all that fag ash falling onto the mixing desk must be bad for the equipment. Still, Charlie swore that Adrian knew his stuff, and we weren't in a position to argue.

The first day was deceptively straightforward. Charlie ushered us into the studio, where we set up our equipment and ran through half a dozen songs, playing each one two or three times. When we broke for lunch I was under the impression that we'd already recorded one side of the album, until Charlie put me straight. The tape hadn't actually been rolling; he and Adrian just needed to work out how to record the songs. I blushed at my naïvety and was thankful that Des hadn't heard. He was walking a few paces behind us, trying fruitlessly to engage Adrian in conversation about the workings of the studio.

He was certainly at home there, to the extent that he was belatedly inspired to write an original track for the album, which was otherwise going to consist entirely of covers. Actually, Des had been playing around with this particular riff for a while now, trying to put words to it. Once Charlie suggested that it might work as an instrumental it was like lighting the blue touchpaper on a firework. Des spent hours working on the track, until we all had every last note of it imprinted on our brains.

By the end of Thursday we were almost finished. True, I was a bit unsure about some of my bass parts, and I'd insisted on a few extra takes just in case. Otherwise I was having a ball. I even enjoyed the boring bits when Charlie and Adrian were fiddling with the equipment, making imperceptible adjustments. If it looked like being a long break we'd go out to the room at the front and sit around drinking tea and talking about what was going to happen when the album came out – who we were going to give free copies to, the party we'd throw to celebrate its release. It was during one of these discussions that we came up with the title of the LP: 'Stinging The Blues'. The pun on 'singing' was my idea, while it was Des who insisted that the word 'blues' should be in the title, to make it absolutely clear to potential buyers what they were getting. By this time (late '67) the music press was full of reviews of albums with titles like 'Mrs Rumbelow's Octagonal Lemonade Shoppe' and 'Bric-a-Brac For A Brontosaurus' by bands with similarly bizarre names. We wanted to distance ourselves from all that and make a stand for good, honest blues.

That evening, Des stayed behind in the studio with Adrian to play around with some effects for his instrumental, which he'd decided to name after the LP (though journalists and fans always assumed it was the other way round). The rest of us went off to the Rose and Crown, and I didn't waste any time putting my plan into action.

"Listen, Charlie," I said as we sat down in the corner with our pints of bitter, "the recording's going well, isn't it?"

Charlie agreed that it was.

"It's just that, well, if we've got some spare time, I thought we could try something." I ploughed on before he could object. "I was thinking about 'Hoochie Coochie Man'. It's good already, but I think it would sound even better with piano on. You know, like the way Otis Spann plays on the Muddy Waters version."

"Uh-huh," said Charlie noncommittally. "And do you have anyone in mind who could play that kind of piano part?"

"I do, as a matter of fact," I replied, as casually as I could manage. "I could bring her down to the studio tomorrow if you like, so you can see what you think."

Charlie raised a quizzical eyebrow at that 'her', but he didn't say no.

I suppose it was a bit mischievous of me not to tell Des what was going on. Childish, really, but I wanted to give him a taste of his own medicine – to see how he liked it, not having a say in a decision that involved all of us. Steve was in on the plan too, but Des was under the impression that Susie was just coming along on Friday as a spectator.

Charlie was a little late, and we were already tuning up when he walked into the studio. I immediately introduced Susie, and Charlie shook her formally by the hand and said: "Ah, so this is your mystery pianist, is it?"

"You what?" said Des with a start, looking up from his guitar.

"We just thought we could try a bit of piano on 'Hoochie Coochie Man', see what it sounds like," I said airily. "Didn't I mention it? Sorry."

While I was talking, Steve and Jacko had gone over to the upright piano that stood in the corner of the studio and moved it away from the wall.

"Where's the stool?" Steve asked.

"It doesn't matter, I can play standing up," said Susie hurriedly. In an instant she was at the keyboard playing a few experimental chords. I was relieved to hear that the piano seemed to be in tune.

Charlie was watching all this with an air of detached amusement. "Look," he said, interrupting the beginnings of an objection from Des, "it's going to take a while for Adrian to mic up the piano properly, so why we don't just have a run-through first to see how it sounds. Okay?"

Des looked as if he was about to say something, then thought better of it. But as we took our places he muttered: "This had better be good."

It was. Susie had been practising this song ever since I'd discovered her secret, and she'd seen us play often enough to know our version inside out. Ignoring Des's glare, she came in perfectly on Steve's count of four, her delicate hands pumping the keys like she'd been doing this all her life, and when we reached the guitar solo her fluid, rolling accompaniment sounded so natural, I wondered how we'd ever managed to play the song without it. As the final notes melted away into the soundproofed walls of the studio, we all turned expectantly to Des.

"Well, all right, I suppose we can try it with the piano," he said slowly, and then his face broke into a big smile and he added: "Nice going, Susie. Why didn't you tell me you could play like that?"

That was the thing about Des; all that really mattered to him was the band, and anything that made us better was okay with him. And so, later that day, my girlfriend made her recording debut, playing along with the version of 'I'm Your Hoochie Coochie Man' that we'd already laid down, while I stood in the control room watching, beaming with pride.

When I arrived at the studio the following morning and discovered that I wasn't needed, I was acutely disappointed, like a schoolboy learning that he's been left out of the football team. But as Charlie pointed out, my bass and harmonica parts and backing vocals were "in the can". Des wanted to tinker a bit more with his instrumental, and there were a couple of his guitar solos he thought he could improve on, but apart from that we were done.

"I'll tell you what you can do, though," Charlie added. "We need to find somewhere to shoot the cover. Des told me about the jackets, and I think it's a great idea to photograph you in them, but we still need a good background for you to pose against. Why don't you go off in the van and have a scout around? Jacko will drive you."

So a few minutes later we were off, armed with a scribbled list of potential locations Charlie had given me. Steve had decided to stick around at the studio, so it was just the two of us. I spent the morning listening to unlikely anecdotes from the brief glory days of Ray And The Romantics as we puttered around north London in the autumn sunshine, stopping periodically to weigh up the photographic possibilities offered by a disused gasworks, a canal towpath or a cemetery. I think Jacko had assumed that we'd just pull up, have a quick look and drive on, but I took my new duties as *de facto* art director seriously and insisted on getting out and having a walk around so that I could consider each location from a variety of angles. When we walked into the Rose and Crown at lunchtime, I'd already listed all the locations in order of preference, with reasons for and against using each one.

(In the end we didn't use any of them. The cover was shot the following week at the Watford football ground, with the three of us facing the wall of the Vicarage Road End as a tribute to the fact that we'd first met there. You couldn't actually tell that was where it was, but there is a clue in the piece of graffiti, just legible over Des's shoulder, that reads 'Stewart Scullion rules OK'.)

Des had done what he wanted to do in the studio, so after a pint and a sandwich we headed for Vicarage Road, where we saw Watford beat Bristol Rovers 4-0 with a goal from Scullion, one from Terry Garbett and two from Tony Currie on his debut. If I remember that match more clearly than most, it's because I was unusually conscious of my good fortune that afternoon. The sun was shining, my team was trouncing the opposition, I was with my best friends, we'd recorded an album and were going to be famous, and that evening I was going to see my girlfriend and have sex with her. For an eighteen-year-old, life really couldn't get any better.

I was so pleased that my plan to have Susie play on the album had worked, I forgot that her original motivation had been to join us on the road. Fortunately we'd planted a seed in Charlie's mind. He soon realised that having a pretty girl on stage would provide an extra focal point for the audience – not to mention reviewers. Using a keyboard player to flesh out our sound wasn't a bad idea, either.

So he turned up at band rehearsal one day to announce that Susie would be coming with us on tour. The only one this came a surprise to was Des (Susie had told me and Steve every last detail of the telephone conversation she'd had with Charlie the previous day), and you could see he wasn't enthusiastic. Quite apart from the fact that another decision had been taken without consulting him, it spelt the end of his plan for The Hornets to become a power trio. Still, he didn't argue. It helped that Charlie had brought along some money so that we could buy an electric piano and other equipment – Des had been after a new amp for months.

The week before we were due to set off, Charlie summoned us to Natchez HQ. Puffing and panting as usual after climbing all those stairs, we were delighted to find the table in Charlie's office covered with bottles of beer and plates of sandwiches. While we were opening the beer, Charlie went out and returned with a large, square cardboard box that was evidently rather heavy.

"Susie, as the newest member of the band, would you like to do the honours?" he said as he dumped it on the nearest chair. Patting his brow with a handkerchief, he handed her a penknife. Susie carefully drew the blade through the tape and then pulled open the flaps to reveal a pristine copy of an LP. But not just any LP. She held it up and showed it around like a game show hostess displaying a prize, and that's just what it was to us, the reward for all the hours of practising and gigging – our very own album, 'Stinging The Blues'.

Susie quickly dealt out copies and the room went silent as we contemplated the physical proof of our status as recording artists. I handled my copy like fine china, holding it by the edges and gazing at it in wonder. The whole of the front cover was taken up by the colour picture of the three of us posing against the wall, so that all you could see was the backs of our heads and the denim jackets adorned with our blues-playing cartoon hornets. Des was in the middle, and since he

112

was the smallest it looked a bit like we were his bodyguards. The title and the name of the band were in the top left-hand corner, in a red typeface that looked sort of handwritten, giving the impression (if you didn't look too closely) that the letters had been scrawled on the wall.

On the back there was another picture of the three of us, this one in black and white and facing the camera. We'd had it taken the same day as the cover shot, in the cemetery just up the road from the football ground, and it showed us trying our damnedest to look mean and moody.

The photo took up the top half of the sleeve. Below it was a white panel with the credits and a list of the twelve songs that we listened to over and over for the rest of that afternoon as we drank and ate and then drank some more:

Side One:
1. Dimples (Hooker/Bracken)
2. You Can't Judge A Book By Its Cover (Dixon)
3. Don't Start Me Talking (Williamson)
4. Flying Saucer (Jacobs)
5. It Hurts Me Too (James/Marshall)
6. I'm Your Hoochie Coochie Man (Dixon)

Side Two:
1. Stinging The Blues (Armstrong)
2. Bright Lights, Big City (Reed)
3. How Many More Years (Burnett)
4. My Babe (Dixon)
5. It Serves Me Right To Suffer (Mayfield)
6. I Can't Quit You Baby (Dixon)

What is there to say about our choice of songs? Well, one reviewer called it "the least imaginative selection of Chicago rhythm'n'blues tracks you're likely to hear in this or any other year". Looking back now, I can see his point. At the time, though, we were all angry about that assessment of what was basically our live set transposed onto vinyl. We did know more obscure tracks, of course we did. Des was always bringing in old blues albums he'd dug up in some obscure Soho jazz emporium and suggesting we try this or that song. But our audiences went wild for the obvious stuff: Muddy Waters, Bo Diddley, Howlin' Wolf, John Lee Hooker. It was no accident that a third of our album was made up of songs written by the undisputed master of Chicago blues, Willie Dixon. Besides, Charlie had signed us on the basis of seeing our live act. If it was that good, it made sense to record it, right?

Of course, it would have made even more sense to record it live, as Des pointed out repeatedly over the next few months, citing the example of his beloved 'Five Live Yardbirds' over and over until Steve threatened to make him eat the bloody record if he didn't shut up about it. Funnily enough, no one could remember Des ever suggesting a live album when we first signed the deal with Natchez.

These recriminations came later, once Charlie had reluctantly conceded that 'Stinging The Blues' was unlikely to make the top forty in the LP charts, let alone the top ten, and had admitted that maybe we should have been more adventurous. It was a lesson we were already learning the hard way, on tour, where we often found ourselves playing on the same bill as other up-and-coming blues bands. There were plenty who soon disappeared from view, but a few went on to make a name for themselves, and you could see why when you watched them play. It wasn't just that they had that indefinable something that marks out a good live act; charisma, presence, whatever you want to call it. They also expanded on the basic Chicago blues template, either by bringing in other styles – a a bit of country blues or boogie-woogie here, a touch of soul or gospel there – or by writing their own songs. We often whiled away the hours in the van arguing over what we were going to do about it.

The trouble was, there never seemed to be time to work on new songs. The itinerary didn't look too bad at first: "Straight up one side of the country, back down the other and home in time for Christmas," as Charlie put it. But closer scrutiny revealed that it wasn't quite that straightforward, and we soon found ourselves zigzagging around the map. One week in November, for example, we travelled up through the Midlands from Leicester to Loughborough to Derby to Nottingham, then back to London for a gig at The Marquee before heading all the way north to Leeds the next night.

These London appearances, designed to increase our chances of being reviewed in the music press, were sprinkled through our schedule at irregular intervals. Sometimes there were a couple of days off either side of them and we had a chance to go home, remind our parents what we looked like and give them a pile of festering clothes to wash. I was uneasily aware that Mum and Dad found these visits upsetting, especially my increasingly unkempt appearance. Mind you, if I had gone to university that autumn, things probably wouldn't have been much different.

I always tried to be bright and positive while I was at home, but the truth was that touring was far more boring than I'd ever imagined. For a start there was all the time we spent in the van; Jacko (who had now officially been appointed Road Manager) behind the wheel, Susie beside him and the rest of us in the back. We sat on hard wooden benches that Steve and his dad had installed specially, two of us facing the other one across the pile of drums and amps and guitar cases. You couldn't see much from back there, and there was nothing to do but talk, about music and football and anything else we could think of, anything that helped to pass the time.

In American songs, touring always used to sound glamorous – cruising along Route 66 on the way to Albuquerque, that sort of thing – but it's hard to get excited about taking the A69 to Carlisle. Still, there were a few incidents I'll always remember. Like the time Des got a small electric shock from the mic stand and was thrown backwards into the drum kit, which the rest of us found hilarious; the bonfire party we played on Guy Fawkes' Night in Sheffield, when it was so cold that I put on every item of clothing I had with me, and Steve played the drums wearing thick woollen gloves; and best of all, jamming with Fleetwood Mac in the back room of a pub in Dudley, vamping away on the harp while Des traded licks with Peter Green. For a few days, Green almost supplanted Clapton at the head of Des's personal pantheon. Then the new Cream album came out and the world shifted back onto its axis again.

Most of the best times we had were on stage, where we had the chance to expunge all the long hours of travelling and hanging around with a blast of pure energy. We often topped the bill, which meant that we could play for longer, and we took the opportunity to stretch out. Each of us got one showpiece number. Mine was the Little Walter instrumental, 'Flying Saucer', that we'd included on the album; Des's exquisite, soulful guitar playing on 'I Can't Quit You Baby' was always one of the highlights of the show; and Steve had developed a drum solo that could be worked into any uptempo number. As for Susie, she got a chance to show what she could do on the electric piano during 'Hertfordshire Blues', which we still played every night. Trying to work in local place names wherever we went kept me busy in the back of the van, but audiences loved it. Maybe that's why, when Charlie decided to release 'I'm Your Hoochie Coochie Man' as a single in a belated effort to boost sales of the LP, he put my song on the B side. The record entered the charts at number eighty-seven in its first week, and I was as proud as a parent watching their child in a school play.

I was just as proud of Susie, though that sounds wrong – too proprietorial. The fact is, she deserved her place in the band. She practised hard and played faultlessly, adding a new dimension to our music. Sometimes, in the middle of a song, I'd turn to watch her playing, head bent over her keyboard, an expression of intense concentration on her face. Then she'd look up and I'd catch her eye and she'd grin at me, a grin that said, "*now* I understand why this is so important to you," and my heart would turn somersaults in my chest and it would be all I could do to remember to keep plonking away on my bass.

It was great having Susie with us, but I did yearn to spend more time alone with her. Steve didn't need to devise stratagems to thwart us any more: most of the day, most days, we were thrown together with the rest of the band. If we were lucky we might slip away for a couple of hours in the afternoon, or get to sit at a table on our own in a pub while Des and Steve played darts.

Still, there were always the nights. Jacko generally tried to find us a b&b with three rooms: he shared with Steve, I was in with Des, and Susie got one to herself. So almost every night on that tour, about half an hour after everyone had gone to bed, I would leave my room and join Susie in hers, and we would make love as quietly as possible (b&bs tend to have thin walls) and then talk for a little and fall asleep in each other's arms. Some time around dawn, I would stumble back to my own bed, just in case Steve took it into his head to pop in before breakfast. As for Des, he drank so much after a gig that my tiptoed exit from the room was superfluous. The way Des snored, I could have tap-danced round his bed without waking him.

All this subterfuge was exciting at first, but that soon wore off and gave way to intense frustration. I wanted to have Susie to myself, and I wanted to live with her, and I wanted to be able to make love to her properly. What's more, I was unhappy about the number of young men who came sniffing around her after gigs, flattering her and asking her out. She always turned them down of course, and she had a cheerful way of doing it so that none of them turned nasty. Still, I didn't like it.

I suppose that's why things happened the way they did. It was in Blackpool that things came to a head, the day after we'd played a gig there. Our next destination was Preston, not far away, so we'd decided to stick around by the seaside for the rest of the morning. Susie and I tagged along with the others for a while, but when Jacko suggested a visit to an amusement arcade we took the opportunity to head off on our own. We ended up on the promenade, leaning on the rails and gazing out at the wide expanse of the Irish Sea, watching ships drifting by in the distance. Then Susie spotted a man down on the beach giving donkey rides to children, and she said something about how nice it would be to bring kids here, even at this time of year.

"Our kids, you mean?" It was something we talked of sometimes in those blissful, hazy moments before drifting off to sleep at night.

She nodded. "But that's not going to happen for a long time, is it? With the band and everything, I mean."

There was a sadness in her eyes, a sadness that I wanted to drive away immediately. "Not necessarily," I said. "We could get married."

"What?"

I thought she hadn't heard me. "I said, we could get married – that is, if you want to."

There was a silence that seemed to last an eternity, and then she flung her arms around my neck and kissed me and said something in my ear. And what she said was: "Yes."

We spent the next couple of hours in a kind of fever, making plans that would have seemed like pure fantasy just a day earlier. I think we were both busy convincing ourselves that we really had agreed to get married – that this was something we could do of our own free will, without reference to anybody else. It seemed too easy, somehow.

Finally we strolled, hand in hand, to the pub where we'd arranged to meet the rest of the band for lunch. And that's when we learnt that Des had been on the phone to Charlie, who'd told us to head back to London at once: our single had climbed into the top twenty and the BBC wanted us to appear on 'Top Of The Pops'.

I knew then that life would never be the same again.

BAR FIVE: STEVE, 1968

Yeah, I was surprised when they told us. In fact, the first thing I thought was that he must've knocked her up, but she said no, it was nothing like that. They were in love and they were going to get married. Simple as that. Well, I knew better than to try and talk her out of something once she'd made up her mind.

That's the thing about Susie, she's always been stubborn. Clever, too. People used to wonder what she had in common with Trevor – I mean, he went to that poncy public school to do A levels, and she only got a handful of CSEs. But she was clever all right. She's always been good at deciding what she wants and then working out how to get it, which is a useful skill to have if you ask me. You know what, I always reckoned she only learnt the piano 'cause she wanted to join the band, and she only joined the band to make sure of getting Trevor. But don't tell her I said that.

She needn't have bothered. The first time he clapped eyes on her, you could tell he fancied her. No, more than that. Blokes like Trevor, educated blokes, they don't just fancy girls, they 'fall for' them. And Trev fell big time. Well, that was all right. I mean, of course I was suspicious at first, what with him being from a different kind of background and everything. But he didn't seem like the type who was only in it for the one thing, if you know what I mean, so I didn't say anything. Besides, he was an improvement on most of the pillocks she went to school with, and I thought she'd be safe with him. Mind you, I kept an eye on the two of them, just in case, especially in the early days. Tried to make sure they weren't left alone together for too long. Trev must've got sick of the sight of me.

Still, I never reckoned it would get as far as marriage. Either she'd get bored of him, or he'd bugger off to university like that Keith had and they'd drift apart – that's how I figured it would happen. And they were still so young, neither of them much over eighteen by the time they got engaged.

That's another thing: it turned out they weren't planning on staying engaged for long. Oh no, they were all for finding a registry office and getting hitched there and then, before anyone could try and stop them. I soon put the kibosh on that. While the rest of them were drinking cheap fizz in this tacky pub in Blackpool, I went and found a phone box and got hold of Ma. She told me to fetch Susie and put her on the line, and a few minutes later Susie was back in the pub, wiping her eyes and asking Trevor if he'd mind if they waited till the spring so they could get married with all their friends and family there. Which was pretty much what I had in mind, too. Like I say, I knew I couldn't talk her out of it, but at least I could make sure she did right by Ma and Pa.

The wedding didn't happen until the middle of the summer anyway, as it turned out. That was mainly Charlie's doing. He came to see the last gig of the tour, at some poxy club in Colchester, and took us out for an Italian meal afterwards. We were just starting to relax and look forward to Christmas, and then he told us he was sending us back out on the road in the first week of January. He gave us some bollocks about "targeting key markets", but Jacko let me know what was really going on. Seems the album hadn't sold as many copies as Charlie expected, so we had to keep touring to make up the shortfall. It was all covered in our contracts, apparently. I hadn't bothered reading mine, so I couldn't really argue.

'Course, it was all right for Charlie, shacked up in his office in Soho with his dolly bird of a secretary to keep him warm. He didn't have to freeze his nuts off in the back of a Transit van for the next two months, did he? And he certainly wasn't there to help dig us out of a snowdrift when we skidded on black ice on the way to Inverness. Inver-bloody-ness! I don't know much about business, but if anyone can prove to me that Inverness was a "key market" for The Hornets, I'll paint my knob orange and start supporting Luton.

When we finally got there, the venue wasn't much bigger than a church hall. This busybody in a suit and a silly tartan hat with a pompom on the top was waiting for us outside. He told us we were late, and if we weren't ready to go on stage in half an hour we wouldn't get all our money. Well, for a moment there I thought Jacko was going to thump him. He was still pretty shaken from the accident, though no one had been hurt, give or take a few bruises. Since he'd been with us, he'd developed this sort of protective instinct, like I've always had towards Susie. He'd've hated himself if anything bad had happened to us. Maybe that's why he changed his mind about throwing a punch. It would've got us into almost as much trouble as him, in the end.

So we trooped into the dressing room and started to get ready. My hands were so cold from holding the shovel that I spent most of the time warming them on the radiator, trying to get some feeling back. Des and Trevor copied me, and Susie took a picture of the three of us sitting there in a row. It looked like we were trying to pull the thing off the wall.

To tell the truth, it wasn't one of our best shows. It didn't help that there were only twenty or thirty people in the audience. Perhaps the 'new blues boom' Trevor kept going on about hadn't reached this far north yet. They were enthusiastic enough, I suppose, and we went through the motions, numb hands and all, but that was it. Even Des couldn't get himself up for this one. You could always tell when he was pissed off 'cause he kept his solos down to the bare minimum, twelve bars and then back to the verse.

Afterwards, we didn't even bother looking for a pub. (Mind you, I did see Des take a few crafty nips from the bottle of scotch he kept in his coat pocket. He didn't offer it round though, the tight bastard.) We just drove straight to the nearest b&b and went to bed. It wasn't very warm there, either. The hatchet-faced landlady said she always turned the heating off at nine o'clock to save money, and I wondered if any guests had ever frozen to death in one of her beds. To be on the safe side I slept with my clothes on that night, with my overcoat on top of the blankets.

There were plenty of miserable days and nights like that. The main thing I remember about those first few months of 1968, driving round

Scotland and then back down through England, is being cold the whole time. We didn't have much money, so we all bought ourselves sweaters and overcoats from charity shops. When it came to vests and long johns we did splash out on new stuff, though. Des and Trevor even wrote a song about the long johns. 'Chilly Willy', that's right. Audiences loved it.

I reckon it was mainly our sense of humour that kept us going. The novelty of touring had worn off, and what with the weather, and being a long way from home, and our second single selling sod all, there wasn't a lot to laugh about. But we still managed, somehow. A lot of it was just banter, stuff about football or other bands we'd met on tour, silly jokes. Not rude ones, though, not with Susie around. She and I had our own routines too – family in-jokes we'd learnt when we were kids, things no one else would understand, never mind laugh at. Trevor, well, he was always coming out with puns and clever stuff like that, and though Des was never much of a comedian, he did have this sarcastic sense of humour that could be sort of cruel and funny at the same time.

The one who really stopped us going round the bend was Jacko, though. I'd only ever met him once before that day he turned up at the garage, but at family parties his name would always crop up sooner or later, usually with some wild story attached. The thing is, just when you thought you'd found out something concrete about him, somebody would come up with another version. Like, why had he come down south in the first place? My cousin Kevin claimed that Jacko was on the run from the old bill, which everyone believed, 'cause let's face it, Scousers do have a bit of a reputation for being light-fingered, don't they? But then Uncle Pat said no, it was something to do with a woman; he'd been knocking off another bloke's wife, and this bloke had got wind of it and threatened to top him. I do know one thing; when we played in Liverpool, Jacko disappeared for a couple of hours and came back with a suitcase full of clothes...

After spending so much time with him, I could see why people were confused. He couldn't half tell a good story, and he told them so well that you wanted to believe they were true. Once, while we were eating fish and chips in this caff in Llandudno, Susie asked him if he'd ever played at The Cavern while he was in that Merseybeat group of his.

"Oh yeah, loads of times," he says, stuffing a forkful of chips into his gob. "But you know, there was lots of other places on Merseyside too, like. We did shows at the Alexandra Hall in Crosby, the Aintree Institute, the Jive Hive – all over the shop.

"I'll tell you a funny thing, though," he goes on, and we all know that means there's a story coming. "We're down at the Aintree this one time when a new band comes in to audition for the promoter. They were just kids really – the guitarist didn't even look old enough to shave – but cocky, I remember that. Scruffy so and so's, they were. The bass player was wearing a moth-eaten old fur coat and the rhythm guitarist had this baggy sweater on that was covered with spots of paint. Whereas Ray And The Romantics, well, we were always dead smart. We wore these matching shiny suits on stage, thought we were the bee's knees. So we didn't really pay these guys much attention.

"So we're hanging around backstage and there's this big yell from the dressing room, and we go in and it's the rhythm guitarist, stomping around and swearing like – well, I won't repeat what he said in front of a lady," says Jacko, winking at Susie. "Turns out the silly bugger's shut his fingers in the khazi door, and now he can't bend them.

"Well, these kids are panicking now. They're supposed to be auditioning in twenty minutes, and here they are without a rhythm guitarist. And I felt a bit sorry for them – I remembered what it was like when you were just getting started. So I said, no problem, I'll fill in if you want. Just tell me what you're going to play, like.

"We did five songs in the end, four rock'n'roll numbers that everyone in Liverpool was doing in those days – 'Good Golly Miss Molly', stuff like that – and one original. That was a bit of a surprise, 'cause not many people were writing their own songs back then, but they showed me the chords and I picked it up easy enough."

We're all hanging on his every word now and everyone's forgotten about eating – except Jacko himself, who stops to put a piece of cod on his fork, spear a couple of chips and smear the whole lot in tomato ketchup before shoving it in his mouth. Finally he carries on.

"They must've failed the audition, even with me helping them out, because we didn't see them around for the best part of a year after that. Then we bumped into them at a gig at Orrell Park Ballroom, and we didn't even recognise them to begin with. They were all dressed from head to toe in black leather, expensive-looking stuff, and they had new instruments that must've cost a pretty penny, too. I got chatting to the bassist just before they went on and he told me a bit about how they'd been playing in Hamburg, and how it was all sex and booze and pills over there, like. Whatever it was they'd been up to, it seemed to have worked – they went on stage and blew the place apart. That was the night I realised Ray And The Romantics weren't going anywhere. We hadn't really improved at all in those ten months, you see. And funnily enough, Ray buggered off to Hamburg not long after, and that was that."

Another pause, winding up the tension.

"Still, at least I've played guitar with The Beatles, and not a lot of people can say that, can they?"

Music seems to run in our family, one way or another. That's why no one was surprised when our Susie picked up the piano so fast. The piano she learned on, the one in our front room, that was Grandad's. He bought it in the Thirties, when they were living off the Holloway Road. Ma used to tell us how when she was younger, her parents used to do duets every evening, him playing and her singing. Ma and her sister, that's my Auntie Eileen, they loved it. One evening in 1940, they were halfway through 'Pennies From Heaven' when the air raid siren went off, so they all trooped out to the shelter at the bottom of the garden. One bomb dropped so close that Ma says the ground under her feet shook like there was an earthquake going on. When the all-clear went, they came out and found that the house next door had been flattened, and half of theirs with it.

Once they'd cleared away all the rubble they found that the piano was still there, with barely a scratch on it. Grandma, being a superstitious sort, reckoned it must be a lucky charm, and when they decided to move out to Watford, where there weren't so many raids, she nagged Grandad till he agreed they could take it with them. 'Course, that was easier said than done, what with petrol rationing and everything, but they managed to scrounge enough coupons together to persuade a mate with a lorry to move them.

So one Saturday morning all the men in the street – all those who weren't off fighting, that is – helped them heave this ruddy great piano onto the back of the lorry. Then Grandad and Grandma and Ma and Eileen climbed up with their suitcases and off they all headed up the Great North Road. The way Ma tells it, people kept stopping to watch them go by, and while they were waiting at some traffic lights this young bloke shouted out, "Give us a tune, then!" So Grandad started playing 'We'll Meet Again', and people at the side of the road sang along, and after that they played and sang for the rest of the journey. Ma says it was so much fun that she clean forgot all about their house being bombed and their neighbours being killed. When she remembered, she felt so guilty that the first thing she did when they got to Watford, even before she'd unpacked, was find the nearest Catholic church and go to confession.

Pa wasn't there at the time, though he and Ma were already engaged by then. But once, after Ma had told us that story, he waited until she'd left the room, leant across the table and said: "I'll tell you one thing; your Grandma didn't really have much of a singing voice. In fact, I always reckoned it was the sound of her screeching that drew that Nazi bomber to the street. Never mind the piano being lucky – we should just be thankful they got the wrong house."

Now Pa, he'd been the drummer in his local church's marching band. He was an apprentice engineer when he was called up, so he was sent to work as a mechanic at a depot in Aldershot, fixing trucks and tanks. He'd only been there a couple of weeks when he heard that the regimental band needed a drummer, and he was in there like a shot.

Apart from anything else it meant he had a fairly easy time compared to his mates – better food, fewer duties. He even got out of being sent abroad a couple of times. But that couldn't last forever, and at the end of 1942 he was posted to North Africa.

Obviously that wasn't quite such a cushy number, but he still found himself playing music. Jazz, this time. He was at this camp just outside Alexandria, and there were a few blokes who used to play in the mess on Saturday nights: guitar, double bass, trumpet and saxophone. Well, one evening he got chatting to them and mentioned that he was a drummer. They all looked at each other and one of them said: "At long bloody last!" and clapped him on the back. Then they led him off to a storeroom behind the mess and lifted up a tarpaulin, and there was a proper drum kit, a good one too. This semi-pro band had been touring the Army bases a few months earlier, and one day they'd driven out into the desert to see some ancient temple and never come back. Their jeep was found, but there was no sign of the band, and no one knew if they'd been captured by the Germans or just kidnapped by Arabs. Anyhow, their instruments were still at the camp, and one by one they'd been claimed by the members of this jazz band. They'd just been waiting for someone who could play the drums to complete the line-up.

'Course, Pa had to tell them that he'd never actually played a full drum kit, but they said it didn't matter, he'd soon pick it up. And that's what happened. He practised with them for a couple of weeks, and after that he joined them on Saturday nights in the mess. Soon they were playing other Army camps, and even the odd gig for civilians in the city. They called themselves The Alexandria Quintet.

When we were growing up and we used to ask him about the war, that was what he told us about; the jazz band – the places they played, the other acts they met, the fun they had. He made the North African desert sound like a sort of holiday camp for British soldiers. Me and Frankie, we wanted to hear about battles and bravery and how many Nazis he'd killed. But he always steered clear of all that, or he'd start answering the question and then suddenly he'd be talking about music again. He did once let slip that one of the original members of the Quintet got himself killed, but that was about it.

One time an old Army mate of his came to our house for Sunday lunch, and while Pa was out of the room this bloke told us a story. It seems that their battalion was travelling in a convoy out in the desert, and one of the trucks near the front broke down and blocked the road. The other trucks couldn't drive round it 'cause there were minefields all over the shop, and while the officers were trying to work out what to do, shells started raining down on them. But Pa rushed up front anyway, and he and another mechanic managed to repair the truck in the middle of this barrage so that the convoy could drive on and get out of range of the shelling. Pa got some sort of medal for it, apparently. But when we asked him about it, he just said: "Oh, I was young and foolish then. Bloody stupid, really. I could easily have copped it."

As for the POW camp in Germany where he spent the last eighteen months of the war, he never spoke about that at all. No music there, I reckon.

Still, when he was back in England he got in touch with a couple of the blokes from the Quintet and they decided to start a new band. Pa bought a drum kit on the HP and paid for it by working as a mechanic. Gradually it turned around, so that it was the money he earned playing music that made it possible for him to buy his own garage. It was a good place to practise, too, but in the end he gave up music. He never really liked modern jazz, and he got fed up with spending every Saturday night playing old tunes for old people, as he put it. So the drum kit was moved to the back room in the garage. I think he hoped Frankie would show an interest, but he never did. Not very musical, our Frankie. The exception to the rule.

Me, I always wanted to play those drums. When I was eight or nine I used to sneak into the garage when Pa was out, peel back the dust sheet and bash away on the tom-toms. Just with my hands – I loved feeling the vibrations tingling through my fingers, and the way the skins started off really cold and then slowly warmed up. Anyhow, one day Pa comes back early and finds me there, and I'm thinking I'm in for a smack. But instead he goes off into the house and comes back with a pair of sticks, and then he shows me how to hold them properly and teaches me to play a basic rhythm. I picked it up quickly and asked him to show me something else, and he said maybe another time. So I badgered him for a few days and he ended up giving me regular drum lessons, every Sunday afternoon after lunch, as long as I helped Ma with the washing-up first.

So that day a few years later when me and Des were walking home from school across the park, and Des said he was going to start his own band, I was in there like a shot: "Can I be in it?" I suppose I should've waited for him to ask me, but sod it. You've got to take your chances when they come along, that's what I say. Never guessed what it might lead to, mind you. Christ, how old was I then? Fourteen, fifteen? Fifteen at least, I reckon, 'cause I remember Des saying we were going to play like The Beatles. That didn't last long...

Where was I going with all this? Oh yeah, I was going to tell you about the wedding. Well, it makes you stop and think, something like that, doesn't it? Especially when it's your own little sister standing there in front of the altar, making all those vows that add up to the fact that she's not really your little sister any more, not the way she used to be.

They didn't want to get married at St Peter's at all to begin with. Trev told me just before the ceremony, in the middle of a fit of the jitters, that he hadn't been inside a church since he started wearing long trousers. As for Susie, she only went on Sundays 'cause our parents made her. But once we got back home after that tour, Ma and Pa started nagging her about having a church wedding. She realised agreeing to that was the best way of making them feel happy about the whole business, so she persuaded Trevor to go along with it for their sake.

Not that they didn't like Trevor. He and Des had both spent so much time over at our place that Ma used to say it was like having two extra sons, and she meant it as a compliment. It was just that Susie was so young, barely knew the world, and here she was about to get married already. And she fired back that she'd just spent six months touring the country in an old van with a bunch of blokes, and without complaining too (it's true, she never did), and didn't that show that she was grown-up?

"Ah, but you always had your brother with you then, didn't you?" said Pa.

That was the nub of it. I'd always been there to keep an eye on Susie, ever since she was old enough to leave the house, and we were all worried about what would happen when she was left to manage on her own, with just Trevor to look after her. I even had a quiet word with him before the wedding – made sure he knew what was what, if you know what I mean.

We had the reception in the church hall, and to start with I thought it wasn't going to be much fun. On the one hand you had Trevor and his old 'chums' from public school. I recognised a few of them from Keith Fisher's party the year before, and I hadn't found them easy to talk to then. They were all at university now. The blokes had long hair, and a few of them had beards as well. I tell you, if Frankie and his gang had met them in the street looking like that, they'd've given them a right pasting, likely as not. Luckily Frankie remembered he was meant to be on his best behaviour. Mind you, if any of them caught his eye he gave them a long, hard stare. They soon found something else to look at.

Then there were Trevor's parents. His mum was wearing a plain, dark blue dress, very tasteful, and a big straw hat. She looked a bit nervous. His dad was sweating hard inside a dark suit, waistcoat and everything, even though it was July. The way he held himself, it was like he was standing to attention.

There were some other relatives and friends of the Harrises there too, but I never talked to any of them. The point is, they were all better dressed than us, and quieter too. Pa set the tone for our lot when he marched into the hall and said in a loud voice: "Right, where's the beer then?" The look on Mrs Harris's face at that moment said as plain as anything that she wasn't looking forward to sitting next to him all through the meal.

So like I say, it was a bit slow to start with. We all sat at long trestle tables, Trev's family and friends on one side of the room, Susie's on the other, and the happy couple themselves on the top table with the two sets of parents, the best man and the bridesmaid. Keith was the best man. Trevor told me he couldn't choose between me and Des, and whether that was the truth or he just wanted me to feel better, it suited me fine, 'cause I wouldn't have wanted to stand up there and make a speech. So me and Des were ushers instead.

Later on I had a chat with Keith, and I asked him if he was still playing r'n'b. He looked embarrassed and said no, he'd given up the bass and was "experimenting with keyboards". He seemed to be in a bit of a funny mood, sort of distant, and I thought at first that being at Oxford now, maybe he thought he was better than me, though I'd never had him down for a snob before. Then one of his friends came over and handed him a joint, and I realised he was just high. A bit later, when I went round the back of the hall, I found a whole crowd of them rolling spliffs and passing them round. They offered me one, but I had other things on my mind.

Two other things, actually: Gail Jenkinson's tits. Susie had picked Gail as her bridesmaid – they'd been best friends since junior school. Like Des, Gail had been in and out of our house all the time when she and Susie were growing up. I suppose that's why I'd stopped noticing her, and what with being away on tour I hadn't seen her for a while. So it was a surprise to see her walking down the aisle behind Susie and realise that she'd turned into a bit of a stunner. She had dark hair cut in a fringe at the front, like Sandie Shaw, and her face was nice. But what I really noticed was her knockers. They weren't enormous, but there was something about the size and shape, the way they bulged under that cream-coloured dress she was wearing, that gave me such a hard-on, I had to stick my hand in my pocket to disguise it. At that moment I wished Trevor had made me best man after all, 'cause then I'd have got to dance the first dance with her.

But it didn't matter, 'cause I did get to dance with her in the end.

All through the meal I kept looking at her up there on the top table, and a couple of times I caught her eye and she smiled at me, a really nice smile. So I reckoned I must be in with a chance. Sure enough, when the tables had been cleared away and the hired band had started playing rock'n'roll covers, we found our way to each other. Eventually there was a slow number and we danced so close together that I could feel every curve of her body, and soon after that we were kissing, and soon after that I took her hand and said: "Come with me."

We walked quickly, holding hands but not saying anything. When we got to our house, I remember thinking this must've been the first time in years it had been completely empty. There was usually so much hustle and bustle, people coming in and out and talking and shouting and playing music. Now it was so quiet, you could hear the grandfather clock in the hall ticking away. Even so, we walked softly up the stairs, still not talking, and she went straight into my room without me having to show her the way (of course she knew the way, she'd been up here hundreds of times), and then we undressed as fast as we could and made love.

You know what? It was the first time I'd ever made love. Oh, I'd had sex before, of course. There was a knee-trembler up against the back of the school gym with Nicky Doyle after an end-of-year party, and then there were the girls who came up to me after gigs, the sort who really just wanted to shag a musician. Well, naturally I was happy to oblige... This was different, though. For one thing, I really liked Gail, and maybe I was just caught up in the atmosphere of the wedding, but it felt like it actually meant something to me.

The trouble is, because of that, I wasn't very good. That is – well, it didn't last long. Gail was sweet about it though, and said we could try again in a little while. So we lay there side by side on my old bed and she told me a bit about her job; she was a secretary at a firm of accountants in Market Street. Then she asked me about the band, but not in that starstruck way some people did, the sort who thought that playing a musical instrument and making a record somehow made you special. She seemed genuinely interested. I was ready to try again soon enough, and this time it was much better. Afterwards I lay there with her head on my chest and thought, so *that's* what it's supposed to be like.

I got a shock when we arrived back at the reception. From outside the hall I could hear the blues playing, but it sounded like a band, not a record. Sure enough, we went in to find The Hornets up on stage – only with Pa on drums.

It's a funny thing, but when you're in a band you never get to see yourselves in action – well, unless someone films one of your gigs, I suppose. So this was the first time I'd ever seen The Hornets play live, and I stood there at the back of the hall for a couple of songs, fascinated. It was Des who caught the eye, of course. He was going through all his usual routines, but I'd only ever seen him from behind. I didn't know about all the different expressions on his face, the way he lived every note he was playing. Watching him, I thought I could see something of what other people saw in us.

Behind him, the others were static in comparison. They'd talked Keith into playing bass and he was standing on the left-hand side of the stage, a stoned grin on his face. Opposite him, Trevor and Susie were sharing a mic. He had his harp and she was shaking a tambourine, and both of them were singing back-up. They looked strange in their wedding clothes, but utterly happy. His arm was round her waist, and at the end of one song they kissed and everyone cheered.

Meanwhile Pa was sat at the back, a fag hanging out of the corner of his mouth, keeping perfect time. He kept looking proudly at Susie, and I got the feeling he'd forgotten all that stuff about her being too young to get married. As for me, I was enjoying watching my family and friends making themselves and everyone around them happy, and I was almost sorry when Pa called me up on stage. As he handed me the sticks he said: "Hope you don't mind me sitting in, Stevie. Here, these are yours now." I could feel tears welling up, but I told myself not to be such a soppy sod and counted out the intro to 'Got My Mojo Working'. I concentrated on my drumming for a bit and the next time

I looked up, Gail was standing in front of the stage, smiling at me. At that moment, the whole world seemed right.

Everyone else seemed to agree, and the rest of the evening was a blast. I think Trev's parents must've slipped away while we were playing, and his other relatives too, 'cause I don't remember seeing any of them again. Soon everyone was dancing with everyone else. Not just dancing, either. I spotted a bloke called Terry, a slicked-back greaser I knew from school, moving in on one of the hippie chicks, and later the two of them headed out the back. At around the same time I saw Charlie Maynard chatting up my cousin Imelda. I suppose I should've told him that she was such a strict Catholic, she might as well have been wearing a chastity belt, but I decided it was more fun to let him work it out for himself.

The thing is, all this seemed perfectly natural at the time. It was like everyone was high on something, dope or booze or love or music, and no one wanted the evening to end. Even when Trevor and Susie left, the rest of us kept on dancing and singing and drinking. When we finally had to leave the church hall some time around one in the morning, a crowd of people came back to our house and Pa got out his best whiskey. There were still half a dozen of us left awake, talking quietly in the front room, when I saw the first light coming through a gap in the curtains. Gail and I went outside and sat on the back step, snogging and watching the sun rise. A bit later I walked her home across the recreation ground, where the dew was sparkling in the sunshine. As I strolled home afterwards, I tried to fix as many details of the night as possible in my memory. It stood me in good stead later, I can tell you that.

Trevor and Susie had gone off on honeymoon to the Costa del Sol for two whole weeks, all paid for by Trev's parents. When they got back they stayed with the Harrises for a few days, and then they moved into a rented flat in Borehamwood. Jacko and I helped them with the move, which didn't take long; even with all the wedding presents, they didn't own enough stuff between them to fill the van. The flat was furnished, so it didn't matter too much, though you could tell from the way Susie was talking that she wanted to buy her own furniture. I couldn't see how they were going to afford it, seeing as how we were still on a weekly wage, and not a large one either. What's more, Trev wanted me to help him buy a car – he couldn't actually drive yet, but he'd booked some lessons. In the meantime he and Susie went everywhere by bus. Well, as Trev said, he wasn't going to cycle everywhere now he was a married man – bikes were for kids. And anyway, Susie could hardly ride pillion.

All in all we must've had four or five weeks off, and not before time. I helped Pa in the garage during the day and saw Gail most evenings and weekends. We didn't do anything special, just went to the movies or drove out to pubs in the country. I don't even remember much of what we talked about; I probably just told her stories about stuff that had happened to us on tour, like I used to in those days when I couldn't think of anything else to say. 'Course, I should've told Gail that I loved her and I wanted to be with her, but I could never find the right words. Anyhow, I was more interested in making love. We did that as often as we could, usually in the back of the van. It wasn't very comfortable, but we didn't care. We were just hungry for each other.

It couldn't last, of course. The holiday, I mean. I even knew exactly when it was going to end; the first Monday in September, the day the second album was due to come out. We'd recorded it in May, in the gaps between gigs, but Charlie said the summer was a bad time to release an LP, so he was going to sit on it for a while.

Personally, I thought we should've locked away the master tapes and forgotten about it altogether. For starters, the sound was all over the place. Maybe that was because we'd recorded it in bits and pieces, but if you ask me, the main problem was that Des and Trev wanted to get a bit of everything in there. So we did a few numbers in our old style – fair enough. But then there were a couple where Des wanted it to sound really heavy, like Cream. (I tell you, if Eric bloody Clapton had released an album where he farted old blues songs, Des would've been out bulk-buying baked beans the next day.) I had to keep redoing my parts 'cause he said I wasn't hitting the drums hard enough. In the end I told him I'd hit him pretty bloody hard if he didn't shut up about it, and that did the trick... There was one song where we had to get a brass section in, even though it cost us an arm and a leg, and an Elmore James cover that ended up as The Hornets trying to sound like Fleetwood Mac trying to sound like Elmore James. And somewhere along the line it was decided that Susie would get to sing lead on one number. Now I've always loved my little sister dearly, but even I wouldn't pay to hear her sing. Her voice was good enough for backing vocals, sure, but she couldn't carry a song on her own. They did something fancy with the tapes to make it sound better, but I knew we'd be in trouble if she tried to sing it live.

That was what really worried me: how were we going to reproduce all this stuff on stage? I kept schtum while we were recording the album, but I had to say something when we listened back to the final mix. Charlie wanted to know what we all thought, so I jumped straight in and said it sounded like a bit of a mess. Des and Trev turned on me and said the album was 'eclectic', and I couldn't say anything to that 'cause I didn't know what the word meant. But I got a fair idea from the bullshit the two of them came up with – all this crap about how we had to "turn our audience on to new sounds". Well, that would've been all right if they'd been our own, and not sounds we'd ripped off from other musicians.

When we started rehearsing again, Des turned up with an afro and huge sidies – yeah, just like you know who. But he'd spent a lot of time working out how we could play the new stuff, and I started to think that maybe I was wrong about it. We played The Marquee on the day the LP came out and it was a great gig. The place was packed, and they all seemed to know the old songs and like the new ones. At the party afterwards, Charlie got up on a table, banged a knife against a bottle of beer and announced that by this time next year, The Hornets would be as big as The Rolling Stones. Maybe people would've taken him more seriously if he hadn't fallen off the table soon after that and spent the rest of the evening dozing in a chair.

Over the next couple of weeks we played a few more gigs in and around London and the vibe was good, especially in places where we'd played a lot in the early days. Some nights we had fans calling out for songs we'd forgotten we used to do, and we all had a laugh as we tried to remember how they went, right there on stage in front of everybody.

But once the tour proper started and we moved further from home, things started to change. There wasn't any one gig where I came off stage and thought, this isn't working any more. I just started noticing worrying signs: the seated venues where you could see dirty great gaps, and the standing ones where half the crowd never bothered moving away from the bar; the times when an audience would clap at the end of a song, but there wouldn't be any cheering; fewer teenage girls hanging around outside the dressing room afterwards.

As the weeks went on, it got harder and harder to ignore. There were towns we'd played before where we were now booked into smaller venues, and when we did play the big halls we were hardly ever top of the bill any more. Sometimes we'd swapped places with bands who'd supported us a year before, which was bad enough, and sometimes we opened for groups we'd never heard of, which was even worse.

Des took it hardest, of course. He didn't say much, but he must've seen his dreams of stardom starting to fade. Being Des, he just drank more. He started slipping a half-bottle of scotch into the back pocket of his trousers every night before he went on stage. He didn't drink in front of the audience – that sort of thing could get you into trouble – but between songs he'd turn his back on them, wink at me and take a swig. It didn't have much of an effect on his performance, in fact the audience probably didn't even notice most of the time, but if you looked closely you could see that he wasn't quite with it. Like, he wouldn't be able to manage his duck-walk, or he'd cut a long solo short for no obvious reason.

As for Trevor and Susie, they were too wrapped up in each other to take much notice of what was going on. Wedded bliss, I think they call it. They were certainly at it like rabbits most nights, and boarding house walls being what they were, I heard far more than I wanted to. In fact I started taking sleeping pills so I wouldn't have to listen to them.

The rest of the time I just got on with it, the way I always did. Solid, dependable Steve… Every couple of days I went to a phone box and called Gail. She was often out, but even when she was there I usually came away feeling disappointed. We didn't seem to have much to say to each other when we weren't together, and though I told her about what was going on with the band, I could tell she wasn't all that interested. It seemed like no one was really interested in what I had to say about anything.

The way I remember it, Charlie would post an updated copy of our itinerary to Jacko every Friday, and we had this ritual where he'd collect it first thing on Monday morning and we'd go through it over breakfast, usually in a greasy spoon somewhere. At the start of the tour it was a bit of a laugh. We'd look down the list of venues and it would be: "Aston University… Hey Des, d'you remember that girl who was all over you when we played there last year?" That sort of thing. But gradually we stopped looking forward to the itinerary. It just told us how badly we were doing.

Then there was that business with Ten Years After. They'd been around for a while, in fact they'd supported us a couple of times. Seemed like decent enough blokes. Well, they released their first album the same day as we put out our second, so they were on the road at the same time as us. Charlie did a deal with their management to book the two bands as a package for a few weeks. 'A Banquet of Blues' they called it, which was pretty fucking ironic, since we couldn't afford to eat half the time 'cause of the lousy wages Charlie kept us on.

The first few gigs we did together, the running order was always the same; some local group opened the show, then Ten Years After came on, and we played last. We'd all go out for a pint afterwards, and Des would sit off to one side with Alvin Lee and talk about guitar tunings, and everything was fine. Then, when we got to Nottingham, where

Ten Years After grew up or something, their manager came to see us and said would we mind if they headlined just this once. It seemed fair enough. If the place was going to be packed with their fans, it made sense not to try and follow them.

The night after that, we were sitting around in the dressing room at Leicester Poly, playing cards to kill time before the show, when Jacko came in. I could tell from the look on his face that it was bad news.

"Listen lads, I'm sorry about this," was how he started off. "I've just been on the phone to Charlie. He says Ten Years After are headlining now."

"What, you mean tonight?" asked Trevor. "I didn't realise they were big in Leicester as well."

Jacko looked embarrassed. "Er, no, I mean permanently, like."

Des was furious, and it certainly didn't do much for our pride. But we couldn't really argue with the decision. We played a dozen more dates with Ten Years After and they blew us off the stage every night. In the same way that Cream played the blues heavier than we did, Lee's mob were faster and jazzier. Des knew it, too. You could tell, 'cause for a couple of days he tried to get us to raise the tempo on the upbeat numbers. It didn't work, though. Trev's bass playing wasn't up to it, and we had to go back to the way we were before.

I can tell you the exact date when I knew the game was up: October 19th, 1968. I know that 'cause I kept a copy of the poster, in fact it's still there on the wall of my music room. It was a week or so after we'd waved goodbye to Ten Years After, and I remember thinking that the two bands were heading in opposite directions, and not just 'cause we were going north and they were due back in London. Anyhow, we arrived in Liverpool a day before we were due to play there, 'cause Jacko reckoned he knew someone who could put us up for nothing. Some time in the afternoon, while he was off "seeing a man about a dog", we were walking round the city centre when we saw this poster announcing that The New Yardbirds were on at Liverpool University that evening.

Des immediately got all excited, till Trevor pointed out that it was nothing to do with Clapton and that lot. According to Trev, this was Jimmy Page, the last one left from The Yardbirds proper, and a bunch of blokes no one had really heard of before. You could see that Des was well pissed off, 'cause he thought he should've known that. Anyhow, we all agreed that going to a gig sounded a lot more fun than hanging around in some dingy pub with Jacko and his Scouse mates.

To be honest, my first reaction to The New Yardbirds was, what a bunch of poofs. I mean, I know everyone had long hair in those days, but the singer and the guitarist both had these curls coming right down over their collars. And the singer had his shirt open to his waist, though I don't know why, 'cause he didn't have a lot in the way of chest hair to show off.

His voice was another thing altogether, though. I couldn't believe how powerful it was, this high-pitched moaning and shrieking coming from this skinny bloke. The guitarist, Page, he was shit-hot too. He could do a slow solo that got right into your guts or play so fast that it took your breath away, and he even switched to an acoustic for a couple of songs, which was unusual for a blues band. I'll tell you something for nothing, they blew me away, and as we trooped out of there afterwards, I had a fair idea the others felt the same way.

The thing is, we all knew we couldn't do that. We just weren't good enough musicians, when it came down to it. And if we carried on doing what we were doing, would anyone still be interested? The way the tour was going, it didn't seem likely. That Liverpool crowd had gone wild for a group who hadn't released a record yet – imagine what it would be like when they did, and the whole country got to hear them. You didn't have to be a genius to see that The New Yardbirds were going to be massive.

The only thing I didn't predict was that they'd change their name, just after that gig in Liverpool, to Led Zeppelin. But sure enough, within a couple of months they were touring the States, selling out gigs and causing riots wherever they went.

Mind you, by that time The Hornets were playing abroad as well.

BAR SIX: STEVE, 1969

It was in February '69, a month to the day after we'd arrived in Hamburg, that I got the 'dear John' letter from Gail. And there was me thinking things couldn't get any worse.

I'd woken up around lunchtime, the way I did most days. I lay there for a few minutes trying to focus, listening to Des snoring. He was making a noise like a rusty chainsaw, which usually meant he'd drunk himself legless the night before. Sure enough, there was an empty schnapps bottle lying on the floor by his bed. I suppose he might've knocked it over and spilt it on the carpet, but that wasn't very likely. Even when he was off his face, Des always looked after his booze.

I got dressed as fast as I could. The flat was freezing as usual, and I didn't need to pull back the curtains to know there was snow on the ground. There'd been snow on the ground the day we got off the train from Hook of Holland, and there'd been snow on the ground every bloody day since. A couple of times the temperature had risen a few degrees and it had started to turn to slush, but then it snowed overnight and we were right back where we started.

Sure, it was fun to start with. On our second day we found a park and built snowmen and had a snowball fight, mucking around like we were eight years old. That soon wore off though, I can tell you. You get fed up of always having cold feet and hands, no matter how many layers of socks and gloves you wear, and getting chapped lips, and bruises on your arse 'cause you've slipped on the pavement.

The daft thing is, I hadn't expected it to be cold at all. As far as I was concerned, West Germany was on the continent, which meant it was south of England, which meant it must be warmer than England. But one day I was walking through the main station and I saw this big map of Europe, and I discovered that Hamburg was actually about the same distance north as Hull. That explained a lot – I knew for a fact that you could freeze your balls off up there.

There was no sign of Trevor and I wasn't about to wake Des, who was always a miserable git after a night on the sauce, so I decided to go for breakfast on my own. On my way out I checked the post box. Although the only letter in there was for me, I didn't recognise the handwriting – Gail had never written to me before. Even so, I sort of guessed who it was from. But I didn't read it straight away, just stuffed it in my pocket and braced myself to go outside, waiting for the blast of icy air that always shot up my nose and made my eyes water.

The Imbiss on the corner, a sort of cross between a greasy spoon and a snack bar, was full of students, yakking away like students do. Des and Trevor were really pissed off that we were staying near the university. 'Course, those two had read all about The Beatles, hadn't they, all that stuff about sleeping in the back of a fleapit off the Reeperbahn surrounded by tarts and pushers and off-duty sailors, and I suppose they thought that was glamorous. Me, I quite liked it where we were – it was just about the only thing I did like about the whole sodding business. It was a damn sight better than driving around in that bloody van all the time, never sleeping in the same place two nights running. Okay, we didn't have much money to spend. So what else was new? At least we were comfortable. Just cold all the time, like I say.

Still, the Imbiss was warm enough, which was why we spent so much time in there, trying to make a cup of coffee last as long as possible. The students did the same thing and no one seemed to mind. I found an empty table in the corner and ordered my usual breakfast, a big grilled sausage and two fried eggs. While I was waiting for the food to arrive I ripped open the envelope.

Gail didn't waste any time getting to the point, I'll give her that – didn't bother asking how I was or what Hamburg was like. This is what she wrote:

'Dear Steve,
I am very sorry, but I am writing to tell you that I won't be able to see you any more when you come back to England. This is because I am

engaged to be married in the summer. My intended's name is Edward and he is a junior partner at my firm. He is a bit older than me, but he is very nice and has his own house in Abbots Langley. I'm sure you would like him if you met him. I hope there are no hard feelings.

Best wishes, Gail'

And that was that.

At least I understood now why she'd been so distant when I'd seen her at Christmas – not letting me touch her, making excuses about headaches and it being her time of the month. She must've been seeing this Edward already. What kind of a tosser called himself 'Edward', anyway? Why not Ted, or Ed, or Eddie? It wasn't hard to see what was going on here. Junior partner, house in Abbots fucking Langley, 'a bit older than me': obviously some educated ponce who wanted a good-looking young wife to clean up after him, shove out a couple of kids and wear a low-cut dress when he invited his boss round to dinner. As for Gail, she was in it for the money, simple as that, and I couldn't compete. If it was a straight choice between a junior partner in a firm of accountants and the drummer in a blues band that was going nowhere fast, it wasn't really a choice at all.

That didn't stop me feeling angry, though. As I ate my breakfast and reread the letter over and over, I kept stopping at the bit where she said I'd like this Edward bloke if I met him. Like buggery I would. I'd give him a good kicking for nicking my bird, and I reckon Gail knew that too. That's why she'd waited till I was safely out of the way before giving me the push.

I was going to order a coffee but I changed my mind. All of a sudden I just wanted to be on my own. It was something to do with the students around me; half of them were cuddling and kissing, and even the ones who weren't looked like they were having a much better time than me. I left some money on the table and went outside.

To start with I headed for the U-Bahn station – I thought I'd get on a train and ride round the city for a couple of hours. I'd done that before, it was a way of using up dead time in the afternoons. The lines were mostly overground, so you could watch the world go by and keep warm into the bargain. Then again, that cost money, and I didn't fancy trying to ride for free. It wasn't worth the risk. The bassist from another British group who were in Hamburg at the time had told us how he never paid – the stations weren't manned, you see. Then one day this pair of inspectors gets on the train. There's an old ticket on the floor, so he picks it up and shows them that, but it's obviously the wrong type or something. Then he tries to claim he doesn't understand German... The upshot was that they marched him off to the cop shop and he had to beg them not to deport him.

Besides, the train would be just as bad as the Imbiss, full of happy couples, so I turned around and started walking instead. It was parky, but at least the sun was out. It wasn't too bad as long as you kept out of the shadows. I skirted round the edge of the university, crossed the main road and went into the botanical gardens. I'd been in there once before and I reckoned it was the sort of place where I could be alone.

It was a very German sort of park, if you know what I mean. Orderly. Neat. Flowerbeds with tidy edges, paths that ran dead straight, trees with little notices nailed to them. I wandered around for a while, and then I found this gate that led into a different bit. It was basically a lake with trees around it on steep banks. There were flowerbeds in here too, but they looked more natural somehow. So I walked round the edge of the lake until I found a bench in the sunshine, pulled my tatty overcoat tight round me and settled down to think. Trouble was, all I could think of to start with was Gail: the way she looked in the raw, the feel of those glorious tits under my hands and how she would moan when I squeezed her nipples just right... I realised I was wiping my eyes. Must've been the icy wind making them water. Yeah, right.

I tried to distract myself by focusing on what was going on around me – which was sod all, to tell the truth. The lake was mostly frozen over, but there was a patch of open water in the middle with a few ducks paddling in it. I watched them for a long time as they swam round and round, stubbornly refusing to give in to winter. The poor buggers must've been hungry, and I was sorry I didn't have any bread for them.

After a while I realised someone was looking at me, the way you do sometimes without necessarily being able to see them. I turned round sharply. Sure enough, there was a girl standing a few yards away, and when she saw that I'd clocked her she came closer.

"I'm sorry if I startled you," she said in English, but with enough of an accent that I could tell she was a Kraut. "You are one of The Hornets, yes?"

I obviously looked gobsmacked, 'cause she quickly went on: "I watched you at the Blueskeller on Wednesday night, you see, and when I saw you sitting here, I recognised you. I think you are the drummer?"

So I said yes, I was, and she asked if she could sit down. I shuffled along the bench and made room for her, and we got talking. Her name was Birgit Schneider; she was a student at the university, doing English and American literature. Her parents wanted her to be a teacher, but she probably wouldn't be because she'd rather do something artistic, though she didn't know exactly what... Under normal circumstances I wasn't much of a one for talking to strangers, but she'd taken me by surprise. Besides, when you've just been chucked, any pretty girl who wants to talk to you is more than welcome. And this girl was pretty, though not in an obvious way. She was small, with dark hair cut short and a round face, and there was something about the way her eyes crinkled up when she smiled.

But that first time I met her, what I noticed most was the way she said things an English person wouldn't, 'cause they'd think it wasn't polite or something. We'd only been talking a few minutes when she said: "It must be very lonely for you here in Hamburg, away from all your family and friends, yes?"

I was about to say no, we were all having a ball, but suddenly I couldn't see the point in lying. So I told her how we were only there 'cause our last album had sold fuck all (I had to stop and explain what 'fuck all' meant), and this three-month gig was the only way the bloke who owned the record company could find to get back some of the

144

money he'd spent on us. And I also told her how we were bored with the way every day was the same; you sleep all morning, try to find some way of passing the afternoon that doesn't involve getting cold or spending money, and then play the same songs in the same poxy club every evening.

Don't get me wrong, I wasn't about to spill my guts completely, even to a girl with a pretty smile. I didn't let on about Gail chucking me and how miserable that had made me feel. Or tell her that we were supposed to be a four-piece, only our keyboard player, my little sister, had come over all bolshy when Charlie had told us about the Hamburg gig and said she wasn't about to move to Germany for the winter when she'd just got a home of her own – all of which meant that Trevor went round with a face like a wet weekend. Or mention that Des had finally started to cotton on to the fact that people were never going to mention his name in the same breath as Eric Clapton, and that his way of dealing with this was to take out a season ticket at the local bar and work his way through every variety of schnapps known to mankind, one by one. Or that we were missing Jacko, who hadn't come because, well, there wasn't really anything for him to do, was there, what with us staying in one place all the time. (But still, he was good at cheering us up, and God knows we needed that.) Or that I was just plain homesick, and went down to the station every Sunday morning to sneak a look at the English papers on the newsstand and find out how Watford had got on the day before, and they'd nearly always won 'cause they were looking good for promotion that season, which just made it worse…

No, I didn't tell her any of that, though she must've got the general idea. And anyhow, happy people don't sit in parks in the middle of winter and stare at ducks for hours on end, do they? I don't know why she didn't just leave me to it. I would've, if the boot had been on the other foot. But instead she stayed there and told me how much she'd enjoyed our music the other night. She said she was planning to come back with some friends at the weekend, and they'd be impressed when she told them she'd actually talked to one of The Hornets.

So I asked her something that had been puzzling me: what was it with the Germans and old music? All the British groups who were over in Hamburg were either blues bands like us, or they were playing old-fashioned rock'n'roll. Either way, you'd be lucky to spend an evening in a club without hearing at least one Chuck Berry song. Didn't anyone here want to listen to German music?

"Have you heard any German music, Steve?" said Birgit, and she laughed. "Some people try to copy American pop and rock, but our language is not very good for rhyming, so it does not work very well. And there is also Schlagermusik, which the old people like, but it is *awful*." She made a face like she'd just smelt something disgusting, and I couldn't help laughing too. "So I think that the German people, the young ones I mean, they like to listen to music in English that has a good beat and words that are not too complicated, so that we can understand them.

"Anyway," she went on, "we only *listen* to American music. You *play* it – do you not think that is a bit strange, too?"

"What d'you mean?"

"Well, look: where do you come from?"

I said Watford, and when she looked blank I explained that it was a market town just outside London, sort of in between the suburbs and the countryside.

"So is it not odd that you and your friends play music that was written for people who lived on cotton plantations in Mississippi, and for poor black factory workers in Chicago? What can you possibly have in common with them? Do you really have a right to sing the blues?"

I was about to say that I didn't sing, I just sat at the back and played the drums. But I knew that wasn't what she meant, so I kept schtum.

"You see," she went on, "I think you English are just like the Germans. You like the beat and the sound of the blues, and the words are actually about, what do you say, universal experiences, most of the time. But it is not your music, any more than it is ours."

I didn't have an answer to that, and anyway I was getting a bit pissed off at the way she was lecturing me. So I mumbled something about how I had to go and get ready for the gig, and that was that. I headed straight back to the flat, intensely aware of the cold all of a sudden, hoping one of the others was there and had put the heating on.

I thought that was the last I was going to see of Birgit, especially since she'd mentioned something about having a boyfriend. But she turned up at the club on Saturday night with half a dozen friends, just like she'd said she would. They were all dancing in front of the stage, looking like they were having a great time, and the mood sort of spread so that it seemed like everyone started enjoying themselves more, us included.

Birgit came over to me in the break between sets, while I was getting the drinks in. She wanted to apologise for being rude about us not coming from Mississippi and all that, so of course I had to apologise back for leaving in such a hurry, and after that we got chatting again. I even introduced her to Des and Trevor, though I didn't explain how we'd met. I think they were shocked that I'd actually talked to one of the locals. We'd all kept ourselves to ourselves since we'd been here, you see, apart from a couple of boozy nights out with other British bands.

From then on I saw Birgit regularly, every Thursday afternoon more or less, 'cause that was the day she didn't have any lectures. If the weather was bad we just went for a coffee, but most times she insisted on showing me bits of the city I didn't know. The first day we went out, we climbed up what seemed like hundreds of stairs to get to the top of this church tower and admire the view, though to be honest I was too knackered to admire anything. Another time we took a train to a place out by the river to the west of the city, where all the rich people live up on a hillside. It reminded me a bit of Moor Park, only without the golf course – though why a millionaire would want to pay all that money to watch cargo ships go by, I couldn't say.

Best of all was when we went walking across this enormous lake slap bang in the centre of the city. I was a bit iffy about it, but Birgit said the water froze so hard in winter that there wasn't any danger. Sure enough, when we got out in the middle there were people strolling around, kids skating, all sorts. I was going to tell her I'd never walked across a lake before, but then I remembered that I had, sort of, so I told her the story of what had happened once when me and Des were kids. There was this lake – it was more of a pond really, but we always called it 'the lake' – at the edge of Cassiobury Park, with a little island in the middle of it. This one winter, we must've been six or seven I suppose, the lake froze over, so me and Des decided to walk across to the island. Des went first. He was a bit scared, but it was okay. Now the thing is, even at that age I was a fair bit bigger than him, and I'd only taken about two steps when I heard the ice starting to crack under me. So I quickly go back to the shore, leaving Des on his own on the island. Trouble is, he's too scared to go back on the ice now, even though I keep trying to tell him he'll be all right. In the end it starts getting dark, so I go and fetch the park-keeper, and he comes back with me and tries to persuade Des to walk across the ice, but Des isn't budging. So the parkie goes away and comes back with a couple of ladders and lays them across the ice – 'cause it really isn't that far – and crawls across and gets Des and carries him to safety on his back. The story even made the local paper. Des's old man read it and gave him a proper hiding.

Those Thursday afternoons, Birgit told me stories too, though hers were mostly about the city rather than her own life. Most of the stuff she told me went in one ear and straight out the other, but there was one story I'll never forget. It was about what happened during the war, in the summer of 1943, when the Brits and the Yanks bombed the shit out of the city, and the Elbe was on fire, and the tarmac on the streets started bubbling with the heat until the water mains burst and cooled it again... I didn't say it out loud, but when she told me that story I was glad Pa had been in the Army and not the Air Force.

Apart from that one time in the Blueskeller, I kept Birgit away from Des and Trevor. I never invited her round the flat or asked either of them to come with me when I was going to meet her. That way I had something that was mine, away from the band and our stupid squabbles. Don't get me wrong, there was nothing between us, me and

Birgit I mean. Like I said, she had a boyfriend, some bloke called Lars she'd met at the university, though she didn't talk about him much, and he never came along to the club with Birgit and her mates. I got the impression that he was more your intellectual type.

Anyhow, I didn't really fancy Birgit. And if I did want to get my end away, there was usually some girl in the audience who was happy to come backstage for a quickie in the dressing room, especially on a Friday or Saturday night. That's one thing I noticed about the Krauts; they were very disciplined, even when they were supposed to be having fun. Monday to Thursday they came along, watched us, danced around a bit, had a couple of beers and went straight home. But at the weekend they drank more, stayed later and acted a whole lot wilder. Just on those two nights, you see.

Where was I? Oh yeah, Birgit. Well, after a while I realised we'd become friends, which was a novelty – I'd never had a female friend before. It must've been something to do with the lack of pressure. What with her having a boyfriend and me not fancying her, we didn't spend all our time doing that stupid flirting thing people do when they want to get each other into bed. We just talked properly, and that suited me fine.

Some of the time we talked in German, 'cause she'd decided I ought to learn and I couldn't see any reason not to. It wasn't like proper lessons – she didn't make me read a grammar book or anything like that. She just showed me how to say the sort of things that came in handy when you were going round the shops or you wanted to buy a ticket for the cinema. Mind you, even before I met her I hadn't done too badly. This one time, me and Trev went into a music shop 'cause he needed a new harp. He'd obviously been practising, and he came out with this complicated-sounding phrase. Knowing him, it probably translated back into English as: "Esteemed sir, I am desirous of purchasing a harmonica in the key of G," or some such bollocks. But he must've got something wrong, or maybe the bloke behind the counter just didn't understand his accent, 'cause he rooted around in a drawer and came out with a kazoo. Trev tried repeating what he'd said before but it was no good, so I thought I'd have a go. I waved my arms about a bit and pointed and used most of the German words I knew, which wasn't many, and the bloke smiled and pulled open another drawer and handed me a harmonica in G. You should've seen the look on Trevor's face.

Like I say, that was before Birgit started teaching me. As it turned out, I was – well, not exactly a natural, but "a very good pupil", she used to say. Funny, 'cause I'd been crap at French at school. The teachers always went on and on about grammar, and I just lost interest. Whereas Birgit, she showed me how to say useful things and sort of slipped the grammar in when I wasn't looking, if you know what I mean. And one thing she taught me was that the best way to learn a language is to listen to people speaking it, like when you're on a train or in a bar. Well, that made sense to me, 'cause I'd always been good at that – sitting in the background, saying nothing but listening to everything. The others probably thought that 'cause I didn't say much, I wasn't really interested, but they'd've been surprised. The fact is, I was always very aware of what was going on around me.

Another thing me and Birgit talked about was old bluesmen. Not the blokes Trevor and Des were always going on about, Muddy Waters and that lot, but a whole different crowd, people the others had learned most of their music from. Robert Johnson I'd heard of 'cause we'd learnt a couple of his songs, but the rest were new names to me: Charley Patton, Son House, Blind Lemon Jefferson and a load more. But even Birgit hadn't heard of Little Sonny Carter, which was worrying.

Then again, everything about that whole business was well dodgy, from the moment Charlie Maynard turned up on our doorstep with an overnight bag in one hand and a four-pack of beer in the other. At first he just said he'd come to see how we were getting on, so we took him down to the Blueskeller that night and he watched us do our thing. We tried a bit harder than usual, 'cause we didn't want him to see how bored we'd all got, and afterwards he clapped us on the back and told us it was criminal that Fleetwood Mac had become stars and we hadn't, but he was going to change all that, just wait. I think he was pissed. It turned out he hadn't booked a hotel room, so he came back to the flat with us and kipped on the floor.

The next day he took us all out to lunch, and that's when he told us what he called "the good news"; we were going to make another album, right here in Hamburg. Des started to say that we hadn't actually got any new songs ready to record, but Charlie interrupted him and explained what the deal was. Natchez had signed up this old American blues singer called Little Sonny Carter, and Charlie wanted us to back him on an LP.

This was all a bit unexpected, but it didn't sound too bad, all things considered. When Charlie went for a slash we had a quick confab and decided that even though none of us had heard of Little Sonny Carter, not even Trevor, it would be cool to work with a real bluesman. We'd been going through the motions for weeks, but we actually started to get quite excited about Little Sonny.

That didn't last long once we'd met him. Charlie picked him up from the airport and took him to his hotel (thank God we didn't have to share our flat with the bastard), and later he brought him along to the club to watch our set. Little Sonny turned out to be a big bloke – taller than me, and I'm over six foot. He had this gnarled old face and a grey beard that was going white at the edges, and I got the feeling right from the off that we were never going to be best mates. He must've been old enough to be my grandad, but it was nothing to do with the difference in our ages, or in our backgrounds for that matter. It was just his manner. Charlie introduced him to us before we went on, and we all shook his hand and said "Pleased to meet you". (I think Trevor even called him 'sir'.) He just grunted, and then turned to Charlie and asked where that goddamn drink he'd ordered had got to.

We pulled out all the stops that evening, and it was a Friday too, so the place really came to life. Des in particular fed off the energy of the crowd and showed off all his tricks. Even Trev joined in, playing a harmonica solo flat on his back in one song. But Little Sonny didn't look impressed. He and Charlie were sitting at a table just to one side of the dancefloor, and whenever I caught a glimpse of him through the crowd he seemed to be either slinging a drink down his neck or watching a pretty girl dancing. Once I caught Charlie's eye and he raised his glass and smiled, like he wanted to encourage me. I wasn't fooled.

Sure enough, when we came out front after the show it was obvious something was wrong. Little Sonny was still at his table, with a shot glass in one hand and the other dangling over the shoulder of a top-heavy brunette who'd been dancing down the front all evening. But Charlie was waiting for us by the door with a look on his face like someone had died.

When we'd left the stage, Charlie had turned to Little Sonny and asked him what he thought of us. Apparently the miserable old bastard's exact words were: "The drummer and the guitar player will do, but lose the bassist." And that was that. He'd decided Trev wasn't good enough to play on his record, and nothing Charlie could say would make him change his mind.

'Course, Charlie didn't tell us this straight off, just tried to make out that there'd been "a slight change in plan" and that it was nothing personal. Poor Trev looked devastated though. I mean, we all knew he wasn't the world's greatest bass player, but that wasn't the point. He was one of the band, he'd been in it from the start. No way did he deserve this.

Des tried to cheer him up. "Look on the bright side, Trev," he said after we'd been talking in circles for a few minutes, "at least you can still play harp."

But Charlie was squirming again. "Um, well, no, actually. Little Sonny plays harp himself, you see, he's pretty hot. He was telling me that Sonny Boy Williamson taught him personally when he was in his teens…"

He tailed off and there was this embarrassed silence.

"That's marvellous, absolutely fucking marvellous," said Trev at last, and for a second I thought he was going to cry. Then he pulled himself together. "Well, seeing as I'm not needed here, I'll be off."

And he left. Not long afterwards, Charlie took Little Sonny back to his hotel. The old git didn't say as much as a word to us before he went. Me and Des stuck around and had a few drinks, and eventually we decided that we were going to tell Little Sonny that if he didn't want *all* The Hornets, he could find himself another backing band. But when we got back to the flat there was no sign of Trevor. We figured he must've gone to an all-night bar to drown his sorrows, but in the morning we discovered he'd taken all his stuff and buggered off. I wondered whether to phone Susie, but I didn't want to worry her, so I waited till Sunday evening. Finally I made the call: it turned out that Trev had arrived home that afternoon. Susie was furious on his behalf, so I didn't ask when he was coming back to Hamburg. I had a fair idea he wasn't coming back at all. Who could blame him?

Des and I spent the evening talking about what we were going to do. I still thought we should tell Little Sonny to get stuffed, but Des said Trevor had gone now, so if we turned down the gig it'd be nothing but a gesture – it wouldn't do Trev any good. Eventually I backed down and agreed to do the session. After all, it wasn't like Trev was being permanently chucked out of the band, was it? And I already had an idea that not a lot of people were going to get to hear this album, so what did it matter anyway?

But yeah, I do sometimes wish I'd stood up for Trev that time. I mean, I'd done my best when we were recording the first LP. Charlie and Des had decided we needed to get a session player in to redo all Trev's bass parts; it was my idea to invent an excuse to get him out of the way for the morning, so the poor sod wasn't completely humiliated. Mind you, you'd think he'd have worked out what had happened when he heard the finished album... The point is, he was supposed to be a mate – Christ, he was my brother-in-law – and I could have done better by him.

But I never had the energy to argue with Des when he'd made up his mind about something. He was good at that – deciding what he wanted and going on and on until he got his way. That's why he was always the natural leader of the band, though Trev tried to kid himself he had a say as well. In the end, you're either a leader or a follower, and

I was a follower. That was the cause of all my problems. I'll come on to that in a bit.

When we turned up at the studio on Monday morning we were introduced to Rainer Kaufmann. Apparently he played bass with a local outfit called the Winterhude Blues Band. Funny-looking bloke. He was dressed in black from head to toe, like flower power and the rest of it had completely passed him by, and he had this sort of helmet of straight black hair that made him look like Sonny out of Sonny and Cher, only thinner.

He didn't talk much, which was fine, 'cause we all felt a bit awkward about this whole situation. But when he did talk, we soon realised he only spoke about five words of English. The producer was better, but he disappeared after the first day and left us with a Scottish engineer called Alan whose German was about as good as Rainer's English. I knew enough of the lingo to translate odds and ends, but it did slow things down. Alan would come on the intercom from the control room and say something like: "Can we try that again, please, a bit more slowly this time?"

So Rainer would turn to me and say: "Sorry, please?" which was his way of asking what someone had said.

"Ein bisschen, er, langsamer."

"Ah, okay." But then he'd say something else to me, and Des would ask what Rainer had said, so I'd have to try and translate that, even if he'd just asked me what time it was. It started to get on my tits after a while. In fact, those sessions were a complete shambles all round. The idea was that Little Sonny would re-record some of his songs with an edgy young band (that's us, in case you're wondering), in the same way as Sonny Boy Williamson had done with The Yardbirds a few years back. That explains why Des was so keen on the idea, now I come to think about it... Anyway, the trouble was that Little Sonny usually turned up late and carrying a bottle of something alcoholic – red wine, whisky, schnapps, he wasn't choosy – which he offered round. Well, Des was never one to turn down a drink, and it turned out that

Rainer could put it away as well, and as for me – you know what they say, if you can't beat 'em…

As a result, the sound we produced wasn't so much edgy as relaxed, and often downright sloppy. Alan tried to protest to begin with, but then we started inviting him into the studio to join us for a drink, and after that he couldn't really complain. In the end he settled for getting a few complete takes of each song down on tape and overdubbing various parts afterwards. Except that Little Sonny refused to do overdubs, so his parts were very rough round the edges.

If you're getting the impression that I wasn't Little Sonny Carter's number one fan, you're damn right. Charlie thought he'd found an unacknowledged genius and he was going to turn him into a star. But after spending a week with Little Sonny, I was fairly sure that all Charlie had turned up was a grumpy old bluesman who'd never made it big 'cause he wasn't much cop in the first place. One thing I've noticed over the years: people who are good at what they do, whether it's singing the blues or repairing car engines, have a certain – what's the word? Grace, that's it. They listen to other people's opinions, even if they know better. Whereas the ones who aren't so good cover it up by insisting they know best, and cut up rough when anyone tries to argue with them. That was Little Sonny all over. Even when we could all hear that he was singing off key or slurring his words, he'd claim it was meant to sound like that and refuse to do another take. I reckon the only reason he'd come to Europe to record was that he'd pissed off every half-decent producer in the States.

Like I say, he was a miserable bastard as well. Never bothered talking to us unless he had to, and then it was usually to tell us when something was wrong. Des was hoping to pick up some tips, and maybe even find that magic ingredient we were missing, but the nearest he ever got to advice from Little Sonny was: "Boy, you either got it or you ain't." Which was a fat lot of bloody good.

On our last day in the studio, after we'd finished taping this chugging, mid-tempo song Little Sonny had obviously ripped off from Jimmy Reed, he said: "So, boys, where're we gonna celebrate

155

tonight?"

We told him we had to play at the Blueskeller that evening as usual, and anyway we were knackered, but he was having none of it. "I mean after that," he said, taking a slug of scotch and wiping his mouth with the back of his hand. "Where does a guy go for some real fun in this town?"

Des and I looked at each other blankly. Truth is, what with being poor and bored and tired and depressed most of the time, we hadn't spent a lot of time out on the razz. Then Rainer asked me what was going on, so I explained. He smirked and said: "No problem. I show you, yes?"

So Little Sonny turns up at the club just after we've finished that night, wearing a shiny suit and generally looking ready for a good time. Rainer quickly takes charge, leading us through the back streets, parallel with the river, and of course I know exactly where we're going. Sure enough, ten minutes later we're pushing our way through the crowd of hookers and dealers and gullible tourists on the Reeperbahn. Little Sonny is obviously very interested in the tarts hanging around in the doorways, most of them wearing nothing but their undies – which is pretty damn brave, since it's only March. But Rainer turns off down a side street where it's quieter, and soon we're going down a rickety staircase into a club.

This place is obviously still cashing in on the Beatles connection. There are posters and pictures of the band on the walls, and the group on stage is bashing out old rock'n'roll cover versions the way The Beatles used to, only not very well. Oh, and half the punters look like Rainer, dressed in black and with moptop haircuts. It's all a bit pathetic really, but Little Sonny seems happy enough, especially when Rainer finds us a table and orders a bottle of schnapps and four glasses. Soon we're toasting anything we can think of, and Little Sonny is telling us this long story about how he was seeing three women at the same time, and one night one of them comes in and finds him in bed with the other two, and she asks if she can join in as well... Personally I don't believe a word of it. But for a bloke who can't be far short of sixty, he seems to have sex on the brain.

He obviously reckons he's in with a chance tonight, too. Did I mention that the waitresses are all topless? Well, this is the Reeperbahn after all, or as good as. So of course Little Sonny keeps ordering more and more drinks, to get the waitress to come over so he can try and cop a feel. She seems okay with this to start with (it's probably par for the course in her job), especially when Little Sonny sticks a twenty-mark note down the back of her knickers. Trouble is, the more drinks he has, the more determined he seems to be to get a proper return on his investment, if you know what I mean.

Meanwhile all four of us are knocking back the schnapps at a fair old rate. Des has invented this game where everyone has to down the contents of their glass whenever the band play an obvious Beatles rip-off, and somewhere around the time they kick into a piss-poor version of 'Twist And Shout', things are starting to go out of focus for me. In fact I nodded off for a while. The last thing I remember is Little Sonny saying to the waitress: "Come on baby, just a little mouthful. I promise I won't bite."

When I woke up it had all kicked off around me. I found out later that Little Sonny had finally got a good hold on one of the waitress's tits, and when she tried to break free he held on tight and practically ripped her nipple off. She screamed the place down, and next thing there was this big ugly bouncer standing by the table asking us to leave. Trouble is, I was asleep, Rainer was drunkenly trying to make excuses, Des thought it was hysterically funny and Little Sonny couldn't see what all the fuss was about. So the bouncer did what bouncers always do: pick on the weediest-looking person, which was Des. He tried to haul him to his feet, only Des wasn't really ready to stand up, and somehow the table got knocked over. That must be what woke me up, 'cause my head was resting on it at the time. So the first thing I saw when I opened my eyes was my oldest mate grappling with this bruiser who was twice his size. Naturally I took a swing at the bouncer, who went flying backwards. I was too pissed to do him any real damage though. He came back at me, and soon we were rolling around on the floor in the middle of all this broken glass, and I remember noticing that the band had stopped playing. There was just this confused mess of people shouting in English and German, so that you couldn't make out any individual voices.

And then all that noise died away in the space of a few moments, and the bouncer got up off my chest and stepped back. When I looked up I saw Little Sonny holding this huge knife – the blade must've been nine inches long. From the look on his face, I'd say he'd used it before and wasn't afraid to use it again.

"That's it motherfucker, you just stand there," he said to the bouncer, who didn't need to know much English to have a fair idea what was expected of him. Then Little Sonny turned to Des. "Go on, you boys git on out of here," he said. "I can take good care of myself, don't you worry about me."

Well, I suppose we should've stuck by him. But Des started making for the stairs, and it seemed natural for me to follow him, and Rainer certainly didn't want to get left behind. Once we were out in the street we started running, and we didn't stop until we were well clear of the Reeperbahn. I think that was when Rainer spewed all over my shoes.

And that was the last I ever saw of Little Sonny Carter. Crazy old bastard.

That night in Hamburg wasn't the first time I'd run away from trouble, not by a long chalk. You could say it was an occupational hazard of being a football fan in the late Sixties. Especially if you hung around with someone like my brother Frankie.

One thing that always annoyed me was the way the papers tried to make out that football hooligans were all the same – brain-dead skinheads in Harringtons, braces and bovver boots. But the fact is, there were lots of different types of hooligan. At the serious end there were the real hard cases who went round looking for trouble and weren't satisfied till they found it. They were sort of like your generals, directing operations. Their troops, well, they were the lads who couldn't have come up with a plan to save their lives, but were happy enough to join in a ruck if someone else started it. Beyond that there was another group – teenagers mostly – who stayed on the edge of the action, piling in when things were going well and legging it when they weren't.

And then there were the nutters: men who acted alone, away from the safety of the mob, whenever the mood took them. Vicious bastards. People like Frankie. And this was the bloke who was supposed to be looking after me when I first went to Vicarage Road. I was only nine. 'Course, Pa wasn't to know. Frankie was hardly going to sit down to tea on Saturday night and boast about breaking some poor bugger's nose that afternoon, was he? And I certainly wasn't about to tell on him. I learnt the rules very early on: always help your mates in a scrap and *never* grass them up. So whenever Frankie waded in, fists flying, I was right behind him. I never questioned it. It was just what you did.

Don't get me wrong, it's not like there was a fight every Saturday. A lot of what the media called hooliganism was just mucking about. Like for instance, travelling back from an away match on the football special, you'd unscrew light bulbs from the carriages and chuck them onto the platform as you passed through a station, to give the punters waiting there a bit of a shock. The whole train would be dark by the time you got back to Watford Junction.

Anyway, like I said, when I started going to matches, Frankie took me, and even when I was old enough to go on my own, I still stood with him and his mates. Safety in numbers and all that. Gradually a few of my own friends from school started coming, including Des of course, though he was never a hardcore fan. He did come along to the odd away match, but he wasn't really into it. He didn't seem to feel that adrenaline buzz the rest of us got from running into trouble, or from running away from it for that matter. I think he was more worried about hurting his hands in a fight and not being able to play the guitar.

Trevor wasn't interested in fighting either, though he did enjoy the football. Mind you, it would all have been a bit different if I'd flattened him that first time, when he clattered into me while I was celebrating a goal. I thought for a moment that some idiot was starting a ruck, so I turned round, fists at the ready. Then I found myself face to face with this frightened-looking kid, and I just felt sorry for him. My future brother-in-law, as it turned out, but how was I to know that? On second thoughts, maybe I *should* have punched the stupid bastard.

It got harder to make it to every game once the band got going properly, and Frankie gave me plenty of stick the first time I told him I couldn't come to a match 'cause I wouldn't be able to get back in time for the gig that evening. When we started going on tour I had to miss home games as well, and sometimes I went weeks without seeing the team in action. As for Hamburg, that was sheer torture, especially with Watford going so well back home. I did try watching local sides a couple of times, but it's not the same when you don't give a toss about either of the teams on the pitch. I couldn't even join in with the singing. At least I was back in time to see us get promoted to the Second Division for the first time ever. We beat Plymouth at home to make it certain, and afterwards everyone went out on the lash and we all ended up in the pond at the top of the High Street, singing and dancing. What a night. Shame about the goldfish, though.

But then came America, and everything changed after that. When the next season arrived, I was ready to start following Watford around the country again. It felt like the only thing to do.

Being in a higher division and playing bigger teams meant we got more aggro wherever we went, but I wasn't bothered. Not even when we played Millwall. The last time we'd been there I'd had to run for my life. I reckon there were plenty who'd done the same and didn't want to risk a repeat, 'cause in the week before the game some of the regulars starting coming up with excuses why they couldn't make it. There were so many blokes who said they had to mend things round the house, you'd think the town had been hit by an earthquake.

No, Frankie couldn't even fill his car. He had this crappy Ford Zephyr that Pa had rescued from the scrapheap and fixed up for him. He wouldn't risk it on trips up north – not after the time it conked out in a blizzard on the way to Rotherham and he missed the whole match waiting for the breakdown truck – but he did drive it to away games around London. Normally there were five of us in there, three crammed in the back, so tight that when you got out at the other end you had to shake your arms and legs to get the feeling back. But for the drive to Millwall there were only four of us, me and Frankie and two of his mates, Grapper and Mick, so at least I could stretch out a bit. Grapper was a huge bloke, bigger than Frankie – though most of the extra was beer gut – and useful for putting the wind up opposing fans. To tell the truth, he wasn't up to all that much if it came to an actual fight. Mick was the opposite, a small bloke with lanky hair and a 'tache who looked like nothing but fought hard and dirty.

When we got to New Cross we parked in a side street, pulled our coats up tight around us with our scarves hidden underneath and walked to the ground at a fair old pace. At Millwall you just wanted to get in the away end as quick as possible – then at least you'd be surrounded by old bill. They used to say it was the only ground where the police were there to protect the away fans from the home ones and not the other way round.

It was a miserable afternoon, cold and grey, and a crap game too. Watford lost one-nil, however much we tried to lift them with our singing and chanting, and that all tailed off towards the end anyway. Everyone was too busy thinking about how they were going to get out safely. In fact, some left good and early, taking a gamble that there wouldn't be any nutters waiting for them outside. As for the rest of us, we spent more time watching the home fans than the action on the pitch. Sure enough, a few minutes before the final whistle, gaps started showing on the terraces at the far end.

Finally the game finished and we gave our players a quick clap before turning and heading for the exit to face the music. It was the layout of the ground that made Millwall worse than other places. There was only one way back to the main road from the away end, and it meant going under a railway arch – a narrow one, not much more than one car wide. A perfect spot for an ambush. Sure enough, me and Frankie and the others were still a fair way from it when the mob we were in the middle of stopped moving. That could only mean one thing:

the Millwall fans had got there first, ahead of the old bill, or maybe the old bill hadn't even bothered trying. Either way it meant trouble, and seconds later the first bottle came flying over and broke on some poor sod's head, just a few feet ahead of me. Then there were bricks and stones and more bottles coming down like hail, and suddenly all the Watford fans were turning and running back towards the ground, hoping they could get out at the other end. We went with them, but then Frankie peeled off to one side and the rest of us followed him. 'Course we did. He was our leader, wasn't he?

He was also a nutter, like I said before. My brother the nutter. God knows I'd seen him in action often enough, but even I wasn't ready for what happened next. Still running, but not quite so fast now, he led the three of us in a wide arc until we were facing the arch, a bit off to one side. Most of the Millwall fans had chased after the rest of the Watford crowd, lobbing more missiles as they went, but there were still fifty or so standing around chanting and cheering.

So what did Frankie do? He only led us straight into the middle of them, didn't he. Without breaking stride he yelled out: "Now!" and started running full tilt towards the arch, so fast that I was struggling to keep up. He was banking on taking them by surprise, and it worked. The Millwall fans suddenly saw these two huge blokes – Grapper was just behind Frankie – heading straight for them, and their natural instinct was to get out of the way. As the crowd parted in front of us like the Red Sea, I thought for a crazy moment that we were actually going to get away with it.

We would've done too, if it hadn't been for a bunch of dozy pillocks right at the back. Three of them there were, no more than fourteen or fifteen by the look of them, all in tank tops and huge flares. They'd probably had a couple of pints of cider before the game and weren't quite with it, 'cause they didn't seem to clock what was happening till it was too late. Everyone in front of them had moved aside to let us through, but when these kids saw us, it must've looked like we were coming for them. So they turned and ran. Trouble was, there was only the one road, so even though we were basically running away from the mob of Millwall fans (because a few did come after us once they'd realised who we were), we ended up chasing these three pillocks by accident, if you see what I mean. When we did hit a junction, they turned left, the same way we wanted to go to get back to the car, so naturally it must've seemed even more obvious that we were after them.

This went on for a while, the seven of us pelting down streets of terraced houses. I was starting to get worried now. Even though the other Millwall fans seemed to have given up, there was no guarantee that they hadn't just taken a short cut – they could be waiting around the next corner. Plus, I wasn't convinced we were still going in the right direction. I reckon Frankie had decided that if the kids wanted to be chased, he was happy to oblige. So he followed wherever they led, and we followed him.

Finally one of the teenagers had a brainwave. As they reached a T junction he yelled out: "Split up!" He turned right and the one behind followed him, leaving the third kid to go left. He could've ignored the command, of course, but that probably never occurred to him. Maybe the first kid was his older brother... There was the slightest hesitation, then Frankie went after him, and I did likewise. Mick and Grapper went the other way.

Soon Frankie and I we were closing on the kid, and he panicked and bolted down the first turning he came to. Only it was a dead end: a couple of houses on each side, then what looked like a scrapyard, with a chain-link fence and high corrugated-iron gates. No way out.

There was a moment of stillness as the three of us stopped at the same time. It was like a scene from one of those Spaghetti Westerns – everyone looking at everyone else, wondering who was going to make the first move. We were all panting, and in the distance I could hear the sound of sirens and singing.

The kid cracked first. At first he looked absolutely terrified, but then the expression on his face changed into something wilder and he charged at what must've looked like the only possible escape route, a small gap between Frankie and the side of the road. Another bad decision. Given the chance, I'd've let him go, but Frankie wasn't feeling so generous. He took a couple of steps sideways and grabbed the kid as he tried to get past. There was a bit of grappling and then the kid was on the ground, curled up in a ball with his hands over his head, and Frankie was putting the boot in. I thought it'd just be a couple of swift kicks, but something came over him. I'd seen it happen before and I knew we were in trouble.

"Come on Frankie," I said. "Leave him now, he's not worth it. The police'll be here any second." The sirens were definitely getting closer, but Frankie took no notice, just kept kicking the kid with his steel-toed boots, moving around all the time, trying to find places he'd missed. The kid was whimpering in this pathetic way – no words, just sounds, like an animal.

Then the first police car came hurtling round the corner and skidded to a halt a few yards from where I was standing.

Fair play to the kid, he spoke up for me in court; said I'd never touched him, it was all Frankie. As far as the judge was concerned we were both just common hooligans, but he had to take the victim's testimony into account, so Frankie was sent down for three years and I got nine months. As they led me out of the courtroom I looked up to where my family and friends were sitting. Pa had his arm around Ma, who was crying, and Trevor was hugging Susie, while Des was sitting there with an angry look on his face. That was when it hit me – I'd let everyone down, everyone who cared about me. And I know it sounds corny, but you'll have to trust me on this; I made a promise to myself, there and then, that I'd never do it again.

BAR SEVEN: TREVOR, 1970

It's ironic, if you think about it. When we first started, we had no reason to sing the blues. We were young and the world seemed full of possibilities. Music was a way of exploring some of those possibilities, but when it came to the blues, we might as well have been singing in a foreign language for all that the words meant to us. Of course we had our problems – but being punished for failing to hand in your homework on time hardly amounts to having a hellhound on your trail.

By the start of the Seventies it was a different story. We'd flirted with success and then seen it slip away, found ourselves standing still while the music scene moved on, and as for what happened in Taunton... Now one of my bandmates was in jail and the other was pickling his liver in alcohol. Plenty of material for a few albums' worth of blues songs there, you'd think. Yet none of us ever sat down and wrote them.

And then we lost our recording contract.

It was a couple of weeks after Steve's trial that Charlie Maynard asked me and Des to come to the office. Charlie himself buzzed us in, and when we got upstairs we found that the receptionist had gone. Her desk had gone as well, and the outer office was now full of boxes of LPs, tightly-packed rows of cardboard cartons piled up to the ceiling. Most of them contained copies of our second album.

Charlie got straight to the point. He explained that we'd originally signed a deal for three albums, which we'd now delivered. But 'Buzzin' With The Hornets' had sold poorly, and he didn't plan to release the Little Sonny LP; Natchez was in financial trouble and he couldn't afford to take a risk on an album that, quite frankly, wasn't up to scratch. (I may have permitted myself a bitter laugh at this point.) Our stint in Hamburg had just about paid off our debts to the company, so all things considered, Charlie thought it was best if we made a clean break.

"You know," he said as we were preparing to leave, "I still think The Hornets could have been one of the great British blues bands. I really believe that. But I've got be honest: somewhere along the way you've lost something you used to have."

Well, we couldn't argue with that.

Why didn't we just knock it on the head there and then? God knows we had plenty of good reasons to give up. But the trouble was, we couldn't actually conceive of doing anything else. Somewhere in the depths of his alcoholic stupor, Des still believed in his dreams of stardom, the dreams he'd been pursuing ever since he first picked up a guitar. As for me, I'd given up the chance of going to university for the sake of my musical career; if I threw in the towel now, it would mean admitting that my parents had been right all along. Not that Mum and Dad ever nagged me – that wasn't their style. Whenever Susie and I went over for Sunday lunch, they were much more interested in the question of when they were going to have some grandchildren to dote on. It didn't do much for my morale to know that I was a disappointment to them in that department as well.

There was another fundamental reason that we didn't break up the band: Steve. I mean, it was hard enough for him in Pentonville as it was. He said very little about the conditions there when Susie and I went to visit him, but you could tell from what he *didn't* say that it was no picnic. Can you imagine how he would have felt if Des and I had gone in there and told him we were taking away his livelihood? As it was, he didn't have a lot to look forward to when he came out. The way I saw it, we owed it to him to keep the band going till then at least. After that – well, we'd have to see how things went.

As a parting gift, Charlie had offered to help us out in any way he could. Well, obviously we were going to find it tough playing gigs without a drummer, so he said he'd see what he could do. The upshot was that a week later we were sitting in a pub in Harrow with Vinnie Romero, swapping stories. Vinnie had been in a group from

Boston that had crossed the Atlantic in '67 in the hope of cashing in on the blues boom. It hadn't worked out and the band had returned to the States within a year – all except Vinnie, who'd fallen in love with an English girl. Now he was sharing a bedsit in Wembley with her, surviving on whatever gigs and session work he could pick up, all strictly cash in hand because "technically I'm like, y'know, an illegal immigrant, man".

I flashed Des a questioning look, and he shrugged his shoulders as if to say that beggars can't be choosers. Given the choice, we probably wouldn't have picked an unkempt, unshaven Italian-American with a rank leather jacket, holes in his jeans and a persistent whiff of dope about him. But Charlie had assured us he was a good drummer, and we had a gig that evening, so we weren't going to turn him away. As it happened, the gig went well, so Vinnie became a Hornet, on the understanding that he'd relinquish his seat behind the drums the moment Steve got out of jail.

This temporary incarnation of The Hornets may not have been the best, or the most successful, but it was certainly one of the hardest-working. In the first six months of 1970 we took every gig we could get. We had to – none of us had any other source of income. (Susie had reluctantly gone back to work at Trewin's, but her wages didn't stretch very far.) Without the backing of a record label we were forced to hustle promoters ourselves, just like in the old days. Fortunately there were enough people with fond memories of the band to provide us with regular work. Thanks to one of Charlie's contacts we also played on a couple of package tours, though nowadays we always opened the show. It was a sobering experience to watch from the wings as bands like Foghat and Taste played a brand of blues that was altogether heavier and hipper than the music that had brought us what little success we'd had. We did our best to adapt; we ditched the poppier stuff and Des drew out his guitar solos to previously unimagined lengths. It helped that Vinnie's style relied more on strength than subtlety, too. So we just about passed muster.

What we really needed was a complete makeover, but you couldn't say that to Des. Looking back, it seems to me that he'd taken to heart one of the guiding principles of the Sixties – the idea that anyone can be whatever they want to be – without grasping that this meant popular culture was continually spinning off in exciting new directions. Des didn't want to know about new directions. As far as he was concerned, he was on a long, straight road that would lead him, one day, to fame and fortune. The rest of us were just along for the ride.

Don't get me wrong. I'm not suggesting for a moment that I was harbouring a secret desire to turn The Hornets into the sort of group many of our peers (and some of our idols) were now playing in – the sort who proclaimed that they were 'fusing blues and rock with the classical and jazz idioms to forge a new and more intense form of music', or some such bollocks. God no. And even if I had, I'd certainly have been put off by my one experience of progressive rock in the flesh.

It was late 1971 when I got the letter from Keith Fisher. We'd been in touch sporadically since he'd gone up to Oxford, and we'd even managed to meet for a beer one evening in his first year when the band had played in Maidenhead. But it had been a while since I'd heard from him, so I was pleasantly surprised when the post brought an envelope addressed in his distinctive slanted handwriting. Inside were two tickets to a concert on the South Bank and a note that simply said: 'Do come, it would be great to see you there – Keith'. There was nothing on the tickets to indicate what kind of concert it was, just one mysterious word: Satyricon.

I'd been wondering what Keith was up to these days, and the answer was obvious once we reached the Queen Elizabeth Hall. I'd never been there before, but I had a fair idea that it didn't normally smell of incense and patchouli. Nor, I was prepared to bet, did its regular audiences feature so many long-haired men with beards, wearing army-surplus greatcoats, cheesecloth shirts and loon pants.

When Satyricon finally took to the stage it was under cover of darkness, and the murmurs of anticipation among the crowd were silenced by a bell that tolled repeatedly for some time. Slowly, other instruments – guitar, bass, drums, keyboards – started to come in, forming a crescendo that built to one enormous chord, accompanied by a blinding flare that flooded the stage in light. When my eyes had recovered, I glanced at my watch. The band had been 'playing' for nearly five minutes without managing a riff, let alone any words. Finally they locked into a stop-start rhythm. At this point the singer, who'd been standing at the back by the drum riser, apparently deep in thought, approached the microphone and let out a high-pitched moan that turned into the start of the lyrics. Not that I could make out more than the odd phrase here and there. I found out later that this first number was called 'New Consciousness Dawning', but frankly I was closer to unconsciousness by the time it dribbled to an end after nearly fifteen minutes of tricksy time changes and pseudo-classical keyboard solos.

It didn't get any better. In an hour or so, Satyricon only got through a handful of songs, though I hesitate to use the word to describe such meandering constructions, none of which had anything you could call a chorus. Occasionally the band would settle into a groove that hinted at straightforward rock music, or the guitarist would launch into a solo that betrayed a youth spent listening to Eric Clapton and Jeff Beck. But the rest of it was just pretentious, over-elaborate rubbish.

Keith was on bass, and he'd clearly been listening to a lot of jazz since leaving The Hornets, judging by the complex patterns he played. He also featured on saxophone on one number, playing almost, but not quite, atonally. Susie and I didn't talk about the music at all when we went backstage after the gig, though. Keith probably sensed my disapproval – in my struggle to come up with a vaguely complimentary adjective to describe what I'd just heard, the best I could manage was 'interesting' – but he was too polite to pursue the point. Indeed, the atmosphere in the dressing room as a whole was terribly genteel. Keith introduced us to the rest of the band and their girlfriends, and then we all sat around and chatted about mutual friends, records we'd bought recently, even stuff that was in the news. This must be what it's like being a student, I thought to myself. It certainly wasn't very rock'n'roll, apart from the large joint that was handed round. Keith and I parted with promises to meet up more regularly (promises I don't think either of us intended to keep), and I went home and put on a Muddy Waters album. The music pulsing through my veins felt like the antidote to a poison.

The first half of 1970 was grim, but there were some consolations. For one thing, it turned out that the pervasive odour of dope that hung around Vinnie Romero was no accident. He always seemed to have enough on him to roll a joint, and being a sociable kind of guy, he liked to pass it around. It wasn't long before toking became part of our post-performance routine, the way drinking always had been before. I was hesitant at first, but I soon got into the swing of it. I needed something to help me get through that awful period.

What with gigging so much, we actually got really tight after a while, and there were nights when we played as well as we'd ever done. The trouble was, you couldn't predict when it would happen. We'd put on a series of deeply average shows in front of what we still thought of as 'our' audience in London, then play like demons in Crewe or Swansea a couple of days later for a handful of students who hadn't come to see us at all. Still, those nights when we came close to playing like a proper power trio were just about enough to keep the dream alive. We even had a couple of shows recorded professionally, got the best bits edited together and sent the tape off to a few record companies.

Power trio? Yes, we were back to the basic guitar/bass/drums line-up again. Susie played a couple of local gigs in January, but her heart wasn't in it, and the moment there was any question of going on the road she put her foot down. "I'm not slogging round the country in that bloody van again," was how she expressed it, "not if you paid me."

I pointed out that this was the general idea, but she just laughed bitterly and launched into a rant about how she had a proper job now, and even selling half-price pillowcases in Trewin's paid better than our 'pathetic dreams of stardom'... Funny how I remember that phrase so clearly now. At the time I filtered it out of my consciousness, thinking only about the effect on the band of losing our keyboard player. As for the implication that I should do the same – get a job, forget about music – it went completely over my head.

If that sounds selfish, well, I suppose I was. All I can say in my defence is that for the past few years, my entire life had revolved around the band. It had been the source of my friends, my wife, my income – and my dreams. I was barely twenty-one and it seemed far too early to even think about letting those dreams go, despite the mounting evidence to suggest that it might be for the best. As for Susie, she'd been there all the time, watching and then sharing our experiences, good and bad alike. The band was as much a part of her life as it was of mine – or at least, that's what I thought. Okay, we'd had a similar row when the Hamburg trip came up, but her objections had seemed more reasonable then. Besides, you heard some dodgy things about British musicians and what they got up to in Hamburg, and I wasn't sure I wanted Susie – my darling, my new bride – to be exposed to them. Of course I missed her like crazy the whole time I was over there, but at least it seemed like there was a reason I was paying that price.

Now I had to face up to the fact that Susie didn't want to be in The Hornets any more. I did this by acting as if she'd never been in the band in the first place. Brilliant, eh? What's more, to pre-empt any suggestions that I might want to follow her into the world of nine-to-five and PAYE, I behaved as if playing music was just a regular job. If she told a story she'd heard from one of the salesgirls at Trewin's, I'd counter with an anecdote Vinnie had told us on the way to a gig. If she started enthusing about her promotion prospects, I'd tell her about the latest record company Des and I had sent our tape to, being sure to stress how keen they were to talk to us (though the truth was that they never were). When I wanted to be particularly sarcastic, I even referred to Des and Vinnie as my 'colleagues'. And at the end of each week, Susie and I pooled our respective earnings. We put most of the money into an envelope that Susie took to the bank, setting a little aside for a visit to the pub on Friday night and a takeaway afterwards.

That was married life for the Harrises.

I still loved her, of course, and I think she loved me. Some of the time it was just like it used to be, when we were hungry for each other and the rest of the world could go to hell. And for much of the time we behaved like all young married couples behave; we went shopping for furniture together, ate at the local Chinese restaurant on special occasions, argued about what we were going to watch on TV, visited one or other set of in-laws for Sunday lunch. The main difference between us and any other couple was that my job involved travelling around the country playing music. When I got home, usually after midnight and often much later, the flat would be dark, and I'd undress quickly and quietly and climb into bed, being careful not to do anything to disturb the steady rhythm of Susie's breathing.

One evening in August, the phone rang while I was doing the washing-up after dinner. Susie went to answer it, and when she returned I guessed from the glint in her eyes what she was going to say.

"That was Pa. It's Steve – they're letting him out early. Good behaviour or something."

We took a couple of steps towards each other and hugged. The soapy water from my washing-up gloves must have soaked through the thin cotton of her blouse in an instant, but she didn't seem to mind. After a while, I noticed she was crying softly on my shoulder.

There were plenty more tears on the day we went to fetch Steve from Pentonville. The three of us – Des came too, of course – had been waiting for nearly an hour by the prison entrance on Caledonian Road when a door in the heavy front gate finally opened and a familiar figure appeared, blinking in the glare of the sunlight. He looks well, I thought to myself as he strode quickly towards us. Susie couldn't wait, and ran to embrace him, so Des and I did the same. Then Des took a bottle of beer from one pocket and an opener from another and presented them to Steve, murmuring: "I thought you might like this." Steve grinned hugely, flipped off the top, put the bottle to his lips, tipped his head back and downed the beer in one go. Wiping his lips with one hand, he clapped Des on the back with the other and we all headed for the car.

The O'Briens wanted Steve to spend his first day of freedom with them. So I dropped him and Susie off at their house before driving home, where I put on a Jimmy Reed LP and opened a bottle of beer of my own to celebrate the fact that The Hornets were back together again. The following evening we all met up at Steve's local, where people were queuing to buy him a drink. He didn't seem to want to talk about his experiences in jail, so to begin with we told him what had been going on while he'd been away. Later, once the alcohol had started to take hold, we moved on to reminiscences of the early days of the band, and eventually Hamburg.

"That reminds me," he said, "you remember Birgit?"

"Wasn't she that German bird you brought along to the club once?" asked Des.

Steve nodded. "She wrote to me a few times while I was inside. The thing is, she's dropped out of university and gone to work for a music promoter, and she reckons she can get us gigs over there. Not just Hamburg – all over the place, like a proper tour. What d'you think?"

I thought it would be great – as long as Susie came with us. But by the way she stiffened at the first mention of touring West Germany, I knew that wasn't going to happen. The trouble was, even as I was drunkenly trying to work out how to play this, Des was saying 'yes' on my behalf. As he said, it could be exactly the shot in the arm we needed – but I was more worried about what it would do to my marriage. I looked at Susie and smiled and squeezed her hand. She gave me a thin smile in return, from which I guessed what she was going to say later that night while we were lying in bed, staring at the ceiling: "You go if you want, but I'm not coming with you. That's not a part of my life any more."

The next day we phoned Birgit and started to hammer out the details of The Hornets' German tour. Steve handled the negotiations, actually – Des still acted like he was the one making the decisions, but because Birgit was Steve's contact, he did most of the work and then relayed the plans to Des for rubber-stamping. Itineraries, transport, accommodation, even fees: in each case, Steve would put his hand over the mouthpiece of the phone, tell Des what he'd agreed with Birgit and ask: "That alright with you?" Every now and then, almost as if he felt he ought to, Des would raise an objection, and Steve would nod and say "Okay" and start talking into the phone again. Oh, I forgot to mention that these negotiations took place in German, which Steve spoke quite fluently. Des, on the other hand, had never bothered picking up the language, apart from a few vital phrases gleaned from the 'Restaurants and Bars' section of 'German For Tourists'. For all he knew, Steve could've been telling Birgit how Watford had got on at the weekend.

We played a few local gigs before leaving for Germany, starting with a Friday-night show at the Trades Union Hall in Watford. We knew it would attract a lot of our long-term fans, and we arranged a special stunt to celebrate Steve's official return to the band. We started off with Vinnie on drums and ran through 'I'm Your Hoochie Coochie Man'. Then, just as we were apparently about to begin the second song, the hall lights started to flicker on and off and the room was filled with the sound of sirens. (This thanks to Susie, who was standing by the door with one hand on the light switch and a cassette player in the other.) The door burst open and Steve appeared, dressed in a convict's outfit we'd hired from a fancy-dress shop, complete with plastic ball and chain trailing from one ankle. Casting melodramatic glances behind him as the taped sirens continued to wail, he fought his way to the stage, climbed up and turned to face the audience, most of whom had recognised him by now and were clapping and cheering. Des and I held his arms aloft, the way they do for a boxer who's just won a fight, and Des leant into the mic and announced: "Ladies and gentlemen, he's just returned from a spell at Her Majesty's pleasure, so please give a big welcome to the one and only Mr Steve O'Brien!" The crowd went wild as Steve walked to the drum kit, where he and Vinnie embraced before the American ceded the stool to its rightful owner. Then we launched into a specially rehearsed medley of 'Jailhouse Rock', 'Riot In Cell Block No. 9' and 'Framed' which went down a storm. It was a great night, and the 'Watford Observer' (whose music correspondent we'd tipped off in advance) ran a half-page article on the band the following week, ending with an upbeat paragraph celebrating the fact that we were about to leave for 'a major tour of West Germany'. For the first time in a good while, it felt like our career was on the up.

Susie never wavered from her refusal to tour with us, but she did agree to come over for a few days. We were due to warm up with a week of gigs in and around Hamburg, so the four of us went out early and treated it as a holiday. Birgit had managed to billet us all with various friends of hers, and Susie and I got to stay in a flat whose owner was away for the week. It was in the smart area north of the Alster where the diplomats and bankers lived, and we spent a lot of time walking the wide, tree-lined streets, crunching the leaves beneath our feet, or sitting contentedly in the Alsterpark in the autumn sunshine and watching the boats out on the lake. I showed her round all our old haunts, and we did the things that tourists do; took a trip up the TV tower for the views, went on a boat tour of the city's canals, strolled around the art gallery. We also spent a lot of time making love, eagerly and tenderly by turns. Susie was insatiable, and we joked about how we only had a week to make up for the two months we were going to be apart.

We barely saw the others during that week. I gathered that Steve was spending a lot of time with Birgit (I assumed they were talking about the arrangements for the tour), and Des was doubtless reacquainting himself with the joys of schnapps. Then, on Saturday night, we played a 'homecoming' gig at the Blueskeller and were gratified to find that the audience remembered us. Susie sat down the front with Birgit and her friends, and got up to dance when they did, and I persuaded her to join us on stage for the encores and play the tambourine. It probably didn't mean a thing to the audience, but it meant an awful lot to me.

I saw her off at the station the next day. Waiting for the train, we talked in that stilted way people do when they know they haven't got long together, and when it came, we held each other tight for as long as we possibly could. There were tears in her eyes as she climbed onto the train, and as it pulled away she hung out of the window waving frantically, until a bend in the tracks finally took her out of sight. I stood there in a daze, thinking about something she'd said that morning.

She'd been staring out of the kitchen window while her coffee went cold, and I asked her if something was wrong. When she turned around she looked so sad, it almost broke my heart.

"It's not always going to be like this, is it?" she asked.

It took me a moment to understand what she meant.

"No – no, of course not," I said. "I promise."

But I knew it was a promise it wasn't in my power to keep.

Touring West Germany was a lot like touring England, with a few variations. Like Birgit, for a start. Our new road manager took care of everything – transport, food, accommodation, money – with quiet efficiency, and we quickly learned to leave her to it. She drove us from town to town in a lime green Volkswagen estate, which wasn't as roomy as Steve's old van. We managed to cram most of our gear in the back, but the drum kit had to be strapped precariously onto the roof rack.

As well as clubs and bars we played at several universities, where we found ourselves performing in auditoriums with tiered, fixed seating and desks. The audience would sit facing us in rows rising up to the ceiling, like an enormous jury. There wasn't room for them to get up and dance, but when they were feeling enthusiastic they would beat on the desks with their hands. This threw us the first time it happened, but we soon got used to it. We also had to get used to sleeping on beds with lumpy, sausage-shaped bolsters, and to breakfasting on cold meat and cheese, but it wasn't much of a hardship. In fact, we were enjoying ourselves. The Germans seemed to like our music, even though it bore little resemblance to anything that was currently fashionable in Britain or the States, and we got a kick out of playing together night after night. With no record company to please and no album to plug, making music felt liberating again. Maybe that helps to explain what happened in Berlin.

It was three weeks into the tour and we'd been playing in the far north of the country, places like Lübeck and Kiel. They were quiet, picturesque towns for the most part, pleasant but a bit dull, so we were looking forward to West Berlin. It promised to be an adventure, and the rigmarole of crossing the frontier from West to East Germany only strengthened that feeling. The border police were suspicious of our luggage and insisted on unpacking every last piece of it. Finally, after Birgit had showed them a document that proved to their satisfaction that we had legitimate business in West Berlin, they allowed us to proceed.

As we entered Eastern Europe for the first time, I asked Birgit what the police were looking for. Was it drugs?

She nodded. "Yes, that and illicit literature. The government of the DDR is very careful about what it lets its people read. They might come across a book by George Orwell or DH Lawrence and decide to start a revolution, you know?"

I smiled to myself. With Des and Steve in the car, the authorities would be lucky to find a copy of 'The Beano', never mind incendiary reading material.

Birgit went on to explain why the motorway we were driving along was so wide: apparently it was meant to double as an emergency runway for aircraft in the event of a war, which also explained why there was no central reservation. She also said that if the car broke down, we'd have to wait for a patrol to come and get us, and if anyone strayed off the road – went into the bushes to answer the call of nature, say – they were liable to be arrested and interrogated.

"Maybe we should do it, eh, guys?" said Des. "It might get us a bit of publicity."

Birgit fixed him with a glare that could have cut through solid steel. "These people, they do not mess around," she said sharply. "You might get some publicity, yes. But you might also spend five years in

177

an East German prison. I think that would not be so good for your career, no?"

After that, no one said anything for a long time. And no one suggested that we stop to take a leak.

It was late afternoon when we arrived in West Berlin, where a light drizzle was falling. We got a glimpse of the city centre on our way to Kreuzberg, where Birgit had again managed to persuade friends to put us up – people she'd grown up with who'd come here to study or to escape military service. Kreuzberg, a run-down area of the inner city hard by the Wall, was where these people tended to congregate, the students and the dropouts, as well as artists of every kind. This, Birgit assured us, was where it was all happening.

We ate at a small restaurant in a cobbled square. The food was Turkish, the ambience bohemian, the décor late hippie – multicoloured candles, paisley-patterned drapes, swirly psychedelic murals, that sort of thing. As for the company, Birgit had brought along a couple of female friends to even up the numbers. Maria, a short, large-breasted girl with lank black hair cascading down the back of her purple cheesecloth smock, was Des's 'landlady'. They seemed to have hit it off – apart from anything else, she showed a familiar preference for liquid refreshment over solids. The two of them spent the evening pouring each other large glasses of schnapps, ignoring the rest of us and occasionally laughing uproariously at some private joke.

Ute, my designated companion for the evening, was less congenial. Tall and slim, with a blond bob and pale skin, she seemed determined to be bored. After a few abortive attempts to engage her in conversation, I gave up and focused my attention on the unfamiliar food. When I paused to look around the table, it struck me that Steve and Birgit were sitting very close together, heads inclined towards each other as they talked. But even then, it was only when they actually kissed that the penny dropped. How long had *that* been going on, then?

When we'd finished eating, Birgit lit a joint and passed it round. Des and Maria took a couple of hits each before returning to their schnapps, and with Steve and Birgit getting more lovey-dovey with

178

every toke, I was starting to think about heading off for an early night when Ute finally decided to talk to me. The dope seemed to have loosened her tongue, though you wouldn't say it had made her mellow, exactly.

"So, you play the blues," she drawled, elongating the word 'blues' in a way that made her sound world-weary, and yet at the same time rather sensual. "What makes you think anyone wants to listen to you?"

Immediately on the defensive, I started reciting the evidence that proved that lots of people did: the albums, the tours, the reception we were getting in Germany... Ute interrupted me.

"Yes, there will always be some people who will listen to anything," she said impatiently. "But can you not see that the real music, the important music, has moved on? Have you listened to Pink Floyd, or King Crimson? They make music that is saying something, something deep and meaningful."

"But the blues is meaningful, you must – "

"Oh yes, meaningful to black American slaves, perhaps. But to white Englishmen? Or Germans? I do not think so." She paused to take a hit from the joint. "Tell me, do you write blues songs of your own?"

"Um, well, I have done..." I tailed off, but she'd already picked up the implication.

"Ah, so you do not write songs any more. Maybe that is because you have nothing more to say? Or maybe you do have something to say, something important even, but the music won't let you say it. Have you thought about that?"

I hadn't, and though I was sure there must be a perfect retort, I couldn't think of it at that moment. Blame it on the dope, and on the red wine I'd been drinking steadily since we arrived.

Not long afterwards we all moved on to a nearby bar, where there was more red wine and another joint. It's at around this point that gaps start appearing in my memory of the evening. I do know that Ute had stopped haranguing me about music and moved on to politics. She spent a long time talking about anarchy, the Situationist International and lots of other stuff I didn't really understand. And I remember a moment when I looked around and realised that the rest of our group had disappeared. How long had Ute and I been on our own?

Then I found myself leaving the bar and stumbling out into the night, dumbly following Ute through streets where neon lights were reflected on pavements slick with rain. And then suddenly we were standing in front of a wall in a pool of harsh light, and I realised with a jolt that this was *the* Wall with a capital 'W', the dividing line between East and West, capitalism and communism. My first thought was that it wasn't really all that high. Surely anyone who wanted to could just stick a ladder up against it and climb over? At the same time I noticed the graffiti that covered it, a chaos of brightly-painted pictures and slogans and abstract designs. It didn't seem quite right, somehow – this structure, which was supposed to symbolise all the evil of the communist bloc, looked like something a bunch of rowdy kids had been let loose on. I was getting more confused by the minute.

Meanwhile Ute was leading me towards a wooden platform, like the sort of thing military leaders stand on to review parades, only taller. I clambered up the steps in her wake and found myself looking over the Wall. Immediately on the other side was a wide, empty stretch of grass, then a tarmaced area where a pair of soldiers were patrolling. There were more soldiers in a watchtower almost directly opposite the viewing platform. Further away I recognised the Brandenburg Gate, spotlit from below. In fact, the whole scene was vividly illuminated. The area to the east of the Wall appeared to live in permanent daylight.

"It is fascinating, yes?"

I'd almost forgotten about Ute, who was standing quietly by my side. I turned to her and nodded.

"Listen," she went on, "did you hear about the anti-Vietnam War protesters in America?" She didn't wait for a reply. "There was a big demonstration at the Pentagon – thousands of people came, so the entrance was blocked off by soldiers. I suppose they thought they were going to be attacked. But the protesters just walked slowly towards them holding flowers, and when they got to the soldiers they put the flowers in the barrels of their rifles. The soldiers were so confused, they did not know what to do. They just stood there with their guns full of flowers. It was a beautiful protest, yes?

"I would like to do that here," she went on, "but as you can see, the soldiers are too far away. So instead, I come up here sometimes and do this." And suddenly she stripped off her T-shirt (an action which revealed that she wasn't wearing a bra), turned to face the watchtower, raised her arms above her head and waved at the guards. It was an oddly cheery gesture, the sort you see girls making in those naturist films where they're always playing with beachballs. "I hope that when they see me," Ute was saying, "when they see how free I am, they will start to want some of that freedom for themselves. It is a small gesture, yes, but with thousands, millions of small gestures we can perhaps do something to change this terrible situation."

By now, part of me was thinking that Ute was as mad as a barrel of monkeys. The rest of me was staring at her small breasts, stretched upwards into a pleasing roundedness by the action of lifting her arms, the nipples stiffened by the cool night air.

Then she put her top back on, yawned and said: "It is getting late now. I think we should go home." It wasn't clear whether she actually meant that we should go home together, but in any case I wasn't at all sure that I could find my way back to my lodgings. So once again I found myself following her through the silent streets.

Home for Ute turned out to be a studio apartment; everything was in the one room apart from the loo, which I made immediate and grateful use of. I emerged to find her unfolding a bed from the wall, and while she took her turn in the bathroom I quickly undressed and got under the rather grubby duvet, still wearing my vest and Y-fronts. Even when she came out of the bathroom stark naked, I swear I didn't know for sure what was going to happen. As she turned out the light and slipped into bed, I closed my eyes, more than ready for sleep. Then I felt a hand – a cold hand – reach down inside my underpants and fondle my prick, which responded in the only way it knew how, and moments later Ute was tugging off my pants and swinging herself on top of me and down, down…

I woke to find a weak light shining through the skimpy curtains. A bird was singing outside the window, but my head was throbbing to a John Lee Hooker beat. I dressed quickly, drank lots of water from a glass I found in the sink, and then left. I found the key to my lodgings in the inside pocket of my jacket, and attached to it was a piece of paper with the address on. A shopkeeper broke off from opening his shutters to point me in the right direction, and ten minutes later I was in the bed where I was supposed to have spent the night, sound asleep once more.

Much later in the morning there was a knock on the bedroom door. My host, a long-haired bloke in a tie-dyed T-shirt, came in and placed a mug of steaming coffee on the bedside table.

"You had a good night, yes?" he said. "I did not hear you come home."

I agreed cautiously that it had been a good night. After he'd gone I sat up in bed for a long time, cradling the coffee mug and thinking about what had happened to me. That was how it seemed: something that had happened *to* me, not something I'd actually gone out and done of my own accord. A reflex self-defence mechanism was already kicking in as I ran through all the possible excuses. I was drunk – drunk *and* stoned; I was feeling lonely, and spending the evening with two couples had made it worse; I was in a strange, exciting city with an 'anything goes' reputation; Ute had tricked me into bed with her; I'd never actually got round to telling her I was married; she'd made all the running…

But deep down I knew that all these factors could only explain what had happened, not justify it. The simple fact was that I'd screwed a woman who wasn't my wife, and you didn't have to be a professor of moral philosophy to know that was wrong. By the time I'd showered and dressed, all I could think about was that Des and Steve mustn't find out – especially not Steve. At the same time I was convinced that my guilt must be obvious to others, like a radioactive glow encircling me. So when I walked into the kitchen to find Steve sitting at the table demolishing a plate of ham and eggs while Birgit and her friend chatted away in German, my entire body tensed. This must be what it felt like to face a firing squad – and when the moment of truth arrived, you just wanted the bastards to get on with it and pull the trigger if they were going to.

The moment passed.

"Morning Lucky," said Steve with his mouth full. "Bad night?" I was trying to think of something – anything – to say, but he just grinned and carried on. "You'd better hurry up if you want any breakfast. Des'll be here soon, and then Jens is going to give us a guided tour."

So I sat down and let the conversation swirl around me while Birgit made me fried eggs on toast. The others doubtless attributed my stupor to the after-effects of last night's overindulgence. They were right, too, only they didn't know all the details.

Jens's tour began, naturally, at the Wall. I was convinced I gave a start when I recognised the viewing platform where Ute had exposed herself, but no one said anything as we passed it. We followed the Wall round as far as the Brandenburg Gate, then went across to the ruined Reichstag, through a huge park, down to the Kurfürstendamm, and finally back to Kreuzberg by train. Jens pointed out the main sights in his fractured English and spent the rest of the time talking to Birgit, while Des and Steve and I walked along behind them. Our conversation eventually came round to the previous night, and there was some good-natured banter about Des's 'date'.

"Yeah, well, what about yours, Trev?" said Des when he'd had enough of our ribbing. "Maria reckons she's a bit of a political fanatic. Goes on marches, chains herself to railings, that sort of thing."

"Yeah, she did go on about politics a lot." I paused for just a moment. "To be honest, I got away from her as soon as I could. Got lost on the way home, mind you. I must've been more pissed than I thought."

They both laughed, but there were no further questions, your honour. That was it. I'd got away with it.

I'd got away with it. Over the next few hours my initial feeling of immense relief gradually mutated into something else altogether, a kind of wild elation. I'd been a good boy at school – always handed in my homework on time, never got detention. Now I had an inkling of why some people persistently broke the rules; if you didn't get caught, it felt fantastic.

By the time we took to the stage in a smoky club off the Kurfürstendamm that evening, I was on a high. All guilt forgotten, I played and sang with gusto. I especially enjoyed 'Back Door Man', the Howlin' Wolf classic celebrating the seducer who has his way with women while their husbands are out. As I sang along with Des on the song's punchline – "The men don't know, but the little girls understand" – I was feeling positively smug. If I'd spotted Ute in the audience, I swear I'd have winked at her.

We did more sightseeing over the next few days, ate and drank well and played a series of above-average shows. Everyone agreed later that Berlin had been the highlight of the tour. On our last night, paralytic on pear schnapps, we crept up to a relatively deserted section of the Wall with a pot of black paint and daubed a crude hornet on a patch where there wasn't much going on, as a permanent reminder of our time in the city. Not that I, for one, was ever likely to forget it.

My sense of elation at having put one over on my bandmates gradually diminished, but it didn't disappear altogether. So perhaps it was inevitable that I would stray again when a suitable opportunity arose – and as anyone who's toured a foreign country with a band will tell you, opportunities for sex are never far away.

It was ten days later and we were in Celle, a small town just north of Hanover with a large British army garrison. All through the show, a sexy brunette in a low-cut top had been dancing right in front of the stage, making sure I had ample opportunity to admire her breasts, and she found me afterwards when I was helping to load our gear into the Volkswagen. She asked if I wanted to have a drink with her, the way plenty of girls had asked me before, only this time I said 'yes' and told her to meet me at a bar round the corner in half an hour. She trotted off contentedly just as Steve emerged from the back door of the club lugging his bass drum, and I felt a surge of elation. I'd got away with it again.

It wasn't difficult to lose the others. Steve and Birgit went straight back to the hotel, presumably to shag each other senseless. (Now I knew they were a couple, the noises I'd heard sporadically during the tour made sense.) As for Des, I had one drink with him in the hotel bar and then left, saying I was going to have an early night. Chances were that I'd be in bed before him anyway.

Not long afterwards I was having vigorous sex with the brunette behind a clump of bushes in the local park. (It was a warm night.) If I'd had any illusions that this meant anything to either of us, they would have been shattered when she offered me a condom from a twelve-pack she kept in her handbag. I think she'd just got bored of screwing squaddies. For my part, the whole point was the illicit nature of the act. Lying in bed later, it occurred to me like a revelation that there must be a lot of this going on: sex where the object wasn't to express love or affection for the other person – indeed, where their identity wasn't even particularly important. It was as if I'd stumbled into a parallel universe whose existence I hadn't even suspected, and I was embarrassed by my innocence.

Celle was the turning point. Don't get me wrong, I wasn't shagging groupies every night. It only happened a few more times, in fact. I had to be confident that I could escape detection, you see, and the combination of a suitable opportunity and good timing was all-important. I learnt the value of patience, and it made the transgression all the sweeter when I did eventually get my way.

And yet at the same time I managed to carry on as normal, and to behave like any dutiful husband who's away from his wife. I still rang Susie every couple of days. She'd tell me about her job and what she'd been up to, and I'd tell her about the towns we'd seen and the gigs we'd played, and one of us would say "I miss you" or "I love you" and the other would agree, and then the call would end.

I wasn't lying, either. I *did* miss Susie and I *did* love her. But somehow I'd managed to partition my brain in such a way that these essential facts had no bearing on my repeated adultery. Looking back now, I can see that the main thing going on was me being incredibly selfish. The feminists would probably say that I was just being a typical man, but I think there was more to it than that. I don't know. You work it out.

What I do know is that when I got back to England to find Susie waiting for me on the quay at Harwich, and she threw her arms around me and whispered in my ear that she was pregnant, I made a promise to myself that what had happened in Germany would never happen again.

BAR EIGHT: TREVOR, 1972

When I'd finished my shower I wrapped a towel around my waist and went straight into the lounge. There was no point putting on smart clothes until breakfast was over. Sure enough, Simon was being difficult, throwing his arms around and making outraged faces as Susie, still in her nightie, tried in vain to feed him toast soldiers spread with Marmite. 'Little Willy' was piping from the transistor radio on the sideboard and Susie was singing along, trying to distract Simon from his tantrum. It wasn't working.

"About bloody time," she said when she saw me. "You know we're supposed to be there at ten, don't you? I won't have time to dry my hair at this rate."

And with that she headed for the bathroom, leaving me to take over the task of feeding Simon, who had yet to come round to the idea that breakfast was the most important meal of the day. I turned off the radio and tried talking to him instead.

"Now Simon, you mustn't mind Mummy being in a bad mood," I began in my most soothing voice. "After all, it's not every day her brother gets married, and she's a bit tense." I picked up a finger of toast, then saw the beginnings of a scream forming on Simon's lips and hurriedly put it back on the plate. "Yes, her brother, that's your Uncle Steve. You like him, don't you?" (This was true, as far as I could tell – at any rate, he'd usually allow Steve to pick him up without bawling his head off.) "He's marrying Auntie Birgit, which means that she'll be your real auntie and not just a pretend one." Simon's face was relaxing now, and this time he didn't flinch when I picked up the piece of toast and Marmite. "And then we'll all be one big, happy family. Won't that be nice?" Simon opened his mouth far enough for me to shove the toast in there, then closed it again and looked at me thoughtfully as he chewed, as if considering what I'd just said.

I'd always assumed babies were immune to sarcasm. Now I began to wonder if I'd underestimated my son.

One of the many child-rearing books we'd bought had extolled the benefits of talking to your baby, but I hadn't realised how much I'd enjoy it too. As long as I kept my voice soft and friendly, I could say anything I wanted to Simon without fear of contradiction or ridicule. He seemed to enjoy our little chats as well, even if he sometimes fell asleep when I still had more to get off my chest. Of course, I knew this couldn't last forever. Soon he'd discover the ability to talk himself, and then I'd have to watch what I said in case he repeated it to his mother. But in the meantime Simon was the nearest thing I had to a psychotherapist, and a damn sight cheaper.

I did occasionally wonder how this had come about – that is, why my closest confidant was a 14-month-old baby. But it wasn't as if I hadn't considered the other options. There was Steve, but he was far too busy with Birgit to listen to my troubles – and anyway, I could hardly talk to him about Susie. As for Des, he'd only ever been interested in talking about music. You could try using him as a sounding board, but you had to be prepared to do so in a pub, and spending time in a pub with Des wasn't healthy. Mum and Dad? I'd never been able to talk to them about anything important, don't ask me why. Some children just don't have that sort of relationship with their parents, and it felt like it was too late now to do anything about it. So that just left Simon.

Of course, there was a time when Susie was not only my best friend, but also my lover, my confidante and much more besides. Like that time when I bolted from Hamburg after Charlie told me I wasn't going to be playing on the album with Little Sonny. I left partly because I didn't want to stick around and watch Des and Steve working on a record without me. But the main thing I was feeling that night as I hurried back to the flat, chucked my clothes into a suitcase and headed for the station, was an overwhelming urge to go to Susie. I needed her to comfort me.

She didn't let me down, either. When I arrived home twenty-four hours later, dog-tired and still highly emotional, she listened patiently while I poured out all my woes and then said exactly the right thing. "The thing is, it won't be a Hornets album without you – you're the bassist, you always have been and you always will be. It might say it's by The Hornets on the cover, but you and I will know the truth, and so will Stevie and Des."

I thought about that a lot in the following days, and realised she was right. And when it eventually became clear that the album wasn't going to appear, I couldn't help but feel vindicated.

But you see what I mean about Susie; she used to be someone I could talk to. Now she was the one I needed to talk *about*, because (since we're juggling prepositions here) I seemed to spend most of my time at home getting talked *at*.

I'd hoped Steve's wedding might give me a day's respite, and for a while it looked promising. First Susie was doing her hair while I was hurriedly pressing the shirt I'd forgotten to iron the previous night (all right, I hadn't forgotten, I'd gone to the pub instead), and then I had to search for a tie that went with the shirt while Susie tried to get Simon dressed in the dinky little blue corduroy suit she'd bought him to wear in his capacity as page boy. With all this going on, there wasn't time for an argument. But once we were all safely strapped into the car and bombing down the country lanes, Susie didn't wait long before asking the inevitable question.

"So, were there any jobs in the local paper yesterday?"

"Just the usual," I replied casually. "Factory inspectors, clerks, that sort of thing. Nothing suitable."

The truth was, I hadn't even looked at the jobs. Like I did every week, I'd bought the paper on the way to the park, where I'd read the football news and scanned the entertainment pages to see if there were any decent blues bands playing in the area (there weren't). Then I'd stuffed the paper in a bin, taken Simon out of his pushchair and let him play on the swings for a while. We'd both enjoyed that.

"Well then," Susie went on (and I knew what was coming next), "why not take a job at Trewin's? There are a couple of good ones going at the moment. One of them's in the book department."

"Come on Susie, we've been through this before." My grip on the steering wheel tensed, but my voice remained calm. "If I got a full-time job we'd have to pay someone to look after Simon, so we wouldn't be any better off than we are at the moment." We were racing down a winding lane flanked with high hedges, and my eyes never left the road.

"Ma could look after him." A familiar, stubborn note had entered her voice.

"Your ma has got arthritis. Simon's already walking, and soon he'll be running around all over the place. It wouldn't be fair to ask her to take care of an active little boy – and it wouldn't really be safe, either. You know that."

Susie didn't say anything for a while. I wondered if she'd decided to leave it there, in honour of her brother's big day. No such luck.

"Well, if only one of us can go out to work, why does it have to be me?" She too was staring straight ahead, watching the hedges rush by. "Why can't I stay at home and look after my son? Why can't *you* be the one who earns the money to put food on the table?"

We'd reached the main road, and I waited for a gap in the traffic before pulling out. "But you're doing so well at Trewin's, what with that promotion and everything. You said yourself that you could be managing your own department by the end of the year. Surely it'd be a shame to throw all that away now?" Then I took a deep breath, knowing that I shouldn't say what I was about to say, knowing what the response would be, and knowing that I was going to say it anyway. "Besides, if I was working I wouldn't have time to concentrate on my music."

"Your music!" She was getting angry now. "What bloody music? When did you last write a song? And you hardly ever play any gigs these days. Why don't you face it, it's over. You're never going to be famous. So you might as well – "

I was saved by a wail from the back seat that stopped Susie in her tracks. I glanced in the rear-view mirror.

"He's dropped his dummy," I said, as if I hadn't heard Susie's diatribe. "He won't stop until he's got it back, trust me."

Susie let out an angry sigh, but she knew I was right. Unbuckling her seat belt, she twisted round and groped on the floor between the seats. By the time she'd found the elusive dummy, wiped it on her handkerchief, stuck it back in Simon's mouth and smoothed down her rumpled dress, we were almost there. I parked behind the library, got out, took Simon from the back seat and carefully crossed the road with Susie by my side. To the small group waiting on the Town Hall steps we probably looked like any other happy young couple, revelling in the joys of marriage and parenthood.

The wedding was a low-key affair. The ceremony was over in less than ten minutes, and the entire wedding party fitted comfortably into a single row, and a single shot, without the photographer needing to use a wide-angled lens or stand on the other side of the road. I've got the picture here now, slightly faded and as dated as any Victorian portrait. The newlyweds are in the middle, of course, beaming broadly: Birgit in a simple white dress and Steve in a monstrously flared grey suit and a patterned purple kipper tie, with his wavy, reddish-brown hair right down to his shoulders. Oh, and he's sporting a moustache – I'd forgotten he grew that. He had it for a couple of years before he thought better of it. To Steve's left is Frankie, the best man, whose combination of a suit and a smile makes him look even more menacing than usual. Then come Mr and Mrs O'Brien, and then Des, looking unaccountably serious. On the other side there's Anna, Birgit's sister and maid of honour, who is basically an older and plumper version of her, then me (and yes, all right, my suit had flared trousers and ludicrous lapels too), and then Susie. Simon, who she's holding, is at least facing the camera and not obviously crying, though from his scrunched-up scowl he may well be about to. A protest about the blue corduroy suit, perhaps.

It occurred to me during the service that the last time I'd seen Steve in a suit had been in court. That was a strange day. I'd never been inside a courtroom before, and I was curious to see how it would compare to the ones I'd seen in films and TV programmes. All that dark wood panelling certainly gave the place a sense of gravity, and it was clear from the expressions on the faces of the officials that this was a grim business. Susie was pressed tightly against me and I could feel her shaking as they brought in one witness after another, the boys and the policemen and then the doctor, all of them stony-faced as they talked about this violent act that Steve and Frankie had committed. It was mainly Frankie, of course, but it was still weird to hear Steve being discussed in those terms, as if he was some vicious thug. For a moment I was transported back to our first meeting on the terraces at Vicarage Road, and I remembered how I'd instinctively been scared of him. It was tempting to wonder if my initial impression had been right after all.

The funny thing is that the more serious the proceedings became, the more I felt an almost overwhelming urge to laugh. When Steve was in the witness box, I didn't dare catch his eye in case it set me off. I'd often heard people talk about something they'd seen or heard and say that they didn't know whether to laugh or cry, and I'd never really understood how that could be. But after the trial I realised that there are some occasions where those really are the only two options, and for those of us who don't easily cry, laughing may be the only way of letting out all the emotion building up inside.

As for Susie, she had no problem with crying in public. The tears were already welling up as the judge prepared to deliver his verdict, and all I could do was hold her close and murmur words of consolation in her ear. There was no consoling Des, though. As he passed us on the way out of the courtroom, he looked at me and muttered, "That's the band fucked, then." I didn't hear from him for weeks after that.

Steve had certainly come a long way since that day. At least, I was fairly sure he had, though I still had a nagging feeling that I didn't know him as well as I thought I did. I saw him often enough – most Thursday nights, for a start, when The Hornets practised at the garage, just like we always had. Then there were gigs, and the football, and Susie and I regularly saw Steve at the O'Briens' house (where he was still living right up to the day of the wedding) or when he popped round to ours. But he didn't talk much about what was going on in his life. He never had, I suppose. The best you could hope for was that he'd have one beer too many and go on about how much he loved Birgit. That was, if she wasn't there with him (she'd got a job in London now, working in the promotions department at EMI).

Meanwhile, Steve had recently turned twenty-one. His friends bought him lovingly chosen gifts (Susie and I got him a new drum stool), but my father-in-law trumped us all by giving him a share in the garage. The original plan had been to make Frankie a partner in the business when *he* turned twenty-one. But when the time came, Mr O'Brien was sensible enough to realise this was a recipe for disaster. So Steve became the chosen heir to the family firm and Frankie was left to take care of himself. He seemed to manage all right, though I was never quite sure how he made a living. I didn't really want to know.

The next time Des and I turned up for band practice, the paint was just drying on the sign over the front entrance to the garage. It now read: 'O'Brien & Son, Car Repairs'. I knew all about Mr O'Brien's gift, having been present at the emotional family dinner where he announced it. But it was news to Des, and he didn't like it. I watched while Steve explained what it meant – he planned to work full-time at the garage from now on – and saw the expression on Des's face darken as the implications sank in. When Steve had finished, Des could barely contain himself.

"But what about the band?" he almost shouted. "I thought you wanted to be a musician, not a fucking grease monkey."

I tensed, suddenly aware how much was hanging on Steve's response. He opened his mouth to speak, and for an awful moment it seemed as though he was going to be as forthright as Des had been. But he must've thought better of it, because he paused before finally replying.

"Look, Des, don't worry, I'll still have plenty of time for the band." His tone was reassuring. "But I'd like to earn some decent bread, and the music isn't bringing in a lot right now, is it?"

Even Des couldn't deny that. Steve's words seemed to have a calming effect on him, though he obviously wasn't happy about the situation. The thing is, none of us had ever taken a full-time job before. Even after we'd lost our recording contract there'd been an unspoken assumption that another company would take us on sooner or later, and that we needed to be free to go into a studio or set off on tour at the drop of a hat. In fact, Steve had been helping out at the garage for almost as long as I could remember, and Mr O'Brien had always paid him for his time. It was just that the formalising of the arrangement seemed like an admission that this was it; we were never going to regain the heights we'd briefly scaled before, and there was no point pretending otherwise.

Des wasn't the only one who'd been clinging with increasing desperation to our dream of stardom. Susie had been hinting for a while that it was time for me to find a full-time job, and now that her brother had done just that, my case for holding out looked pitifully weak. It even crossed my mind to suspect Susie of being behind this whole business – of putting the notion in her father's head that a share in the garage would make a fine coming-of-age present for Steve, just to get me out of the flat and into gainful employment.

Unfortunately, as Steve hinted that day in the garage, being a member of The Hornets barely counted as 'gainful employment' any more. For one thing, we'd run out of record companies to send our tapes to, having tried all those that had ever shown any interest in the blues, as well as plenty that hadn't. The response, when we got one at all, was always the same; the only groups they were interested in signing were those that played hard rock or progressive rock, and preferably both. One A&R man replied with a letter that said: "Have you guys actually *heard* Led Zeppelin?" Just that, nothing else. We chucked it in the bin.

The trouble was, we *had* heard Led Zeppelin and we knew we could never be like them. We didn't have their natural bravado, their musical dexterity, their range of influences – we couldn't even aspire to their luxurious heavy-metal hairstyles. (Even so, it might have been worth trying, if only to see Des, shirt open to his waist, trying to play his guitar with a violin bow.) Above all, we simply didn't have the collective willpower to make such a major change in style. We'd found something we could do well and marked out our territory, and we didn't have the guts to venture outside it. Barely into our twenties, we'd already become as musically conservative as the folk fans who'd booed when Bob Dylan went electric. Des in particular – well, I sometimes wonder whether his musical development stopped the night he saw The Yardbirds at The Marquee and chose Eric Clapton as his role model.

(Mind you, that influence finally seemed to be wearing off. Clapton's most recent album, the one that had 'Layla' on it, was still blues-rock, but with a distinct country flavour as well. A couple of years earlier, Des would've taken one listen and then headed for Hammond's to buy a pedal steel guitar and a copy of the Willie Nelson songbook. Not any more – the LP barely rated a mention.)

Don't get the wrong idea – all this stuff about the possibility of changing our style is pure twenty-twenty hindsight. It's not as if any of us ever arrived at band practice and raised it as a topic for debate. Sure, we talked about the music we'd been listening to (and even Des didn't subsist solely on a diet of the blues), but that never translated into any kind of influence. Des would suggest starting off with something familiar by Muddy Waters or Jimmy Reed, and we'd take it from there.

But the writing was on the wall, if only we'd bothered to look. It wasn't only record companies who showed a complete lack of interest in our music; it was also getting harder to find gigs, and by the summer of '72 we were down to less than one a week. Fortunately there were still a few local pubs where the landlord remembered us, and our small but loyal band of fans sought us out and made enough noise (and bought enough beer) to ensure that we got asked back. But the student venues that had once been our bread and butter weren't interested any more, not now there was a steady stream of bands coming through who modelled themselves on Led Zeppelin and Free, or Pink Floyd and Yes; Chicago blues was out of fashion. As for new gigs, they were

195

all but non-existent. Now *there's* a subject for a blues song. It's a shame we'd long since given up trying to write our own material.

What on earth did we think we were doing? It's a fair question, and I can only answer with a simile. When people talk about gambling there's one scenario you hear described again and again. It's the story of a man – it's always a man – who's never had anything to do with gambling or betting. Then, one day, some chance set of circumstances places temptation in his way, and he's drunk or naive enough to think, why not? And what do you know? He gets lucky in a game of poker, or the horse he's backed romps home at 100-1, or he puts all his chips on the winning number on the roulette wheel. Suddenly he's in the money. Of course, he could just walk away: pocket the cash, give due thanks to Lady Luck and get on with his life. But human nature doesn't work that way. Human nature makes him think: hey, that wasn't so hard. I had a bit of money, I gambled it, and now I've got a lot of money. So if I gamble a bit more, I'm bound to win an even larger amount. And he gambles a bit more, and this time he loses. But he's still ahead of the game, so he has another go, and then another. And before he knows it he's lost all his winnings and his original stake as well. So now he keeps on playing in an attempt to get back to the amount of money he started with. Maybe he succeeds, maybe he doesn't. The important thing is that he's hooked, drawn back again and again to the table, to the track, to the casino, by the tantalising memory of his first big win.

Well, that was us: hooked on a precious memory of success, unable to believe that the experience wouldn't be repeated if we just kept on playing long enough.

Naturally, that's not what I told Birgit's sister Anna, who I found myself sitting next to at the wedding reception. Actually, 'post-wedding meal' is a more accurate description, since it only involved the nine of us who'd been at the Town Hall and took place in the back room of an Italian restaurant in Market Street. After a few glasses of Chianti I found myself explaining that the absence of a recording contract was merely a temporary hitch, and that the success of bands like Led Zeppelin was good news for us because it would draw people back towards the blues. Maybe I even believed it when I said it, and if Anna was sceptical she was polite enough not to say so.

Eventually I changed the subject and started quizzing her about Birgit. I knew her only as the confident, sharp and utterly self-possessed woman Steve had just married, and vaguely assumed she'd always been like that. But Anna said no, not at all.

"When she was younger she was very, how you say, studious, yes?" I nodded. "She was quiet, shy. Always in her room, reading, always reading. We thought she would become a teacher, at a university or perhaps a school, like Papa. He taught history, you know, until he became unwell..."

She tailed off, and I made appropriately sympathetic noises. I knew that Birgit's father had been diagnosed with cancer, and that was why her parents hadn't come over for the wedding. Instead, Steve and Birgit were going to spend the first few days of their honeymoon with the Schneiders, who lived in a small town on the Lüneberg Heath called Soltau, before travelling further south to stay at a hotel in the Black Forest. (The only memorable thing about Frankie's best man's speech was his attempt to get a laugh out of some tortured wordplay involving wedding cake and Black Forest gateau.)

After a respectful pause I asked: "So, um, when did Birgit change? Stop being quiet and shy, I mean?"

"Oh, when she went to university, for sure. I don't know exactly what it was. Perhaps it was the people she met, or the things she learned, or just being in a big city like Hamburg, but when she came back to Soltau after her first semester she was different." Anna was becoming more animated now. "She would only wear black, and she told jokes, and when she was in her room there was always music playing. Old music, you know, like you play."

"And what about you? Did you go to university?" I asked, deciding to treat the jibe as an accident of translation.

"No, I was not so clever at school, so I got a job instead. Now I work as a secretary for a firm of book publishers in Bremen. It is interesting, you know. But I think that you have been to university, yes? Steve always says that you are the educated one in the band."

I smiled ruefully. "No, no, I never went to university. Because of the band, actually. We were just starting to be successful when I left school, and I didn't want to give that up."

"Ah, I see," she said, and that was that. There followed a long silence while we both pondered how our horizons might have been broadened by a few years of higher education. It had always seemed such a clear-cut decision on my part. It was only now, in articulating it to Anna, that I realised it might not look that way to an outsider.

Eventually Anna got drawn into a conversation with Birgit and Des, while I was left to the mercy of my mother-in-law, who was sitting diagonally opposite me. I managed a couple of minutes of diversionary chit-chat about food and flowers before she launched into two of her favourite themes: when was I going to get myself a decent job, and wasn't it time I started thinking about giving Susie another child? I got the impression that the two issues were directly linked in her mind – that it was only the lack of a larger income that was preventing us from extending our little family. In fact, it was a bit more complicated than that. True, we both doted on Simon, and in my darker moments I did wonder whether our love for him was the only thing keeping our marriage together. But as far as I could see, adding a second child into the equation would risk upsetting the delicate balance we'd established. I hadn't forgotten how stressful those first few months after Simon's birth had been. Weeks and weeks of broken nights, leading to shortened tempers and, inevitably, shouting matches. I didn't think our marriage could survive a repetition of that. Then there was the question of sex – or more precisely, when we could start again. It had been a difficult birth and the doctor had told us sex was inadvisable for a while. But as the weeks turned into months, I sensed that Susie was using this as an excuse. It wasn't that she *couldn't* sleep with me, but that she *wouldn't*. Not only that, but she wouldn't talk about it either. It was around then that I started going out.

You'll have to trust me on this (and I realise that may be asking a lot), but I really wasn't looking to have an affair. Really. I just needed to get out of the flat, away from the arguments that flared up whenever Susie and I spent too long alone together. So once or twice a week I would literally leave her holding the baby and go out on my own for the evening. Occasionally I drove to a country pub, found a quiet corner and read a book for the time it took me to drink a couple of pints. But mostly I went to gigs – blues gigs, of course. It was getting harder and harder to find them, but using a combination of local papers and the music press I could generally track down a band I wanted to see, even if it occasionally meant driving all the way to Surrey or Essex.

Most of these bands played the same sort of stuff as we did, and my official reason for embarking on these excursions – the reason I gave Susie, and anyone else who asked – was that I was checking out possible venues for Hornets gigs and keeping tabs on the competition at the same time. What could be more natural for a professional musician? Well, I suppose it would've been a bit more natural if I'd taken one of my bandmates with me from time to time. I never asked them, though; I just wanted to be on my own. And I was, for a few weeks. Then I met Alison.

It happened in the back room of the Black Horse in Amersham, and it might not have happened at all if the gig had started promptly. But it didn't and I had plenty of time to survey the scene from my table just off to one side of the stage. The room was an oversized extension that had clearly been built with grander forms of entertainment in mind. Now the parquet flooring was permanently sticky with spilt beer, the cast-iron tables wobbled alarmingly and the low stage sagged in the middle. Having completed my inspection, I was absentmindedly studying a faded black-and-white photograph of a carthorse on the wall beside me when I heard a woman's voice.

"Excuse me, is it all right if I sit here?"

I glanced up and immediately felt a tingling feeling I hadn't had in a long time, like a delicious itch running up and down my body. She wasn't stunning to look at, but she had a great body. I also remember noticing the long, dark-brown hair spilling down onto a Led Zeppelin tour T-shirt, and registering that she was tall for a woman. About the same height as me, in fact. She was older than me – in her late twenties, I guessed – but none the worse for that.

"Um, sure," I said, looking around warily for a boyfriend or husband. At the same time I noticed that the room wasn't anything like full and there were plenty of free tables. She seemed to be alone, anyway, and once she'd sat down and placed her half-pint of cider on the gently rocking table, she said: "You're Trevor Harris, aren't you." It was a statement, not a question.

I was so surprised that I choked on my bitter, and by the time I'd finished spluttering it was too late for false modesty. "That's right," I managed to cough. "Do I know you?"

She laughed. It was a surprisingly hearty, almost mannish laugh. "No, I doubt it. But I've seen The Hornets play a couple of times, and I've got your first album." She paused. "And to be honest, the jacket is a bit of a giveaway."

I turned around and peered over the back of my chair, where my denim jacket was hanging. It was the jacket Des had had made up for me for the cover of that first LP, the one with the picture of a hornet playing a mouth harp. I hadn't worn it in the hope of being recognised, though. Denim jackets were simply the sort of thing you wore to blues gigs, and I'd snatched it from the hook in the hall on my way out – I was leaving in a hurry in an attempt to get the last word in an argument for a change.

I tried to explain some of this, instinctively omitting any mention of Susie, and then Alison introduced herself, and soon we were talking about the blues: bands we'd seen, records we'd bought, favourite songs. It was the sort of conversation I used to have with Des, but hadn't had for a good while now, and I was enjoying it so much that I was almost annoyed when the band finally came on and started playing 'I'm Your Hoochie Coochie Man'. Towards the end of the song, Alison leaned over to me and shouted in my ear: "It's not half as good as your version." I was so pleased that I had an urge to kiss her there and then. But I managed to resist for another half-hour, until eventually I found myself holding her tight as we swayed around the tiny space in front of the stage which passed for a dancefloor. The band was playing 'It Hurts Me Too' and we'd both just agreed that it was our favourite Elmore James song, and the next thing I knew, my tongue was halfway down her throat. It seemed perfectly natural at the time.

Soon afterwards we left the pub and went back to Alison's house a couple of streets away, and soon after that we were having energetic sex in her bed while Jimmy Reed blared out from the stereo downstairs. She was gratifyingly impressed with me. She wasn't to know that after months of Susie rationing our sex life, I was as horny as Warren Beatty on Viagra.

It was only in the car on the way home that it struck me; if Alison knew so much about The Hornets, she must have known about Susie, too. Even if she hadn't seen the band when Susie was playing with us, there was the matter of our wedding, which had merited a small piece in 'Melody Maker' – and it was obvious that Alison was every bit as avid a reader of the music press as I was. Then again, maybe the fact that I was married was part of the attraction for her. Because I did feel as if I'd been deliberately seduced, to a certain extent. It's hard to explain… Well, look: she obviously wasn't like the groupies I'd screwed in Germany, bored young girls who enjoyed boasting to their mates that they'd had sex with a rock star. With Alison there'd been an obvious bond from the moment we'd started talking, and we'd got on so well that I used this bond to justify my actions to myself as I drove back to my sleeping wife and baby. Sure, I'd been unfaithful, but I hadn't just slept with any old slapper. No, I'd slept with a real blues fan, and that wasn't so bad, was it?

I know, I know. Don't say it.

Alison told me not to phone her, but she'd mentioned that she was a regular at the Black Horse's blues nights. Sure enough, when I went back a fortnight later, there she was. It wasn't long before we fell into

201

a routine; we'd meet at the pub, have a couple of drinks, talk about the blues and watch the band, and then go back to her place for sex. Sometimes, if the band wasn't up to much, or if we were just feeling particularly randy, we'd leave the pub early and have more time for sex. This was definitely a good thing, because Alison was excellent at sex.

It had never occurred to me that some women were better in bed than others. Everyone always talked about the man's 'performance', as if it was marked out of ten for technique and artistic impression, but the general assumption was that the woman just lay there and let the man get on with it. I'm talking about the way we'd discussed sex at school, of course, before most of us had actually had it. My subsequent experiences hadn't done much to alter those first impressions, though. I'm thinking especially of the girls in Germany, but Susie wasn't exactly hyperactive in bed either. Warm, tender, loving – all of those, certainly, but not what you'd call enthusiastic.

Alison, on the other hand, was extremely enthusiastic, and versatile with it. I don't know whether she'd read the 'Kamasutra' or just spent a lot of time experimenting, but she knew all sorts of different ways to have sex, most of them completely new to me. I soon realised that the object of the more novel positions was generally to maximise the pleasure *she* got from the act. Maybe it was something to do with women's lib, which was a big thing in the news in those days. Alison was certainly all for equal opportunities. If I was going to have an orgasm, she was damn well going to have one as well, and I wasn't allowed to go until I'd made her come.

If I'm giving the impression that my relationship with Alison consisted entirely of beer, music and sex – well, then it's an accurate impression. We hardly spoke about anything but the blues. She did eventually let slip that she was married, though only after I'd spotted a wedding photo she'd forgotten to hide before bringing me home one night. It turned out that her husband was in the Navy, away at sea most of the time. From various things she said, I got the idea that he knocked her around, but I didn't pursue it. She didn't ask about my home life, so I didn't pry into hers. We'd made a little bubble for ourselves and it was a happy place to live, even if it was only for a couple of hours every fortnight.

As for the place where I lived the rest of the time, nothing much had changed. Susie and I kept on having the same rows about the same issues. That was deliberate, on my part at least. It seemed to me that the quickest way to get found out would be to alter my behaviour so much that Susie would wonder what was going on. As it was, I was confident that she didn't suspect anything. She went to bed early and was usually asleep by the time I got home after a trip to Amersham. One time, though, she did wake up when I came in. She switched on the bedside light and squinted bleary-eyed at the clock.

"You're a bit late, aren't you?" she said drowsily.

"Oh, the Black Horse gets an extension when there's a band on, so they can stay open longer," I replied, slipping into my pyjamas and between the sheets. I kissed her on the forehead, then leaned over and switched the light off again. "Sleep well," I added as an afterthought. And that was that.

By the time Steve's wedding came around, my affair with Alison was all but over. A few months earlier she'd told me her husband was due back in the country soon, and since then I'd only seen her once. I'd started to pick and choose my visits to the Black Horse again, depending on which band was playing. Of course I missed seeing Alison – talking to her, having sex with her – but it didn't hurt the way it would have done with a real relationship. The hardest thing was resisting the temptation to get Susie to make up for what I'd lost. So on the rare occasions when we did make love, I had to keep reminding myself that Susie and I had only ever used the basic positions, and that suggesting anything more adventurous would almost certainly lead to some awkward questions.

I was coming out of the gents' at the end of the evening, absentmindedly wiping my hands on the back of my trousers, when Birgit stopped me. I got the impression she'd been waiting for me. I started to say that Susie had already taken Simon out to the car and that she'd be getting worried, but Birgit interrupted me.

"It's Susie I want to speak to you about, Trevor," she said. "I've been talking to her a lot this evening. She is very unhappy, you know."

I shrugged my shoulders. "Yeah, well, life isn't exactly a bowl of cherries for me either at the moment."

"A bowl of cherries?" She frowned at the unfamiliar idiom, but she wasn't to be distracted. "No, I mean she is *very* unhappy, and you don't seem to understand it. That is why I am talking to you. After all, we are sort of related now, yes?"

I opened my mouth to speak, then realised I had nothing useful to offer and closed it again. Anyway, I was curious to hear what Birgit was going to say.

"It seems to me that you and Susie are at a, how do you say, a critical point in your marriage," she went on. "You are both still young, you have a beautiful son, you could achieve so much together. But you, Trevor, you are threatening all that by making Susie so sad. So I think you have to decide now, once and for all, whether you want your marriage to work. Do you want it to work, Trevor? Do you?"

She looked straight at me, then abruptly turned and went back into the restaurant, her heels clacking on the tiled floor. I stood there for a few moments in a kind of daze, and not just because of the bottle and a half of wine I'd put away during the meal. Then I remembered that Susie was still waiting for me outside and hurried out to join her. It was only later that I realised I hadn't actually answered Birgit's question.

BAR NINE: DES, 1983

Let's get one thing straight; I never had a drinking problem. No way José. Drinking was never a problem for me. In fact, I was damn good at it. Okay, I was never in the same league as Keith Moon or Ollie Reed, but I had my moments. 'Course, I had a good teacher, didn't I? And after all, every boy ends up following in his father's footsteps, one way or another.

It was much harder for Dad, he had to pick it up from scratch. His father wasn't a boozer, not at all. A couple of pints of pale ale in the pub on a Saturday night, that was enough for Granddad, or so I've been told. Never met him myself. It would've been a bit tricky, what with him and Grandma being buried under half a ton of rubble when a bomb fell on their street in 1941. Who'd've thought Coventry would turn out to be such a dangerous place to live? Dad was away on basic training at the time, he only found out when the CO called him into his office after parade the next morning. Thought he was in trouble for not polishing his boots properly. 'Course, that could've driven him to drink – his parents dying like that, I mean. The only thing is, thousands of people must've been in the same boat, millions even, and it's not like the whole country was on the sauce by the end of the war. Leastways, not that I've ever heard. Or maybe booze was rationed. I hadn't thought of that.

Same goes for his time in the Army, out in the east. Burma. He never talked about it much, though he did used to say that malaria got a lot closer to killing him than the Japs ever did. He must've been a lot stronger before he came down with that, I guess. You can sort of tell from the photos of him as a teenager. He wasn't tall – you've probably guessed that already – but he wasn't weedy either. By the time I came along, it was like there was something missing.

Still, I reckon it was what happened to Mum that finished him off. I'd only just turned five when she took to her bed. She was very pale, not like other kids' mothers, so I kind of knew there was something wrong, even though Dad never said as much. He just told me she needed a lot of rest. It was all right to start off with. I was allowed to spend all day in her bedroom if I wanted, sitting in the corner and building things with wooden blocks. But gradually I was in there less and less, and soon it was just a quick visit after I'd had my supper. Baked beans on toast, every bloody day. I'd tell her what I'd been doing and she'd listen carefully, and then I'd kiss her on the cheek and Dad would send me off to my own room to get ready for bed. He'd stay in there with her for a while, talking, and I'd fall asleep to the muffled sound of voices leaking through the wall.

It took her the best part of a year to die, and I got used to looking after myself. Good practice, as it turned out. Well, Dad didn't have the time to take care of both of us, and he must've reckoned that as long as I got fed and had a few toys to play with, I'd be okay. And I suppose I was, really. I didn't know my mum had cancer, did I? Before the funeral, while I wriggled about in a miniature black suit that didn't fit properly, hardly paying attention, Dad tried to explain how I wasn't going to see my mother again. I just nodded when he said did I understand, 'cause I was used to not seeing my mother and I couldn't grasp how the situation had changed. I remember the funeral, or at least the do afterwards, like some sort of strange dream, the little terraced house filled with people in dark clothes speaking in low voices, and me threading my way through them with cups of tea and plates of biscuits. After everyone had gone I watched Dad go to the sideboard, take out a bottle of amber liquid and fill a tumbler with it. He sat in his armchair for the rest of the afternoon, drinking from the glass and gazing at the photo of Mum that stood on the mantelpiece, a photo taken before she got ill, probably before I was born. And I might as well not have been born, that day at least, for all the attention he paid me.

I don't know when the drink stopped being a comfort and turned into a crutch. He held onto his job at Odhams for a good few years, that I do know. He was proud to be a printer, too. I remember him showing me a piece in the local paper that said there were thirty-nine firms of printers in Watford – funny how that stuck in my mind, that it was thirty-nine, not forty – employing over ten thousand people, and Odhams had once had the most modern photogravure works in the world. 'Course, I hadn't a clue what photogravure was, and I couldn't tell you now, but it sounded mysterious and impressive, like something out of science fiction.

But by the time he showed me that article, he wasn't a printer any more. All those years of him working nights, me being looked after in the evenings by his sister, Auntie Vi, who always treated me as if I needed to be wrapped in cotton wool, though it took me years to work out why – all that came to a sudden end one day. I was about ten. I never found out what he did to get the sack. It can't have been too bad, 'cause they gave him a new job as a cleaner. Or maybe they just felt sorry for him. Anyhow, he worked days from then on, tidying up the printing works after the papers had gone to press. Always used to have cuts on his hands from the sharp-edged metal sheets they printed from. It was his job to get rid of them. He was supposed to wear gloves, but I guess he forgot to put them on sometimes. I didn't see much of Auntie Vi any more, and she and Uncle Ernie moved away soon afterwards. But I didn't see much of Dad either, 'cause he always went straight to the pub after work and didn't come back till closing time. That suited me fine, it meant I could play the guitar for hours on end without worrying about him shouting at me. It was Auntie Vi gave me my first guitar, something to keep me occupied while Dad was out, she said. I'll come back to that another time.

Where was I? Oh yeah, I was going to say that maybe it was a bit unfair what I said before, about having a good teacher when it came to drinking. Dad never taught me to drink. By rights, living with him should've put me off the stuff, seeing what it did to him – and feeling what it made him do to me. The hitting, I mean. Not punching, don't get me wrong. Just a slap if I disagreed with him and he decided he didn't like it, though he could slap hard enough if he wanted to. Sometimes I didn't even have to disagree, simply being there at the wrong time was enough. It came to a point where I'd try and avoid him, and what with him spending so much time at the pub, that wasn't so difficult. We could go a week without ever being in the same room at the same time.

When all's said and done, I had a pretty lonely childhood. Does that sound like self-pity? It's not meant to. Thing is, I had no brothers or sisters, no mother, a father who might as well not have been there, and no other relatives apart from Auntie Vi – and like I said, she moved away. For a long time Steve was my only friend, the only kid in the playground who didn't call me runt or weed or worse, the only one who didn't make jokes about my dad later, when it came out about him losing his job because of his boozing. And if Steve was around, he made sure people didn't make those jokes in the first place. So naturally I hung around with him as much as I could. He didn't seem to mind.

It was only when we got to secondary school that I realised that hanging around with Steve might be a good way to find myself more friends. This was before my first band, of course. That's why I started going along to the soccer. I was never really what you'd call a fan – sometimes the guys at school would be talking about a Watford result and I didn't even know there'd been a match – but Steve and all his mates went, so I went too. I suppose I sort of hoped that if they saw me around often enough, out of school I mean, they'd start including me in things.

It worked, too. The way I remember it, we were standing around on the terraces one Saturday afternoon, and a few of the guys from my class started talking about a party they were going to in the evening. I said, whose is it, then? And someone laughed and said you're not invited and then they all laughed, and Steve said leave him alone, like he always did, with just enough menace in his voice that they did what he said.

Then this one guy, I think he was called Tom, he says, tell you what, you can come along if you bring some booze with you. And they all laughed again, 'cause of course I was far too small to get away with buying anything, in fact most of them were too, except for Steve, who was always tall, or so it seems to me now. Anyhow, I guess they forgot about Dad, or maybe they just assumed he locked away all the serious alcohol, the way their parents did. But I just stared Tom down and said sure, I can do that, cool as you like, 'cause I knew all the places where Dad kept the hard stuff and I was pretty sure he wouldn't notice if one bottle went missing. So that evening I turned up at the party with a bottle of Bell's, and they all smiled and someone said well done. They were even more impressed when we passed the bottle round and I took a good swig without so much as a grimace, which is more than the rest of them managed. I'd practised at home, of course. Not that day – before, just curious to see what the stuff tasted like, the stuff Dad treated like it was the be-all and end-all of everything.

My size had a lot to do with my drinking, now I come to think about it. No, straight up. I'm only five seven now, and it took me a long time to reach that height. In the meantime, there was no way I was ever going to get served in a pub or an offie. But there were more parties, and that meant more excuses to raid Dad's liquor stores, and pretty soon I'd developed a taste for whisky and gin. 'Course, I had to be careful not to take so much that he'd notice. So what I did was, I bought a cheap hip flask, and I'd pour the booze into that and then refill the bottle with water. That way there wouldn't be one missing, a bottle I mean, just in case he'd been counting, and there wasn't much chance he'd notice any difference – he only used to hit the hard stuff after a night down the pub, and by that time he was in no state to judge whether a bottle of cheap whisky had been watered down or not. Jesus, most nights he could hardly count up to ten.

Later on, after I'd started The Hornets, I was spending almost as much time in pubs as Dad did, and I had plenty of time to drink all the beer I could handle and then some. I didn't even have to buy my own, half the time. The landlord would throw in a free pint or two as part of our fee, if he liked us that is, or fans would buy us a drink just for the thrill of chatting to a real live musician. I always used to get a kick out of that – the idea that little Des Armstrong had turned into someone people wanted to be seen with. I'll come back to that, too.

Bear with me.

Then I went to Hamburg and discovered schnapps. Fruit-flavoured alcohol, who'd've believed it? There were different kinds that tasted of peach, pear, apple… I hadn't a clue what was in my drink sometimes, and I didn't care either. If variety is the spice of life, I certainly spiced up mine while we were in Germany, no question.

And then there was America. The others have told you all about that, right? No? Fucking cowards. Or maybe they just decided it was my story, so it was up to me to tell it. Well, I will, don't worry. Only not now. Not yet.

You'd think what happened in Taunton would've put me off booze for life, but it had the opposite effect. Drinking to forget and all that. Anyhow, drinking was what I did – anyone'll tell you. What no one told me was that it was affecting my performance, on stage I mean, and maybe they should've. Although fair's fair, I'd probably just have told them to piss off if they had said anything.

And it wasn't my fault the band fell apart. Christ no. I was the one trying to keep it together, trying to find gigs where they didn't want you to sound like Pink Floyd. Prog rock – what was all that about? A load of speccy gits from public school, so ashamed of liking music with a beat that they turned it into something intellectual – all those 'suites' that filled the whole side of an LP, with stupid lyrics about elves and dragons. Jesus! I wouldn't've minded, but some of them were bloody good blues musicians when they started off, before they forgot everything they'd learnt from Muddy and Wolf. And then there was that Keith Fisher. Mind you, I wasn't too surprised about him. Damn good bassist, best we ever had – we wouldn't have had to rerecord *his* parts on the first album the way we did Trevor's, no way. But you could tell the blues was just a hobby for him, a style he wanted to master. So good riddance, we were better off without him. It wasn't his life, not like it was for the rest of us. Me especially.

That's why I was so gutted when we finally ran out of gigs, some-where around '75. There were a couple of places we could still play every now and then, but I was barely earning enough to keep me in guitar strings. I guess I'd always known that when one of us cracked, that would be the end, but I hadn't figured it would be Steve. Mr Reliable. 'Course, now I can see that was the problem. His old man was counting on him to run the garage, what with his health going and everything, and Steve wasn't going to let him down, was he? So I was about to set off for band practice one evening when the phone rang and it was Steve, he said practice was off, there was a Ford Capri with a knackered gearbox he had to fix by the next morning. So I said, no sweat, Trev and I can start without you and you can join us when you're finished with the motor. There was an awkward pause and then he cleared his throat and said, well, the thing is, there's nowhere to practise any more. I said, what d'you mean? And he said business was going well, so he'd had to start putting cars in the back room of the garage again. He'd even had to take the drum kit and store it in the house, in Susie's old room. That's the word he used, store, and that was when I knew it was over.

I couldn't cope at all. Went on a huge bender that lasted a week, till I had to stop 'cause I'd run out of money and drunk every drop of alcohol I could find in my flat. When I finally sobered up, I decided I had to get away. Away from Watford, away from Dad, away from Steve and Trevor and everything that could remind me of The Hornets.

Don't get me wrong, I wasn't giving up. That never entered my mind. So The Hornets hadn't worked out the way I'd hoped. So what? I was only twenty-six – I mean, I was hardly past it, was I? Plenty of time to get another band together and start again. Good music would never go out of fashion, especially not the blues, half a century old and counting. I was right about that bit at least.

So I moved to Camden. Well, I wasn't about to settle in some strange part of the country – and a lot of it was pretty damn strange, judging from what I'd seen on tour – and if I was going to live in London, it made sense to pick an area that was full of musicians and places to play. There was a buzz about the place too, something you could feel in the air when you went round the market on a Sunday morning. It was a while before I realised it was the first stirrings of punk rock.

Anyhow, things went well to start with. I got a job in a second-hand record shop on Chalk Farm Road and found a cheap bedsit nearby. Then I put up cards in all the music shops and venues in the area: Ace blues guitarist seeks cool dudes to join him in bid for world domination. There's no point selling yourself short, is there? I didn't get much response, mind you, and half the people who did answer the ad were complete time-wasters: drummers who didn't own a drum kit, bassists with no sense of rhythm, and far too many people who'd never even heard of Elmore James, for Christ's sake. Yeah, of course I set them a test. I didn't want just any old musicians in my band, did I?

I found what I was looking for in the end, more or less. Phil, the drummer, was a couple of years older than me. He'd been in a band in the first blues boom, then he'd joined the Army – he had the tattoos to prove it. He told me a bunch of other stuff too, but I wasn't that interested. The main thing was that he could keep a rock-steady beat. Same goes for Martin, the bassist: the baby of the group, barely out of his teens. He'd never been in a band, but he'd obviously practised a lot and he loved the blues. That was good enough for me. I thought about all sorts of fancy names, but in the end I called it The Des Armstrong Blues Band. If you've got a name people recognise, you might as well make the most of it.

It was all a bit strange at first, I won't deny it. Not just things like having to pay for a rehearsal room either, though that was a shock to the system. I suppose I hadn't realised how much you take for granted when you play with the same guys for a long time: the way they know what key you're going to do any particular song in without having to ask, know when to play a fill and when to shut up. Suddenly my solos didn't sound as shit-hot as they used to, and it was a while before it dawned on me that it had something to do with what was going on in the background. Who'd've thought Steve and Trev had put so much effort into making me sound good?

Still, we rehearsed for a couple of months and got a few gigs in pubs around Camden and Islington. It felt good to be in a proper working band again. Okay, so people weren't exactly queueing round the block to see us. But at least I was playing the blues. The rest would come. It had to.

Only, I gradually realised there was something missing. Obvious really, when I finally twigged. No mouth harp. Martin didn't play it, you see, and I wasn't about to learn. I reckoned singing and playing lead guitar was enough to keep me busy. Trouble is, it just didn't sound like the blues to me any more without a harp. Piano, that's an optional extra, but you *need* a harp player. So I bunged Martin a couple of quid, lent him a copy of Little Walter's Greatest Hits and told him to get himself down to the nearest music shop and buy himself a harp.

Apparently he started practising every day, but I never got to hear the results before I fired him. Well I had to, the little prick was far too bolshy for my liking. He started questioning things. Why do we have to play My Babe that way? Can't we change the tempo of Help Me, rock it up a bit? I ask you. He didn't seem to understand that I was in charge. I was the one who'd been in a successful blues band. I knew what I was doing.

The final straw came one evening in the Dublin Castle, where we'd gone to watch Dr Feelgood. They weren't bad, as it happens, but Martin was going on and on about how amazing they were, how we should copy their aggression and their attitude. The only way to shut him up was to send him off to the bar to buy me a pint of Guinness and a whisky chaser, and whatever he wanted of course. When he brought the drinks back, I noticed he hadn't got himself anything. He was obviously still fired up, and then he started saying I shouldn't drink so much, my guitar playing was sloppy, and loads more besides. So I sacked him. Just like that. Told him to fuck off out of my band and not come back. Which he did. Never returned my Little Walter album either, the bastard.

After that I never seemed to be able to keep a stable line-up for long. I advertised and found a new bassist, but then Phil upped and left to join a punk band called Wally And The Wankers – no, I'm not kidding. So I had to look for another drummer, and when I'd got one I lost the bassist – he was arrested for dealing in drugs, which I'd had no idea about when I hired him – and so on and so on. It all became very time-consuming, I can tell you. Whenever I wasn't working in the record shop I was auditioning or rehearsing musicians, or on the blower trying to find us a gig, and it was so stressful, I started keeping a hip flask of whisky with me at all times, just to calm my nerves. One day I realised that more than two years had gone by, two years of scrabbling around for musicians and work, and The Des Armstrong Blues Band was still playing the same grotty gigs in the back rooms of pubs in Kentish Town and Tufnell Park where the carpet stuck to the soles of your shoes and you risked electrocution every time you plugged in your amp, and most of the punters would rather play darts than listen to a song by John Lee Hooker anyway. And it was a long time since anyone had come up to me and said, didn't you used to be in The Hornets?, and though that pissed me off, I sort of missed it now it didn't happen any more.

'Course, all this was pretty hard to take. To be honest, seeing things clearly was too much for me to deal with, so I went on a three-day bender to make sure it didn't happen again. And when that was over, I carried on exactly like before.

And then I found out about Dad.

It was Bill Boyd who called, Dad's next-door neighbour. He and Gladys had lived there as long as I could remember. They didn't have any kids of their own, and I've got vague memories of them being nice to me after Mum died. Bill was a bus driver, used to drive the 258 down to Harrow and back. Once when I was in my teens, I got on Bill's bus and found I didn't have enough money for the fare, but he let me on anyway.

It turned out the Boyds had been keeping an eye on Dad ever since I'd moved out. I suppose someone had to, and I wasn't in a fit state to look after anyone. Truth is, I'd barely spoken to the old bastard in the past couple of years. It wasn't that I hated him, not exactly, but whatever ties had once connected us had long since broken. Now he was just this old guy who owned the house I'd grown up in. The last time we'd talked had been a few months ago, when he'd rung to wish me happy birthday. That was surprising in itself, and maybe I should've twigged then that something was up. I do remember thinking he sounded frail and sober – an unusual combination. He asked me how I was and I told him about my band, which probably wasn't what he wanted to hear at all. Then I had to ring off 'cause I was supposed to be somewhere, and that was that.

Bill had plenty to say. A lot of it was about me, and it wasn't very complimentary, but the bottom line was that Dad was dying. Had been for over a year now – not that you'd know, would you?, as Bill put it. It was his liver, of course. One way or another, the Boyds had ended up looking after him, and Dad had said not to tell me, but they thought it was only right I should know that the doctor said he might not make it past the end of the week. I tried to remember what day it was. Tuesday? No, Wednesday. Shit.

When I put the phone down it seemed like there was only one thing to do. Maybe those family ties hadn't snapped completely after all, I don't know. I chucked a few clothes in a bag and caught the first train I could get to Watford, and an hour later I was looking down at a tiny, wrinkled old man who was barely recognisable as the bad-tempered drunk who'd knocked me about when I was a kid.

I've never been one for soap operas or soppy scenes in movies, so I'll spare you the details of the next three days. Let's just say we managed a kind of reconciliation. Sitting in that musty bedroom with the curtains closed, me on a chair and him propped up in bed, we talked mostly about Mum. He told me stories about what it'd been like when they first met, stuff he'd never spoken about before. It was like catching up on a part of my childhood I'd missed the first time round. So when I went into his room on Sunday morning with a cup of tea and found that he'd slipped away overnight, my first reaction was anger that he'd gone before I had a chance to ask him everything I wanted to. Then I sat on the end of the bed and cried for a bit.

Eventually I roused myself enough to go next door and tell the Boyds what had happened. They called the doctor, who turned up half an hour later and did whatever it is doctors have to do when someone dies. He came and found me out in the back yard, standing in a patch of trampled-down weeds, swigging from my hip flask. After he'd finished telling me all the official stuff about death certificates and whatever, he looked at me real close for a few moments and said, you'll go the same way, you know, if you carry on the way you are. He was obviously one of those doctors who say what they think.

I asked what he meant and he said, you know what I mean; you're a drinker, just like your father, I can tell by looking at you. I started to explain that the whisky was just 'cause I was upset, but he interrupted and said that wasn't what he was referring to – it was obvious from my eyes, my skin. 'Course, he wasn't the first person to tell me I drank too much, but what with him being a doctor, and bearing in mind the timing, I don't mind admitting it made me think.

There weren't many of us at the crematorium. I hadn't been able to track down Auntie Vi, so it was just me and the Boyds, plus Steve and Trevor. I hadn't actually asked them – hadn't spoken to either of them since moving to Camden, to tell the truth – but I guess word gets around. The fact is I was glad to see them there, because of what I was planning. Afterwards the three of us went to the pub. Even though he'd been round our house dozens of times, Trev had never actually met Dad, so Steve and I ended up telling stories about him, and they were mostly funny ones. What you might call black humour, given the circumstances – the time he was so pissed that he fell asleep in his cottage pie and woke up with a face full of mash, that sort of thing. We also talked about what we'd all been up to, which was a bit awkward, to be honest. It was pretty obvious that Trevor wasn't with Susie any more, but no one said anything.

Finally, when it was getting near closing time, I went to the bar and brought back a round of large brandies and proposed a toast to my dad, who was still my dad even if he was a miserable old soak. Then I announced that in honour of him, I was going to make this my last drink; I'd already signed up with Alcoholics Anonymous, my first meeting was the next day, and I was never going to drink alcohol again. I downed the brandy in one, savouring the tang of sweetness on my lips to the very last, and then settled back to enjoy the expressions on my friends' faces. Trev just looked shocked, like I'd announced I was moving to the Moon – which I could understand, I was shocked myself that I'd gone through with the idea that had taken root in my mind after the doctor had gone. As for Steve, he was trying to look like he approved, and I'm sure he did, but I could tell he didn't think I could do it. Well, that was fair enough too. I wasn't sure I could do it either, and if I'd known how hard it was going to be – how much my body had come to expect regular, large doses of alcohol – I might not have given up at all.

The fact is, Steve was partly right. I have fallen off the wagon a few times over the years – but I've always managed to clamber back on. I won't pretend it wasn't sheer bloody torture to begin with, though. After the funeral I moved back into Dad's house full-time, and me and Bill Boyd combed the place for secret stashes of booze. Bill reckoned Dad had kept on drinking almost to the end, even after the doctors had forbidden it. I'd told Bill about my plan and asked him to be tough with me if he saw me drinking. Well, we did unearth a couple of bottles, so Bill made me pour the contents down the drain outside the back door. Just the smell of the fumes was enough to give me a craving, and I said as much, so he went into the kitchen and fetched some bleach and poured it down after the alcohol, and that helped. It was a long time before that drain blocked up again, I can tell you.

My new life meant making a lot of adjustments. For starters, I had to knock The Des Armstrong Blues Band on the head. I didn't trust myself in a pub, not yet anyhow, and pubs were the only places that ever hired us. The band was going nowhere anyway. I didn't give up playing the guitar, though. In fact I ended up spending more time on it than ever before, sitting on the bed in my old room and playing along with records like I had when I was a kid, or just jamming on the blues. Oh, and I learnt to play with a slide, which I'd been meaning to do for years, and I practised until I sounded more like Elmore James than Elmore himself. I also learnt that all those people who'd told me the drink affected my playing had been right, only now I had ears to hear it for myself.

'Course, I wasn't playing guitar all day. I had a job for one thing, another record shop gig, in a second-hand joint down Market Street. And I'll tell you something funny. When I worked in Camden I just turned up – late and half-cut, half the time – racked the records in more or less alphabetical order and worked the till. Now I actually started paying attention. Well I'd always had a head for business, hadn't I? Good job someone did, too. But I'd only ever applied it to the band I was running. This time I took an interest, worked out what sold and what didn't, and began making suggestions to Ray, who owned the place. He realised I had a bit of specialist knowledge and put me in charge of the blues section, which consisted of a few dog-eared old Chess LPs and not a lot else.

I knew exactly what to do. I soon got in the habit of going round Camden Market on a Sunday morning looking for blues albums that might be worth a bit. Most of the stallholders didn't have a clue, which was what I was counting on. The very first time I went there I found an original 1962 copy of Robert Johnson 1936-1937 – the album in the Classic Jazz Masters series, the first time anything by Johnson had been available in Britain. Just looking at the sleeve took me back to that day I'd played my own copy to the band, and we'd ended up driving round the countryside looking for a crossroads where Trev could sell his soul to the devil. Shame it didn't work... The stallholder was asking £1.50, but I knew that a serious blues fan would pay at least a tenner for it. Ray was sceptical when I brought it in the next day, along with a few other odds and sods, but by the end of the week I'd sold the lot at a decent profit. I was up and running. Only trouble was, the stallholders soon got wise to me and put their prices up. Didn't matter, I just moved on to other markets – I ended up travelling all over London. And you know what? I really enjoyed it. Turns out there was more than one way of making a living from music. I don't know why I hadn't realised that years ago.

Another thing that changed after I moved back to Watford was that I started reading. I'd never bothered before, not since school, but I needed another hobby, something to stop me slipping back into bad habits. Even I couldn't play guitar all night. So I started going to the library, wandering around looking at books until I saw a title or an author's name I recognised. Then I'd read the blurb on the back and if it sounded interesting, I'd give it a go. I read a bit of everything to start with: biographies of famous people, poetry, and loads of classic novels – Dickens, Hardy, you know the sort of thing. Eventually I latched onto philosophy, the sort of stuff I'd heard people talking about back in the Sixties, when it seemed like everyone was trying to open themselves up to new levels of experience. Well, everyone except me. The Doors Of Perception, that was the first one I tried. The Doors had taken their name from it, and Jim Morrison had a way with the blues when he wasn't fannying about pretending to be a lizard, so I thought it might be worth reading. Can't pretend I understood every word, but it gave me a taste for books that make you think about why things are the way they are. I was obsessed with Buddhist ideas for a while, especially the theory of karma. You know – what goes around comes around, you get what you deserve, all that. It seemed to make a lot of sense with reference to me and my Dad, when I got to thinking about it. And I did spend a lot of time thinking about stuff like that. Looking back, wondering where I'd gone wrong, how things might've been different. When all's said and done I guess I was living in the past, which isn't healthy, I can see that now, but maybe it was a stage I had to go through.

It wasn't long after I'd got into all this Buddhist stuff – around '83 I think it was – that Trevor rang me. That was unusual in itself, I didn't hear from him much since he'd gone off to be a student. And when I did, he always sounded down – the divorce had hit him hard, real hard. But this time he sounded excited. Some record company had

219

bought up the rights to our stuff and they wanted to reissue the LPs. Well, I wasn't about to argue. I'd always been proud of the first two at least, even though Buzzin' With The Hornets didn't really work out the way I wanted, so it was only proper that more people should get a chance to hear them. And if I got a few quid in royalties as a result, that was all right too. I asked Trev to check out exactly what the deal was, to make sure we weren't going to get screwed again. Charlie Maynard seemed like a nice guy, but he saw us coming. All right, he saw me coming – I was so desperate for a record contract, I didn't read the small print. Big mistake.

But you see what I mean about karma? It was like, I turn into a drunken arsehole, the band splits up: I clean up my act, we get another shot at the big time. Or at least, a chance to make a few bucks.

The next thing that happened was that I got a call from a guy called Nigel Scullion. Said he was a journalist and he'd been hired to write the sleevenotes for the reissues. He also reckoned there was a chance of an article about the band appearing in one of those record collectors' magazines if he got enough material. No problem on that score, I thought, so I told him to come round the next day.

The following morning we're sitting at my kitchen table, him and me, with a pot of tea and a tape recorder in the middle between us, shooting the breeze about stuff that happened nearly twenty years ago. This Nigel – big bloke, round specs that make him look like an owl – seems nice enough, and though I can tell he's not a diehard blues fan, he knows a fair bit. So I tell him everything I can remember about how the band started, and Keith and Susie, and Reading and Natchez, and how we recorded the LPs. And then there's a pause and he looks at me kind of funny and says, now, can you tell me what happened in Taunton? Only, I asked Trevor and Steve and they both said I should ask you.

Well, I say I need to go to the loo, and when I get to the bathroom I find I'm trembling. I want a drink – a large brandy, that'd do it – more than I have at any time since I quit. I'm standing at the sink, gripping the sides real hard to try and stop the shakes, and I glance up and see myself in the mirror and realise just how old I look – and I'm still the right side of thirty-five, for another few months anyhow – and I think: sod it, it's time. So I go back and tell Nigel what I'm about to tell you now.

The tour in the summer of '69 was Charlie's idea, of course – a final desperate attempt to drum up a bit of interest. It looked impressive in the music papers, for sure; Hornets to tour US, that was the headline in the NME. You had to read on to learn that we were only actually going to tour one small corner of the country. When we looked at a map we found that we were sticking so close to the east coast, we might as well hire a boat to travel between gigs rather than a van. It wasn't so much another British Invasion as the rock music equivalent of a bunch of kids ringing a doorbell and running away again. Trev came up with that one.

The story was that Charlie had an old pal who booked bands on the New England college circuit, and he'd talked this guy into fitting us into his schedule for a few weeks. We'd do a couple of gigs in New Jersey and then work our way up to Boston via a bunch of college towns in Connecticut, Rhode Island and Massachusetts. Not quite what I'd pictured when I dreamt of conquering America. But once I'd got over my initial disappointment that we weren't going to see Chicago or Memphis or the Mississippi Delta, I was still excited. This was it: the promised land. I thought the American air might breathe new life into the band.

Jacko got to come with us this time, and everyone agreed that was a good thing. 'Course, we did wonder what sort of tall tales he'd have about touring the States – no doubt he'd played in Elvis's backing band, or taught Chuck Berry a few new chords – but no, he said right up front that he'd never been there before, and he was as wide-eyed as the rest of us.

Mind you, once the novelty of hearing American accents had worn off, touring the US was pretty much like touring the UK. The main difference was that we usually had a lot further to travel between gigs, and I actually started feeling nostalgic for the Newcastle to Edinburgh trip we used to see as a long haul. On the plus side, there was no shortage of teenage talent hanging round after the shows. It obviously wasn't purely down to our musical prowess, though the music went down well enough too – and so it bloody well should've, seeing as how some pretty ordinary British blues bands were making a healthy living over there at the time. I liked to think we were giving audiences a taste of what they'd been missing – your genuine Chicago blues.

Where was I? Oh yeah, the groupies. I got the impression they'd open their legs for anyone with an English accent. I guess we had The Beatles to thank for that, along with every half-arsed beat group who'd ever followed them across the Atlantic. Jacko in particular got more offers than he knew what to do with, though he did his best to keep up. He was soon laying on the Scouse accent thicker than ever, all wack this and la that. I overheard him telling more than one cheerleader type that he was related to Ringo Starr, but he soon realised he didn't even need his shaggy dog stories. The accent alone did the trick.

If you're thinking all this sounds like another tawdry example of rock'n'roll excess – well, damn straight, that's what it was, and we loved every minute of it. One of the tapes we played to death in the van was a Muddy Waters compilation I'd made, and Mannish Boy became our anthem, except that we changed the line, I'm way past twenty-one, and sang …just past twenty-one instead, 'cause that's all we were. Mind you, since Hamburg we felt a whole lot older.

That reminds me. Early in the tour, when we were staying in New Jersey, we had a day off and took the train into New York. Went up the Empire State Building, took the ferry out to the Statue of Liberty, all that tourist stuff. Then I wanted to go hunting for rare blues albums in Greenwich Village. The others weren't interested, so I went on my own.

Late in the afternoon I was walking down Bleecker Street when I saw a busker on the corner of the next block. I heard him first, actually – there's nothing like a wailing blues harp to grab my attention. As I got closer I saw it was an old black guy singing a Jimmy Reed number and accompanying himself on the harp, with a coat crumpled on the sidewalk in front of him. I rooted around in my pocket for a few coins, and as I dropped them onto the coat I glanced up into his face and realised – bugger me, it's Little Sonny. As our eyes met he faltered for a moment, then carried on blowing hard into his harp, so I went and stood a little way off till he'd finished the song.

Yeah, it's me all right, he said, wiping his lips and slapping the harp against the palm of his hand to shake out the spittle, no reason to stare. What the fuck are you doing here in my country anyways? So I explained about the tour, and he snorted and said ain't that fucking typical, I'm playing on street corners to rustle up enough dough for a quart of whisky, and then some motherfucker brings a bunch of motherfucking white kids all the way over from England to play to another bunch of motherfucking white kids who don't know the blues from their ass.

He had a point, sort of, so I said why don't I buy you a drink, and I thought he was going to tell me to fuck off but then he said okay. So we went to a bar on the other side of the street and drank neat bourbon, and gradually he relaxed and told me how he'd been arrested after that fight in the club in Hamburg, the one where he'd pulled out his knife, and how he'd spent the night in a holding cell with a bunch of drunks and a couple of transvestite prostitutes who kept looking at him funny. Once the cops had worked out that he didn't have any money they sent someone to his hotel to fetch his luggage and then loaded him straight onto the first plane to the US of A, after putting a stamp in his passport that said, and don't come back! or something like that. 'Course, it wasn't any good to him being back in the States, seeing at how the only record company that had shown any interest in him was Natchez, and they were in London. So he called Charlie long distance, but Charlie said they'd had a one-album deal and that was that, thank you and goodnight, and Little Sonny gave him a piece of his mind and then slammed the phone down and realised he didn't have a cent to his name. So here he was in New York, sleeping on a friend's couch and playing on street corners while he tried to find a gig.

He was more angry than feeling sorry for himself, as far as I could tell, but I don't mind admitting that I felt sorry for him. For a moment I was even thinking of inviting him to come and play at a couple of our shows. Then I remembered what a miserable old bastard he was, sank the rest of my whisky, bunged him a couple of bucks to buy himself another and left him sitting at the bar. We were a blues band, not a charity. At the end of the day, Little Sonny Carter wasn't even a particularly good bluesman. He had the attitude all right, but not the chops. And he didn't love the music the way we did. So fuck him.

I know, I know, I'm still putting it off. But Nigel the journalist seemed happy enough, 'cause he hadn't been able to find out what had happened to the old sod after Hamburg. Oh yeah, something I forgot to mention; Deuce were even going to release the LP we made with Little Sonny. Not re-release – it never saw the light of day at the time. Quality control, that's what Charlie said when we asked him why, and I sort of knew what he meant. I doubted it would sound a whole lot better a decade and half later, but hey, what did I know, I'd only played lead guitar on the album. Anyhow, that's why Nigel wanted to know about Little Sonny, he was writing the sleevenotes for the LP that Deuce were planning to call Little Sonny And The Hornets In Hamburg. Must've taken them weeks to come up with that one.

Okay, yeah, right. I think I've filled in most of the background: why we were sent to the States, where we went when we got there, the frame of mind we were in. And you can take it as read that I was drinking heavily. Jack Daniel's, that was my latest discovery. Tennessee Sippin' Whisky they call it on the label, and when I first tasted it I could see why. Put a match to your lips after a swig of that and you'd be breathing fire. But naturally, with a bit of practice I found I could work my way through a bottle at a respectable speed.

No, this isn't another digression. And anyway, I'm not much of a storyteller, you must've realised that by now. That's why I never wrote any lyrics, I suppose. I still should've tried, though. Should've taken Trev's lead – surely I could've come up with something better than

Hertfordshire Blues, for Christ's sake, though fair play to him, that song worked well enough on stage. But expression, that's my speciality. Wringing the emotion out of a song. My guitar does the talking. This is hard for me.

But that last bit wasn't a digression. Mr Daniel's product played a key part in what happened in Taunton, though I wouldn't go so far as to blame him entirely.

Taunton, Massachusetts: that's where it happened. We'd fetched up there after playing a gig at Brown University. It was an Ivy League joint, the local promoter explained, full of clever rich kids who were going to end up running the country. Not that you'd guess it from the way they were throwing themselves about, but that might've had something to do with it being their end-of-term party. That's mostly what we were playing, graduation balls and parties. It suited us fine. The students who came along got pissed and danced up a storm, and that meant we enjoyed it more. You could tell they were pretty randy, too, so we started sticking a few of the raunchier blues numbers into our set list. Stuff like I Just Want To Make Love To You, and almost anything by Jimmy Reed, 'cause his songs have that lazy, sexy rhythm to them.

Anyhow, Taunton was the next stop. We were due to play two gigs there, the local college on the Thursday evening and then a club in town on Saturday night. It meant we got a day off when we didn't have to travel, which was rare, and we celebrated by doing something we'd been talking about for a while; we hired a car.

Ever since we'd got off the plane, Steve had been drooling over pretty much everything with four wheels. Huge motors most of them, much bigger than we were used to. But he liked the older ones best, and I could see his point. You couldn't help marvelling at all those Cadillacs and Chevrolets covered in gleaming chrome, with outrageously shaped radiator grills and tail fins and all kinds of weird stuff. Just looking at them made you feel like you were in a Chuck Berry song.

So on the Friday morning, Steve and Jacko – who was the only one of us who was actually licensed to drive in the States – went down to this car rental place in the centre of town and came back with a '59 Chevy convertible, powder blue, a real cool-looking motor. Jacko said the owner had kept trying to give them the latest model, but Steve insisted on having the oldest car in the lot.

We all piled into the car, put the top down, stopped off to buy some booze and then headed for the coast. It was further than it looked on the map, but we got there in the end. We had a swim in the sea, lounged around on the beach eyeing up the girls, then finally, reluctantly, we got back into the car, drove up the coast road for thirty miles or so and returned to Taunton. When I remember that day I think of us barrelling down a highway in the sunshine: Jacko driving, Steve beside him trying to navigate, and me and Trev in the back, passing the bottle between us and singing along with the songs on the FM station we'd found – Stones, Creedence, Hendrix... I remember the feeling of the wind whipping through my hair, the taste of the bourbon on my lips, the towns and the countryside speeding by, looking just like I'd always imagined they'd look. I tell you, it was one of the best days we ever spent together.

Back in Taunton we went out for some food, had a few more drinks and set off for the party. We'd been invited the night before by a bunch of kids we'd got talking to after the gig. I say kids, but they were about the same age as us – it's just that at the time, all our experiences on the road had made me feel incredibly mature. These three guys had been right down the front all night, singing along, and when we came out front afterwards they were still there. We chatted about the blues for a while and then they said, d'you want to come to a party tomorrow night? And we had nothing better to do so we said sure, we'd love to.

I wasn't exactly the life and soul of the party, to be honest. We'd been drinking all day and I needed to kind of tune out for a while. I remember sitting on a cushion on the floor of a large, dimly-lit room, with incense burning and a conversation going on around me about Vietnam. I had nothing to say, but I was happy to swig from a bottle of beer – not even caring that it was American beer and tasted like piss – and listen in. There was a joint going round too, and after a few tokes I must've fallen asleep.

I don't know how long I was out for. When I came round, the room was just the same, only there weren't so many people in it. I wandered round the house till I found the kitchen, grabbed a bottle of something and decided I ought to look for the others. I was feeling pretty good now, like the sleep had revived me.

The three of them were out in the garden, smoking and talking to a bunch of guys I didn't remember meeting before. Hey Des, said Trevor when he saw me, you're just in time. We're going to watch a race. His eyes were gleaming with excitement.

I was about to ask, what kind of race?, but then I realised I knew exactly what kind. It was the kind of race Chuck Berry and The Beach Boys and Jan And Dean wrote songs about – two guys in souped-up cars racing flat out, head to head, winner takes all. It sounded like a great way to round off a great day, so I said count me in.

We stayed outside, drinking and toking and chatting, for a while longer. It must've been later than I thought, 'cause I looked round and there was a faint strip of light just above the horizon, and then someone said let's get going, the race starts half an hour after sun-up, out at the old airstrip. People started moving out to the front of the house and getting in their cars.

Somewhere along the line we'd decided that Steve and Trevor would ride with the guys we'd been talking to, while Jacko and I would follow on behind in the Chevy. But when I got out front it seemed to me that most people had already left, while the rest of our party were still messing around, taking far too long for my liking. So I jumped into the driver's seat of the Chevy, turned the key and revved the engine. Still no reaction from the others, who were standing on the lawn talking about who knows what, so I tooted the horn and started to pull away from the kerb.

That got their attention all right. Jacko came running up alongside and said what the hell do you think you're doing, and I said I'm going to watch the race, are you coming? I was driving along slowly, but fast enough that Jacko had to trot to keep up with me. Then I stopped

227

so that he had time to haul himself into the passenger seat, and then pulled away sharpish before anyone else could get in.

I ought to mention at this point that I'd never actually passed my driving test. Never taken it, for that matter. Sure, I'd messed around in cars a bit, and Steve had given me a few lessons, but that was it. Jacko must've known this, 'cause he kept trying to reason with me, telling me to slow down, pull over to the side of the road, let him drive. Well, that wasn't going to happen. Apart from anything else, he'd drunk almost as much as me, so he had no right to be behind the wheel of an automobile, none whatsoever, and I told him so. It was around then that he tried to grab the wheel, but all that happened was that we shot diagonally across the road, narrowly missing a parked car. He didn't try that again.

Thing is, I was scared too – but at the same time, I was loving every minute of it. In my mind I was writing myself into every song I'd ever heard about a guy in a car. I made a mental note to get the band rehearsing Key To The Highway as soon as possible.

The road seemed to go on for miles, with big houses set back behind huge lawns on either side, so I didn't have to worry about taking a wrong turn. I was still trying to get us to the airstrip in time for the race. Then a car pulled alongside and Trev leaned out and said, Des, turn left at the next junction and follow us, all right? While I was listening to him, I must've unconsciously steered towards him too, so that the other driver had to veer to the left to avoid a collision, and after that he quickly accelerated ahead.

I did what Trev said, hanging a left when we finally reached a junction. I barely slowed down – hell, there wouldn't be anything coming at that time of the morning – 'cause I didn't want to give Jacko the chance to take over. We passed a few more houses and then we were out on the open road, farmland as far as I could tell, with the other car off in the distance ahead of us and the slowly widening crack of dawn on the horizon off to our right. I was enjoying myself, I don't deny it, and even Jacko had calmed down a bit now. He must've been thinking that maybe it was going to be all right after all. Trouble is, I still had all those old song lyrics running through my head, and somehow I got to thinking that I couldn't let the car ahead of me get away, like I was in a race myself. I speeded up, just a little at first, but that didn't seem to make any difference. So I put my foot to the floor, and now the engine was making so much noise that I couldn't make out what Jacko was saying, though I got the general idea that he was protesting.

Sure enough, the other car's tail lights started to get closer, bit by bit. Then they disappeared, and by the time I'd realised they must've gone round a bend in the road, we were hurtling towards that bend at top speed. As stoned as I was, even I could tell that we weren't going to make it, but I started to turn the wheel anyway. And somewhere at the back of my mind, Jan and Dean were singing: you won't come back from Dead Man's Curve...

BAR TEN: STEVE, 1983

It was Trev who raised the alarm. Chuck was driving and Bruce was alongside him, both of them singing along with the radio, while me and Trev were sat in the back, whacked out on beer and dope, not saying much. We were worried about Des driving, 'specially in the state he was in, but there was sod all we could do. The sun was starting to shimmer on the edge of the horizon, and I was gazing at it absent-mindedly when Trev turned round to look out of the back window. After a moment he said: "Hey, shouldn't we be able to see them by now?"

Chuck looked up at the rear-view, Bruce squinted at the side mirror and I twisted round to join Trev, and we all agreed that the last time we'd noticed, Des and Jacko hadn't been *that* far behind us.

"S'alright, they've probably just taken a wrong turn somewhere," I said drowsily. "Des never did have any sense of direction."

There was a pause. The pair in the front exchanged glances.

"Dude," said Bruce, starting to sound worried, "there aren't any turnings off this road, not for miles."

That was when Chuck slowed right down, did a u-turn in the middle of the deserted highway and accelerated back the way we'd come.

I should've known what to expect. I'd seen plenty of crashed cars before. People used to bring them to Pa's garage all the time, with crumpled bumpers and wings bent out of shape, doors caved in, you name it. All I ever thought about was the damage to the bodywork.

Mind you, no one had ever brought Pa anything half as mangled as the Chevrolet was when we found it. There wouldn't've been any point. When the road curved round, the car had carried straight on, through a wooden fence and on into a large oak tree at the edge of a field. It looked as if Des had tried to swerve at the last minute, though (or was it Jacko, wrenching desperately at the wheel?), 'cause only the right-hand side, the passenger side, had concertinaed into the tree trunk. And Jacko, my poor cousin Jacko, he must've shot out of his seat like an arrow from a bow at the moment of the collision, through the windshield and into the tree, which was stained with what looked like – oh God – his brains. Even thinking about it now makes me want to puke, which is what I did when I got out of the car and saw his body sprawled across the hood of the wrecked Chevy.

From that moment I sobered up fast, and the same goes for Trev. He'd gone really pale, but he was also the first one to ask where Des was.

Our frantic search didn't take long. Des was round the other side of the huge oak, propped up against the trunk, and at first I thought he must be dead too, 'cause he was covered in blood and his clothes were torn. But then I saw his eyelids flicker and I knew that however bad it looked, it could've been much worse. We never did work out how he'd escaped Jacko's fate. Whatever had happened at the moment of impact, he'd obviously stayed conscious long enough to crawl round the tree before blacking out. As Trev and I knelt by him, his eyes opened fully for a few seconds, but from the vacant look in them I reckoned he didn't know who we were or where he was. Still, he was awake enough to feel pain. I found that out when I touched him on the arm and he let out a loud groan.

We were interrupted by Bruce, who'd been checking out the car. "Uh, guys, if your friend's okay we ought to move him," he said. "The Chevy could blow, y'know. We all need to get away from here."

So we picked up Des the best we could, pretending we couldn't hear his agonised moans, and laid him in the back seat of Chuck's car. Trev was all for taking him straight to the nearest hospital, but Bruce pointed out that once he'd recovered, the cops would most likely lock him up and throw away the key. Christ, it turns out Des wasn't even old enough to *drink* legally in Massachusetts – none of us was – never mind driving without a licence and manslaughter, or whatever the hell it was that had happened here. If Bruce was right we didn't have much time. Another car might come by at any moment, and once the driver had found a payphone and called the cops, that would be that.

So we hurriedly cooked up a plan. Bruce would drive Des to his frat house, leave him there with a medical student he thought he could trust, and then go on to the nearest police station. (I had no idea what a frat house was, but I was past caring, just as long as we did *something*.) Trev volunteered to go with him, to help carry Des at the other end – and, I reckon, 'cause he didn't want to stay and look at what was left of Jacko a moment longer than he had to. Who could blame him? Me and Chuck would stay there, reassuring anyone who stopped that the police were on their way, and then we'd tell the cops our version of what had happened. This meant leaving out any mention of Des, and of the fact that we were in a band. To the cops we'd just be three guys from England who'd been visiting friends in Taunton. We'd stayed up all night talking (and yeah, maybe Jacko *had* had a drink or two, but that was okay 'cause he was legal) and then decided to drive to this place our friends knew for breakfast. Jacko had taken the Chevy, but somehow he'd crashed. End of story. A tragedy, for sure, but no one would go to jail.

The plan worked well enough. Once the others had driven off, Chuck and I went and stood a safe distance from the wrecked Chevy, with our backs to it. We didn't talk much – didn't know what to say – just stood there watching the sun come up over the low, wooded hills. It was only when I felt its warmth on my skin that I realised I was shivering. I'd been lost in thought; confused memories of Jacko flickered through my brain, in between bouts of wondering how the hell we'd got here. I didn't have any answers.

Occasionally cars did come past, and some of them slowed down when they spotted the Chevy. A couple of drivers pulled up alongside us and asked what was going on; once they heard the cops were on their way, you could see the relief in their faces and they drove away sharpish. After what seemed like forever, a black and white police car arrived with Trevor and Bruce looking nervous in the back seat, and a minute later an ambulance too. The cops only asked me a couple of questions. Over their shoulders I caught a glimpse of Jacko's body being transferred into a big black bag and then carried to the ambulance. That drove away, then another police car came and we were all driven back to Taunton… and suddenly we were free to go, apart from some stuff about formalities that I didn't pay much attention to. By now I just felt numb all over, like I'd been wrapped up tight in cotton wool, and when I got back to the motel I slept like a baby.

In a strange sort of way, the need to protect Des and keep the truth from coming out helped us get through the next few days without breaking down. There wasn't time to sit around moping. When I knocked on Trev's door the next afternoon he looked bleary-eyed, whether from sleep or crying I couldn't tell and didn't ask. I went and got us both some strong black coffee from the diner next door, and then we sat down and tried to work out what to do. It felt odd, drawing up a plan between the two of us. It wasn't Jacko we were missing, it was Des, like he was the one who'd died.

The first thing was to cancel the gig we were supposed to be playing that evening, so Trev phoned the club and told them we'd all come down with food poisoning and there was no way we could go on. Then he called the promoter in New York and fed him the same line, laying on the olde-worlde English politeness good and thick and assuring him that we'd be healthy and raring to go in time for the next date. The promoter blustered a bit and made a big thing about us not getting paid, but he didn't seem to suspect anything.

Now what? We decided it would look suspicious if we flew straight back to England, which was what we really wanted to do. Anyway, that was out of the question if Des was as badly messed up as we feared. But if we stayed in the States and pulled out of the tour, the promoter would definitely start asking questions, so we had to make it look as though we were carrying on as normal. There were only a handful of dates left; we'd just have to play them and hope that by the time we'd finished, Des'd be well enough to travel.

That was as far as we'd got by the time we arrived at the frat house that evening. Bruce led us up to an attic room where Des was lying in bed sleeping – sedated, according to the student they'd persuaded to look after him. An earnest bloke with a straggly beard, he seemed nervous, like he was expecting the cops to burst in with machine guns any minute and drag him off to jail. But Des wasn't half as badly off as he could've been. He had a couple of fractures in his left arm, which he must've landed on when he was thrown from the car, and a bit of concussion, but no internal injuries. The rest was just cuts and bruises that would heal in a few days. The plan was to keep him doped up to the eyeballs and let time do the rest. I didn't bother asking where they'd get the medication from, 'cause Bruce and Chuck obviously didn't have a problem getting hold of prohibited substances. They were both stoned already and it was only seven o'clock.

So anyway, Trev and I told them what we were planning to do. It turned out they knew this bloke who played guitar, and half an hour later we were jamming on old blues songs with Danny. To begin with he was more interested in showing off the tricks he'd learned from watching Jimi Hendrix – playing the guitar behind his head, all that crap – but once we'd explained the situation and promised to pay him the going rate, he calmed down a bit. We ran through all the main styles he'd need if he was going to play with us and he seemed to be able to cope, so we shook hands and welcomed him as a temporary member of the band.

Twenty-four hours later we were on stage in a lecture theatre in Cambridge, Massachusetts, with Trev on vocals as well as bass and mouth harp. Danny stood by the drum kit so I could feed him cues. It wasn't one of our greatest performances – after all, we did have one or two things on our minds – but we got through it, just about. You could tell from the puzzled looks they gave us that a few members of the audience had spotted that the faces on stage didn't quite match the line-up pictured on our album covers (unless you could believe that Des had grown six inches, put on three stone and dyed his hair blonde), but we'd decided not to say anything during the show. Afterwards we told the handful who asked about Des that he was ill, which was true enough.

And that's how it went on for the rest of the week. We tried our best to put on a decent show every night, and we didn't do too badly after Trev suggested letting Danny off the leash. Well, with Des out of the picture we needed someone to be the focus of attention and even Trev, bless him, had to admit that he wasn't a natural front man. So the crowds left happy enough and the promoter stayed in New York. We got away with it, though it didn't exactly feel like a triumph.

Back at the frat house in Taunton we found Des sitting up in bed reading a copy of 'Rolling Stone'. His left arm was in a sling, but the cuts on his face were already starting to heal and the shaggy student said yes, he was well enough to travel. So we thanked him, and Bruce and Chuck of course, and paid Danny his wages, and then we helped Des into the van and set off on the long drive back to Newark. We didn't talk much on the journey. I had the feeling that if any of us had started speaking about what'd happened, the floodgates would've opened, and we were all too scared of what might come out. So we listened to the radio and watched America go by, and on the plane we read magazines or slept, and at Heathrow we loaded all the gear into the Transit and headed for Watford. After I'd dropped the others off I steeled myself to break the news to Pa. I was hoping he might have some idea how you go about organising a funeral when the body's in a morgue five thousand miles away.

I spent a lot of my time in prison going over that trip in my mind. On my very first night in the cell, after the door slammed shut, I lay on my bunk staring up at the roof and thinking all sorts of things, but mainly that I was only there because of what had happened in Taunton – because of Des, in fact. But one thing about being in the nick, there's time to do a lot of thinking, and it wasn't long before I stopped feeling sorry for myself and realised it was more complicated than that.

You want to know something? I reckon getting sent to Pentonville may just have been the best thing that could've happened to me at that point in my life. Straight up. I didn't see it like that at the time, mind you. But the truth is, I was lucky the way my porridge panned out – and not just 'cause it gave me a chance to get my head sorted.

Number one, it was lucky that I was in for ABH, and that I looked as if I could handle myself. All sorts went on in that place – you heard about stuff happening in the showers that you wouldn't wish on your worst enemy – but no one ever tried to mess with me. In fact more than one would-be big shot tried to recruit me for their gang, but I always turned them down flat. I'd had enough of being part of a gang. One of the things I worked out when I was doing all that thinking: I'd always let other people make the big decisions, even when I didn't agree, even though I'd have to take the consequences. Maybe it was time to do something about that.

My second stroke of luck was my cellmate, Norman. He was in for robbery (and not for the first time), halfway through a four-year stretch. Nearly twice my age but he looked older, with a bulging gut, greying hair and eyes that were sort of kind, which was a rare thing in the nick, I can tell you. He was friendly, but sharp as well. He knew how the system worked and wanted to get through his time without any hassle. I think he appreciated the fact that I felt the same way.

But the best thing about Norman was his guitar. A battered old acoustic, it was. The second evening I was inside, we'd just come back to the cell after eating the slop that passed for supper, and Norman pulled this thing out from under the bottom bunk and said: "I'm going to play for a bit. You don't mind, do you?"

I was still feeling my way into prison life, so naturally I said no, anything he wanted to do was all right by me. Then I lay back and listened while he strummed a few old tunes. Folky stuff – 'Scarborough Fair', that was one of them. It turned out he'd shared a cell in Strangeways with a student radical a few years back, and this bloke had taught him to play. When he was released he left his guitar behind, and now it was Norman's prize possession. He said playing it made things seem better than they really were, and I could see how that might be.

So we got talking about music, and of course I told him all about The Hornets. He seemed to be quite impressed, especially when he heard that we'd made albums and appeared on TV. He hadn't actually heard of us, mind you, but I didn't really expect that he would've.

"So, do you play the guitar?" he asked.

"Nah, like I say, I'm just the drummer."

"Not much chance of playing the drums in this place, son," he said. "How's about I teach you to play this thing? I can show you enough to be getting on with. And you'll need some sort of hobby to keep you sane, take it from me. Unless you're thinking of writing poetry or taking up needlework."

I laughed and said no, I wasn't interested in anything like that. Then one of the screws came round and locked us in for the night, so we agreed that Norman would give me my first guitar lesson the next evening.

Well, I took to it like a duck to water, didn't I? It was a bit tricky holding the strings down to begin with, but once my fingertips had hardened up I got on fine. Norman showed me a few chord shapes and taught me some basic tunes, and it wasn't too long before I was working out songs for myself. Folk music has the same kind of structure as the blues, so it wasn't much of a jump from the stuff Norman knew to the sort of songs I'd been playing with the band. In fact, after a couple of months he said he might as well stop teaching me, seeing as how I'd caught him up. He sounded pissed off to tell the truth, but once I'd buttered him up a bit he relaxed and said it was all right, he just wished he was naturally musical like me.

Naturally musical? I'd never thought of myself that way, and after lights out that night my mind started working overtime. One thought or memory led to another, until I realised that no one had ever given me any praise for the music I'd been playing all these years. I mean, sure, I knew the band was halfway decent, but I couldn't remember anyone ever saying how good *I* was. Not Des or Trev, not Charlie, no one in the studios where we'd recorded – not a single sod had ever told me I was good at playing the drums. At least when I helped Pa in the garage, he'd lean over an engine after I'd finished working on it and take a good look at what I'd done, and often he'd say: "Nice job, Stevie. Nice job." But in the band, everyone took me for granted.

Once I'd got the idea in my head, I couldn't shake it off. Sitting there in my cell, away from all my friends and family, I was gradually putting together a picture of how my life worked. It was like when you strip down a car engine: you take it apart, make a note of how the pieces fit together, give them a clean, maybe replace a few that are worn out, and then you reassemble the whole thing and it works much better. Well, after a few months inside I began to see how all the pieces of my life fitted together and which ones needed changing.

(Years later I was at this party and I got talking to some bloke who was about my age. I was a bit pissed and I found myself trying to explain all this to him. When I'd finished he laughed loudly, and I asked him why.

"About the same time as you must've been in Pentonville, I was hitch-hiking to Afghanistan with a couple of mates," he said. "We were searching for enlightenment, you know, and we thought we'd find the key to happiness if we consulted the wise men of ancient tribes and smoked lots of dope." He paused and laughed again. "Now it turns out I'd have done better to steal a car and get myself locked up in jail for a few months. You've got to admit, that is bloody funny.")

Anyhow, all this navel-gazing still wouldn't've come to anything if it hadn't been for my third piece of luck. The biggest piece of luck I ever had, in fact.

Birgit.

When I left Hamburg in the spring, she promised she'd write to me, and to my surprise she did. Her first letter was nice. Friendly. She told me what she'd been up to, the bands she'd seen and the records she'd bought, and said things in Hamburg were less interesting since The Hornets had left. I spent ages working on a reply. Well, I'd never written a proper letter before, unless you count those stupid thank-you notes Ma used to make us write after Christmas to all the relatives who'd bothered to send us a two-bob postal order. But eventually I got something down on paper and sent it off. A week or two later I received a reply, and soon we were carrying on a proper correspondence. It got so that I looked forward to the post arriving every morning in case there was something for me.

Then we went to America. I'd told Birgit we were going, of course, and I sent her a cheery postcard from New York, so it was natural that in the first letter I had from her after I got back, she asked lots of questions about what it'd been like.

Well, to start with I wasn't going to tell her anything much, the same way I didn't say anything much to anyone who asked me about the trip. A bit of old bull about the sights we'd seen and they went away happy enough. Why bother them with gruesome stories? But gradually I started to feel this urge for confession. Maybe it was the Catholic in me coming out, though God knows, if that was the case it was the first time in years. Sure, I went to church with Ma and Pa every Sunday, but I never bothered with confession, hadn't done since I was thirteen and I was stupid enough to tell the priest me and my mates had been at the communion wine.

No, this was different. Confessing to a priest, that always seemed to me to be about owning up before you were found out, by God I suppose. But this was just about me, no one else. I had this feeling deep down inside that it would be better – better for me – if I told someone what had happened. What's that old saying? A problem shared is a problem halved. That's sort of what I was thinking. And Birgit was the perfect person to tell, 'cause I didn't have to look her in the face while I was doing it. I could put it all down on paper, just the way it happened. So that's what I did. And then I wrote how confused I was feeling, how much I missed Jacko, how I felt like Des had betrayed our friendship and how I wondered if I could ever really forgive him – stuff I'd never told anyone. And when I finally slipped the letter into the pillar box, it did feel like some of the weight had lifted off my shoulders.

Even so, I was nervous about her reply. Nervous about whether she'd reply at all, in fact, even though I knew I hadn't done anything wrong. Well, apart from telling the cops a pack of lies, obviously. It was more to do with what the crash said about my life, about all our lives. So when she did reply to my letter, and near the end she wrote:

239

"This incident must have made you think very much about your mode of living" (so what if her English wasn't always perfect?), I thought, yes, thank God, she understands. It was a very understanding letter all round, the sort only a good friend can write. That's what Birgit was, I realised, a good friend. It came as a bit of shock.

'Course, nothing she wrote could stop me carrying on like a prize pillock, which is how I ended up in the nick. But now I didn't hesitate to tell her what had happened. I poured out the story of the day of the Millwall game – covered three sheets of writing paper, front and back. I was hoping for another understanding letter in return, but I had another think coming – Birgit wrote back saying she was shocked and disappointed that I would get involved with violence, especially about something as trivial as football, and she thought I was a better person than that. She went on like that for a couple of pages, till I was almost in tears, slumped on my bunk thinking I'd lost my friend, wishing I'd kept quiet about the whole business. But then, right at the end, she said she knew I wasn't a bad person really, and asked me to tell her how I was coping in prison, and I realised she hadn't given up on me after all. So we carried on our correspondence, writing to each other so often that Norman and the other blokes I hung around with noticed and started making jokes about my 'bit of Kraut stuff'. No one believed me when I said I'd never screwed her, she really was just a friend.

I was so grateful to Birgit for not giving up on me, I couldn't have begun to explain it to anyone. So I didn't try. One thing I did do, though, was sign up for German classes. I wanted to be able to talk to her properly in her own language the next time we met, whenever that was.

As it turned out, I didn't have to wait all that long. The way Birgit told it in her letters, coming to see The Hornets every week and hanging around with me had got her so enthusiastic about music, she'd decided to make it her career. She asked around, and eventually she landed a part-time job working for a promoter. To start with she wasn't much more than a secretary, but soon she was making touring arrangements for foreign bands and helping to draw up contracts, and her boss realised he was onto a good thing and offered her a full-time job. 'Course, that meant dropping out of university, but she'd lost interest in studying anyway, and it didn't bother her if she didn't get a degree. It bothered her parents, mind you, and they didn't talk to her for months afterwards – literally, not a word. I couldn't imagine what that was like, what with me always having been so close to Ma and Pa, so in my next letter I tried to comfort her, telling her they'd come round when they saw how successful she was.

And she was successful. She didn't exactly boast, but from the way she wrote about her job it sounded like she was practically running the place. She must've been persuasive, too, 'cause she managed to talk her boss into letting her arrange a tour of West Germany for The Hornets. She didn't say anything in her letters until she'd got him to agree, and when she did tell me, I was so happy that I danced a little jig around my cell. (Luckily Norman wasn't around at the time.) Part of me was thinking this was the perfect way to get the band back on its feet, the four of us doing what we did best, playing music to live audiences. Another part of me was just looking forward to seeing Birgit again.

From then on I made damn sure I didn't do anything that could damage my chances of an early release. I must've been the best-behaved prisoner in Britain, those last couple of months. And sure enough, in September I found myself on a train pulling into Hamburg station, and I could see Birgit standing on the platform waiting for me. Well, obviously she was waiting for all of us, and once we'd got off and unloaded our bags we each hugged her in turn, even Susie, who'd never met her before. But while I was hugging her, I put my mouth close to her ear and whispered "Danke schön," and my heart jumped as I felt her pull me a little bit tighter in response.

There wasn't much time to talk right then, what with so much to sort out. Birgit had found places for everyone to stay, so we spent a couple of hours driving around town in the knackered green Volkswagen estate that was going to be our transport for the tour. (I think Birgit was counting on my skills as a mechanic to keep it on the road, and I certainly needed them.) We dropped Trevor and Susie off first, in a posh street near the Alster, and once Birgit had shown them round the house we went on to some place north of the airport, where Des was going to stay with an artist friend of hers. Finally there were just the two of us left in the car, but even then we didn't talk about anything personal – just the arrangements for the tour, stuff like that. Then we pulled up outside an apartment block in a street in Altona, and I recognised the address and realised I was going to be staying with Birgit herself. We went inside, up two flights of stairs, into number 11 – I knew exactly where to go, I'd written the address often enough – and I put my bags down in the hall. The next thing I knew, we were in each other's arms and kissing like we'd just invented it. And you know what? It felt right. Simple as that. It felt like this was the only possible way things could've turned out.

Me and Birgit spent most of that week together, kissing and cuddling and, oh yeah, screwing like we were making up for lost time. Which we were, I suppose. It carried on that way once the tour started. Mind you, we were discreet about it, for a while at least. How come? I think it was 'cause I knew that Trevor and Des were both unhappy. Trev was missing Susie, that was obvious. I could sympathise with that – I'd always enjoyed having my little sis around, and I was sorry that she hadn't come on the road with us. As for Des, he was drinking like it was going out of fashion, and you didn't need to be a trick cyclist to know what had brought that on. So it seemed like flaunting the fact that me and Birgit were so happy together would only make the pair of them even more miserable, and there was no need for that. But then, one evening in West Berlin when we were all getting drunk and high, I forgot that our relationship was supposed to be a secret and French-kissed Birgit in front of everyone. I suppose Des and Trev knew something was going on after that. Truth is, I was too happy to care about them any more.

The hardest part of that whole tour was saying goodbye to Birgit at the end of it. Still, we'd already come up with a plan for another German tour, just so's we could spend more time together. There wasn't really the demand, to be honest, but Birgit made the figures look good enough. That second tour was the last time The Hornets played on the Continent, but by then I knew Birgit and I were going to be together whatever happened, so it didn't matter. I started working longer hours in the garage and saved up so that I could go and stay with her as often as possible. She came to stay with me sometimes, too, but that wasn't so much fun, seeing as how Ma and Pa were old-fashioned about the idea of an unmarried couple sharing a bed. But finally, once I was sure I could look after her properly, I asked her to marry me.

Sorry – I'm rushing through this a bit, aren't I? Trouble is, I've never been much good at talking about the way I feel. Even with Des, my oldest friend, it's always been unspoken. Well, apart from the odd time when I've got completely hammered and said more than I meant to. But otherwise Birgit's the only one I've ever really opened up to. I think it's something to do with the fact that she never assumed she knew what I was like. Does that make sense? You know how I was saying before about being taken for granted – well, Birgit never took anything about me for granted. She took me as she found me, and luckily for me she liked what she found.

The truth is, all that navel-gazing I did in the nick wouldn't have made much difference if it hadn't been for Birgit. I'd probably have slipped right back into my old life: bashing the drums with The Hornets, hanging around with Frankie and his mates at the football, helping Pa in the garage. Actually I did go back to all those things, apart from Frankie's gang of course – and anyway, he was stuck in Parkhurst for another couple of years. The difference was that now I could see a life beyond all that. I didn't know what it was going to be, exactly, but with Birgit's support I reckoned I had a shot at making something that was mine.

I want to be clear about this: there was never a masterplan, nothing like that at all. After we'd got married, me and Birgit rented a little terraced house off Whippendell Road, not far from the football ground. Pa let me have the old van for nothing and I used it to drive to work at the garage in the morning and to ferry the band to gigs in the evenings. I kept that van going for years, you know, patching it up and replacing parts when they wore out, till finally it just died, late one night on the A41 when we were coming back from a show in Hemel Hempstead. The RAC had to tow it back to Pa's, and somehow I knew the poor old thing would never run again. I'll tell you something, I almost cried.

Where was I? Oh yeah, married life. Well, Birgit started looking for a job as soon as we got back from the honeymoon, and it wasn't long before she was working at EMI, bringing in a good wage. What with Pa having given me a share in the garage as well, we were doing nicely, nicely enough to buy our own house just around the corner from where we'd been living. This would be in '79, I think. Yeah, that's right, I remember 'cause it was the year Watford got promoted to Division Two and the goldfish in the High Street pond got stomped again.

It was also around then that my solo career began. Yeah, I know. It's not a phrase I thought I'd ever find myself using, to be honest.

What happened was this. After I got out of the nick, I bought myself an acoustic guitar and carried on playing, just like I'd done when I was inside, practising a bit every day. I never told Des or Trev, though.

But I had no problem with telling Birgit, and I played for her sometimes when she came to visit. I was still doing folky stuff at the time 'cause that was what Norman had taught me. But I was getting bored of Donovan and Dylan, so it wasn't hard for Birgit to steer me towards country blues. Back in Hamburg she used to talk about people like Blind Lemon Jefferson and Son House, and now she started sending me albums to listen to.

One of the first was a Robert Johnson compilation, and I recognised it 'cause Des had played it to us years ago. I remember 'cause it was the same day we ended up getting plastered and going off to look for a crossroads where Trev could sell his soul to the devil. We used to have a laugh in those days, before it all got so serious.

Mind you, Robert Johnson's music was serious stuff, I could tell that straight off. There was something about that record that had really got to me when I first heard it, and I often thought we should play songs like that – songs with a bit more depth, you know? But there was no point in me even suggesting it. Des decided what we did and didn't play (though Trev liked to kid himself that his opinion counted for something), and he knew what he liked. Now I got to pick my own songs, and I ended up choosing 'I Believe I'll Dust My Broom'. I listened to it over and over again until eventually I figured out how the main riff worked. It took a long time – we're talking months here – but in the end I got it down well enough.

I spent a lot of my spare time over the next couple of years building up what I suppose you'd call a repertoire. I'd listen to one of the LPs Birgit had given me, pick a track I liked and practise till I'd mastered it. Then, one evening, Birgit came home and found me sitting on the sofa, crouched over the guitar, concentrating so hard that I didn't even notice she was there at first. When I'd finished the song I was playing I found her watching me intently, and there was a look on her face I couldn't quite figure out. There was surprise in there, but something else as well.

"You know, you sing very well," she said. Then she came over and kissed me, and soon I forgot all about the guitar. It was only later that I remembered what she'd said. I was barely aware that I *was* singing, you see. It's true that I'd started singing along with my guitar playing, but just as a way of keeping track of where I was in the song. The important thing was what my hands were doing.

It was only a few weeks later that I found out the meaning of that strange look Birgit had given me She said she had something to show me, and handed me a piece of paper. It was a handbill for a gig at a club in Charing Cross Road. 'An Evening of Acoustic Music', it said in big letters, and then there was a list of names. That bloke who used to be on the telly with Jasper Carrott was at the top – Loudon Wainwright, that's it – and then a few others, and right at the bottom: Steve O'Brien.

I didn't get it at all. "So there's some bloke out there playing gigs who's got the same name as me," I said, shrugging my shoulders. "No skin off my nose."

"Not some bloke, Steve. You." She gave me a friendly poke in the chest with her index finger and smiled.

Now I was starting to get it, and I didn't like it. "You mean I – you want me to – now wait a minute, I can't do that. No way."

"Of course you can do it. You're really good, you know? Maybe you don't realise it, but I do. I played your tape, the one I recorded last month, to the guy who runs the club, and he's really keen for you to play there. Oh, and by the way, I'm your manager now. So don't let me down."

She looked deadly serious for a moment, but then she burst out laughing, pointing at me and saying: "Oh Steve, your face, you look so scared." Then I started laughing too, and I knew there was no point in arguing any more. I realised Birgit had the whole thing worked out and I'd just have to go through with it. Once she'd decided something was going to happen, it usually did.

And so, six weeks later, I found myself standing at the side of a tiny, low stage, gazing nervously round a dimly-lit room where forty or fifty people sat cradling bottles of beer. Then the compere went up to the microphone and welcomed everyone to the venue and said: "To start us off we've got a guitarist who's playing his very first gig. So let's give a big hand to Steve O'Brien!"

'Course, it wasn't anything like my first gig, but no one had asked me or Birgit about The Hornets and we hadn't told them anything. Anyhow, I felt so nervous, it might as well have been my first time on a stage. There's a big difference between sitting at the back, half-hidden behind a drum kit, and standing there alone in the spotlight. But somehow I made the step up onto the stage without my legs collapsing under me, and managed to sit on the stool and adjust the mic to the right height and mumble something that was meant to be "Hello". For a second or two I was completely paralysed by fear, but then I saw Birgit sitting right down the front, smiling up at me like a proud parent at the school play, and I just thought, "Fuck it," and started playing the first song. And you know what? It was okay. I concentrated hard on my playing and remembered to sing properly, and three songs later I was leaving the stage and everyone was clapping. I mean, it was hardly a standing ovation, but it was proper applause, like people meant it.

After that it all sort of happened naturally. The club-owner booked me straight away for another gig and I ended up playing a residency there, every Thursday evening for six months. Meanwhile Birgit got me occasional dates in clubs that specialised in acoustic music. I tell you what, she was a bloody good manager (which didn't surprise me at all). She seemed to know instinctively what the next step should be, all the time pushing me gently, making me extend myself, so that I was constantly surprised by what I was capable of. She had the right contacts, too. She'd got to know a few music journalists through her job and she soon found out how to get the right kind of person to review one of my shows. So one evening this bloke from 'Folk Roots' magazine came along; he wrote some nice things about me, and that led to a few more bookings. And it was in 'Folk Roots' that Birgit read about Niall Molloy.

Molloy was a DJ who was making a name for himself on Radio One. He had a late-night show, just a couple of hours every Wednesday, but it seemed like people were talking about him more than the other DJs. He was playing all kinds of stuff: folk, country, rock'n'roll, blues, and a lot of what they call 'world music', though I don't think the term had even been invented back then. Birgit and I listened to the show one evening and it was a real eye-opener. In one half-hour he started off with Willie Nelson, followed that with a country-punk band I'd never heard of, and then played Son House, a strange piece of African music with instruments I didn't recognise, and Elvis doing 'That's All Right Mama'. Apart from the unconventional playlist, the other thing you noticed was his enthusiasm; he talked about the records in a way that made you want to go out and buy them. He reminded me of Des back in the beginning, before he started on the sauce.

So Birgit posted off a demo tape of my stuff to Niall Molloy with a copy of the 'Folk Roots' review and a list of my next few gigs. A couple of days later Molloy himself phoned up, and the following week I was on the show. I played a couple of numbers right there in the studio, sitting facing him across the mixing desk, and in between he talked to me about the music and my career. It turned out he knew all about The Hornets – he'd even been to see us play – and he seemed particularly impressed by the fact that I'd switched from the drums to the guitar. Not many people do that, he said, and I suppose he was right, though I'd never looked at it that way. So I explained, a bit embarrassed, about how I'd come to learn the guitar, and he got excited about that too – he went on about how some of the great blues musicians had done time. Well, I wasn't so sure about that, and for a while there I started thinking he was a bit of a wanker, but I didn't say anything. You meet people like that, people who seem to think there's something cool about having been in prison. The best way to deal with it is to ignore them.

Anyway, the day after I appeared on Molloy's show I got two phone calls from people who'd heard it. One was a bloke who said he ran a small specialist record label (and he wasn't kidding – it turned out to be such a small operation, it made Natchez look like CBS). The other was Trevor.

I was a bit worried when I heard his voice. The thing is, I still hadn't told him or Des anything about my solo career. I started off wanting to keep it to myself, and after a while it got so that I couldn't think of a way of breaking the news without it looking odd. Me keeping it a secret, I mean. And I didn't want it to look like I was crowing about my success, either.

Still, Trev didn't sound pissed off. He was more surprised than anything else, which was understandable, though the way he went on about it you'd think I'd split the bloody atom. We met up for a drink a few days later and though it was always going to be awkward, what with him being my sister's ex and everything, it went okay. He told me about his job and asked me lots of questions about my solo stuff, and I got the impression he was genuinely pleased for me. I enjoyed the evening too, and it wasn't just relief at having come clean at last. I'd forgotten how satisfying it was talking about music with Trevor. Birgit knew a fair amount of course, but with her there was always more of business angle. With Trev I could talk about stuff I'd been listening to and songs I was thinking of including in my set.

We ended up arranging to meet again the following week and it became a regular thing, the two of us sharing a few pints and chatting about music. It was sort of like we were learning to be friends again. I know I've often taken the piss out of him over the years – well, he can be so slow on the uptake sometimes, it's like shooting fish in a barrel – but I've always had a soft spot for him. That's why I decided Trev should be the first one to hear about the latest unexpected development in my career.

It had all happened on the spur of the moment, at a Sunday night show at a folk club in the West End. Before the interval they opened the stage to floor singers – that's where anyone who wants to can come up and do a song. Most floor singers are newcomers hoping to get noticed, and often as not it's the first time they've played in front of an audience. You can see the fear in the eyes, watch their hands shaking as they fit the capo onto their guitar.

The last of the three floor singers that evening was different, though I didn't see it straight away. He'd been sitting at the table next to mine, and I didn't have him down as a performer at all. He'd slouched in his seat while the first two singers were on, so still that I thought he'd nodded off. He was wearing a moth-eaten overcoat and tatty black jeans and he had long, messy hair and a wispy beard. My guess was that he was a student who'd come here for a cheap night out. It was only when he got up that I saw the guitar case propped against his chair, and as he shuffled onto the stage I noticed how scrawny he was. He didn't look well, was my first thought. That or he was on something.

But he started to play, and then he started to sing, and it was like – well, it was like nothing I'd ever heard before. It sounded like a traditional acoustic blues at first, the sort of thing I played myself, but then these strange rhythms crept in. I thought I recognised them as coming from African music, and something Niall Molloy had said on the radio came back to me. He'd been explaining how African music was the original blues, 'cause that was what the slaves took with them when they were carted off to America, what they sang on the plantations, and what eventually turned into the music we recognise as the blues. I couldn't see it at the time, but listening to this kid it made sense. And he had this high, clear voice that swooped up and down the scales. I couldn't tell you what he was singing about, but it sounded lovely.

When he'd finished there was a moment of stunned silence and then scattered applause, and he ambled back to his chair as the PA tape came on. I was stunned myself – by the brilliance of the music, but also by the fact that the rest of the audience couldn't see it. Meanwhile the kid was putting his guitar away. He looked as if he might be about to leave, and I made a snap decision to go over and talk to him.

So I offered to buy him a beer, and he hesitated and then said "Thanks very much," and while we were standing at the bar I told him how much I'd enjoyed his song. He relaxed a bit then and answered my questions willingly enough. He hadn't been in London long, he'd recently moved down from Sheffield – I had a feeling he might've run away, or at least left under a cloud, but I didn't ask for details. He was eighteen and quite shy, though he livened up when we started talking about music. It turned out he listened to Niall Molloy too, and when I told him I'd been on the show a couple of weeks ago he came over all embarrassed, 'cause he hadn't realised who I was.

"Don't worry, I should've introduced myself properly," I said. Then I asked him his name, and he did a funny thing; instead of just telling me, he pointed to the sticker on the side of his guitar case. Well, I got a shiver down my spine, I can tell you, 'cause the sticker said 'Tommy Barnett'.

Tommy Barnett was one of the all-time Watford greats, you see. Well before my time, but I knew all about him 'cause he was the club's record goalscorer. So I reckoned it must be some sort of omen, and even as I was asking the kid if he had a manager (and I was sure the answer would be no), I'd made up my mind what I was going to do.

'Course, by the time we got round to drawing up contracts I'd found out that his name was Jimmy Barrett, not Tommy Barnett; what with his bad handwriting and the dim lighting in the club, I'd misread the sticker. (Trev laughed long and hard when I got to this part of the story – he said he'd always known I was obsessed with Watford, but this took the biscuit.) Anyhow, it didn't matter, 'cause after talking to Jimmy some more and getting him to play a few tunes for me I reckoned my instinct had been right, omen or not. He probably wasn't going to have much in the way of hit singles, but I had a feeling there was an audience out there for his kind of music. Birgit agreed with me, too. When I went home and told her what I'd done she looked doubtful, but once she'd heard Jimmy play she kept telling me how clever I was. Mind you, we both knew I'd never have done anything like this if it hadn't been for her.

The next time I met Trev for a drink, he was all excited about something, and he could hardly wait for me to get the beers in before telling me. Turns out our albums were going to be rereleased – they were even going to send some bloke round to interview the three of us for the sleevenotes.

"So, what do you think?" Trev asked. He looked flushed.

I took a swig of my pint and tried to decide what I thought. "Well, it's good, isn't it?" I said eventually. "I'm not even sure I've got a copy of the originals any more. But Trev, I wouldn't go hiring a tux for the Grammies just yet, all right?"

"I know we're not going to get in the charts or anything like that. But there's quite a market for stuff from the Sixties these days, Birgit must've told you that. We could cash in. We could – "

He stopped suddenly, a wary look on his face.

"We could what?" I asked, though I already knew what he was going to say.

"Well, it's just that I was thinking... Maybe we could get the band back together, play a few gigs. Show everyone that it's not all about nostalgia. That the story of The Hornets isn't over."

"But it is, though, isn't it?" I said. "I mean, I've got the garage, and Des is putting his life back together again, and you, well, you're..."

And that was the point, of course. The poor sod hadn't found anything to fill the dirty great hole the break-up of the band had made in his life. He looked so forlorn that I felt guilty about what I'd just said, so I promised I'd at least think about his idea.

I did a lot of thinking over the next couple of weeks. I also phoned Niall Molloy, who said he'd definitely play a track or two from the reissues on his show. He added that it would be a better story – and we'd sell more albums – if the band was still playing. Then that journalist came round to interview me, and I found I actually enjoyed talking about the old days. The questions he asked me about the band reminded me how popular and successful we were, for a while at least. I suppose I'd forgotten that. Lots of other stuff came back to me then, some of it good, some not so, but the upshot was that I realised that despite everything, despite all I'd said and done about carving out something that was mine alone, I did miss that feeling of being part of a group.

So the next time I saw Trev I told him that if Des was up for it too, I'd play a Hornets reunion gig to celebrate the albums being rereleased. Just the one.

BAR ELEVEN: TREVOR, 1983

You know 'The Lost Weekend', that old film about an alcoholic writer? I can top that – I had a lost *year* somewhere in the mid-Seventies. If I was a religious man, I might have believed I was being punished for my sins. After all, adultery is one of the big no-nos, isn't it? As it was, it just seemed like my life was crashing down around me, and it reached a point where I couldn't cope any more.

It's hard to pinpoint an exact date when things started to go wrong – or rather, *more* wrong – but there is one disturbing incident that stands out in my memory. It was September 1974 and I'd spent the evening with Alison at the Black Horse. We weren't seeing each other as often as we used to (her husband was spending more time at home now), but when we did meet the evening still followed the same pattern: drink, music, sex. The comforting, routine aspect of it all was one of the things I liked most about the affair now that the novelty had worn off.

After the band had left the stage and last orders had been called we prepared to leave. Alison paused to light a cigarette when we got outside, and I noticed her shivering in the autumnal chill. She was only wearing a T-shirt and jeans so I offered her my jacket, the old denim one with the cartoon hornet on the back. It was a bit ragged round the edges, but still wearable. Then we set off across the car park.

We'd only taken half a dozen paces when three men emerged from behind a parked car and attacked Alison. It was wordless, quick and brutal. One of them punched her hard in the face, and as she went down they all kicked her in the ribs and in the head. Then one of them spat: "You've been warned," and they ran off. As I told the police, it happened so fast, it wasn't like there was a chance for me to intervene. Besides, I was taken by surprise – by the time I'd realised what was going on it was almost over. I think I shouted something stupid like "Hey, wait a minute!", but that was the sum total of my involvement. And I wasn't much more help when it came to identifying Alison's assailants. It was a cloudy night and the only light in the car park was a 100-watt bulb at the far end, so I was never going to be able to give an accurate description of the men. All I could recall was a series of images: a cropped head, a leather jacket, a pair of lace-up boots. That and the sickening sound of ribs cracking.

I went with Alison in the ambulance, but I had to leave her in Casualty and go home to Susie – I couldn't think of a plausible excuse for staying out all night. Also, I panicked. Simple as that. Something bad had happened and I wanted to get away.

The next morning, after I'd dropped Simon off at nursery school, I went straight to the hospital. To my relief, Alison was conscious, and a nurse assured me she hadn't suffered any permanent damage. She wasn't exactly pleasant to look at, though. Most of her upper body was heavily strapped, there was a bandage round the top of her head, and her face was covered in bruises. She wasn't in any state to talk, so I just sat with her for a while, holding her hand, and then left to go and give my statement to the police. When he'd established that Alison and I were both married to other people, the sergeant raised a quizzical eyebrow, and from that point on I had the feeling that he wasn't planning to devote a great deal of time or effort to tracking down Alison's attackers. Well, why should he? They obviously didn't present much of a threat to society at large; they'd set out to deliver a warning and they'd achieved their aim. It was unfortunate for Alison, but then again she'd been cheating on her husband, so she'd had it coming.

Of course he didn't actually say any of this, but I couldn't blame him for thinking it. Christ, I'd even been thinking it myself. Oh yes. With my usual genius for ascribing guilt to anyone but me, I found myself wondering what Alison had said or done to give the game away. And after I'd been so careful with Susie…

I visited her several times, in hospital and then at home. We talked a lot about the attack without coming to any firm conclusions, but overshadowing all our conversations were those ominous words: "You've been warned." I think we both knew we were going to heed

254

the warning. Our affair had been fun, exhilarating even, and we were very fond of each other, but not fond enough to risk further physical injury. The last time I left her house, my parting words were: "See you." But I knew I wouldn't. And you know what? It was a relief not having to carry around that particular guilty secret any more. That day I vowed to try to be a better husband in future.

Then my father died. Not immediately, but it was just a couple of weeks after I'd seen Alison for the last time. In its own way this was as shocking as the assault in the pub car park – he was only sixty-one and he'd never had any serious health problems. I was leafing through the papers on a dreary Sunday morning when the phone rang. Moments later I was listening to Mum telling me Dad had collapsed in the back garden, in the middle of digging up some potatoes for lunch, and she thought he was dead. By the time I got over to Chorleywood they were carrying his body into an ambulance, covered in a sheet. It turned out he'd had a heart attack, nothing more complex than that. Mum mentioned that his father had died of the same thing, and the GP said it might be genetic. That gave me pause for thought, I can tell you. And after I'd stopped thinking about myself I looked at Simon, playing with his Dinky toys on the living-room floor, and wondered if I'd passed on the fatal gene to him too.

The funeral was a strange occasion. I felt removed from events, as if I was watching myself taking part. There was a hollowness at the centre of it all, as far as I was concerned – holding a religious rite for a man who'd scarcely been inside a church in forty years, and then only for weddings and christenings. We sang the sort of hymns people sing at funerals, and a vicar who'd never met my father read a eulogy based on a handful of facts we'd given him. It didn't seem to have a great deal to do with my Dad, an outwardly stern and reserved man who was fundamentally kind, and proud of his work and the way it had enabled him to look after his family.

In fact I spent most of the service feeling guilty about the way I'd neglected him – and Mum, for that matter. I'd always told myself it was because they disapproved of the life I'd chosen, but the truth is, they'd never done much in the way of expressing that disapproval. It wasn't in their natures to say what they thought about anything important, which had always frustrated me. When Susie was pregnant we'd go to their house for Sunday lunch; Dad would spend the meal fulminating against the neighbours who kept parking their car across the end of his drive, or boring us rigid with a minute description of the progress of his vegetables, without once asking how Susie was or giving any indication that he was looking forward to becoming a grandfather. Some weekends we'd spend one day with Susie's parents and one with mine, and the contrast between the boisterous, welcoming warmth of the O'Brien household and the reserved politeness we were greeted with in Chorleywood was embarrassing. So we gradually started spacing out our visits to my parents, making excuses, often blaming Simon (or rather, some illness or injury Simon had supposedly suffered) for our non-attendance. Which was cruel, not least because my parents took an obvious pleasure in playing with their grandson, even if they never said as much. When Dad picked Simon up for the first time, I saw a tenderness in him I'd never glimpsed before. "It was the same when you were a baby," said Mum later that day. "Especially when he thought no one was looking, he could be as soppy as anything." I remember thinking, why did he have to wait until no one was looking?

That damp November day at Dad's funeral, as I walked away from the grave over a carpet of rusty leaves, I made another promise to myself: I resolved to be more attentive to Mum, and in particular to take Simon to see her on a regular basis. I didn't have much of an opportunity to keep that promise, though; within a year, Mum too had passed away. And in between the two funerals my marriage finally fell apart.

I suspect the timing of Dad's death was rather inconvenient for Susie. She'd probably intended to chuck me out earlier, but she wasn't completely heartless, and in the aftermath of the funeral she was sympathetic and attentive when I needed her to be. I even began to wonder whether our marriage had bottomed out. Then, after what she'd obviously decided was a decent interval – about three months, in case you're taking notes – she went through with her original plan.

I say she chucked me out, but it wasn't really like that at all. One evening, after she'd put Simon to bed, she came into the living-room, sat down in the chair opposite mine and got straight to the point.

"Trevor, I think it's time to put an end to this," was how she began. Even thinking about it now, all the hairs on the back of my neck are standing to attention. "Our marriage, I mean. I want a separation."

She paused as if to give me a chance to say something, but I was so surprised, I couldn't speak. So she went on, her voice steady and almost – almost – empty of emotion.

"I've been thinking about this a lot, for a long time, and I really believe it's the only way for – well, for either of us to be happy. Because we're not happy together, are we? You know that, don't you?"

I didn't know anything any more, and all I could manage was a desperate "But – " before she carried on.

"Let me finish, please. What I'd like to happen is for you to move out as soon as you can. I know you've got as much right to stay here as I have, but I'm hoping you won't want Simon to be without a home. You can still come and see him, of course. I'm sure we can come to an arrangement. But for his sake, it's best we do this now, as soon as possible. It can't be good for him to be growing up in such a – such a loveless atmosphere."

A loveless atmosphere? Something struck me that I ought to have realised much, much earlier.

"But – Susie – you…" I tried to gather my thoughts. Finally, pathetically, I managed to ask: "Don't you love me any more?"

"No." She looked me straight in the eye and there was no possibility of doubting her words. "No, I don't love you any more."

And that was that. In the face of such an overwhelming declaration, there was no point in arguing. So I didn't.

* * * *

In hindsight, there was plenty I could have argued with, and maybe I should have. Take Susie's assumption that she was going to keep Simon, for a start. Okay, she was the breadwinner in the family, but I was the one who'd looked after him almost from the day he'd been born. Surely that would have counted for something in the eyes of a court? But it didn't come to that, so I'll never know. The same goes for that tear-jerking line about Simon being without a home. It wasn't as if the pair of them would have been walking the streets – Susie could have moved back in with her parents at the drop of a hat, and she knew it. The bottom line was that she wanted me out of her life as quickly as possible, and getting me to leave achieved that with the minimum amount of fuss.

Move where, though? I should have gone to stay with Mum, that much seems obvious now. We'd have been good for each other, I'm sure. Looking after her might have stopped me spending so much time brooding about my marriage, and my company would have helped to distract her from her grief at losing Dad. But I was too proud to even consider it. Moving back to my parents' house, even with Dad gone, seemed like admitting that I'd failed completely, and I wasn't prepared to do that.

I didn't have a lot of other options, mind you. In the circumstances I couldn't turn to Steve, and Des was incapable of helping himself by this stage, let alone anyone else. I suddenly realised how few friends I had. My entire life since the age of seventeen had centred on the band, and I'd long since lost contact with anyone I'd known at school. I felt very lonely, so I did what lonely people traditionally do and went to live in a bedsit. A succession of bedsits, as it turned out. Money was the main problem, of course. Susie had been supporting me, and when she threw me out I got a quick and brutal lesson in personal finance. What little money I had soon ran out and once I was on the dole I found myself endlessly calculating what I could afford. If I bought an LP, would I have to go without lunch for the rest of the week? If I walked to the social security office instead of taking the bus, how long would it take me to save enough for a new pair of jeans?

It was obvious that I needed a job. But what was I qualified to do? Play music. And how did musicians make a living if they weren't in a band? Session work, of course. Well, that shouldn't be too difficult to find, I thought to myself, and the idea perked me up no end.

An idea was all it was, though. If I'd ever bothered making friends with any producers, engineers or studio owners, things might have turned out differently. But I hadn't, and it took a series of increasingly pathetic phone calls to distant acquaintances before I finally landed my first job, playing guitar on a radio advertisement for a car dealership. It took two hours and I earned thirty quid for my troubles, but at least I had a foot in the door. Or so I thought. In fact, that ad turned out to be the pinnacle of my session career. I soon discovered there were plenty of musicians out there with years of experience, and far better contacts than I had. They got first pick of the good jobs and I was left scrabbling around for scraps. After a couple of even lower-profile gigs and many more phone calls I threw in the towel. It looked like I was never going to be asked to play on one of Eric Clapton's solo albums after all.

After that I swallowed my pride and started applying for jobs advertised in the local paper, just like Susie had been nagging me to do. That's how I found myself working in the tax office in Watford as an 'administrative assistant'. The bloke who interviewed me seemed to be impressed by the fact that I'd taken some A levels and offered me the job on the spot. I thought it might at least be moderately interesting, but it turned out to involve a great deal of filing and photocopying and little else. Still, my colleagues were affable enough, and when I forgot about how heartbroken I was, I even got round to flirting with the secretaries every now and then.

It didn't last though. The trouble was, I didn't have anything to occupy my free time any more. (Simon had been very useful in that regard – the need to look after him had generally kept me out of mischief.) I couldn't even play the guitar at home, as my irascible landlady wouldn't allow it. So every evening I went back to my shabby room, drank cheap whisky and listened to old blues albums – and I had to do that through headphones if I wanted to listen at any volume above a whisper, or Mrs Pearson would be up the stairs and banging at my door. The amount I drank depended on how sorry for myself I was feeling that day, and I often fell asleep in my armchair.

Eventually the inevitable happened; I got through an entire bottle and didn't wake up until noon. When I rang the office I could tell my boss was suspicious, but he accepted my explanation that I'd got a temperature and hadn't been in any state to call earlier. I should have taken that as a warning, but I didn't. I kept on drinking, and after a few more missed days, and an official warning, I was called in to Mr Pleat's office for "a serious talk about your persistent absenteeism". Even then I might have been able to save myself with a display of contrition, but I didn't manage that. The moment he started lecturing me on my behaviour I launched a volley of swear words and told him where to stick his job, which saved him the bother of having to sack me. It was all very rock'n'roll – and bloody stupid.

The job had lasted four months, and it was a record I never bettered. Each time I started with a new employer I'd get on all right for a while, but they'd soon begin to tire of my feeble excuses for not showing up on time (or at all) and get rid of me. Unemployment was high in those days and I was a long way from being irreplaceable, particularly in the type of unskilled office and shop jobs I was taking. I even worked in a pub for a while, but that was doomed from the outset. The temptation to keep sipping the spirits was irresistible, and no landlord wants a barman who drinks more than the punters.

As for landladies, they too tended to take exception to my habits, especially when I threw up on the furniture, broke treasured ornaments or, in one case, set light to the curtains. (Look, it was an accident, and I put them out again as quickly as I could.) So I moved fairly often, and rarely through choice.

The funny thing is, I didn't realise my drinking was the main problem. The way I saw it, I'd spent too long being a creative artist to settle down in a dreary nine-to-five job, and that was all there was to it. I know, I know... The real trouble was that after spending so much time with Des, my idea of what constituted an abnormal level of alcohol consumption had been hopelessly distorted. A bottle of whisky a day? Nothing to worry about. As long as I could still dress myself and I didn't forget my name, I wasn't in any danger of becoming an alcoholic. What's more, I was capable of looking respectable if I needed to. When I visited Mum for Sunday lunch, or went to Susie's to pick up Simon, I always managed to shave and put on clean clothes, and I could lie convincingly enough to make them believe I was building a new life for myself.

But were they convinced? Maybe Susie wouldn't allow herself to acknowledge what I was turning into, but I think Mum knew. She never said anything, but as I was leaving she would press a bundle of ten-pound notes into my hand and refuse to listen to my protests that I was doing all right, really I was.

If I have one major regret about my lost year, it's to do with Mum. As spring turned into summer and I turned into a shambling drunk, I was dimly aware that my mother was changing too. She'd always had an ample figure, but now she was getting thinner and her clothes were hanging off her. That should have alerted me; if she'd been dieting (as she often used to when I was growing up), she'd have bought new clothes to show off how much weight she'd lost. No, she was just wasting away. When I went to her house for lunch I was so busy stuffing myself with nourishing food – a rare treat – that I barely noticed her pushing a tiny helping around her plate. And if I did notice, I didn't draw any conclusions, just as I ignored the fact that she always seemed to have a cough or a cold.

So it was a shock when Mum's GP phoned me to say that I should come and see her at once if I wanted to see her at all. He sounded irritated – it turned out that I'd forgotten to give Mum my latest address and it had taken him an hour to track me down. When I got there, he took me to one side and told me she'd caught pneumonia; it shouldn't be fatal in a healthy woman of her age, but she wasn't a healthy woman. Her immune system was weak and she wasn't responding to treatment.

What's more, he wondered if she really *wanted* to get better.

When I was finally allowed into the bedroom to see her, I was horrified. This pale, frail skeleton of a woman – had I really been blithely taking advantage of her all these months? She'd been so keen to look after me, when she was clearly the one who needed taking care of. I broke down there and then, knelt by the bed and wept, until Mum (who I'd assumed was asleep) put a hand on my head and said: "There there, don't cry, it's not your fault." Maybe it wasn't, but I hadn't exactly helped.

She died the next day. On the death certificate, under 'cause of death', the doctor put down "complications arising from pulmonary pneumonia". But we both knew it was really grief that had killed her.

I'd like to be able to say that Mum's death prompted me to take a long, hard look at myself and what I was doing with my life. But if anything, I sank even further into the morass of self-pity. I was an orphan at twenty-six – another to add to the litany of woes I recited as I drank.

And I could afford a better class of whisky now, thanks to Mum's life insurance policy and the proceeds of a lifetime of careful saving – not to mention the money I got for selling the house in Chorleywood. On the advice of the family solicitor I put most of it in a savings account, on the basis that I needed to decide how best to use it in the long term. But all I did was start drinking my way through my inheritance. What's more, I could do so in the relative luxury of a rented flat, without any pressing need to look for work. And I dare say I could have gone on like that indefinitely if it hadn't been for Mrs O'Brien.

I didn't see much of my in-laws any more, but we were still on good terms. Even if they weren't sure exactly why I was no longer living with their daughter, they knew I hadn't knocked her about or anything like that. So when I was invited to lunch at the O'Briens' house to celebrate Simon's fifth birthday, I was grateful for the hearty welcome they gave me. It was almost as if I was seventeen again and I'd cycled over there to rehearse with Steve and Des.

By way of contrast, Steve now treated me with an awkward coolness. He'd struggled to reconcile his friendship with me and his loyalty to his sister, and the latter had won, as it always had and always would do. I couldn't blame him for that. Birgit was there too, but she was just cool. Every time I caught her eye, I could read the expression as clearly as if the words were written on a sign hanging round her neck. I told you so, it said. You've only yourself to blame.

As for Susie, she was cordial but reserved, as she always was around me these days. We'd agreed at the start of our separation that we weren't going to argue in Simon's presence, and we'd managed to stick to that. The trouble was, it meant we both bottled up all sorts of feelings that hadn't gone away just because we'd split up. It led to an uncomfortable tension that we'd learned to defuse simply by avoiding spending time alone together.

So in the middle of that mild spring afternoon I found myself out in the garden, reading with Simon while Mrs O'Brien was busy tending to the narrow flowerbed that ran along the fence. She had a little cushion that she knelt on, and an old plastic ice cream carton that gradually filled up with the weeds she teased out of the soil with her plump fingers and a trowel. As I listened to Simon picking his way through Dr Seuss's tongue twisters, my gaze kept drifting to her broad backside, which wobbled gently as she worked.

Now Kathleen O'Brien always was one of those maddeningly intuitive women. I swear she never saw me watching her, but eventually she turned round, looked me straight in the eye and said: "You know, I wouldn't feel smug if I were you, Trevor. You're not so slim yourself these days."

Taken by surprise, I mumbled something about how I was actually thinking about taking up jogging. Which was true, insofar as I'd seen some athletics on TV a week or two earlier and thought that maybe I should do some form of exercise. I just hadn't got round to doing anything about it.

"Well, you've certainly got enough time on your hands," said Mrs O'Brien, hauling herself to her feet and wiping her hands on her apron.

She came and sat in the deckchair opposite me while Simon, sensing that I was no longer paying full attention to his reading, slipped off his seat and started racing a pair of toy cars round the edge of the lawn.

"You know, I was sorry to hear about your mother," she went on, and then paused as if in respect of her memory. "Susie tells me you're quite comfortable now?"

"Yes, that's right, thank you." I wasn't sure where this was leading.

There was another pause. Mrs O'Brien smoothed her apron down over her knees. "I know it's very sad, but this is a great chance for you, isn't it? To make a fresh start, I mean."

"Well, yes, I suppose so," I said cautiously. I wasn't about to tell her I'd become accustomed to a life that consisted mainly of drinking and sleeping – though she'd probably guessed anyway. It would take more than a quick shave and a clean shirt to fool *her*.

"You should be a teacher," she said, as if the thought had just popped into her head. "I've watched you with Simon, you're very patient."

"A junior school teacher? I don't think that's really – "

She cut me off, shaking her head. "No, no, the age of the child isn't important. A schoolteacher I mean, any kind. Now, what lessons did you enjoy most when you were at school?"

I thought for a moment. "English. That was always my best subject."

"Well then, you should be an English teacher." She folded her hands in her lap and looked me straight in the eye as if to say, there, that's settled then. And in a way it was. Because although I protested that it wasn't as easy as that, I didn't have the right exam grades, and I wasn't sure I wanted to spend all that time studying anyway, Kathleen O'Brien wasn't having any of it. As far as she was concerned I had the time, the money and the ability, so what was the problem? And over the next few days, as I thought about what she'd said, I slowly came round to her point of view. So, in the absence of any other external guidance, I let my mother-in-law determine the future course of my life. No jokes, please.

I arrived at the University of East Anglia in the autumn of 1977 to study English and Education. Why there? Well, why not? I remembered Norwich from my touring days as a pleasant city with a river, a castle and a half-decent football team, and it seemed like the sort of place where I might enjoy spending four years of my life.

Apparently, mature students often have difficulty making friends with other undergraduates. I didn't even bother trying. I didn't go out of my way to be unfriendly, but I just didn't have much in common with a bunch of eighteen-year-olds who were living away from home for the first time.

Surprisingly, the one area where we might have found common ground turned out to be the line in the sand that separated me from the younger generation. Punk rock was at its peak and all the fashion-conscious students were ripping holes in their clothes and refastening them with safety pins. I wasn't such a blues purist that I wouldn't listen to anything else, but this stuff was so far removed from my twelve-bar roots that I simply didn't get it. So although UEA attracted a lot of big-name punk and new wave bands, I stayed away, preferring to spend Saturday nights at a city-centre pub that put on blues and soul bands. But I spent most of my free time alone in my rented flat, listening to old LPs and playing my guitar.

I did think about joining a group, or even forming one of my own. I dare say a postcard stuck up on the right noticeboards ('Wanted: guitarist and drummer for blues band. Must be into Muddy, John Lee, Wolf, etc') would have lured a few fellow enthusiasts out of the woodwork. But the truth is, I felt the same way about my band as I did about my wife: The Hornets might be in the past, but that didn't mean I was ready to replace them just yet. The very fact that I was at university meant I was moving on in one sphere of my life. That would have to do for the time being.

In the end, the four years passed quickly enough. I worked hard, especially when it came to my periodic bouts of teaching practice; I indulged in a kind of low-level socialising with other people from my course, making a few friends I didn't expect to keep in touch with after graduating; I went to watch Norwich City play every now and then and developed a soft spot for them, though it wasn't the same as supporting Watford; I bought a second-hand Ford Escort and drove back to Hertfordshire once a month to see Simon; and I had a succession of girlfriends, after discovering that my policy of keeping my distance from mainstream student life had invested me with the air of a man of mystery – something attractive young women found, well, attractive. But they were always short-term relationships. Some girls were put off when they learnt that I had a young son, while others lost interest when I failed to pay them as much attention as they were used to receiving. The fact is that I wanted sex and companionship (in that order, most of the time), but I didn't want to be part of a couple.

I graduated in the summer of 1981 and landed a job at a comprehensive school in Hampstead. The first time I walked into that staff room I remember thinking: this is it, a new beginning.

But of course it wasn't really. Life doesn't work like that; elements of your old existence have a habit of intruding. I was just getting into the swing of being a schoolteacher – learning how to get the best out of my pupils, going to the pub with colleagues after work, flirting with the art mistress – when the phone rang one evening. It was Susie. The conversation went something like this:

Susie: "There's something I need you to do for me."

Me: "What's that?"

Susie: "I've met someone and I'm going to marry him. So I need to get divorced."

Me: "Oh. Well, okay, I suppose."

Susie: "I don't want this to get nasty. Shall we just call it 'irreconcilable differences' and leave it at that?"

Me: "Um, all right."

Susie: "Good, that's settled then. I'll get my solicitor to send you the papers. Are you coming over to take Simon out on Sunday?"

Me: "That's right."

Susie: "Okay, I'll see you on Sunday."

Me: "Yeah, see you."

And that was that. It was only after I'd put the phone down that I thought of all the questions I should have asked. Who was this man who was going to marry the one true love of my life? Was he a suitable person to look after my son? How did Simon feel about this? And then there was the one question I really wanted to ask, even though I already knew the answer: does this mean we're never going to get back together?

Because all this time, ever since Susie had asked me to move out, there'd been a small part of me that had assumed this was a temporary arrangement. After all, we were only separated, it wasn't like we were getting divorced or anything. One day she'd realise she really did love me, and then we'd be a family again.

Only now we *were* going to get divorced, and then it would be over for good. Well, I wanted a new beginning, didn't I? And that was what I was getting, wasn't it? So why did I feel like I'd been kicked in the crotch?

The divorce itself was painless enough, just a series of documents shuttling back and forth between two sets of lawyers. Susie didn't want much from me apart from her freedom, and all I was concerned about was getting regular access to Simon, which she was happy to give me. My solicitor said he'd never seen such an amicable settlement, and though he was smiling when he said it, I could tell he was thinking that it was a good thing too. If all divorces were like ours he'd soon be out of business.

But underneath the facade of friendliness, I wasn't taking it well. If Susie wasn't going to suffer, everyone else around me was. Especially my pupils, who got fewer jokes and more punishments for minor misdemeanours. More set books about unhappy marriages, too, whether or not they were on the syllabus – I made my sixth-formers read both 'Anna Karenina' and 'Madame Bovary', despite their protests that these weren't actually part of the canon of English literature.

I took my frustration out on women too, like the art mistress I

267

mentioned a moment ago. Lucy had a steady boyfriend when I joined the school, but over a period of several weeks I worked hard to persuade her to go out with me. Finally, in the drunken aftermath of an end-of-term party, I got her to admit that her relationship wasn't everything she wanted it to be. Once she'd conceded that much, it wasn't too difficult to persuade her to come back to my place for a 'nightcap'. She seemed to enjoy it enough at the time, but I woke in the morning to find her sitting on the edge of the bed sobbing her eyes out. The rest was predictable enough: she blamed herself for cheating on her boyfriend (who she really did love very, very much, whatever she'd said the night before), and she blamed me for leading her astray – yes, she really did use that phrase. We never went out together again, or had a civil conversation for that matter.

My next conquest was Chantal. She was an 'assistante' – a student from Toulouse who'd opted to spend a year in London helping English teenagers learn French. Since Chantal was really rather beautiful, the teenagers at my school didn't learn a lot of French from her. The boys spent all their time trying to impress her, while the girls spoke to her as little as possible and slagged her off behind her back.

I'd see Chantal sitting on her own in the staff room at lunchtime, reading 'Le Monde' and ignoring the conversations going on around her. It might have looked as though she was unsociable, but it wasn't hard to guess that she was actually lonely. So she was grateful when I started paying her a little attention, and a relationship based on the occasional friendly conversation soon expanded to include visits to the cinema, walks on Hampstead Heath and cosy evenings in Italian restaurants. Finally, one Friday night I managed to get her drunk enough on cheap red wine to persuade her to come back to my flat, and a couple of brandies later she was all but comatose as I led her into the bedroom.

This time I awoke to the sound of vomiting coming from the bathroom. Finally Chantal emerged, wrapped in my tatty cotton dressing gown and looking even paler than usual, and asked me in a tremulous voice whether we had done "zat zing" the night before. (Her English accent hadn't improved as much as it might have.) I could have lied and told her that no, she'd been drunk and I'd simply put her to bed, but I didn't see the point. So I said yes, we did have sex, and very nice it was too. Maybe I should have lied after all. It turns out she was a Catholic, and a strict one at that, and having sex before you were married was a mortal sin in her book. (I was tempted to point out that it had never bothered Susie, but this didn't seem to be the time to mention my ex-wife.) Nothing I could say was going to make this situation any better, so I stayed in bed while she hurriedly dressed and left, still crying.

Chantal wasn't in school on Monday morning and I heard that she'd phoned in sick. For a few days I worried that she was going to make a formal complaint to the headmaster, though I hadn't really done anything wrong – we were both consenting adults, after all. But when she finally reappeared, nothing happened. Like Lucy, she simply gave me the cold shoulder for the rest of the term, and when it was over she returned to France, a little older and wiser than when she arrived, though not a great deal better at speaking English with a convincing accent.

And then there was Nicki. She was one of my pupils – though before you get the wrong idea, I should point out that in sexual terms she was a lot more mature than Chantal. I knew this from the graffiti in the loos, much of which concerned Nicki's extracurricular activities. Now I know the wall of a toilet cubicle isn't exactly 'Hansard', but even if only half of what was scrawled there was true, Nicki was a very confident girl. She was attractive in an uncomplicated way, with a pretty, freckled face and large breasts that she wasn't shy about showing off. Just watching her walk down a corridor you could tell that at seventeen, she was already used to getting what she wanted.

And what she wanted, that summer term, turned out to be me. (Don't ask me why – maybe she was just bored of horny teenage boys.) I first became aware of it one morning when I found her sitting on my desk, chatting to one of her girlfriends. While the rest of the class grudgingly moved to their own desks, Nicki stayed put, so that when

I sat down I found her milky white thigh disconcertingly close at hand.

"Oh, would you like me to move, Mr Harris?" she asked, as if she'd only just noticed my presence.

"If you don't mind," I said, but I couldn't help smiling. As she slid off the desk, her skirt rucked up just enough for me to catch a glimpse of something lacy underneath.

The next day I was walking down Haverstock Hill on my way home when Nicki emerged from a shop and almost walked straight into me. This time it was her breasts, clearly visible under her artfully unbuttoned white shirt, that were suddenly unusually close. "Sorry!" she said cheerily and sauntered off up the hill without so much as looking back, doubtless confident that I'd be watching her. Which I was.

We continued in this fashion for a couple of weeks, and Nicki's flirting became more and more blatant as she realised I wasn't going to object. Because I'd decided that if she was up for it, so was I. It wasn't as if she didn't know what she was doing.

Finally she made her move. She came to find me at the end of the day and asked for extra tuition to help her prepare for the end-of-year exams. We weren't supposed to offer this service, but I was fairly sure she had something else in mind besides 'Sense And Sensibility', so I said okay and suggested she come round to my flat the following evening.

"Why wait till tomorrow?" she said with a sly grin, and I conceded that there was no reason, I just thought she might be busy today. It turned out that she did have plans, and they involved pleasuring me in ways that most seventeen-year-old girls didn't even know about, let alone practise.

Whatever other people might have thought if they'd known about us, Nicki was the seducer in this relationship, not me. She came round a couple of times a week for the best part of a month, cheerfully showing off different elements of her repertoire each time. And she was the one who decided when it was over, a decision she announced one afternoon shortly before the end of term. As she was buttoning up her shirt, she explained that she wouldn't be coming round any more. She'd started going steady with a bloke who lived down her street, and he was asking questions about where she kept going after school, and she didn't want to tell him she was shagging her English teacher in case he came over all jealous and decided to do something about it, and that was about the size of it. A couple of minutes later she was gone, and that was that.

Soon the summer holidays were under way and any risk that I might have started seducing fourth-formers was averted. No, I'm joking – nothing like that was ever on the cards. In hindsight, it's obvious what was going on here. In my relations with women I'd been reaching back into the past, towards a time when I'd been happy – and specifically, towards the magical time when I'd first started sleeping with Susie. Now that I'd screwed a seventeen-year-old, I'd achieved my aim. Mind you, I'm still not sure what it proved, or who it proved it to.

My affair with Nicki must have satisfied something inside me, anyway; I certainly didn't spend the holidays prowling the streets of north London looking for sex. No, I just mooched around – drank too much, slept in most mornings, went up to Hampstead Heath with a book if it was sunny, watched TV and listened to old records if it wasn't. I also discovered a great show on Radio One where this Irish bloke called Niall Molloy played a really interesting range of music. And one evening late that summer, while I was running a bath, I turned on the radio and heard Niall Molloy interviewing my friend Steve.

You know all about his solo career, of course – I'm sure he's given you the lowdown. But I didn't have a clue. I'd barely seen Steve over the past four years. Deliberately so: I'd wanted to cut myself off from my past life while I sorted myself out. So it was just the weirdest experience to tune in to Radio One and find this DJ talking to Steve about the blues. I didn't actually twig that it was him playing live in the studio, not at first. Not until Molloy asked him why he'd decided to cover 'Crossroads Blues', anyway. Then Steve told the story of how Des had played us that Robert Johnson album in the back room of his dad's garage, all those years ago.

I think the interview ended soon after that, but I'd stopped listening anyway. I was off in some other place entirely, and when I came to, there was an old rockabilly song crackling on the radio and I was sitting in the bath crying, the water going cold around my legs.

You know how it is when you haven't spoken to someone in a long time; I must have stood by that telephone for half an hour before I finally plucked up the courage to dial Steve's number. Talking to him was a bit odd at first, like getting back on a bike you haven't ridden for years – but you soon remember how to do it, and that's how it was with me and Steve. Before I knew it, we were arranging to meet up for a drink on Sunday night.

That was okay, too. We talked a bit about Susie (it turned out that Steve wasn't keen on his brother-in-law-to-be, which cheered me up no end) and about Simon, who Steve doted on almost as much as I did, and I told him about my job. But we mainly talked about music. We started with Steve's new solo career and the songs he was playing, and from there we just ended up talking about the blues.

I realised afterwards how much I'd missed that. I hadn't had anyone to share my enthusiasm with for a long time, though there had been a mad moment when I'd half thought Nicki was interested. One afternoon I'd emerged from the bathroom to find her kneeling on the floor, flicking through my LP collection.

"What *is* all this stuff?" she asked, looking up from the cover of a Slim Harpo album with a perplexed expression.

Now over the years I'd developed a sort of potted history of the blues to explain my passion to people who didn't know anything about it. So I began to tell her how the blues was the authentic music of black protest in the United States, and how it had moved north from the cotton fields of the Mississippi Delta to the factories of Chicago and Detroit… I hadn't got very far when she interrupted me.

"Black protest?" There was an unmistakable note of scorn in her voice. "Maybe back in the fifties or whenever, but not anymore, granddad. Don't you listen to the radio? Hip-hop, rap, that's where it's at now. No one listens to this shit any more."

So much for recruiting a new fan.

But that was what was so good about meeting up with Steve; we could take that mutual interest in the music for granted. It wasn't just about the blues, either. The great thing with old friends is that there's so much you don't have to explain, don't even have to say out loud. It's like you're locked onto a common frequency, in a way that simply doesn't happen with people you've just met. After that first reunion, Steve and I started meeting regularly for a drink or two and it became the highlight of my social life, something I looked forward to for days beforehand. I'd drive up to Watford or he'd come down to Chalk Farm, and occasionally we checked out blues bands in Camden pubs, comparing their versions of the classics with the ones we used to play.

It was around this time that I received a letter from a company called Deuce Records. In it, they explained that they'd bought the rights to all recordings previously owned by the long-defunct Natchez label, including both albums by The Hornets, which they were planning to rerelease in the spring. I soon realised that the letter was really just for my information; it didn't seem as if I had any say in whether the albums were rereleased or not, though I was assured that all previous arrangements with regard to royalties would be honoured. The main thing Deuce actually wanted from me was contact numbers for Steve and Des.

Well, I admit I probably over-reacted. Blame it on the pleasure I took from my renewed friendship with Steve and on the increased amount of time I was spending listening to, talking about and playing the blues again – but it really did seem to me that this was a sign, a sign that it was time to reform The Hornets. It was all I could do to stop myself phoning Des and Steve there and then, but I forced myself to spend some time thinking it through properly first. I went out and bought a pile of music magazines and started listening to radio stations I hadn't bothered with before, and the more I read and heard, the more I became convinced that the time was right for a reunion.

It seemed that Niall Molloy's show wasn't an isolated phenomenon. More and more people were investigating what was loosely called 'roots' music, a term that included everything from traditional English folk to Chicago blues. What's more, Deuce was just one of a number of labels dedicated to reissuing forgotten classics from the Fifties and Sixties.

I told Steve all this when I saw him a couple of days later, but I could tell he wasn't persuaded. The trouble is, I'd been so busy thinking of valid reasons for reforming the band that I'd overlooked other considerations, like the fact that Steve had a solo career now. But at least he promised to think about it

The following Monday evening a journalist called Nigel Scullion came round to do the interview for the sleevenotes, and I ended up talking to him for hours. It was almost midnight when he left, doubtless dreading the task of transcribing two C90 tapes full of me rabbiting on about the old days. A lot of memories came back that evening, more good than bad. I think it must've been the same for Steve, because Nigel Scullion was due to talk to him next, and it was on the Wednesday that Steve called and said, okay, if I wanted to organise a gig to celebrate the album reissues, he'd come along and play the drums. I called Des as soon as I'd put the phone down, and it didn't take long to persuade him to sign up as well.

I stayed up late that night working on a set list. The Hornets were back in business.

BAR TWELVE: DES, 1989

Like I said before, I spent a lot of time on my own when I was a kid. I wasn't the type to sit with my nose buried in a book, and we didn't have a telly in those days, so the radio was my best friend, up until I met Steve anyhow. I'd listen to any old crap to start with, but then I discovered Radio Luxembourg and rock'n'roll. You could only get it in the evenings, and the signal used to fade in and out, but even so – well, I mean, wow. We're talking '58, '59 here, and every other record they played was a classic. Man, I loved it. I was ten years old and rock'n'roll was like a signal from outer space.

I must've told Auntie Vi about the music I'd been listening to, 'cause one day she and Uncle Ernie turned up with a surprise for me. Ernie had been to the States on business and he'd come back with a stack of rock'n'roll records. You know what, that's still the best present I've ever had. My eyes must've been wide as saucers as I went through the pile, 'cause I remember Auntie Vi laughing as she watched me, but in a kind way. There were singles by Elvis, Chuck Berry, Little Richard, Fats Domino, Gene Vincent, Buddy Holly… It was an instant rock'n'roll collection, and I played those records till the grooves wore out.

It was Christmas that same year when Auntie Vi gave me the guitar – an acoustic, but still – which runs the records a close second in the all-time best present stakes. Dad looked at her kind of quizzically as if to ask, what did you want to buy him something like that for?, but he didn't object. I guess he reckoned anything that kept me off the streets was okay.

It did that all right. I bought a book on how to play the guitar and spent every evening practising, and hour after hour at the weekend, until my fingertips were so callused, you could've stuck a needle in there and I wouldn't've felt a thing. Be Bop A Lula was the first rock'n'roll song I tried. It was nice and slow, you see. My version was on the basic side, sure, but close enough that I knew I'd soon be able to play it properly if I just kept practising.

Now the thing is, when I first heard those great rock'n'roll records I loved them all equally, but gradually I started to differentiate between them. For starters, the slow songs didn't excite me as much as the faster ones like Great Balls Of Fire or Sweet Little Sixteen. It was the energy that turned me on, I can see that now.

There were other factors too. Like, Buddy Holly just seemed a bit too nice when you saw those pictures of him in his smart blazer and his heavy-rimmed glasses. The same with Elvis – even I could see that by the end of the Fifties he'd already lost whatever it was that had made him special. He was an entertainer, not a rocker any more. Now Little Richard, he was at the other extreme, too wild, with that huge hair and those crazy nonsense lyrics – I didn't have the foggiest what he was on about. Jerry Lee was all right, but he played the piano so I couldn't imitate him.

That left Chuck Berry. He had everything: energy, speed, rhythm, great lyrics that I wrote down by listening to the records over and over, and he played the guitar, just like me. Listening to Chuck in 1960 I wanted to *be* him, or if that wasn't possible I wanted to be American. I'm sure I wasn't the only one. It was those lyrics that did it for me, all those songs about high schools and hot rods and record hops. I spent hours puzzling over Too Much Monkey Business as if those garbled verses contained the keys to some mystery, and I learnt more about geography from three minutes of The Promised Land than I ever did at school. Then there were words and phrases that baffled and intrigued me – the coolerator in You Never Can Tell, the gunny sack in Johnny B Goode. And the cars: Cadillacs and Chevys and whatever the hell a cherry red Jidney was. God, I'm getting excited just thinking about it now. You've got to remember, America wasn't so familiar then. Hollywood films were the only clues I had to go on when it came to life in the States, and most of them were no use, Westerns and gangster movies I mean. Rock Around The Clock gave me some idea, that and a few other films, but it was Chuck's songs that filled out the picture, and if it was a limited picture – limited to cars, girls, rock'n'roll and dancing – what did I care? I was about to become a teenager, though they didn't really use that word in Britain at the time, and those were the things I was interested in.

So Chuck Berry was my hero, no question, and when it came to copying riffs off records I concentrated on his. I had an electric by now, and a little amp I'd bought by saving up the money from my paper round and other odd jobs. The great thing was, once you'd mastered one, the rest came easily enough 'cause they all followed more or less the same pattern. I didn't know or care that his songs were based on the classic twelve-bar blues progression, I just copied them the best I could. Same goes for singing; I imitated the way Chuck sang, and it didn't occur to me that I was singing with an American accent, and a black American accent at that, instead of using my natural voice. I was just pleased I sounded like my idol – well, leastways, the way he might've sounded before his voice broke. And when I sat on my bed and played Roll Over Beethoven at top volume, so that the neighbours started banging on the walls, I felt good, real good.

I'll tell you another thing too. As you might've noticed, I'm not exactly a six-footer. Even as a small kid I was unusually small, and it was soon obvious I was always going to be a shortarse. Sure, having Steve around stopped the worst of the bullying, but kids said stuff all the time, and I can't deny it used to get to me. So yeah, there was an element of, well, I'll show *them*, in the way I went about becoming a musician. It made me more single-minded, for sure.

So there I am in 1963, fourteen years old, five foot five in my socks. A skinny kid with a quiff, a pair of secondhand winklepickers and a head full of Chuck Berry riffs. Not much in the way of friends, but that doesn't bother me. What I really want now – no, what I really *need* – is a band.

I didn't have much idea what I was aiming for when I started out. I mean, I knew I wasn't going to find three guys who were mad about Chuck Berry the way I was. Apart from anything else, he'd been in prison for the past couple of years and people had forgotten about him. Everyone was listening to Merseybeat now, but that was okay 'cause those groups just nicked ideas from Chuck and the others. So when I put the word around school that I was getting a band together – well, me and Steve – I said we were going to be like The Beatles. That was enough to attract another guitarist and a guy who could just about play the bass, and we started rehearsing. We tried Rock'n'Roll Music and Twist And Shout, and I think we had a go at Please Please Me as well, but it wasn't working, and the others lost interest after a couple of sessions.

After that the line-up kept changing. Except for Steve, of course, he was always there. Just as well, 'cause we needed that room at the back of his dad's garage to rehearse in. But rhythm guitarists and bassists came and went, kids who wanted to be Lennon or McCartney but turned out to have sod-all talent. That was okay so long as they were enthusiastic and ready to learn. Trouble is, people got intimidated. I mean, there's me ripping into Johnny B Goode while they're still struggling to get through a basic chord transition at medium tempo – you can see why they'd be discouraged. But the thing is, I knew where I was going, and if anyone else wanted to come along for the ride they had to be able to keep up.

Finally we settled on a regular bassist, a chubby guy with a Beatles bowl cut who Steve used to call Porky Pete. Pete Gallimore, that's right. I didn't much like him. He was always clowning around, telling stupid jokes, dirty ones that sounded odd coming from the mouth of this boy who looked like butter wouldn't melt. But he could hold down a bassline well enough, so we stuck with him. He joined just in time for our first gig, a two-song set in the school canteen on the last day of term. We played Rock'n'Roll Music and Twist And Shout and we called ourselves The Rolling Beethovens – which is a shit name, obviously, but I was proud of it at the time.

Meanwhile I was still listening to Radio Luxembourg, and I bought at least one single every Saturday morning from an electrical shop on St Albans Road. They had a little box of records on a shelf at the back, behind the cookers and the washing machines. But I wanted to see live music as well, so I used to go up to town on a Friday or Saturday night.

Just me on my own, on the tube, then hitching back to Watford – or as near as possible – if it was late when the gig finished. The Marquee was my favourite venue, they got all the best bands. I didn't always get in, mind you, 'cause of my size. Eventually I got to know one of the doormen, Big Dave – he was a Chuck Berry fan, so I was okay if he was there, but otherwise it could be a bit iffy. And even if I did get in, I couldn't afford to drink anything stronger than Coke, which was a drag. But the music was worth all the hassle, yeah, definitely.

There was always something I could learn, too. It wasn't just about the way the guitarist played a solo. I wanted to see how the singer worked an audience, watch the way the band segued from one number into the next, study how they structured a set and which songs they chose to cover. If I'd spent as much time and energy on my schoolwork as I did analysing bands at The Marquee, I'd've got better marks than Trevor.

Then I saw The Yardbirds and everything came into focus. Sure, I'd seen plenty of groups playing Chicago-style blues before, but most of them did it like it was an afterthought. They'd play a Muddy Waters song, but it'd be sandwiched between a Little Richard number and something by Ray Charles, as if they thought that all American music was the same. 'Course, there were bands out there playing nothing but the blues, but I steered clear of them. I still thought of myself as a rock'n'roller.

The Yardbirds changed all that. December 1963 it was, and I'd gone all the way down to the Station Hotel in Richmond, where they had a residency at the Crawdaddy Club. The Legendary Crawdaddy Club they always call it in books, but that's bull. Back then you could've stopped a hundred people in the street and ninety-nine would never have heard of the place. The hundredth would've been me. I wouldn't normally have made that much effort to see a blues band, but Big Dave kept telling me I should, he said they always played a couple of Chuck Berry songs and they'd recently got this shit-hot guitarist who was worth the price of admission on his own, whatever he was playing.

Big Dave wasn't kidding. The band came on, five of them in

matching grey suits, and before I knew it they were tearing into the fastest version of Too Much Monkey Business I'd ever heard. From that moment I was blown away. I loved Keith Relf's singing, that husky voice he had – and the fact that he was on the short side didn't go unnoticed either – but it was the guitarist who really caught my eye. Eric Clapton. Slowhand. God. Tall, dark and handsome, fingers flashing across the strings. There was one solo he played, on Smokestack Lightning, that nearly reduced to me to tears – I even forgot to study his chord shapes. And when they'd finished, with a Bo Diddley song that went on and on as if they couldn't bear to leave the stage, I was numb with emotion.

On the journey home I decided what I was going to do; I was going to have my own blues band. From that night on I ate, slept and dreamt the blues. I bought every record I could get my hands on, went to see The Yardbirds whenever I could, taught Steve and Pete the principles of the twelve-bar blues and copied Eric's solos till my fingers were ready to bleed. But deep down I knew we weren't a proper blues band yet. We were just three teenagers practising in the back of a garage.

Then Trevor came along. Well, all right, first time round he didn't make a lot of difference. Now I come to think of it, I never did apologise for the way I stitched him up at that stupid grammar school dance. It wasn't his fault no one in the audience recognised my genius when they saw it – and I'm prepared to admit that maybe there's a slight possibility I wasn't *quite* as good as I thought I was. But I had all sorts of chips on my shoulder, and when things went wrong I suddenly decided to take it out on him. Poor sod, he looked like he was going to cry.

Still, he got over it. Must've done, or he wouldn't have suggested giving the band a second chance. Yeah, he was the one who made the difference, I will say that much. Without Trev, The Hornets would never have got off the ground.

I tried to tell that Nigel guy all this, but I obviously didn't explain it properly 'cause it doesn't come across in the sleevenotes. Don't get me wrong, he's had a good stab at it and the facts are all there. It's the *feeling* that's missing. I'm talking about that feeling of being young and knowing you're about to conquer the world, knowing with an absolute certainty that it's there for the taking. Trouble is, he approached it as a historian. To him The Hornets were just one of dozens of British r'n'b groups knocking around in the mid-Sixties. But to me – well, it was my life, wasn't it?

So, was it a success? That's the question I kept asking myself after the albums were reissued. I mean, I'm 35 years old and suddenly it feels like I'm all washed up: a former musician, a former alcoholic for God's sake, barely making ends meet. Hardly a successful outcome for someone who was going to be the next Eric Clapton, is it?

But then I'd look at those two LPs and I'd think, I made these, and people bought them. People who liked music, people who could've spent their money on any album in the shop, a Beatles LP maybe, or if they were into the blues, an original by Muddy Waters or Howlin' Wolf, picked a Hornets record out of the racks, took it to the counter and handed over one and six or whatever it was, carried it home and listened to it. No one forced them to do that. Okay, so maybe there weren't as many of them as there could've been, certainly not enough to make us rich or famous, but does that matter? It's like playing a gig; you might not get mobbed at the end, but even if only a section of the crowd are clapping and cheering and shouting encore, you've succeeded. Even if it's only temporary, you've touched something inside of them, and that's success in my book.

Then again, I'd take one of the albums out of its sleeve and put it on the turntable, and suddenly success was the last word that sprang to mind. Blame the producers, blame the quality of our musicianship – Christ, you can blame me for most of the lousy ideas that made it onto vinyl. The truth is, we might've been a shit-hot live band when we were on song, but we didn't do ourselves justice in the studio.

Stinging The Blues isn't bad, I suppose, for a first attempt. There's a youthful energy that comes across, a feeling that we were grabbing our chance with both hands. But the choice of covers is clichéd, the originals are feeble and the playing's okay at best. As for Buzzin' With The Hornets, it's just a mess. What the hell was I thinking? Oh sure, there are lots of ideas in there. Trouble is, most of them are other people's. That was our downfall, in the end. We were so enthusiastic about our influences, we never broke free from them. My fault mainly, I can see that now. While other bands ditched most of their covers after a year or two, we kept on playing them. Sure we wrote a couple of things, but it was just messing around. We should've taken it more seriously, locked ourselves in a room until we'd written a few decent songs of our own. Without that The Hornets were just a covers band.

So ask me again – was it a success? Even now, my answer will depend on how I'm feeling at the time.

I was never all that bothered about girls when I was a teenager. No, straight up. I know a lot of guys only learned an instrument to impress the birds – and I don't think Trev would've been quite so keen to join my band if he hadn't met Susie – but it wasn't like that with me. The music was the be-all and end-all. Then we started having a bit of success, just locally, and all these girls started coming on to me and I didn't know what to do. I suppose I was shy. Sounds crazy, doesn't it? How can someone who stands up on a stage every night, singing and playing the guitar in front of crowds of strangers, call themselves shy? But I guess there are different kinds of shyness. There are millions of people who'd shit their pants at the thought of performing in public, but they're confident enough in private. Whereas for me, performing was what I was meant to do, so it never occurred to me to be nervous. Anyhow, it wasn't really me those audiences saw up there on the stage, just a persona: Des Armstrong, blues guitarist extraordinaire, the character I'd settled on to take me to the top.

But that wasn't the same Des Armstrong who'd be sitting backstage after a gig when girls would come along and say they wanted to meet the band. Some of them did just want to chat, and maybe share a drink and a fag, but there were others who were bolder – they weren't going to leave until they'd made some sort of intimate contact, if you get my drift. To be honest, I couldn't see what was in it for them, but I never tried to stop them. I had my first proper shag in the back of the van outside a pub where we'd just played. I didn't have to do much, she sat on top and did all the work. I never saw her again, never even knew her name.

Until the booze kicked in big-time, I got more sex than the average single bloke, I reckon. But only sex. Nothing more. I had no idea how to take the lead with girls, you see, so even if I did meet someone I fancied – 'cause I still had urges like anyone else – I wouldn't do anything about it. If she didn't come on to me, that was the last I ever saw of her. I did try a few times, but the thing about being shy is that somehow the words in your head won't come out of your mouth. It's as if there's something swallowing them before they turn into sounds. Even simple things, like asking a woman for her phone number, turned out to be impossible. After a while I stopped trying.

And that's the way it stayed, even after I quit drinking. Trouble is, without the booze I discovered loneliness – proper, gut-wrenching, I-think-I'm-going-to-slit-my-wrists loneliness – for the first time, and it was worse 'cause I didn't know what to do. The best I could manage was to keep busy, with work and music and books. I guess I thought it was always going to be like this, so I might as well get used to it.

Then I got the letter. It wasn't the first fan letter I'd had, not by a long chalk. At our peak we all used to get fan mail, though after the first few batches we barely bothered to look at it. A lot was from girls putting down in writing, and in frighteningly precise detail, exactly what they intended to do to us if we'd give them the chance. Then there were the boys who wanted to know how to be in a hit group, like there was some simple formula. Some wanted to roadie for us, or even join the band – fat chance. Some just wanted me to tell them how I played the solo on It Hurts Me Too, note by note. For a while the letters piled up in the Natchez office, then the pile got smaller and smaller until we stopped getting mail altogether – another sign that we'd passed our sell-by date. Like all the others, we failed to see it.

The letter I got in 1984 had been sent to Deuce, and they'd forwarded it on to me. It was written in small, neat handwriting on smart paper – cream with a deckle edge – and it went like this:

Dear Des,

I hope you don't mind me being so informal, but I feel as if I know you personally, even though we've never met. I've certainly seen you often enough, and you've probably seen me, though you won't recognise my name. Back in the Sixties I was a Hornets fan, one of those girls in black who used to stand in front of the stage when you played at King's Langley Youth Club. We'd shout out the titles of our favourite songs, hoping that you'd play them. We hoped that you'd notice us, too, and although I was far too timid to do anything about it, I did have a serious crush on you. There, I've said it!

I bought both your albums and played them over and over again. So when I was in a record shop the other day, looking for a new Muddy Waters compilation I'd read about, and I saw that The Hornets' LPs had been reissued, I just had to buy them. I took them home and played them straight away, one after the other, and the music took me back to the days when I was an awkward teenager, a bit tomboyish and not at all sure what I wanted out of life – the days when the opportunity to lose myself in music on a Friday night was the highlight of my week.

I apologise for rambling on about myself. The thing is, I got the impression from the sleevenotes that things haven't gone so well for you in recent years. So I wanted to write and let you know how important your band and your music were to at least one confused teenager, back in the days when it sometimes seemed that if you didn't know exactly where you were going, you were in danger of getting left behind. Does that make any sense?

Well, that's all I wanted to say. I hope this finds you well and happy.

Best wishes
Gillian Lewis

I must've read that letter four or five times, sitting at the kitchen table as the light faded outside. Then I set about composing a reply. It took me the rest of the evening and most of a pad of writing paper before I had something I was happy with. In the end I decided that since this Gillian had been so open with me, I should do the same. So I told her about my dad dying and me giving up the booze, and a little about my job in the record shop, and what Steve and Trevor were up to, and of course I thanked her for her letter and told her how much it meant to me that she'd written it. And finally I said that if she wanted to relive her youth – and was prepared to risk being disappointed – she should come along to our reunion gig the following week.

A couple of days later I got a second letter from Gillian, and this time she told me more about herself. The best bit was where she said that although she couldn't really claim to have had a hard life, no harder than average anyway, she'd always related to the blues and found it a comfort in hard times. Oh, and she said she'd definitely be coming to the concert, and she was sure she wouldn't be disappointed.

By this time I was feeling something stirring inside, the kind of excitement I hadn't felt for a long, long time. So I wrote Gillian a note asking if she'd like to meet me before the gig, and then went out to post it before I had time for second thoughts.

I knew it was her as soon as she pushed open the door of the coffee shop. Well, the way I was feeling, I wasn't going to risk going near any place they sold alcohol. As it is, I was on my third cup by the time Gillian arrived. She cracked a big smile when she saw me, and I noticed the corners of her eyes crinkled up when she smiled. That appealed to me for some reason, and I felt a shiver of anticipation. As she walked over to my table I gave her the once-over. She was petite, maybe an inch or two smaller than me – that was a relief, I'd been worried she might be taller – and she was wearing a black polo neck and tight blue jeans. She wasn't exactly beautiful, I decided as I tried to look her up and down without being too obvious, but there was definitely something attractive about her face.

I stood up and held out my hand, trying to stop it shaking. Too much coffee. Hi, I'm Des Armstrong, I said.

I know, said Gillian, smiling that crinkly smile again, I'd have recognised you anywhere. You haven't changed that much since the last time I saw you play. Brunel University, September 1970, she went on before I could ask. It was the night before I went off to college myself, and I couldn't think of a better way to spend it than watching The Hornets with a bunch of really good mates.

Then she looked at me and laughed. You're blushing, she said.

There was an awkward pause until the waitress rescued us by coming to take Gillian's order. When she'd gone I said, You're very, what's the word, open, I suppose. Even in your first letter.

I know, people are always telling me that – I've got a bit of a reputation at work. The thing is, I realised a few years ago that if you're thinking something, you might as well go ahead and say it out loud. Well, most of the time at any rate.

It goes back to my marriage, you see. Back then I didn't say what I thought, not at all. My husband, Mike, he was a heavy drinker. He used to roll in late every night stinking of beer, and I never said anything. Not a word. I just acted as if nothing was wrong. I was miserable as sin, but I didn't know what to do about it. Finally I plucked up my courage, sat him down and told him he either had to stop drinking or I was going to leave him. And it felt so good to say those words. It was really liberating.

She paused, so I asked, What happened? Did he stop?

I think he was so shocked that he actually did try for a while. He couldn't stick with it though, so I did what I'd said I'd do – packed my bags and went back home to my parents. Last I heard he was living with someone else, still drinking every night. He won't change.

All the time she was telling this story she'd been fiddling with a bag of sugar. Now she looked up, looked me straight in the eye.

That's one reason I wrote to you, you know, she said. I read that you were a reformed alcoholic – you don't mind me using that word, do you? – and I thought, I know how hard that must be, having watched

Mike and everything. And I suppose I was curious about you, and I decided I wanted to meet you.

So you were relying on me answering your letter, then?

Oh, absolutely, she laughed. And if you hadn't suggested that we meet, I certainly would have done, don't you worry.

I didn't know what to say. It didn't matter though, 'cause Gillian was happy to lead the conversation, and soon we were chatting away like old friends. By the time we'd finished I'd completely forgotten my nerves – well, my nerves about meeting her, anyhow. I was sorry when I had to leave for the soundcheck.

Sure enough, Gillian was right down the front that evening, and seeing her there helped me through. 'Cause it was tough, real tough for me. It was the first time I'd played with The Hornets since joining AA, and I realised how much I used to take a pre-gig drink or two for granted. Backstage beforehand I was in pieces, wondering if this was going to work. We all were. Sure, we'd been rehearsing, but playing in front of an audience was something else altogether. Only Steve seemed at all relaxed. Ever since we'd talked about doing this he'd given off this vibe as if he was doing us a favour by taking part, you know? Truth is, he probably was. He didn't need it as much as me and Trev did.

It went okay, that's the main thing. Not our best gig ever, but far from the worst. We played a lot of the old favourites, and what with the average age of the audience being nearer forty than twenty, they went down well. Near the end I took a big risk by leaving the set list we'd planned and dedicating I Just Want To Make Love To You to my new friend – honest, that's what I said. I knew Trev and Steve could cope, it was a song we used to play a lot in the old days, but I was more worried about Gillian. I was rewarded with another of those smiles, though, and at that moment I knew I'd found what had been missing from my life.

I could fill a whole book telling you about Gillian and what she means to me, but you'd think I was a soppy old git. Just so's you know, we've got a kid now, a little girl we named Etta, after Etta James obviously. If it was a boy it was going to be Elmore, and Gill's pregnant again now, so that may still happen. Or he may be a John Lee, I'm quite keen on that. No, we're not married – Gill decided she didn't want to risk it again. I don't care, I'm happy with her and that's the only thing that matters. The rest is all just forms and stuff.

There's plenty more I'm going to gloss over, mainly about the band and how we picked up again where we'd left off. We're still together, the three of us. We do fifty or sixty gigs a year these days, that's at least one most weekends. So if you find yourself in a pub in Camden on a Friday night and three middle-aged guys come out and start playing I'm Your Hoochie Coochie Man, the odds are it's us. A big guy on drums, muscular-looking, barely breaking sweat, a look of concentration on his face; a paunchy bloke with fair hair on bass and harp; and a shortarse up front, singing and playing guitar, wearing a Hawaiian shirt or a snazzy waistcoat, his receding hair tied back in a ponytail. Ladeez and gennelmen, I give you The Hornets.

Our other big market is student unions. If your son or daughter is at university, there's a fair chance they'll get their first taste of the blues from The Hornets. So if they come home in the holidays raving about Muddy Waters, blame us. We can take it. Not that we're on a mission to convert the world to the blues or anything like that. We don't expect to become famous or make bestselling records either, not any more. We set our sights much lower these days – or much higher, maybe. We just want to make people happy. If they go home from one of our gigs feeling the joy and the power in the music, the way we feel it, then we've done our job.

So I'm not going to go into a lot of detail about the last few years. We're all well into our forties and I think we've settled down into our personalities, accepted ourselves for what we are. Well you do, don't you? You have to or you're in trouble. We're not going to change much now, I reckon. 'Course, I could be wrong. I often am.

But I do just want to tell you one more story, a story that kind of sums the whole thing up.

It's April 1989, nearly five years since we got back together to celebrate our albums being rereleased. Now they're coming out again, on CD no less. But this isn't a straight reissue. Oh no. This time we're getting the deluxe treatment, a three-CD set in a special box. The first disc contains both the original LPs, which have been remastered; the second has the album we recorded in Hamburg with Little Sonny, plus a few B sides and outtakes; and the third is a recording of our live set from the Blueskeller, one we never even knew about. Charlie must've organised it, I guess. I've heard the rough mixes and it sounds pretty good. Then there's a booklet full of old photos, details of the recording sessions, interviews with the three of us and other people who were involved, and even – get this – an essay by a journalist who writes for a specialist blues magazine. Who'd've believed it, eh?

So we've decided to celebrate with a party for friends and family and supporters. Everyone gets a copy of the box set, some food and drink and a bit of live music. Not a bad way to spend a Saturday night.

We spent ages trying to decide on a venue. We talked about all sorts of pubs and clubs, but finally we decided to go back to our roots and hired St Peter's Church Hall. Yeah, that's right, where Trevor and Susie had their wedding reception. Trev wasn't too keen at first, but he came round. He told me the other day that he'd thought about it and realised that his wedding was still one of the happiest days of his life, even if it did all go pear-shaped later.

I'm the first to arrive and the caretaker has to open up for me. Steve's already been in to set up, so the instruments and mics are all in place. There's a row of trestle tables down the right-hand side of the hall too, ready for the refreshments. Birgit's in charge of that, she's got caterers coming. I don't really need to be here this early, but Ian, the guy from Deuce, is supposed to be delivering the CDs at six o'clock – the very first batch, straight from the factory – and I'm impatient to see them. To pass the time I go up on stage and double-check the equipment, then plug in my guitar and start jamming on the blues, the way I always have done when I've nothing better to do. I must've got lost in the music, 'cause next thing I know there's a burst of laughter from the back of the hall and I open my eyes to see Steve and Simon standing by the door, pissing themselves. I suppose I must've been doing what Gill calls my blues face – eyes closed, face scrunched up like I'm in pain. It's something I copied from Clapton, way back when, but I do it naturally now. I guess Steve doesn't get to see it too often.

The pair of them have been to Vicarage Road, of course. They never miss a home game. Steve's been taking Simon for years, and now the kid's a bigger fan than he is, if that's possible. Simon's coming up to his A levels, and Susie says he was reluctant to apply for university 'cause he didn't want to risk missing Watford games. Eventually she persuaded him though, and he'll be off to Warwick in the autumn. She's happy enough – she reckons if he comes back down for the football, it means she'll get to see him once a fortnight or so.

How'd they get on? I ask, unplugging the guitar and putting it back on its stand.

We won two-one, says Steve, hanging his coat on a hook by the door.

So what d'you reckon Si, are you going to get promoted?

We're still in with a chance, but if not we should make the play-offs, says Simon earnestly. He's quite a serious boy, I've noticed. Always thinks before expressing an opinion, works hard at school, never gets into trouble. I reckon it's something to do with his parents being divorced. I read a book once about the effects of divorce on the kids, though I'm buggered if I can remember the details. I don't know anything about these play-offs, either – they didn't have them when I used to go to games – but I'm not about to get into a long conversation about football with Simon right now. I've made that mistake before.

So instead I ask him how he's getting on with the guitar I gave him for his birthday last month. He's been playing for a while now. Trev taught him, actually – it was something for them to do on the days they got to spend together, once Si was too old to be taken to museums and stuff like that. To tell the truth, he's pretty sharp. Not instinctive or inspired, but solid. I guess he takes music as seriously as he does everything else. So I get him up on the stage, hand him my guitar, plug in the bass and play a basic twelve-bar pattern while he runs through the changes. After a while we have a go at Bright Lights, Big City, and when we finish I look up to find Trev standing there in front of the stage, smiling at us but with a strange look in his eyes. I think I know what he's feeling. My daughter's a lot younger than his son, but I'm a parent too. It's something to do with circularity, the past and present coming together for a moment, so that you look at your kid and see yourself. It's spooky shit, I'm telling you.

Anyhow, Simon leaves off playing and we all say our hellos, and that's when I spot that Trev is wearing his band jacket, the one with the cartoon Hornet on the back. It's a bit tight on him now, mind you. I don't think he could do it up if he wanted to. I exchange glances with Steve, and from the way he grimaces I know he's noticed as well. Thing is, Steve got pissed one night a couple of years ago and told me the story; how he'd found out that Trev was cheating on Susie, and while he was trying to work out what to do about it he told Frankie, and a few days later Trev's girlfriend got the shit kicked out of her in a pub car park by a gang of Frankie's psycho mates. He'd lent her his jacket, you see – yeah, *that* jacket – and in the darkness they thought she was him. I find myself wondering if the bloodstains still show, but I'm not about to look too close.

'Course, Trev doesn't know the truth, and he never will if me and Steve have anything to do with it. Though you'd think he might've worked it out by now – same as you'd expect him to have listened to the first LP and noticed how professional the bass playing sounded, much better than he was capable of. I know what you're thinking, by the way, but don't worry – the booklet that comes with the box set lists him as the bassist. With a bit of luck he'll never know any different.

But that's the thing about Trev; he's a clever bloke – good at passing exams and stuff – but he's not actually that bright, if you know what I mean. Doesn't see what's going on around him, or if he does see it he doesn't understand it. Personally, I reckon part of the problem is that he's always let his dick do too much of the thinking for him.

Still he's not doing too badly, all told. He's Head of English now at that school and from what I hear, he's popular with the kids. He's even persuaded some of his sixth-formers to come along and watch us a couple of times. But he's still single and it gets him down sometimes, you can tell. Shit, I know what that kind of loneliness is like. Sure, he's had a few girlfriends, but none of them ever looked like becoming permanent. The way I see it, he's looking for another Susie, or at any rate someone he feels about the way he felt about Susie in the beginning. Good luck to him, I say. He's going to need it.

Birgit's the next to arrive, and the five of us – Trev and Simon, Steve, Birgit and me – are sitting around a table, nattering away, when Ian finally arrives lugging a heavy cardboard box. While he's cutting through the packing tape, Steve gets out a bottle of champagne he's brought along specially and pours four plastic cups-full. I have to make do with water from the tap in the gent's, but I'm not bothered. The main thing is seeing the CDs, and once Ian's got the box open we all cluster round him impatiently, like kids waiting for gifts from Santa.

The picture on the front is from the time when we were recording our first LP – I remember the photographer coming into the studio and shooting off a few reels while we were on a break. One of the pictures he took was going to be used on the back cover of the original album, until Charlie changed his mind and went for something moodier. This one is a black and white shot of the three of us mucking around; Steve's pretending to stab Trev with a drumstick while I try and hold him back.

The one on the cover of the box set is different, we look more relaxed. I'm standing in the middle with my guitar still strapped on, holding a coffee mug in one hand while I talk to Trev, who's on the left of the picture. It may have been coffee in the mug, but I'm willing to bet there was a slug of brandy in there too. Maybe I'd just told a joke or something, 'cause Trev is laughing, looking as youthful and happy as I've ever seen him. Meanwhile, on the right of the picture, Steve is sitting behind his kit, smoking a fag and watching the two of us. It's hard to read his expression, but then it always was.

Meanwhile Trev has put one of the discs into the CD player at the side of the stage, which is connected to the PA. It starts with a few seconds of crowd noise and I realise he's picked the live CD, just like I would've. That's the one we really want to hear. There's an announcement in German, then you hear me saying, Good evening, we're The Hornets, from England, and this is our theme tune. And then we're off, playing a lazy, loping rhythm. I'm thrown for a minute, but then the vocals start and I remember that we always used to kick off our set at the Blueskeller with I'm A King Bee, only with the first line changed to say I'm a hornet. It didn't make much sense 'cause we didn't bother rewriting the rest of the song, and it's full of references to hives and honey. We only played it while we were in Hamburg, and now it's been immortalised on CD. Weird.

While we're listening to the music the caterers arrive, and Birgit goes to help them unpack and show them how she wants everything laid out. The others have moved away from the table too. Trev's poring over the booklet that comes with the box set, while Simon and Ian are asking Steve questions about the music that fills the room. But I'm still sitting there in the midst of the caterers' bustle with my eyes closed, listening closely to every note, every line, imagining myself playing those songs in a shitty little club in Hamburg, twenty years old and at my peak – a bloody good guitarist, if I say so myself.

The climax of the set is our version of First Time I Met The Blues. I was listening to Buddy Guy's original cut just the other day, and my first thought now is that I never really put across the desperation in the lyrics. In case you don't know the song, it's about a man who's out in the woods, being hunted by something he calls the blues, and you can tell from the pitch of his voice, high and shaky, that he's scared witless. It catches up with him in the last verse and he greets it like a real live person: Good morning Mr Blues, what're you doing here so soon? You can tell Buddy's not pleased to see him.

Like I say, I never quite got the voice right, but I reckon I made up

293

for it in other ways. The original recording was released as a single: three verses, three bursts of Buddy's stinging guitar and it was over. We used to string it out with a solo after the second verse, and that was when I really went to town. Something about that song brought out the best in me and some nights I'd just go on and on, lost in the music, letting the feeling flow through my fingers and out onto the strings. We had this arrangement that when you were coming towards the end of a solo you stamped your foot twice and the others knew to be ready to kick into the next section of the song. Steve told me once that when I was playing that solo he used to get so mesmerised, staring at my feet and waiting for the cue, that he almost forgot to play the drums. I swear that song often lasted fifteen minutes.

The version on the live CD isn't quite that long but it's a good one all the same, and my solo is spot on. I picture myself with my blues face on, eyes shut, head thrown back, one leg slightly in front of the other so as to raise the fretboard to the level I like it at. When the song ends I open my eyes and find I'm crying. Thankfully no one's seen me, so I nip out the back of the hall and take a walk round the block to pull myself together.

When I get back the guests have started to arrive, and soon the party's in full swing. So many familiar faces, including some I haven't seen in years. Like Frankie O'Brien for instance. He hasn't been inside for a while but from what I hear, that doesn't necessarily mean he's a reformed character. Maybe he's just a bit more careful these days, if you know what I'm saying. His parents are here too, of course – they wouldn't miss this for anything, even though Francis has to walk with a stick these days on account of his hip, and Kathleen says her cateract has made her half blind. Watching her smiling face as she talks to Simon, the thought pops into my head that she's the nearest thing I've had to a mother all these years. It's all I can do to resist the temptation to go over this minute and tell her so and give her a big hug, but I don't want to interrupt her conversation with her grandson. I'll do it later.

There are some people I don't even recognise at first. Well, we tried to track down everyone who'd played a part in shaping the band, even if none of us had seen them for years. So when this fat, balding guy in baggy chinos and a Gap sweatshirt walks up to me and pumps my hand, I'm struggling. Seeing that, he grins this huge grin and suddenly I'm there: Porky Pete Gallimore, in the flesh and porkier than ever. He's a financial adviser now, lives in Berkhamsted with his wife and three kids. Does he still play music? Nah, he gave that up years ago, barely even listens to the stuff, apart from the odd Tina Turner LP, maybe a bit of Phil Collins. I say nothing and pass him on to Steve first chance I get.

Another of our old bassists is here too: Keith Fisher. Looking pretty smart as it happens, in a fashionably tatty leather jacket. I'm not so sure about the ponytail though. He tells me he made enough from Satyricon to buy into a recording studio, and now he owns it outright and produces all kinds of stuff. Any blues? No, there aren't many record companies prepared to throw money at blues bands these days.

We get talking about our old record company and Keith tells me that after he decided not to sign with them, he wondered whether he'd blown his only chance to make a record. Whatever happened to Natchez, anyhow? he says, so I tell him we asked the same question, and a researcher at Deuce uncovered a sad story. It seems that after Little Sonny had been deported from Hamburg, Charlie went back over to the States in search of more undiscovered bluesmen. He travelled to Chicago and then on to Memphis, and that was where he was found one night, lying dead in an alley with a knife wound in his chest. The cops said he'd probably been mugged, but who knows? Charlie had a liking for wine, women and song, and I wouldn't put it past him to drink too much wine and come on to the wrong woman. A dangerous thing to do in a black part of town when you're a white man with a funny accent. Poor Charlie.

As the evening wears on and the drink flows, I have that strange sensation of power I've often experienced since I gave up the booze: a feeling of being the only person in control in a room full of people who are out of it. I wander round the hall with a glass of orange juice in my hand, listening to conversations, occasionally joining in. I spend a while with Steve and Ian, who's enthusing about a new collection of obscure Delta blues singles Deuce is releasing. Apparently someone came across a stack of 78rpm records in the basement of an old plantation house in Mississippi, and we argue about whether whoever stored them there thought they were special, or just junk, and whether it matters. Then I move on to Trevor and Susie. They seem to get on well enough these days – especially when Susie's husband isn't around. They're talking about Simon going to university, but then they get on to reminiscing about what he was like as a baby and I decide to leave them to it. Keith has just found out that Birgit works for EMI – she's a big shot these days – and he's cosying up to her, probably hoping she'll be a useful contact for his studio. Simon is chatting with Jimmy Barrett, that guitarist Steve discovered, and I move closer in the hope that they might want to benefit from my expertise. Turns out Jimmy's giving Si tips on student life and how to have a good time on a grant, so I move on without stopping, over to where Porky Pete is showing pics of his equally porky kids to Kathleen O'Brien, who's squinting at them through her glasses. I figure she might need rescuing, so I sit down beside her and when Pete's finished with the family snaps I start chatting to her about the old days.

Tell me something Kathleen, I say after a while. What did you think about our band? When we first started rehearsing, I mean. Did you think, wow, my son and his friends are going to be big stars?

She doesn't laugh like I thought she might, but considers the question seriously for a moment. No Des, to be honest I never thought that. But then, what did I know about music? She pauses for a moment. I just thought it was nice that Stevie had a hobby, and friends like you who cared about him. That was what was important to Francis and me.

So now I finally say what I was going to say earlier, about her being like a mother to me, and we hug and then I move off quickly before

I start crying again. It's that sort of evening. But I need to get myself composed 'cause it's almost showtime.

At around ten o'clock, Ian gets up on the stage and introduces himself. He says a few words about how proud Deuce are to have produced this box set and how they hope it'll restore us to our rightful place in the history of British blues. Then he announces me and I get up beside him and shake his hand before taking the mic out of its stand.

I've been thinking about my speech for days and I've written out version after version, none of them quite right. I have the last one in my back pocket, but in the course of the evening I've decided I don't need a script. I know what to say now.

Ladies and gentlemen, I start off, thank you all for coming here tonight, and thank you Ian for your kind words. I'm not sure about our place in the history of British blues, though. To be honest, I reckon The Hornets probably weren't much more than a footnote, not when you look at what other bands did. I mean, I know original copies of our albums fetch a good price these days – I should do, I own a second-hand record shop after all. And I can tell you that a lot of the records that sell well to collectors are crap. Anyone who's ever listened to the stuff David Bowie released in the Sixties will know what I'm talking about.

I wait for the laughter to die down before going on. I think what I'm trying to get at, I say, is that it doesn't really matter whether or not The Hornets' music is important in the greater scheme of things – sorry, Ian. What matters is that the music on these CDs is our lives, mine and Steve's and Trevor's and Susie's, and a few other people's as well. These shiny little discs contain the – oh, I don't know – the essence of ourselves, I suppose, when we were younger and keener and a hell of a lot more innocent than we are now. And I'm very grateful to Deuce Records for the chance to relive those years, so please raise your glasses and let's drink a toast to Deuce.

When that's done, and before people can start talking, I pick up the mic again. You're probably getting sick of the sound of my voice by now, but there's just one more thing I want to say. When we started playing music, we didn't have a clue what the blues was. Not a fucking clue.

Shit, I didn't mean to swear. I press on quickly.

I mean, of course we knew all about twelve-bar patterns and bending notes and the history of the blues, but we didn't know the thing itself. Maybe young people shouldn't even be *allowed* to play the blues, you know? Maybe they should be made to wait till they've lived a bit.

Well, we've lived a fair bit now, me and Steve and Trevor, and I reckon we know what the blues is, and the good thing is that we've come through it all, come through it stronger than we were before. I think we're playing better than ever before, too. We may not be making new albums or storming up the charts, but we know what we're talking about now, and we're going to give you a demonstration in a minute or two.

But before that I'd like to propose another toast, a toast to someone who isn't here to celebrate with us tonight, someone who didn't make it through at all. And the ironic thing is, it wasn't even his fault.

I'm choking up now, but I just about manage to get to the punchline.

So please will you drink to the memory of Jacko Hawkins, the best bloody roadie in the world.

The tears are stinging my eyes and I can tell the others are feeling the same way. The O'Briens are looking upset too, so I quickly beckon to Steve. He fetches a stool from the side of the stage, picks up his acoustic guitar and launches into Crossroads Blues, a stark, almost scary version: our tribute to Jacko. Everyone stands and watches in silence, and there's no movement except for Steve's fingers flickering across the strings.

When he's finished, Trev and I join him on the stage and launch into I'm Your Hoochie Coochie Man, and from then on it's a blast, two hours of good-time Chicago r'n'b, 'cause the best way to respond to death and disaster is to celebrate life, and that's what playing the blues is all about when it comes down to it. Defiance, that's the word

I'm looking for.

So we play all the old favourites, and after a while we manage to persuade Susie to get up there. She claims she hasn't even played the piano in years, but she picks it up again soon enough and we rattle through Mannish Boy and a few more besides. There are other guest appearances too, from Jimmy Barrett and Keith and even Simon, though they have to take it in turns 'cause we haven't got room for everyone on the stage, or enough guitars for everyone to play. But the funny thing is, the more people that join in, the more that feeling of defiance grows, like we're flicking a V sign to everything bad in the world. We may be playing in a church hall, but I reckon this music is a greater force for good than any hymn that's ever been sung here.

Mind you, at one point near the end of the evening things do get almost religious with a version of Got My Mojo Working that blows away pretty much anything we've ever played before. Steve's on drums, I'm on lead guitar and Trev's on harp, plus we've got Jimmy on acoustic rhythm guitar, Susie on piano, and Simon standing beside her with a tambourine, and the six of us rip into the song like there's no tomorrow. For the first couple of verses it's just the rest of the band that sings the response: I sing, I've got my mojo working, and they sing, Got my mojo working! straight back at me, just like Muddy Waters' band does on the classic recording from the 1964 Newport Festival. But soon the whole audience is joining in and I milk it for all it's worth, leading them in different keys and tempos and variations on the words, and I feel like a gospel preacher, the power and the joy and the sheer exhilaration.

Because that's the one thing you need to know, when it all comes down to it; playing the blues is the best feeling in the world. When you're up on that stage, nothing can touch you. It's a paradox, if you like – you can't play the blues and have them at the same time. It's when you stop playing that your troubles start.